D0260768

MR. BONES

BOOKS BY PAUL THEROUX

FICTION

Waldo
Fong and the Indians
Girls at Play
Murder in Mount Holly
Jungle Lovers
Sinning with Annie
Saint Jack
The Black House
The Family Arsenal
The Consul's File
A Christmas Card
Picture Palace
London Snow
World's End
The Mosquito Coast
The London Embassy
Half Moon Street
O-Zone
My Secret History
Chicago Loop
Millroy the Magician
My Other Life
Kowloon Tong
Hotel Honolulu
The Stranger at the Palazzo d'Oro
Blinding Light
The Elephanta Suite
A Dead Hand
The Lower River
Mr. Bones

CRITICISM

V. S. Naipaul

NONFICTION

The Great Railway Bazaar
The Old Patagonian Express
The Kingdom by the Sea
Sailing Through China
Sunrise with Seamonsters
The Imperial Way
Riding the Iron Rooster
To the Ends of the Earth
The Happy Isles of Oceania
The Pillars of Hercules
Sir Vidia's Shadow
Fresh Air Fiend
Dark Star Safari
Ghost Train to the Eastern Star
The Tao of Travel
The Last Train to Zona Verde

PAUL THEROUX

Mr. Bones

Twenty Stories

HAMISH HAMILTON
an imprint of
PENGUIN BOOKS

HAMISH HAMILTON

Published by the Penguin Group
Penguin Books Ltd, 80 Strand, London WC2R 0RL, England
Penguin Group (USA) Inc., 375 Hudson Street, New York, New York 10014, USA
Penguin Group (Canada), 90 Eglinton Avenue East, Suite 700, Toronto, Ontario, Canada M4P 2Y3
(a division of Pearson Penguin Canada Inc.)
Penguin Ireland, 25 St Stephen's Green, Dublin 2, Ireland (a division of Penguin Books Ltd)
Penguin Group (Australia), 707 Collins Street, Melbourne, Victoria 3008, Australia
(a division of Pearson Australia Group Pty Ltd)
Penguin Books India Pvt Ltd, 11 Community Centre, Panchsheel Park, New Delhi – 110 017, India
Penguin Group (NZ), 67 Apollo Drive, Rosedale, Auckland 0632, New Zealand
(a division of Pearson New Zealand Ltd)
Penguin Books (South Africa) (Pty) Ltd, Block D, Rosebank Office Park,
181 Jan Smuts Avenue, Parktown North, Gauteng 2193, South Africa

Penguin Books Ltd, Registered Offices: 80 Strand, London WC2R 0RL, England

www.penguin.com

First published in the United States of America by Houghton Mifflin Harcourt Publishing Company 2014
Published in Great Britain by Hamish Hamilton 2014
001

Copyright © Paul Theroux, 2014

The moral right of the author has been asserted

'Mr. Bones', 'The Furies' and 'I'm the Meat, You're the Knife' first appeared
in the *New Yorker*; 'Incident in the Oriente', 'Our Raccoon Year' and 'Long Story Short'
(under the title 'Twenty-two Stories', which won a 2009 PEN/O. Henry Prize) in *Harper's Magazine*;
'Neighbor Islands' in the *Sunday Times* (London); 'The First World' in *Precious Stories*;
'Siamese Nights' and 'Voices of Love' in the *Atlantic*; 'Another Necklace' in *Subtropics*; 'Minor Watt'
appeared in the *Virginia Quaterly Review* and in 2011 received a National Magazine Award for Best Story

All rights reserved
Without limiting the rights under copyright
reserved above, no part of this publication may be
reproduced, stored in or introduced into a retrieval system,
or transmitted, in any form or by any means (electronic, mechanical,
photocopying, recording or otherwise), without the prior
written permission of both the copyright owner and
the above publisher of this book

Printed in Great Britain by Clays Ltd, St Ives plc

A CIP catalogue record for this book is available from the British Library

HARDBACK ISBN: 978-0-241-14674-3
TRADE PAPERBACK ISBN: 978-0-241-14675-0

www.greenpenguin.co.uk

Penguin Books is committed to a sustainable future for our business, our readers and our planet. This book is made from Forest Stewardship Council™ certified paper.

CONTENTS

I feel very shy and blushing at being let in for that thing at my venerable age.

— JOSEPH CONRAD AT FIFTY-THREE,
in a letter to a friend, on finding out that his wife, Jessie, was pregnant

Minor Watt

MINOR WATT, THE real estate developer and art collector, was seated at the Jacobean dining table with the fat baluster legs that served as his desk, waiting for his wife – soon to be ex-wife – to arrive. He had been thinking of himself, but the graceful Chinese vase with a tall flared neck, resting on the antique table, made him reflect that, as with so many things he owned – perhaps all of them – he was able to discern its inner meaning in its subtle underglaze, the circumstances of his acquiring it, its price of course, its provenance, all the hands that had touched it and yet left it undamaged, its relation to his own life, its secret history, its human dimension, almost as though this pale porcelain with the tracery of a red peony scroll was human flesh. And then after this flicker of distraction he thought of himself again.

How people said, "You're the calmest man in the world."

He always replied, "As I made more money my jokes got funnier." And when they laughed, he added, "And I got better-looking."

"You're amazing," they said, and with a glance at his collection – the Noland painting *Lunar Whirl* on the wall behind him, the objects glinting on side tables and shelves and in the glass cabinet. Was that a human skull?

"And my collection got more valuable."

"One of a kind," they said.

The only gift anyone can make to a much wealthier person is an extravagant compliment, often in the circumstances the opposite of what the poorer person feels, yet inevitably with a grain of truth and a stammer of ambiguity. The visible fact of his wealth, Minor Watt knew – his collection like a set of trophies – made these people at times incoherent and yet obvious. Instead of "He has this great thing," they thought, "I don't have this great thing."

He lifted his gaze to the works arrayed in his office, a sampling of his areas of collecting: the Noland, a Khmer head of Vishnu in stone, a Chola bronze Shiva Nataraj, an old Dan mask with red everted lips, and a squat Luba fetish figure bristling with rusty nails; a greenish celadon salver propped on a stand, a massive Marquesan *u'u* club with small skull-shaped bas-reliefs for eyes, and beside it, like an echo, an Asmat skull. More human skulls were ranged on a backlit shelf. Among collectors of tribal art, skulls constituted a silent trade, and they were an early and lasting passion with Minor Watt: New Guinea ancestor skulls with cowries lodged in the eye sockets and others overmodeled with clay and painted like masks, some of them shiny from use as headrests, like large chestnuts, the same rich color; Kenyah skulls from Sarawak scratched with scrimshaw lizards on the cranial dome; smoke-dark Ifugao enemy skulls sitting side by side on a smoky plank; Tibetan skulls and skull cups, chased in silver; and more, all of them saturated with mana.

No one said "One of a kind" with surprise. Minor Watt had grown prosperous in the roofing business in New York, city of flat roofs. "A flat roof is designed to leak," he said, and his familiarity with the bones of these buildings led him to speculate successfully in real estate. From the age of thirty or so, Minor Watt had had everything he'd ever wanted, every dollar, every woman, every serious business deal, every artifact – his eye fell upon a standing bodhisattva, a mustached Maitreya from Gandhara carved in schist, second century, Kushan period, clutching a plump vial that contained the elixir of immortality. A duplex on Park Avenue, a house by the sea in Connecticut, with a set of buildings that served as his personal museum. A loving wife – where was she?

His artworks were not for warehousing but for display – showing them was his incentive to collecting. He'd loved taking his wife to the opera, Inca gold glittering at her throat. Even more than the joy that drove his collecting passion was the knowledge that in buying a rare object he had prevented someone else from owning it. Another pleasure in his collection was his certainty that, even as he was examining a piece, its value was rising, no matter what the stock market was doing. He had bought a small Bacon in London – a head of George Dyer. Over the years its value had increased two hundred-fold. Those human skulls: if similar ones could be found, which was doubtful, they'd cost twenty times what he'd paid.

One of the paradoxes of the people who praised these objects was that in most cases they had no idea what they were looking at. At first Minor Watt's pride made this almost a sorrow to him; and then, out of snobbery, such ignorant remarks delighted him. "I love this African stuff," someone would say, smiling at a fierce-faced Timor house post. The Gandharan piece from the Swat Valley was taken to be Greek. "Byzantine," an art historian said of an eighteenth-century Lalibela painting of the Ethiopian saint Gabbra Menfes Qeddus. His old cartoonish reverse-glass paintings done by itinerant Chinese in Gujarat baffled all viewers. "Indonesia? Bali?" A bulb-headed Fijian throwing club known as an *ulu* was assumed to be a Zulu knobkerrie, and no one ever noticed that the ivory inserts on its lobes were human molars, from its five victims.

And which of them would know that this Chinese vase was Ming? Minor Watt and his wife had bought it together after much discussion in Shanghai, after a Yangtze cruise in 1980, and had hand-carried it back to the States. The vase, treasured, as all these objects were, like members of their family, had accompanied them through six changes of address. As though demanding custody, she'd included it as part of the divorce settlement. Had she noticed it glowing in the display cabinet on her previous visit with her lawyer?

Thinking of the woman, he heard his intercom buzz, and then his secretary's voice: "Your wife is here."

Already it was an odd word, since they'd agreed to the divorce months before and had now signed most of the papers. In mentally moving her out of his life he was reminded of his mood when he sent a piece to be auctioned, how he had no feeling for it; even though it still had monetary value, it was dumb and mummified, and, the thing having lost all meaning and hope, he smiled as he let it slip away.

He had wondered which woman would show up – the angry woman, the sad woman, the wild-eyed woman, the oversensitive woman, the rejected one, the triumphant one, the sulker, the smirker, the old friend.

She was none of these when she entered the room. She looked thinner – all the fury was gone, leaving her pinched, the anger wrung out of her. Such corrosive emotion was unsustainable over so many months: she looked cured of an illness, weaker, subdued, much paler. The fighting had ended, and now, like people who knew each other far too well, they were rueful with disillusionment, meeting merely to observe a few formalities, wishing they were strangers.

"Hello, Minor." She spoke in the spongy voice of languor and abandonment, and her eyes were drawn to the vase.

She was here to pick up the valuable old keepsake and then to go. She had been reluctant to come. He had told her it was too fragile to risk mailing, but this was turning into a formal ritual of farewell. He would pass her this lovely vase and she'd carry it away in its cushioned box – the Chinese purpose-built cushioned coffin with the sliding lid and the rope-like handle – carry it as they had done more than twenty years ago in what had been one of their many treasure hunts, but an important one: he'd also been an early investor in the Chinese economic miracle.

"Sunny." Her name was Sonia.

She sat down in the antique Savonarola-style chair, in the same knees-together posture, as she had done many times, but this was perhaps the last time – not perhaps. It was all at an end, a true breakup. No more wifehood for her – she'd probably never remarry and forfeit the alimony. He smiled thinking of his rich pretense of complaining about money, knowing in his heart that money never mattered, because there was always money; but such a vase as this was, even as the philistines guessed, one of a kind. It was promised to Sonia, and yet he could not see beyond the finality of this handover to any future for himself.

She hadn't been a trophy wife: he had loved her, she had been part of his great luck and his achievement, and he had educated her in appreciating his vast art collection. Now she knew what a Scythian chariot finial was, and she knew why this Ming vase was precious for its copper-red underglaze, so fragile and yet unmarked. Knowing his collection this well, she was the only person who truly knew him.

"I can't stay long."

Saying this, still looking at the vase, it seemed that she had moved on, and she had the unimpressed body-snatched look of a woman who was perhaps newly involved with another man.

"I understand. I've got things to do. I'm still in business, in spite of what's happening." Not until he spoke did he realize he was resentful. He went on, "You expected to see me ruined?" She wasn't listening. So he said, "I hate these people who are complaining about the economy. They created the downturn. I did too. That's why I saw it coming. Only a fool thinks it's straight north forever. I'd love to find a way to show them how foolish they've been." She didn't react. He leaned toward her. "It wasn't straight north with us. It's south now."

Her eyes were dark and unperforated.

He said, "So here it is."

"It's beautiful," she said. "Thanks."

She meant, Thanks for agreeing to give it to me – because she knew its value. It had symbolized that long-ago trip, the best phase of their marriage, as well as the taste that she had acquired from him and her insight into his personality.

But she didn't know that he had already surrendered it, that he was merely going through the motions. He didn't care about it anymore. He was surprised that she had agreed to this meeting, which was trouble for her, since she'd gotten the Connecticut house in the settlement, but had put it up for sale and now lived elsewhere – she refused to give him her address. Yet the thought of her being inconvenienced gave him some satisfaction.

"I know just what I'm going to do with it. I have the perfect place for it."

This annoyed him. It meant that she had a house or an apartment that she loved – a shelf in that place, perhaps someone to admire it with her. *I found it in Shanghai when China was just opening up.* He resented her certainty, the way it seemed to represent a part of her future that she'd already begun to live without him. He was wrong about her seeming to be weakened after an illness; she was strengthened in her recovery.

"I've got the old box for you to carry it in." He tapped the lid.

The pale cedar box was still crusted with the red wax seal from the antiques dealer in Shanghai, the folded export permit, a tissue-flimsy certificate, marked with chops and stiff at one corner with glued-on stamps. The box was as venerable as the vase, though Sonia didn't seem to think so. It held as many memories, perhaps more, for being unregarded, plainer, and more durable.

All this time he had been sitting behind the great carved dining table that was his desk, talking across his blotter as if to an employee. He got up and walked to the front of it, avoiding Sonia's side, circling, so that he stood apart, facing the vase.

"If you're pressed for time – you've a place for it, huh? – you might as well take it away."

He leaned, reached, and lifted it, then turned to her. Startled by his sudden offer, she raised both her hands to receive it, a mother's gesture, to bring it to her body and cradle it like a baby. With a sudden warp of nausea in his throat he let it drop, and before she could grasp it, it plunged in a blurred column of its own pale light. As it smashed, she clawed the empty air with feral fingers and a second later put her futile hands to her face.

"Sorry," he said softly, the word no more than a breath in the aftermath of the smash.

She let out a sharp cry, as though she'd seen a precious creature die. Even in the worst moments of their marriage he had never seen that look of loss on her face, an expression of pain amounting to agony. But the exaggerated expression seemed comic, as terror sometimes does to a bystander. He surprised himself by laughing – and because it was involuntary, like the reaction to a wisecrack, it was full-throated, a great guffaw, a joyous snort-honk of gusto that was like a sound of health.

Hearing him she began to cry, bobbing her head with sobs, and when he stepped nearer to comfort her, he lowered his foot onto the broken pieces, rocking his shoe, grinding them smaller, like a big jaw masticating nuts. Any hope that the fragments could be glued back together ended with the heavy molar-crunch of that footfall.

She did not say another word. When she left – he could see in her posture, in her shoulders, the angle of her neck and head – she was a different and defeated woman.

He said sorry again, and it was like the eloquence of the richest satire. The exhilaration was still rattling in his throat. He had not thought he was capable of such an elaborate undoing of the ritual. He shouted again across his office as the door shut: "Sorry!"

"An accident," he murmured after she'd gone. But was it? People said, There are no accidents. They would have added, It was an unconscious wish to break the vase and upset Sonia.

And she had been – devastated. He had not realized how passionately she must have craved it until the thing broke and her face fell, until she left the office, moving stiffly, wounded, her posture altered, one shoulder higher than the other. She would not have looked more punished if he had physically assaulted her, beaten her head against a wall. Yet – for the sake of melodrama, he lifted his hands in a slow sacramental way – he had not laid a finger on her.

It was one thing to withhold an irreplaceable piece, or to sell it; it was another thing entirely to destroy it. Fascinated to think that the vase – such a live presence moments ago – no longer existed, he felt a thrill that very nearly undid the ache of incompleteness he'd sensed in himself that morning, the vase on his desk, knowing that Sonia was on her way. In the past, the nearest he'd come to this feeling was in a casino, stacks of chips piled in front of him, the roulette wheel spinning, Sonia round-shouldered behind him, horrified that he might lose it all. But he hadn't cared – he was giddy at the prospect of losing. The thrill was visceral, an access of strength, a physical lift, an intimation of perverse power that drained from him when he won. In defiance, he put all his winnings on one number, and he was so exultant when he lost that he could recall each witnessing slack-jawed face at the table.

The memory of Sonia and the vase was most of all a memory of her fear: how scared she looked, wild-eyed in terror as the thing fell, and not just by the shattering of the vase, but by his laughter – the insult of it – and she had hurried away as though from a murderer. The act undid everything she knew about him; it made him a stranger to her. He was well aware of being self-taught and inarticulate, yet this smash showed virtuosity.

"The Ming vase," he told friends. "It got T-boned. By me."

He smiled at their shocked silence. People at the periphery could be possessive of someone else's treasures, as if these things were aspects of the friendship. Did they think he was so rich that he would hand them over?

These memories buoyed him through the rest of the divorce, the last of the paperwork, the depositions, all the signatures, the summing up, the attorneys' fees. Whenever he became glum – wondering What next? – he summoned up the moment in his office when the vase slipped from his fingers, the finality of its breaking, the shoe crunch, and the look of loss on her face.

Minor Watt had a collector's caressing habit when alone, of padding around his apartment in slippers, picking up the smaller objects in his collection, holding them to the light, and turning them slowly, as you were forbidden to do in museums. He savored the details that made them unique, the subtle flourishes, not only the texture carved into an elephant tusk but the buttery hue of old ivory, the tiny human stick figure like a petroglyph incised into the shaft of a Tongan war club, the scarification represented on the cheeks of a Chokwe *pwo* mask, the lizard gouged into the dome of a Kenyah skull, the diamond in the forehead of a small seated silver-cast Buddha. Leonard Baskin sometimes wrote a note in pen strokes on a watercolor in his elegant hand. Minor Watt owned three such Baskins – three different notes. No two Francis Bacons were alike; many seemed provisional and splashed. Minor Watt's *Study for Head of George Dyer* was overpainted in one corner, streaked in another, rubbed with the dust from Bacon's studio. The painting was not large, but all Bacons were valuable, almost absurdly so. Some collectors kept them in vaults, with albums of Krugerrands and taped blocks of hundred-dollar bills.

He'd been eating. He rose from the table and lifted the *Study for Head of George Dyer* from the wall and propped it against the silver Victorian wine cooler near his plate of meat. Imitating the George Dyer pout, he braced and gripped his steak knife and raked the canvas, two swipes, then held it on his lap. He marveled at the sight of his own knees through the slashes he'd made – the real world framed by the rags of the painting. He poked at the long slashes. Hearing him grunt, his servant, Manolo, opened the dining room door. "You okay, boss?"

But Minor Watt's feeling was muted. He'd wished someone had seen him, as Sonia had. Not Manolo, who had no idea, but a true witness – even better, a connoisseur.

He called a friend, Doug Redman, who owned several Bacons, but prints, the limited-edition signed lithographs. Redman had often remarked on this painting.

Redman came over that same night, because Minor Watt had said, "It's about my Bacon. I want you to see it."

Minor Watt was sitting before his fireplace when Redman entered the room. At first he did not believe that the slashed painting in his lap was the *Head of George Dyer.* The profile was familiar, the frame unmistakable.

Minor Watt said, "It's the Bacon. You know it's the Bacon."

"But what fuckwit damaged it?"

"I did!" Minor Watt cried out, giddy from hearing his own shrieky voice. The man leaned closer and looked pained, seeing that it was the Bacon. Minor Watt threw it into the fire and at once the canvas caught and flames rushed over it, making a black hole in the slower-burning frame.

Redman groaned and made as if to snatch at it, but the canvas was just smut and soot.

"What's wrong with you?" he said in a tentative voice, too fearful to be angry, as though dealing with a crazy man who might run at him.

He'd expected this art collector's shock, but Redman's terror made Minor Watt even happier.

"Gone!" Minor Watt said, and Redman stepped back. "Totaled!"

"How can you do a thing like that, especially in this economy?"

"Your objection is that I'm wasting money, not destroying a work of art. You're the fuckwit. You don't deserve to live."

Afterward Redman talked, word got around, but no one asked straight-out if Minor Watt had destroyed the painting. To several friends Minor Watt said, "By the way, I fried the Bacon."

A witness gave the destruction a greater meaning and made it all the more satisfying. But the problem was to find someone who knew enough about such an eclectic collection to care. Most of the idiots had no idea. What good was it to smash something in private? Someone else had to know, someone had to care. Who better than the painter himself? The Noland target painting was an early one from 1965. Minor Watt invited Kenneth Noland to his house and encouraged the softly smiling white-haired man to admire his own painting. "One of my favorites," the old man said. And then, with Noland watching, Minor Watt stepped close and shot an arrow into the bull's-eye. Before the startled Noland could protest, Minor Watt threw down his bow and swiped at the painting with a dagger.

"Whoa," Noland said, staggering a little and raising his hands to protect his face, as though he expected to be assaulted. And then, cursing, he hurried from the room.

"It was like wasting one of his children," Minor Watt told Noland's dealer, because the dealer had once asked to buy back the painting.

The dealer said, "I don't think anyone has ever done what you've done."

"People used to tell me that all the time," Minor Watt said, "but for once I think you're right."

He owned a set of crockery, a dinner service for eight, that had been used at Vailima by Robert Louis Stevenson. He invited seven friends, Manolo served a gourmet meal, Minor Watt told the story of the plates, how they had been brought by old Mrs. Stevenson, visiting from Edinburgh ("They'd been in the family for years"), explained the monogram, called attention to the gilded rims. Over dinner the talk was of selling valuables and budgeting. "We're selling our plane." "We've auctioned our Stella." "We've put Palm Beach on the market."

When the meal was over, he asked the diners to carry the plates out to the upper deck of his penthouse. He stacked them and, fascinated by the oddity of the pile of plates resting on a rail, a pillar of bone china, the diners watched him push them over the edge onto the tiled terrace below.

As a woman screamed, Minor Watt said, "Now we don't have to wash them."

That look of joy meant he had to be insane, probably dangerous – they were afraid. They would never forget this, he knew. And he saw how they sidled away, made excuses to leave.

About fifteen minutes later, one of them, Irby Wilders, came back.

"Minor – you okay?"

"Never better. You?"

Irby's mouth was shut tight, his eyes narrowed, like a man on the deck of a ship in a gale. He said, "I'm wondering where the bottom is."

"It's down there," Minor Watt said, pointing to the smashed plates.

He knew this disillusioned investor thought he was crazed by the recession. But "never better" was exactly how he felt. He was strengthened by the dropping of the irreplaceable plates.

Minor Watt did not say the word, but he knew the feeling that preceded this act of violence. It was disgust. Disgust had made him drop the Ming vase. What was the origin of his disgust? He did not know. It wasn't money, but it was related to wealth, a kind of fatness. Many people he knew were embarrassing themselves in their economies. Now they believed him when he said, "None of that for me." He was well aware that by ridding himself of the rare objects all the sourness in him was gone, and he had an appetite again.

He saw the point of murder now, and not simple homicide, but cannibalism. He'd found the cabinet of skulls an aesthetic satisfaction, like a rare ossuary. He'd never understood the pleasure of eating the bodies of these men, of emptying these skulls of the brain and spooning it into a bowl and gorging on the gray jelly sponge. Now he appreciated the magnificence of eating flesh, the great appetite, the ritual devouring. The destruction of the vase and the plates and paintings – pieces as unique as any man – was not vandalism. It was enrichment, a source of power. He was eating art.

Two couples, dinner guests at the plate-drop, the Diamonds and the DeSilvas, called separately, expressing concern, pretending to sympathize. "You must be under a lot of pressure." And they suggested to Minor Watt that if there were any other items in his collection that he wanted to get rid of, they would be glad to accept them. He'd smashed the plates, therefore – their reasoning went – he didn't care about them, and would probably hand over a precious object for nothing or very little.

"But I do care," Minor Watt said after he'd hung up. "That's why I did it."

You do something spontaneously, perhaps accidentally, with no thought of the consequences, he thought, and sometimes you're surprised at what you've provoked. His roofing career leading to real estate had proven that. Smashing china was a revelation, and a cure.

The Diamonds said they had always been very fond of Minor Watt's Tang celadon bowl, smuggled out of Cambodia, perhaps stolen from the National Museum in Phnom Penh. The man who'd sold it to him had remarked on its solidity, how this thick piece of pottery had survived through twelve centuries.

"That piece could take a direct hit."

Minor Watt had always smiled, and felt small and somewhat in awe, remembering those words. He invited the Diamonds for tea. He called attention to the jade-colored glaze, the inimitable crackle, and allowed them to salivate at the prospect of the gift – they were actually swallowing, gulping in anticipation. Then he asked them to put on protective goggles. "You'll see it better." Humoring him – he was insane, wasn't he? – they put them on, and Minor Watt took a hammer to the bowl and, with his tongue clamped in his teeth, pounded the celadon to dust.

The DeSilvas had hinted on the phone of their liking for an Edward Lear watercolor of the Nile depicting Kasr el-Saidi among some riverside palms. These people, too, pleased to be invited for tea, let their covetous gaze wander over the painting.

"The color is brighter without the glass," Minor Watt said, and removed the painting from its frame. He served tea, and after filling their cups he dribbled the pot of hot tea over the watercolor, as the man held his sobbing wife.

Minor Watt said, "Sorry," as mockery, but he thought, Of course I know what I'm doing. Power over works of art that he owned, but also power over these people. He had the power to terrorize them, too, without ever touching them.

Each thing he destroyed strengthened him; each person he terrified through his destruction made him someone to be feared. It had never been his intention; it was all a revelation. Money had no meaning anymore. He'd amassed his art collection believing it would inspire respect – and it had, to a degree; and it had inspired envy, too. The assumption in New York was that he would eventually give the collection to a museum. To these people, and perhaps to a museum, these objects represented wealth – the absurd bias toward money. Even a museum would not regard them as collectors' items, one of a kind. These days a museum would sell them, to stay afloat, and Minor Watt would be forgotten. It disgusted him to think that, transformed into money, they were replaceable. The collector's conceit was always that he or she was a temporary custodian.

"No – I am the owner – the last owner!" Minor Watt said.

Destroying them meant that he was the equal of the person who made them – more than that, he was more powerful. He wiped these rare things from the face of the earth, leaving only a memory in which he mattered; and a memory was the more evocative, even mystical, for its vagueness. After centuries of use and veneration, of being handled and crated and resold, catalogued, photographed, admired, the small thin-rimmed jade bowl balanced on Minor Watt's fingers, in his lovely kitchen, before the blinking eyes of the museum curator, was tipped into a blender. And before the man could react, Minor Watt clapped the lid on and poked the button labeled *Liquefy*.

More ingenious in devising ways to destroy these works of art, each one appropriate to the object, his intention was to make the destruction as memorable as the object itself: the memory of its extinction.

He had some supporters, all of them art students, video artists, creators of installations, one who worked with decaying food, another with human blood, who interpreted Minor Watt's destruction as a form of art, a kind of ritual theater, performance art. They sent him letters. They praised him for turning his back on art history to create something new.

"You are a total hero," one of them said – a pretty purple-haired woman, very thin, black fingernails, neck tattoo, torn black clothes, greasy boots.

Her praise alarmed him, though her look kept him watching. She had come with a group to his uptown office. He had agreed to meet them in the foyer, his security people in attendance.

"You got a Rauschenberg?" a man in the group asked – spiky hair, mascara, the same boots.

"An early one," Minor Watt said. "Birds, animals."

"Wipe it! Whack it! Know what Rauschenberg did? Bought a de Kooning drawing and erased it. Erased it! Exhibited it as his own work. It's in a museum. Is that radical?"

"You're way beyond that, man. You're like a whole new movement – iconoclasm."

He smiled and sent them away. Iconoclasm was nothing new. The word had been in use for five centuries. Minor Watt continued destroying because destruction itself gave him a greater appetite for shattering a whole lovely thing. The breaking of each piece meant the breaking of a barrier that admitted him to a region of cold ferocity. The act of destruction had nothing to do with art. He laughed at the students who claimed his destruction as a form of conceptual art. No, he went on breaking his collection because – he felt sure – he had entered a realm of self-indulgence he'd never guessed at before. He was gluttonous for more. He was not an artist, he was a child smashing a doll, and he was also a ruler punishing a province, a tyrant carrying out a massacre. He did it with a smile, and knew that the great destroyers were smilers – destruction was the certain proof of wealth.

He went on smiling and never uttered the simple truth that he had discovered: "No matter how outrageous my assault on art, no one can stop me."

He still bought art. And at auctions, when he saw how passionately someone wanted to acquire something, he wagged a finger and outbid them. Later, he contrived ways to show these people that he'd destroyed the thing they had craved. Other bidders hated to see him enter at a sale, but he could not be banned – and he knew that the auctioneers were secretly pleased that he was bidding, because he bid without limit.

Who could prevent him from destroying a thing he owned? He jeered at his critics. "You'd think I was committing murder!" It was worse than murder for some of these people. And these were the same people who'd stood by, indifferent to the cruelty of the Taliban rule in Afghanistan – stoning women to death for adultery, hacking the hands from thieves, and after Friday prayers, the beheadings. And who cared? But when the Taliban dynamited the sixth-century giant standing Buddhas in Bamiyan, these hypocrites howled in pain, demanding military action, the overthrow of the Taliban, the siege of Kabul – and it had happened!

But Minor Watt now understood the Taliban, and their earlier incarnation, the White Huns of the fifth century, who'd taken their saddle axes to the Buddhas and stupas of Gandhara, not far from Bamiyan. (He had such an ax, a *tabar-i-zin,* with *Victory from God and Imminent Conquest* engraved in gold on its blade in Persian. He used it on one of his Hockneys.) What lay behind these furious acts of purification was a demonstration of will. Never had these destroyers seemed stronger, fiercer, less sentimental, more resolute, more intent in their mission: inaccessible, unappeasable figures of pure horror and domination. It was certain that invaders or rulers who would dynamite a beautiful work of art placed a much lower value on human life, because artworks were one of a kind and people were pretty much the same. Even those people whom Minor Watt knew seemed to feel this way.

So in vandalizing his artworks he was regarded as worse than a crank. He was a homicidal maniac.

He told people he knew, who objected, that he might have stopped had the reaction against him not been so strong. He wondered if what he said was the truth, because the reaction – the sense of outrage, the condemnation – energized him. What right did they have to say "How dare you"?

Though it was unimaginable to the art collectors and connoisseurs, the destruction became easier for him. "Why am I doing it? Why am I so effective and precise? Because I am a connoisseur!"

How fragile, how insubstantial these objects were. A Japanese woodblock print was made of rice paper. Even his greatest Utamaro hardly raised a flame before the astonished and insulted eyes of Mr. Harada, and it left a mere smudge of ash. The value of a gourd cricket cage was its lid, a deeply carved cookie of ivory that could be pinched apart, and the gourd was easily crumbled. In a gesture of strangulation he broke these things in his hands, and to be certain they wouldn't be reassembled, he stamped his shoe on them, grinding them with his foot sole. He slashed paintings, he crushed porcelain, he hammered silver pots flat.

And he required witnesses – the effort was almost wasted without someone watching, especially someone who cared, who would report it.

These witnesses believed they could persuade him not to destroy the thing. They tried (as they saw it) to talk him off the ledge. "Think of the implications of what you're doing." He thought of the implications. They were his motives. Their concern only made him more intent on finishing the job.

Minor Watt never raised his voice; he was not angry. His calm way in this destruction unnerved anyone who watched him, as though he was about to stick a knife in their eye. There were always plenty of willing witnesses these days, since their hope was that at the last minute he'd have a change of heart. But the witnesses themselves roused his conviction.

Something else that animated him was the desire to destroy each thing differently. "I could simply set my house on fire," he told one collector. "I could stack everything I own onto a pile and set it alight. But that would be meaningless."

And he wanted to add that a massacre can mean less than a single execution.

"So what you're doing has a meaning?" Doug Redman had asked.

"Yes, I think so. The experience of seeing a lovely thing leave the world forever. The drama of extinction, so to speak. It's a death."

He was not, he said, the first person to destroy works of art. The Vandals had given the world a word by doing it. The Chinese emperor Ch'in Shih-huang had burned every book in his kingdom in 213 B.C. Spanish conquistadors had stolen golden ornaments from the Inca people and hammered them into crucifixes. In 1942 bombing raids by the Germans had targeted specific churches and museums, not only to demoralize the British but to demonstrate German might. Baron Gustav Braun von Sturm said, "We shall go out and bomb every building marked with three stars in the Baedeker Guide." The devastating raids on Britain called the Baedeker Blitz leveled thousands of ancient buildings, their contents – paintings, furniture, silver – reduced to ashes. Most of the Old Master paintings stolen by Irish terrorists in the 1970s from English houses and museums had never been found and had probably been kicked to bits or sold for guns.

Compared to this, trashing a Francis Bacon was negligible. Bacon himself regularly destroyed paintings he'd done that didn't suit him, and laughed when the critics howled. The destruction had not diminished him; it had made him loom larger.

But though the historical precedent for the destruction of artwork was ancient, the novelty that Minor Watt introduced was his using his own art collection, piece by piece; and while it seemed a form of insanity, it was both unprecedented and lawful.

He felt no remorse – far from it. He was suffused with an unexpected sense of power, greater than anything he'd felt in acquiring the works. He knew the joy of a winning bid, the cry of "Sold!" The arrival of the wooden crate, the dismantling, the revealing of the painting, the urn, the skull, the statue, the goblet. But destroying any of these things gave him the intense pleasure that could only compare with devouring something rare – eating an endangered animal, the feeling the Chinese had when feasting on a bear paw or a moose nose or the liver of a tiger.

He envisioned no end to it. He had enough money to go on buying art. The disgusted foretaste of destroying a thing he saw in a salesroom or a catalogue filled him with an urgency to buy it.

The discouraged Bennett Hembergs said, "It's not yours – art belongs to the world. We are merely the preservers, keeping these pieces for future generations."

"I disagree," Minor Watt said in his quiet way. "I am disproving that. By destroying them I am making them mine."

He did not say (though he implied it) that it was his intention that no one would ever see them again. Or hold them or touch them or smell them – the smell of such antiques was distinct and musty, like that of leaf mold or dried meat. No one would bear witness to them. Knowing they were irreplaceable, he did his best to prevent anyone from photographing them whole.

"You're like a murderer, a rapist who kills his victims!"

He laughed – the tyrant laugh. "You don't know what murder is!" These were things that belonged to him. "No one can prevent me from destroying my own property, providing I do it in safety."

The great pity, in Minor Watt's mind, was that he was the true connoisseur: he had studied these pieces with such care that no one saw as deeply into them as he did. "What a loss," they said, but they didn't know the half of it. The witnesses, the gallery owners, the collectors, were not ignorant, but neither did they fully understand the works – their historical importance, even their monetary value.

Art critics condemned him; his name became a euphemism

for gratuitous violation. He was denounced and vilified. Yet he gloried in the abuse. It proved how successful he'd been: he wanted his efforts to be known. And, by the way, it showed how wealthy he was – the word "potlatch" was used for his destruction made into a ritual. He'd caused the moneymen to be afraid and, in their cowering, to look small and mean.

Not everyone howled. Some women were attracted to him for these acts of destruction. Unstable women, on the whole, too eager, excited by the danger, by being so close to the fires that scorched his paintings, the dazzle of the knife blades, the clubs that smashed the pots. They were like the panting people who chased fire engines or joined window-breaking mobs or wrote letters to serial killers, falling in love with them, marrying them on death row. The women were perhaps destructive themselves and had lived by ruining other people – but not on this scale. The ingenuity of Minor Watt shredding his paintings, smashing his porcelain, crushing the decorated skulls, microwaving his majolica, roasting his Polynesian clubs in his fireplace, had not occurred to them – they didn't own any works of art. He avoided these women. What did they know?

And at the parties he attended he was treated as notorious. Stab a Stella and people flee – or hang around, transfixed. He stopped going to parties. "Charisma vampires," he said; they sapped his energy.

What alarmed the art world was that Minor Watt had the means to replace these works. When he showed up at auctions the other bidders glared at him, and when he was successful gloom descended on the salesroom, for it was known that the piece he'd bought – painting, book, pot, sculpture, dueling pistol, helmet, whatever – would be shattered to bits. And if it happened to be a rare South Indian bronze, it would be blowtorched into a sorry lump of unrecognizable metal. Ownership to Minor Watt meant oblivion.

Some works cried out to be destroyed. Certain statues, certain paintings, the carvings that collectors referred to as "exquisite." They seemed defiant, and not just the delicate ones but the robust images too. The broad black strokes in a wall-sized Rothko seemed to stare at Minor Watt and say, "Kick me."

Had these artworks been people, he would have been arrested, convicted of murder, and imprisoned. But what he did was regarded by most people who knew of it as worse than murder. Yet he was almost delirious in his innocence, free to slash paintings and shatter gold Mayan ornaments and all the rest, because the objects belonged to him.

Furious people visited him to vent their feelings. Even a policeman: "Your neighbors are complaining . . . smoke . . . noise." He laughed: what noise? Even stepped on, a Meissen shepherdess made less noise than someone chewing corn flakes. "Your neighbors said they heard gunshots."

"Yes. I blew holes in a Jasper Johns. It seemed created to be shot at. Then I burned it. I have a permit to carry a gun."

"I'll need to write it up. It was a painting?"

"It was a target."

The sound of the gunshots had rippled through him and swelled him with a sense of power. He felt bigger, stronger, more visible; his name was on people's lips. He was better known, more famous, as a destroyer of art than he'd ever been as a collector. And that was another motivator, the conceits of the other collectors, the presumption, the calculation. He laughed when one of them said, "A piece just like that sold at auction for a million-two." In the past they had ignored him, taken him for a philistine. What philistine? His eye was unerring in choosing the greatest works to destroy – the best went first, then the lesser works. In this way he proved that he had taste. Had he been a philistine, he would not have discriminated. But he was a connoisseur, and he brought all his connoisseurship to his destruction.

Some dealers – not many – avoided him. Some auction houses tried publicly to bar him from sales. But because of the money he was willing to pay, in a period when business had never been worse, he was discreetly welcome, usually after hours, in the galleries and studios. And he was willing to pay more than anyone else. He didn't haggle. If he saw a thing he liked, he bought it without hesitating.

He grew to love the twitch of greedy anticipation in the moist eyes of the art dealer on his entering the gallery, the subtle hints that a certain object might be worthy of his attention – not the best piece in the place, but always the most expensive.

This afternoon the dealer was Tony Faris. He had an early Hopper. He called to his assistant, Mara, to prop the painting on an easel.

Buyers and collectors said, "Can you make me a price?" or "What's the best you can do?"

Minor Watt smiled at Faris and said, "How much?"

The price was named. He studied Faris's mouth uttering the big number, the dry lips, the licking tongue, the jerking head.

"I'll write you a check," he said. Then, because Faris had hesitated and Mara had glanced at her boss, he said, "How do you want me to pay for it?"

He loved the way Faris said, "Cash is good."

"Send it to me. Pack it well."

He knew he was sending the piece to its doom. They all did. Collaborators!

"I know you'll be happy with it."

Happy, yes, because if it were not of such great quality, he would not have bought it, would not trouble himself to slash it, burn it, pour acid over it, melt it, batter it with a hammer.

Mara brought the Hopper to him in a taxi. He invited her up to his apartment and led her through part of his collection, his usual challenge, daring her to identify this or that piece.

"Naga," she said, correctly, of a red-beaded necklace in a framed box. "Reverse-glass painting, Hanuman," and "Mughal *khanjar,* real jewels in the hilt." She seemed reverential, even moved by the objects. "And that is a *dah,*" she said of a silver dagger.

"You know what you're looking at."

"Many of these things have a practical use." She was glancing from the Marquesan club to the Dan mask to a Zulu headrest. "Not art objects, but useful tools," she said. "To you they are emblems of power."

He lifted the Marquesan *u'u* and wondered if he should smash it.

"The language of things," she said.

He knew why the dealers were so willing to consign these artworks to oblivion. The money he paid was one incentive, but there was a larger issue: the scarcer the work, the rarer the masterpiece in any area, the greater the demand and the higher the price. A finite number of Hoppers existed. Minor Watt's Hopper was an oil the painter had executed in Rockland, Maine, in the summer of 1926 – moored fishing boats, a clutter of drooping telephone wires, the serene old culture, the ugly tilted crosstrees. Hopper had spent less than three months in Rockland. He'd done fewer than a dozen paintings. The destruction of this painting increased the value of all the rest of them, probably a better one that Faris had kept for himself.

The Noland prices rose on the news that he'd wrecked two early targets. He pounded his Gandharan Maitreya figure, a "Buddha of the future," into fragments and the market for these strangely Hellenic central Asian sculptures became buoyant.

He had never collected coins, inros, netsukes, perfume bottles; apart from a few pieces he'd given Sonia, jewelry left him cold. And what sort of spectacle would they make on a bonfire or in a crucible – a sparklet, a fizz, a bad smell. Even melted, the heaviest earrings – West African or Indian – would amount to no more than a twisted nugget of gold. He craved a visible triumph, a blaze, a marble statue reduced to powder, to be sneezed into nothingness.

The painter Tristram Cowley invited him to his studio, and Minor Watt sat while Cowley showed him his latest work. Minor Watt admired the detail, made comments. He knew what these painters wanted him to do – buy a picture, not the best one. They held back. Minor Watt was patient. He chatted, waiting until the better pictures were slid out and leaned against the wall. Cowley's pieces were based on x-rays. Minor Watt chose *Compound Fracture.*

"You know where to send it."

Cowley knew what would happen to *Compound Fracture.* And he knew what would happen to his reputation, to the value of his work: it would be a breakthrough.

But such a painter was not the best witness to the destruction. Critics were excellent – they grieved. And the most knowledgeable critics were the best. They were able to appreciate the worth of the pieces. They could put a price tag on them, but few of them could afford to buy them, and so they were truly shocked to see Minor Watt slash them to rags.

After a nighttime visit to the New York studio of another painter, Minor Watt was walking to the corner to find a taxi when he was set upon and pushed to the sidewalk by two men. At that moment, a police cruiser happened to drift past, interrupting the assault, though the two attackers slipped between buildings and got away.

"You okay?" one cop asked. "They get anything?"

"I'm fine. I have my wallet. My watch." Patting himself, Minor Watt was glad that he felt no pain.

"I guess we got here just in time. Lucky. They could have done some damage."

Minor Watt smiled at that notion – that they might have broken his bones. Maybe they were men who objected to what he was doing. Or maybe they were thugs looking for trouble.

It happened again – this time a gunshot fired into his car, which was parked in a public lot. He was not in the car, but the bullet through the windshield entered at the level of his head. That was a message: not a random act of violence but an attempted murder. He lost count of the people who would be glad to see him dead. Sonia would smile and tell people what a bastard he was – and never mention how they had loved each other. He bought a bulletproof car and hired a bodyguard, and, secure, he was gleeful, thinking that there were people who were so outraged by the destruction of his artworks that they were prepared to kill him.

The phone rang in his bulletproof car, a woman. "This is the Tony Faris gallery. Mr. Faris would like to speak with you."

"Put him on," Minor Watt said.

"Right away. But I just wanted to say that I read about that trouble you had and I'm really sorry."

"Thanks for noticing. You're Mara?"

"You remember."

"'The language of things.' I liked that."

Then Faris was on the line, saying, "Are you all right?"

Other people called – dealers, galleries, auctioneers, painters, sculptors. In almost every case, they were people who wished to sell him work, all of them well aware of his plans for the piece: the knife, the hammer, the acid bath, the crucible, the bonfire, the oven.

Sonia called. She sounded terrified, and her anxious questions told him that she was afraid he might hurt her.

After the mugging and the gunshot, his protective measures took so much of his time that for three weeks or more he did not destroy anything. In this period of reflection he realized that he would never run out of works to destroy. He felt a twinge of inhibition. Faris's sale of the Edward Hopper gave him his first intimation. Even if he concentrated on, say, Chola bronzes – a niche of Indian art – he'd only find at most a dozen masterpieces. Museums and die-hard collectors had the rest, which would be the more valuable for his destruction of the others.

And so he stopped and pondered what to do next. This pause proved accidentally helpful. He saw that he was regarded as a dominant force in the art world, almost as though his destruction was a form of art criticism, causing fear and gratitude. His spell of doing nothing created suspense. He liked the idea that he was spreading alarm by not lifting a finger, that he'd become a symbol of intimidation.

I have not drawn blood, he thought, not one drop. I have not hurt a single person physically. I have not put a hand on anyone. I have never raised my voice. I have not cursed, nor shown anger, nor damaged anyone else's property.

The paradox he saw in the partial destruction of his collection was that he had helped to stimulate the art market and inflate some prices. This was a drawback, if not a defeat. In his period of inaction and watchfulness, his phone warbled all the time – dealers chattering to do business – and he was tempted. But he knew their motives. He was being used. Perhaps this was to be expected, but he saw it as a diminution of his power. He despised them, but he began to doubt himself for having set a wayward impulse loose.

Escaping his apartment, leaving his phone behind, he walked the New York streets in dark glasses and loitered in the open spaces where other anonymous people were idling – Central Park, Union Square, Battery Park. He strolled, sensing that he was being watched, possibly followed; the shutter click of someone ducking out of view whenever he turned. Maybe one of those demented art students.

Sitting on a bench one day in Central Park, near the zoo, he became aware that it was trembling beneath him – the slats, even a gentle rocking of the frame. At the far end of the bench a young woman sat with her face in her hands, her shoulders heaving. She might have been crooning a lullaby softly to herself, but she was sobbing.

At first Minor Watt turned away and prepared to go. What

made him linger was the suspicion that the woman would think, in his abrupt departure, he was rejecting her – and that might make her feel even worse.

Seemingly grief-stricken, she turned her smeared face to him and said, "I'm so sorry."

Now it was too late for him to leave. Nodding at her with a look of consolation, he saw that she was beautiful. Her misery made her fragile and pretty, her sorrow creasing her features with complexity.

"You're Mr. Watt," she said.

He was not surprised. He felt that the world knew him, even in his dark glasses and his oblique outings.

Looking closer, he recognized her as the woman from the gallery – Faris's assistant, where he'd bought the Hopper he'd destroyed. The language of things.

What he'd first noticed about her – her Asiatic pallor, the porcelain smoothness of her skin – was more emphatic, probably because of her weeping. She had the ageless look of someone who'd been kept in a darkened room her whole life: the luminous delicacy of her face, her small shoulders, her slender hands. In contrast was the fullness of her breasts, which seemed to have a personality of their own – when she leaned they seemed to swing for him. Why had he not noticed her beauty before?

"I know you," he said.

"Mara," she said.

"How about a cup of coffee?"

At the nearby outdoor café, she told him she was being evicted for not paying her rent. And the reason she had no money was that Faris had laid her off after Minor Watt had stopped buying pictures. "No one's buying art these days."

In this period, Minor Watt felt responsible for much that was happening in the world of business, and in the city generally. He sensed that had influenced great shifts of money, not just in the art market but all over, because art was linked to so many areas of the economy. His destruction had made art an even more valuable commodity.

"I used to destroy my artwork," he said. "You know I'm famous for that. I sometimes think that it was my wish to be an ascetic."

"No," Mara said, and got his attention – no one ever disagreed with him. She went on, "Ascetics are driven by pride, the desire to be like gods. You are different from anyone else."

He stared at the pretty lips that had said this. He thought of installing Mara in his apartment. He had plenty of room. But he said, "How much are we talking about?"

Mara mentioned a round figure. It was nothing to him, yet with facial expressions and movements of his head he made his habitual show of puzzling over the amount.

He normally carried a quantity of ready cash, in case he might see a piece he wanted to buy, and dealers almost swooned when they saw real money. He picked out the amount she had named from his wallet, folded it, and pushed it across the table, the way he might ante up in a poker game.

Palming the money, Mara began to cry again, and then, dabbing her eyes, she wrote something on a napkin and put it into his hand. And, as though overcome by his kindness, she hurried away without another word.

He saw that a telephone number had been stabbed into the limp napkin. But he didn't call her. Almost a week went by, and she called him, asking him whether he wished to visit her.

"Because you're responsible for my being here," she said. "I make good coffee."

Had she forgotten saying that? Because when he visited her, she opened a bottle of wine and poured him a glass.

"How have you been doing?"

"You know this economy better than I do. I've sent out a million résumés."

He understood what she meant: I don't have any work.

"I know the art galleries are hurting."

"You did them a huge favor," she said. "But my background is finance."

She was a banker, reduced to flunkying for Tony Faris. To make it easier for her, he said, "How much do you need?"

She mentioned a figure, she raised it by a third, she smiled sadly. She said, "I'll pay you back with my first paycheck."

She took the money and made it disappear in her pale hand. She was beautiful, perhaps the more so for looking submissive, with her slightly tangled hair, wearing her best dress. She had a dancer's legs, slender and yet strong, like her fingers, and her head was small and well shaped on her long neck.

As he was reflecting on her doll-like beauty – thinking, Chinese? Cambodian? – she said, "The first time I saw you with Faris in the gallery I knew you were powerful, the way you carried yourself. I knew you by reputation. I hadn't realized how young and handsome you were."

"Very kind of you," Minor Watt said. "Made my day."

And as he got up to leave, Mara said, "You don't have to rush off."

He said, "I'm tempted to stay."

But he kissed her lightly and left, wondering at this turn of events.

Then it was he who called her, and met her again at the café in the park. He offered her more money, and she took it without mentioning that she'd pay him back. This happened two more times. It seemed that his giving her money kept her from finding a job, though at the third meeting she said she was still sending out résumés.

"Anyone interested?"

"Sporadically," she said, and held his hand, tugging. She told him about her family, from Mizoram, next to Assam, all Baptists, yet with an ancient pedigree. Her full name was Mara Lal Pawl. That was how she'd known the Naga necklace and the *khanjar* and the silver *dah*. But she was alone here; she had not found another Mizo in New York. Minor Watt thought, Imagine!

"Meet me tomorrow," he said, and specified a store on Madison Avenue.

He took her to buy jewelry. He helped her pick out shoes. She selected some clothes. He sat while she tried them on, and he thought how she was like a small daughter saying, "How do you like my new dress, Daddy?" He paid for the clothes.

They left the last store – Barneys – and walked around the corner to the Pierre for a drink. He said, "You should have a boyfriend, pretty girl like you."

"Fired him," she said. "Besides, I have you."

He did not reply, just kept walking, and he could see that she was thrown. He said, "Would you do something for me?"

Mara didn't hesitate. She said, "Anything."

He let her move into an empty apartment in one of the buildings he owned that was visible from where he lived. Using binoculars he could sometimes see her at her window. He began to live for these glimpses, Mara flashing past, or lingering to look out, not knowing that she was being caressed by his gaze.

Minor Watt went on visiting in the oblique way of a wealthy and secretive friend. He sat and held her in a scrutinizing way, thinking: What is it about her that makes her lovely? The only way to possess her was not to love her, but to support her, to satisfy her with money, and yet to keep her a little hungry and apart. He knew that feeling – the poor might be content with the little they have, but the rich always want more. Sonia had always resisted, her defiance subdued him, and he loved her, but he had never truly possessed her.

By the second month Mara, in her acceptance, became entirely dependent on him.

"I saw Faris the other day," he said. "He told me I was ruthless."

"He doesn't know anything. You're really very compassionate."

"You think so?"

She had a beautiful smile. "Oh, yes."

She didn't know him. He was a stranger, as featureless as a bank, which was all he was to her, a source of light and money, her sole support.

But with the connoisseurship he'd acquired over many years, he knew her well. She was as familiar to him as any object he'd studied, and like those objects she was an empty vessel, self-regarding, inward-looking, even smug and needing to be held, like all the art he'd ever owned. But that didn't matter. She was also one of a kind, exotic for being a Mizo, lovely in her own way, perhaps lovelier, more delicate and fragile, more breakable than any piece that had ever passed through his hands. And she belonged to him.

What Minor Watt imagined happening, and what he rehearsed in his mind, was that on the anniversary of Sonia's leaving him, the beginning of the stock market slide, he would take out the *dah* that she had once recognized and named. He would carry it to the apartment that Mara occupied, and he would confront her, gripping the foot-long dagger by its silver hilt. And then, as before, when facing Sonia with the rare vase, he would hope for inspiration. Perhaps nothing would happen. Perhaps in dramatic finality he would lift his hand and slash Mara's throat and watch her bleed to death on the carpet from Khotan. And he would say to all the people who condemned him, "Now do you see?"

What actually happened was that he visited the apartment, the *dah* tucked inside his jacket. Mara smiled when she let him in, but she also seemed to notice that his posture was odd. He was slightly canted to one side, favoring a crease in his jacket.

Minor Watt touched her, smoothing her pale slender neck with his fingers, a characteristic gesture.

Then he said, "I'm not going to hurt you."

Mara stepped back with widened eyes, moving her lips, as though translating what he had just said into her own language, and terrified by it. Surprised by her reaction – why wasn't she reassured? – Minor Watt slipped his hand beneath his jacket and located the knife. But Mara was quicker. She moved on him with an old-fashioned slap, an efficient Asiatic chop, and the knife clattered to the hardwood floor. She dived at it and with a sweeping gesture grasped the handle, shook off its scabbard, and poked the blade at him. Flapping his hands in distress, Minor Watt shrieked. His own voice scared him: she had cut him, she had drawn blood. No one had ever injured him. Fearing for his life, he grew small as Mara loomed. In that moment she ceased to be ornamental. She was a horror to him, as though one of his pieces of art had come alive. Turning into a tribeswoman, suddenly feline, with blazing eyes, she pointed the dagger at him.

Minor Watt was murmuring as if in prayer, pleading for his life, as Mara said, "This is a Burmese *dah,* but we have similar knives in Mizoram. Some are well made. Most of them are tools," she went on, examining the blade, "instruments for cutting – for killing." Now she held it to his anguished face. "They are not trophies. Not art, but useful objects. Now I think you know that."

Minor Watt backed away, looking at the ugly thing in her hand, reminding her that he had been kind to her.

"Here's what I want you to do for me," Mara said.

"Anything," he said.

"Remove all your clothes," she said.

Without raising her voice, Mara repeated her request. And he obeyed, undressing slowly, and finally stepping out of his boxer shorts, one hand cupped at his groin for the sake of modesty, the other raised to protect his face, at the level of the blade.

Begging her now, he was gabbling, and Mara's look of disgust convinced him that she meant to kill him. She made as if to slash him, but only nicked his chin. Even so, he howled at the sight of the blood that dripped on his pale belly.

She prodded again, moving him with the blade into the elevator and down to the ground floor, then let him run. And – grateful, eager – he fled from the apartment, out of the building, naked, his hands and body smeared, absurd, from his touching his wounds, a laughingstock on the busy street, a hilarious news item in these anxious times.

Mr. Bones

WHENEVER I GET sentimental and take on a reminiscing tone and talk about how my father used to read to me and encourage me, I realize that I'm lying. Is it a way of being kind to his memory, like "You look marvelous," something he used to say? "Pretty as a picture"– seldom true. "Looks good enough to eat," over my mother's gristly meatloaf. But then generosity can often seem to verge on the satirical.

My father, apparently a simple cheery soul, seemed impossible to know. His smiles made him impenetrable. In his lifetime I found it hard to see through his niceness, and even now, ten years after his death, he seems more enigmatic than ever. There he stands, at a little distance, jingling coins in his pocket, waiting for someone to need him, a satisfied man with the sort of good humor and obliging manner I associate with an old-fashioned servant. "Glad to oblige!"

A smile is the hardest expression to fathom – you don't inquire, you don't even wonder. He must have known that. I never thought: Who is he? What does he want? He said he was happy. He would not have said otherwise, but though I believed him, there were things I didn't know. At the period I am thinking of, he had just lost his job. Never mind, he found another one. Did he like it? "I'm tickled to death!"

He was so thoroughly nice it did not occur to us that we did not know him. He didn't drink, he didn't smoke. He never went out at night except to church. Bowling and the movies he abandoned after first becoming a father. He had few friends, no close ones, no confidants – he wasn't the confiding type. He wasn't a joiner.

I was eleven. With two older brothers and a younger sister –

there would be three more children eventually – I was invisible, in the lower middle of the pack, always a few steps behind, beneath notice. And my father was the insubstantial presence he wished to be, merely a voice, a man who lived in the house. Dramatic entrance, and then silence. A hush. Dramatic departure, and then silence again.

This all sounds harmonious, yet there was disorder and tension and conflict in our household. It was crooked in the angular splinters in the woodwork, pulsing in the air, a disturbance that was deep, subtle, and without any voice, a noiseless bewilderment and uncertainty, the vibrant presence of low-pitched rivalries, and it was all masked by politeness, or sometimes hostile displays of affection. The quiet-seeming household is often more turbulent or intimidating than the household of the tyrant or the drunkard.

One of the unspoken conflicts in the house was the house itself, a constant reproach in the cabinets that failed to catch, in every creak of the floorboards, the peeling wallpaper, the stains on the ceiling like mocking faces, every draft that scuttled under the doors. All these awkward reminders. My mother's version of the story, which was the blaming version – the one that my mother wouldn't let him live down – was that having decided that we had to move (four kids in a tiny house and a fifth on the way), my father would be the house hunter. My mother was pregnant and busy, but she was also the sort of person who provoked us to make a decision, so that if we failed she could say, "Whose fault is that?" Deniability was a defense she mastered long before such a word was coined.

By directing my father to look for a new house, she became the one to be propitiated: a scolding silence if it was a good choice, loud blame if it was a bad one. Dad was like hired help, the house hunter. "And it better be a good one."

Unused to the trick of spending a large amount of money, risking this big decision, Dad became more affable, more genial than I'd ever seen him. It was sheer nervousness, a kind of helpless hilarity, like that of an almost ruined gambler at the blackjack table risking everything on the turn of a card.

He saw three or four houses. They were unsuitable. He liked all of them. My mother was vexed. This was dinner table talk: we were discouraged from speaking during mealtime, so we listened. Buying anything involved endless deliberation. "What's good about it?" my mother would say. "It'll be hard to heat," or "It's not on a bus line," or "That's a bad neighborhood."

One winter night Mother was in tears. Dad had seen another house he liked. He was told the price. He was in the nervous affable mood, his gambler's anxiety. He did not bargain, or say "My wife will have to see it," or "We'll think it over."

He said, "We'll take it!" with a sudden flourish of money that startled even the seller of the house, who was a cranky old woman in a soiled apron.

That was my mother's version, in the oral tradition of the family history, the only version that was ever allowed, all the blame on Dad. In a matter of an hour or so my father had seen the house and agreed to buy it. Another detail to his discredit was that he had seen it in the dark. Because it was January and he worked until five-thirty, he would have driven there after work, tramped through the snow, looked it over, and by seven or so it was a deal.

The reason for my mother's tears was that, anticipating his finding the right house, Dad had been carrying five hundred dollars in small bills around with him, and the papers he signed that very night (the old woman had them handy in the pocket of her apron) specified a deposit of that amount, nonreturnable.

"Our whole life's savings!" my mother cried, thumping the table. "How *could* you?"

Obviously he'd liked the house, he didn't want to risk losing it, he wasn't a bargainer, and he was pressed for time, house hunting after work. It was: buy the house, pay the rest of the money with a mortgage, or lose the deposit. "Our life's savings – wasted!"

My father suffered, smiling sheepishly through a number of scenes at the dinner table – and other times too. I heard bedroom recriminations, rare in our household. But in a short time the mortgage was granted, the house was bought, and we moved – a huge disruptive event in a family with few, almost no, events that involved a substantial outlay of money. It was the only time we moved house, and what made it memorable were my mother's tears. After it was done, her father and mother paid a visit. Her father – sententious, pinched and pious, a self-proclaimed orphan – looked at the house, surveyed the street, pronounced it a disaster, and said, "Poor Anna."

The house was large but odd-shaped, bony and tall and narrow, like a cereal box, the narrow side to the street, the wide side a wall of windows, and somehow unfinished – the kitchen not quite right, the doors either sagging or poorly fitting or missing, varnished cabinets of thin wood, the floors creaky and uneven. But it had four bedrooms. Fred and Floyd shared a room with bunk beds. "There's room for the piano," my father said in a voice of hollow enthusiasm.

"Life's savings" was probably an exaggeration, but not much: my father's new job was menial, a shoe clerk. He was grateful for the job, but a man selling shoes spends a great deal of time on his knees.

He never stopped smiling that winter. His smile said, All's well. Mother banged the kitchen cabinets to demonstrate the loose hinges, the broken latches. She tugged at the front door, exaggerating the effort, saying she was coming down with a cold because of the drafts, sighing loudly, all the sounds and gestures in the theater of discontent.

Dad said, "Say, I'll see to that."

He was imperturbable, not so chummy as to cause offense,

but deferentially amiable. "How can I help?" A kind of submissiveness you'd see in the native of a remote colony, with the wan demeanor of a field hand or an old retainer.

Spring came. The roof began to leak, the gutters were rotted, the nailed-on storm windows proved hard to take down. Now that we were less confined by winter, we could see that the house was big and plain and needed paint.

Dad began to paint it, with a borrowed ladder and a gallon of yellow paint. A neighbor saw him and said in a shocked voice, "You're not going to paint that house yellow!"

So Dad returned the yellow and bought some cans of gray.

"That's a lot better," the neighbor said.

My mother pointed out that he'd dripped gray paint onto the white trim. He corrected it by repainting the trim.

Mother said, "Now you've gone and dripped white paint on the shingles."

Dad smiled, repainting, never quite getting it right.

Anticipating warm weather and insects, he put up screens. The screens were wobbly and rusted; holes had been poked in them.

"Didn't you look at the screens before?"

She was talking about January, when he'd bought the house. This was mid-March.

The stove was unreliable. The fuel oil in the heater gurgled and leaked from the pump, and that had to be replaced by a plumber, Dad's fellow choir member Mel Hankey. He worked for nothing, or for very little, groaning in wordless irritation as he toiled, like giving off a smell.

My father's new job was a problem: long hours, low pay, my mother home with the small children, and pregnant – due in June. She was heavy and walked with a tippy, leaning-back gait, supporting her belly with one hand, seeming to balance herself as she moved.

"I lost a child two years ago."

As though she was threatening to lose this one.

Dad said, "It's going to be fine."

"How would you know?"

He smiled, he had no reply. As a sort of penance he washed the dishes, calling out, "Who's going to dry for me?" And because of the tension, each of us said, "I'll do it!" and pushed around trying to be helpful, like terrified children in a drunken household. But there was no drunkard here, only a disappointed woman and her smiling husband.

I said he had no recreations. He had one, the choir, legitimate because it was church-related. He had a strong, confident, rather tuneless voice, with a gravelly character, and even if thirty other people were singing, I could always discern my father's voice in the "*Pange Lingua*" or "*O Salutaris.*"

"You're not going out again?"

"Say, I've got choir practice."

He prays twice who sings to the Lord was printed on the hymnal. He believed that. Choir practice was more than a form of devotion, an expression of piety; it was a spiritual duty. But Dad always went alone, never taking any of us as initiates to the choir, and he always came back happy – not in anything he said, but his mood was improved, you could tell by the tilt of his head, his movements, his breathing, the way he listened, with a different sort of smile, a relaxed posture, his walk. He weighed less. He was always happier after he sang.

April came.

"The house is full of flies."

"I'll take care of that."

He patched the screens with little glued-on squares of screen.

"And the paint's peeling."

Instead of priming it or waiting until the summer, he'd painted over the grime and the paint hadn't stuck.

"The faucet drips."

"Say, I'll pick up some washers on the way home from choir."

"This is the second time I've mentioned it."

Dad was putting on his hat, snapping the brim, looking jaunty.

"You never listen."

All he did was listen, but there's a certain sort of nagging repetition that can deafen you. We didn't know we'd come to the end of a chapter, that we were starting a new chapter. And after it was over we knew Dad much better, or rather knew a different side of him.

The wickedest episodes of revelation can have the most innocent beginnings. This one began with a song. It seized my attention at the time, but looking back on it, it seems even weirder, scarier, almost unbelievable, except that I witnessed it all and even now remember it with reluctance because of my crush of embarrassment. I came to understand that my father's smiles made him an enigma; but for a brief period I knew him, and though it was a kind of comedy, I was frightened and ashamed and shocked. The revelation unfolded obliquely, growing worse.

He came home carrying a large envelope with a tucked-in flap. Trying to look casual, he got his fingers inside and with a self-conscious flourish took out some pages of sheet music. The illustration on the cover showed a black man in a gleaming top hat, white gloves, mouth smilingly open in the act of singing. I could see from his features that he was a white man wearing makeup.

"Say"–Dad was rattling the pages–"can you play this, Mother?"

Asking a favor always made him shy. Being asked a favor made Mother ponderous and powerful. *Oh, so now you want something, do you?* she seemed to reply in the upward tilt of her head and triumphant smile.

She looked with a kind of distaste at the sheet music, plucking at it with unwilling fingers, as though it was unclean. And it *was* rather grubby, rubbed at the edges, torn at the crease where it was folded on the left side. It showed all the signs of having been propped on many music stands. Old, much-used sheet music had a limp cloth-like look.

After a while, Mother brought herself and her big belly to the piano. She spun the stool's seat to the right height and, balancing herself on it, reached over her pregnancy as if across a counter. Frowning at the music, she banged out some notes – I knew from her playing that she was angry. Dad leaned into his bifocals.

Mandy
There's a minister handy
And it sure would be dandy . . .

He gagged a little, cleared his throat, and began again, in the wrong key.

He could not read music, though he could carry a tune if he'd heard it enough times. In this first effort he struggled to find the melody.

"You're not listening," Mother said.

"Just trying to . . . ," he said, and clawed at the song sheet instead of finishing the sentence.

He started to sing again, reading the words, but too fast, and Mother was pounding the keys and tramping on the pedals as though she was at the wheel of some sort of vehicle, like a big wooden bus she was driving down a steep hill with her feet and hands.

Mandy
There's a minister handy . . .

Hearing the blundering repetition of someone being taught something from scratch was unbearable to me, because, probably from exasperation, I learned it before they did. I was usually way ahead while they were still faltering. I was always in a fury for it to be over.

I left the room, but even two rooms away I heard,

So don't you linger
Here's the ring for your finger
Isn't it a humdinger?

Against my will I listened to the whole thing until the song was in my head, not as it was meant to be sung, but in Dad's tuneless and halting rendition.

Later, over dinner, in reply to a question I didn't hear, Dad said, "Fella gave it to me – loaned it. I'll have to give it back afterwards."

"Who loaned it?"

"John Flaherty."

"Why?"

"Mel Hankey loaned it to him."

"What's it for?"

"Minstrel show."

Mother made a face. He was eating. As though to avoid further questions, Dad filled his mouth with food and went on eating, with the faraway look he assumed when he didn't want to be questioned. *I'm busy thinking,* his expression said. *You don't want to interrupt.*

Then, out of the side of his mouth, he said, "Pass the mouse turd, sonny."

We stared at him. He was chewing.

"Tell you a great meal," he said. "Lettuce. Turnip. And pea."

He winked. We had no idea.

"Minstrel show," he seemed to feel, explained everything – and perhaps it did, but not to me. Words I had never heard before had a significance for him, and a private satisfaction. But "mouse turd"?

After that, he practiced the song "Mandy" every night, singing with more confidence and tunefulness, Mother playing more loudly, thumping her pedaling feet. His voice was strong, assertive rather than melodious. Within a week, he grew hoarse, lost his voice, and from the next room it was as though another man was singing, not Dad but a growly stranger.

Around this time, having mastered the song, he revealed his new name. This was at the dinner table, Mother at one end, Dad at the other, Fred, Floyd, Rose, and me between them.

"Fella says to me, 'Wasn't that song just beautiful? Didn't it touch you, Mr. Bones?' I says, 'No, but the fella that sang it touched me, and he still owes me five bucks.' "

"Who's Mr. Bones?" I asked.

"Yours truly."

"No, it's not," Fred said.

"Only one thing in the world keeps you from being a barefaced liar," he said to Fred.

We were shocked at his suddenness.

"Your mustache," Dad said, and wagged his head and chuckled.

"I don't have a mustache," Fred said.

Mother got flustered when she heard anyone telling a joke. She said, "Don't be stupid."

"You think I'm stupid," Dad said eagerly. "You should see my brother. He walks like this." He got up from the table and bent over and hopped forward.

He did have a brother, that was the confusing part.

"You're so pretty and you're so intelligent," he said, striking a pose with Mother, using that new snappy voice.

"I wish I could say the same for you."

Dad laughed, a kind of cackle, as though it was just what he wanted to hear. He said, "You could, if you told as big a lie as

I just did." He nudged me and said, "She was too ugly to have her face lifted. They lowered her body instead."

With that, he skipped out of the room, his hands in the air, and I thought for a moment that Mother was going to cry.

He had become a different man, and it had happened quickly, just like that, calling himself Mr. Bones and teasing us, teasing Mother. She was bewildered and upset. The song he mastered he kept humming, and his jokes, not really jokes, were more like taunts.

"Maybe it's his new job," Fred said in the bedroom after lights out.

Floyd said, "It's this house. Ma hates it. It's Dad's fault. He's just being silly."

"What's a minstrel show?" I asked.

No one answered.

Trying to be friendly, Mother asked Dad about his job a few days later.

"They said I'd be a connoisseur, but I'm just a common sewer."

Then that gesture with the hands, waggling his fingers.

"Said I'd be a pretty good physician, but I said, 'I'm not good at fishin'.' Or a doctor of some standing. I says, 'No, I'm sitting – in the shoe department.'"

Mother said coldly, "We need new linoleum in the upstairs bathroom."

"And you need new clothes, because your clothes are like the two French cities, Toulouse and Toulon."

"Don't be a jackass."

"*Mister* Jackass to you."

"I wish John Flaherty hadn't given you that music."

"Lightning Flaherty said I needed it. Tambo gave it to him. Play it for me again, I need a good physic."

Mother began to clear the table.

"I love work," Dad said. "I could watch it all day."

Mother went to the sink and leaned over. She had turned on the water, her bent back toward us, and I associated the water running into the dishpan with her tears.

He was a new man, even my brothers said so, though, being older than me, they were often out of the house in the evenings when Dad – Mr. Bones – was at his friskiest. He had swagger and assurance, and if I tried to get his attention, or if he was asked a question, he began to sing "Mandy." He had somehow learned two other songs: "Rosie, You Are My Posie" and "Rock-a-Bye Your Baby with a Dixie Melody" – Lightning's song, and Tambo's, so he said.

I was used to my father singing, but not these songs; used to his good humor, but there was anger in these jokes. And he, who seldom went out at night except to Benediction or choir practice, was now out most nights. He stopped asking Mother to play the piano for him; he would simply break into song, drawling it out of the side of his mouth.

When you croon, croon a tune,
From the heart of Dixie . . .

He didn't look any different, he dressed the same, in a gray suit and white shirt and blue tie and the topcoat he disparaged as "too dressy." One day the sleeve was limp. He flapped it at Mother and said, "I know what you're thinking: World War Two," as though his arm was missing. Then he shot the arm out of the sleeve and said, "Nope. Filene's Basement. Bad fit!"

The variation that night and for nights to come was the tambourine he had somehow acquired. When he made a joke or a quip he shook it and rapped it on his knee and elbow and shook it again. *Shika-shika-shika.*

"RSVP," he said, holding up a piece of mail. "Remember

Send Vedding Present," and he jingled and tapped the tambourine.

One day after school I went to the store where he worked. Instead of walking in, I kept my head down and crept to the side window to get a glimpse of Dad. He was sitting in one of the chairs in the shoe department, his chin in his hand, not looking like Mr. Bones but sad and silent, a man trying to remember something. Other clerks in shirtsleeves had gathered at the back of the store and were laughing, but not Dad. Were they ignoring him? He paid no attention. He was reading – unusual, a shoe clerk reading. I didn't know this man either.

I began to be glad that he was out most evenings. At the other, smaller house we'd moved from, he was always at home after work, and in the early days of this new one – the bigger house that Mother hated – he was usually in his chair, dressed in flannel pajamas and a fuzzy bathrobe, reading the *Globe* under a lamp in the corner. But after that first night, with "Mandy," and then the jokes, and the tambourine, as Mr. Bones, he was out at night, sometimes didn't come home for supper, or if he did, it was "Pass the mouse turd" or, holding the pepper shaker, "This is how I feel, like pulverized pepper – fine!"

"The oil burner's back on the fritz," Mother said.

Any mention of a problem with the house these days made Dad smile his Mr. Bones smile and roll his eyes.

"Heard about the King of England? He's got a *royal* burner."

"We'll have to get Mel to look at it."

"Tambo is a busy man, yes he is. Says to me, 'What is the quickest way to the emergency ward?' I says, 'Tambo, just you stand in the middle of the road.'"

Mother did not react, except to say, "It's giving off a funny smell."

"Giving off a funny smell!" Dad said, and put one finger in the air, what I now recognized as a Mr. Bones gesture – he was about to say something and wanted attention. "Mr. Interlocutor, what is the difference between an elephant passing wind and a place where you might go for a drink?"

"I don't think you understand," Mother said in a strained voice. "This house hasn't been right since the day we moved in. First it was the roof, then the paint, then the plumbing. Now it's the heat. We're not going to have any hot water. Everything's *wrong.*"

Dad held his chin in his hand, as I'd seen him do at the store. He thought a moment, then looked around the table and said, "Mr. Interlocutor, the difference between an elephant passing wind and the place where you might go for a drink is – one is a barroom and the other is a *bar-rooom!*"

He said it so loud we jumped. He didn't laugh. He drew his chair next to Mother and sang.

Rosie, you are my posie,
You are my heart's bouquet.
Come out here in the moonlight,
There's something sweet, love,
I want to say.

Mother looked awkward and sad. She wasn't angry. In a way, by clowning, Dad took her mind off the problems of the house. She could not get his attention. And who was he anyway? He had a different voice, a jaunty manner.

It wasn't any kind of joking I'd heard before from him. His teasing was more like mocking and bullying. He wouldn't call Mel Hankey anything but Tambo, and John Flaherty was Lightning. They had never been close friends before – he had no friends – but now he had Tambo and Lightning and Mr. Interlocutor.

"Morrie Daigle said he'd help you fix the roof."

"Mr. Interlocutor is too hot to do that. He is so hot he will only read fan mail."

That was how we found out who Mr. Interlocutor was.

"Have you lost your wallet?" Dad said to Floyd.

"No," Floyd said, and clapped his hand to his pocket.

"Good. Then give me the five dollars you owe me."

Floyd made a face, looked helpless, thrashed a little. It was true that Dad had given him five dollars, but he had not brought it up before this.

Dad said, "Hear about the Indian who had a red ant?"

I didn't understand that one at all. I pictured an Indian with an insect. It made no sense.

There was something abrupt and deflecting in his humor. He made a joke and seemed to expand, pushing the house and his job aside. He'd been at the new job for six months now and never mentioned it. I had seen him in the store, not working but sitting in the chair where the shoe customers were supposed to sit, and instead of waiting on them, or talking to the other employees, he was reading.

Mother seemed to be afraid of him. Before, she had always made a remark, or nagged, or blamed. But these days she relented. She watched him. When he made a joke she became very quiet and blinked at him, as though she was thinking, What do you mean by that?

Floyd was on the basketball team, Fred played hockey, so they were out most evenings – practicing, they said. I knew it was an excuse to stay away from home and Mr. Bones. Rose was just a little kid of seven, and she actually found Mr. Bones funny, and let him tickle her.

But I had nowhere to go, and I didn't like the angry jokes or the cruel teasing. Mr. Bones was always laughing or singing, and he never listened, except when he was thinking up another joke. He was a stranger to me, and for the first time I began to think, Who are you? What do you want?

What happened next was more shocking. Dad's change was a surprise, but when he changed again he seemed monstrous. We thought, What next? It frightened the whole family, but maybe me especially, because I went to bed thinking, Who are you?

The light went on and I had the answer.

Most of the lights in the house were bare bulbs with no shades, hanging on frayed black whips from the ceiling – another source of Mother's complaints – and the brightness of the one dangling in my bedroom made it worse. I had been woken up, so the light blazed and half blinded me. Yet I saw enough to be terrified.

A disfigured villain from a horror comic was bending over my bed – I realized only later that it was Dad – his whole face sticky black, a white oval outline around his lips. He wore a cap that even afterward I could not imagine was a wig, a red floppy bow tie, a yellow speckled vest, and a black coat, and he was emphatically holding his hands out in white gloves. He was smiling under that blackness that shone on his face, and he leaned over me and spoke, seeming to shriek.

"Give us a kiss, sonny boy!"

Then he laughed and stood up and waved his gloved hands again and jerked the light chain, bringing down darkness.

His voice had matched his face. He was so black that I dreamed he was still in my bedroom, standing there invisible in his floppy tie: Mr. Bones. I had not heard the door shut.

I even said into the menacing gloom, "Dad – are you there?"

Giving no answer was just the sort of thing he'd try as Mr. Bones.

I said again, "Dad?" And in a trembly voice, "Mr. Bones?"

I had not heard him leave. For all I knew he stayed there to scare me. But in the morning the room was empty.

At breakfast he was eating oatmeal as usual. He had a decorous way of holding his spoon. I looked closely at him and saw some streaks of black makeup caked in the lines on his neck. I sprinkled raisins on my oatmeal.

"Pass me the dead flies, sonny," he said in his Mr. Bones voice.

These days his remarks silenced the room. We all felt the effect of his angry humor. I didn't know how deeply Mother was upset – though I knew she was. Floyd and Fred were startled but sometimes pretended to find it funny, and occasionally they teased back. When Dad made his "Toulouse and Toulon" joke, Floyd said, "Well, you're like a town in Massachusetts – Marblehead." Instead of being insulted, Dad smiled and said, "I like that."

But he kept on worrying Fred about college, and Floyd about trumpet lessons. We didn't know what was coming next. We had not foreseen the songs or the jokes; we had not expected the black face. Maybe there was more.

His voice was hoarse from practicing, and now every night he came home in black makeup, his wig like a too-big woolly hat. He talked about Tambo and Lightning and Mr. Interlocutor, and he told the same jokes. Hearing it again and again, I came to understand the one about the Indian and the red ant – red aunt was the point of it. We never pronounced it "ant," always "awnt."

I felt embarrassed and fearful. We were afraid to ask him about his job in the shoe department these days. If Mother mentioned the house, that there were drips to be fixed, the oil burner to be mended, linoleum to be laid, painting to be done, I didn't hear it. All our attention was on him, who he was now, Mr. Bones. To almost any question, he began singing.

A million baby kisses I'll deliver
If you will only sing that "Swanee River"

The rhythm was there, a confident slowness and drawl, yet his voice was strained from overuse. He lifted his knees and did dance steps as he sang, and he raised his white gloves. And Mother sat at the piano, looking anxious, playing the melody.

It seemed so wrong, I was always glancing at the door, scared that someone – a neighbor, the Fuller Brush man,

Grandpa – might come in and see him swaying and singing with a black face and that wig.

He had another song too:

When life seems full of clouds and rain,
And I am filled with naught but pain,
Who soothes my thumpin' bumpin' brain?

He would always pause after that, and lower himself and put his head out and say, "Nobody!"

His voice was gargly and cross, as though he was in pain. The weeks of rehearsals had taken away his real voice and given him this new one.

When all day long things go amiss,
And I go home to find some bliss,
Who hands to me a glowin' kiss?

He was standing over Mother at the piano, and her bleak plunking notes, and smiling angrily, his wig tilted, one glove in the air.

"Nobody!"

The next time I sneaked after school to the window of the store and looked in, I saw him sitting where I'd seen him before, in the chairs reserved for customers, reading. He was not in blackface, yet his assurance, his posture, the way he sat, like the owner of the store, made him seem more than ever like Mr. Bones. He looked thoughtful, his fist against his mouth, a knuckle against his nose. And the other clerks and floorwalkers seemed to avoid him, talking among themselves, as though they knew he was Mr. Bones.

At a funeral in church one Saturday, I stood beside Ed Hankey, both of us altar boys, in starched blouse-like surplices, holding tall smoking candles, preparing to follow the coffin down the main aisle. The priest was swinging a thurible – more smoke – and the relatives of the dead man were howling.

Hankey said in a whisper, "You going to the minstrel show?"

"I don't know. Are you?"

"My old man's in it. So's yours."

"I don't even know what it's supposed to be."

"It's a wicked pisser. Just a bunch of old guys singing, like a talent show," Hankey said.

Then we saw the priest glaring at us. We straightened our candles and approached the coffin.

This big event was just a talent show to Hankey. And his white-haired father, who worked on the MTA buses, was just an old guy singing. Yet in our house Mr. Bones had taken charge and intimidated us all.

He had a different complaint about each of us. These objections were clearer when he was in blackface and a wig than when he was just Mr. Bones in name. He was now a man in a mask, someone to fear, saying things he normally avoided, singing strange songs. In his minstrel show costume he could be as reckless as he wanted.

It was true that Fred told fibs and didn't want to go to college, true that Floyd owed him money and hated trumpet lessons. And it was easy to see that Mother's nagging caused him to tease her and change the subject. His jokes were more than jokes; they were ways of telling us the truth. The yellow mustard in big quart jars was cheap and tasteless; "mouse turd" was a good name for it. The stale raisins that Mother bought cheap in the dented-package aisle were like dead flies. But it was so odd hearing these things from his gleaming black face, his white-outlined mouth, his woolly wig askew, and rapping his tambourine after he spoke.

"Dad," we said, pleading.

"Dad done gone. 'That was prior to his decease, Mr. Bones.' I says, 'He had no niece.'"

Shika-shika-shika went the tambourine.

He was happy, not just smiling but defiantly happy, powerfully happy, talking to us, teasing us in ways I'd never heard before. He had once been remote, with a kindly smile that made him hard to approach. Now he was up close and laughing at us and he wouldn't go away.

He was someone new, convincingly a real man, as though he'd been turned inside out, the true Dad showing. Swanking in the role of a comical slave, he'd become a frightening master to us, and because he was so strange we had no way of responding to his tyrannical teasing.

Something else I discovered, because I kept going to the store to lurk and spy on him, was that instead of sitting silently alone in the shoe department he'd been hired to run, he now had company: Mel Hankey, John Flaherty, Morrie Daigle, and two men I'd never seen before. All of them with their heads together, sitting in the customers' chairs, whispering, as if they were cooking something up. So odd to see this in a store where everyone else was working or shopping or being loudly busy.

That was his secret. Mine too. The whole affair looked more serious than just black faces and songs and jokes. These men were like conspirators, with a single plan in their minds, and the sight of them impressed me, because Dad was in charge. I could see it in his posture, sitting upright like a musician holding an instrument; but the instrument was his hand. Wearing white gloves, he seemed to be giving directions, issuing energetic commands. Mr. Bones was their leader.

So, after all, he had friends – these five whispering white men, who were black conspirators. We had taken him to be a man with no friends outside the family, no interests outside the house and the church; but here he was with his pals, Tambo, Lightning, Mr. Interlocutor, and the rest whose names I didn't know.

But that same night, as though to dispute all this, he came

home after dinner in blackface and floppy coat and wig, and said, "Listen to Mr. Bones."

Fred was fiddling with the radio, Mother was at the sink with Floyd, I was looking at a comic book.

"I says, listen to Mr. Bones!"

He spoke so loud we jumped, and as we did, he banged and clicked his tambourine. He was like a drunk you couldn't talk back to, yet he hadn't had a drink.

I ain't never done nothin' to nobody,
I ain't never got nothin' from nobody, no time!
And until I get somethin' from somebody, sometime,
I don't intend to do nothin' for nobody, no time!

He searched us, shaking his head, and moaned, "Nobody, no time!"

Was it a song? Was it a poem? Was it a speech? It was too furious to be entertainment. We sat horrified by the sight of Dad in blackface, rapping his tambourine on his knees and his elbow and then bonking himself on the head with it.

Even though it was painful to hear, it was being spoken by a man who had our full attention. We had to listen; we couldn't look away. That proved he was the opposite of the poor soul he was describing – he was stronger than we were, but I recognized the "nobody" he spoke of. It wasn't Mr. Bones, it was Dad.

After that, he went over to Fred and said, "What are you going to do for Mr. Bones?"

"College," Fred said, blinking fiercely.

"Know the difference between a college professor and a railway conductor?"

"No."

"No what?"

"No, Mr. Bones."

"One trains minds and the other minds trains. Which one do you want to be?"

"College professor, Mr. Bones."

But Mr. Bones had turned to Floyd. "What are you going to do for Mr. Bones?"

"Trumpet lessons, Mr. Bones."

"You always were good at blowing your own horn. Ha!" Then he had me by the chin and was lifting it, as Dad had never done. "Who was that lady you saw me with last night?"

With his white-gloved hand gripping my chin, I couldn't speak.

"That was no lady. That was my wife!"

Mother muttered as he shook his tambourine.

"You'll need some Karo syrup for that throat," Mother said, and handed him a bottle and a spoon.

He took a swig straight from the bottle, then said to Fred, "Here, want to keep this bottle up your end?"

I didn't know it was a joke until he lowered his shoulders and swung his arms and shook his tambourine.

I had been dreading going to the show for weeks, and when the day came I said, "I don't want to go. I've got a wicked bad stomachache."

"Everyone's going," Mother said, trembling with a kind of nervous insistence that I recognized: if I defied her, she might start screaming.

On a wet Saturday night in May we went together to the high school auditorium in our old car, Mother driving. I could tell she was upset from the way she drove, riding the brake, stamping on the clutch, pushing the gearshift too hard. Dad had gone separately. "Tambo's stopping by for me."

I hurried into the auditorium and slid down in my seat so that no one would see me. When the music began to play and the curtain went up, I covered my face and peered through my fingers.

Dad – Mr. Bones – was sitting in a chair onstage, and the

others, too, sat on chairs in a semicircle. Mr. Bones looked confident and happy; he was dressed like a clown, but he looked powerful. He was wearing his floppy suit, shiny vest, big bow tie, white gloves and tilted wig, and his face was black. All of them were in blackface except Morrie Daigle, in the center, who wore a white suit and a white top hat.

"Mr. Bones, wasn't that music just beautiful? Didn't it touch you?"

I pressed my fingers to my ears, closed my eyes, and groaned so that I wouldn't hear the rest. I wanted to disappear. I was slumped in my seat so my head wasn't showing, and even though I kept my hands to my ears I heard familiar phrases: *physician of good standing* and *that was prior to his decease.*

The songs I knew by heart penetrated me as I sat there trying to deafen myself. Mr. Bones sang "Mandy." "Rosie" and "Rock-a-Bye Your Baby" were sung by others. Someone else sang "Nobody."

I heard, *You should see my brother, he walks like this,* and knew it was Mr. Bones. I heard, *bare-faced liar.* I heard, *Toulouse and Toulon.* Even so, my eyes were shut, my palms stuck against my ears, and I was groaning.

There was much more, skits and songs. People laughing, people clapping, the loud music, the shouts, the tambourines, the familiar phrases. This was silly and embarrassing, yet the same jokes and songs had intimidated us at home. And Mr. Bones had been different at home too, not this ridiculous man clowning, far off on the stage, but someone else I didn't want to think of as Dad, teasing us and making fools of us and getting us to agree with him and make decisions. That was who he was – Dad as Mr. Bones.

When the people onstage were taking their bows and the auditorium was still dark, I said, "I have to go to the bathroom," and ran out and hid in our car.

Back home afterward, no one said anything about the show. Dad was in his regular clothes, with the faint greasy streaks of black on his neck and behind his ears. He was excited, breathless, but he didn't speak. The strange episode and uproar were over. Later, I got anxious when he hummed "Mandy" or "Rosie" while he was shaving in the kitchen, but he didn't make any jokes, didn't tease or taunt anymore. Looking through the side window of the store, I saw him standing near the cash register, in the shoe department, smiling at the front door as though to welcome a customer.

The following year there was talk of a minstrel show, but nothing happened. We had a TV set then, and the news was of trouble in Little Rock, Arkansas, integrating the schools, black children protected by National Guardsmen, white crowds shouting abuse at the frightened black students who were being liberated. The bald-headed president made a speech on TV. Dad watched with us, saying nothing, maybe thinking how Mr. Bones had been liberated too, or banished. It was not what he had expected. The expression on his face was vacant, stunned with sorrow, but before long Dad was smiling.

Our Raccoon Year

THEY WERE LIKE hissing animals, blinded by the dark, thinking that no one knew. So we pretended we didn't and hoped they'd stop. Then he'd say something, and she'd say something, and – Don't say anything more, I thought, and held my breath – he'd say something sharp, and after a gasp and some crackling, their talk swished back and forth in furious whispers. Sometimes a thump, and a swelling silence that terrified Sam and me more than the hisses.

It was not a question of our being happy or sad, but a condition, worry without a payoff, as though the house was always the wrong temperature. Then one muddy March day Ma said she was going away, she didn't say where. She looked at us with bright anxious eyes and swallowed whatever she was about to tell us. Soon she was gone, down the driveway, where someone was waiting, under the sky like a low ceiling.

"She's where she wants to be," Pa said. "With her friend."

I did not know it at the time, but that was when our raccoon year started, the first feature of it, Pa stopping whatever he was doing to squint, and wrinkle his nose, with a listening tilt to his head.

"There's this funny smell."

He had been an attorney. "My partner Hoyt used to say, 'I bite people on the neck for a living.'" He smiled. "That wasn't me." He had been the first man in our state to gain full custody of his children in a divorce settlement, his best-known case. It happens these days, but years ago it was unheard of, the divorced husband holding on to the house and the children. I was one of the children, my younger brother Sam the other child, both of us still at the Harry Wayne Wing Elementary School in town. Pa was now a financial counselor, working from home, handling investments.

"I'm a bottom feeder in the money business," Pa said. "Just pawing through it like a scavenger." But he was more than that: a reasonable cook, sometimes painted pictures, kept a boat on the creek in the summer. He gave us his wind-up Victrola and his collection of old 78 rpm records, which we often played – "South American Joe," "One Meat Ball," "Shanghai Lil," Hawaiian tunes.

After Ma left, he would not hire a babysitter for Sam, or a cook for us, or a cleaner for the house. He waited with us for the school bus on the main road, and then – as he explained in the evening – he cleaned the house, did the laundry, and went grocery shopping. His office was at home, so he could easily combine housework with his business. He stopped sketching and sailing. He took up fancy cooking, the sort of cooking that makes a person bossy, using recipes out of books, talking about his sauces and his fresh ingredients. He used expressions like "my kitchen" and "my garlic press," and of some dishes, he said, "Those beef tips pair nicely with a Merlot," or "Anything with a mouth would eat that."

But there was nothing he could do to fill the empty space that Ma had made by leaving. Watching him trying so hard made me sad. And so I ate the food he prepared with frowning attention, even when I was not hungry.

Our house sat on the brow of a hill, allowing us to see that we had no neighbors. But we had visitors. Just after Ma left, we began to find twists of scat like heaps of blackened sausages in corners of the porch, or we'd forget a plate of half-eaten food – it might be a leftover lump of risotto Milanese on the picnic table – and it would be gone in the morning, the plate licked clean. We found scratchings and evidence of prowlings, clawed earth, overturned buckets, but saw nothing of the perpetrators, as Pa called them. They were like phantoms. Even when he was wrinkling his nose, Pa praised them for being invisible, ripe-smelling ghosts that were about to arrive or had just left, content to live among themselves, never showing their faces, and shadowing us and living on our scraps.

"Probably doing us a favor, cleaning up after us."

As well as the main house, where Pa slept and cooked and kept his library, we had two other houses: the office house where Pa worked, with a guest room downstairs, and another whole house at the far end of the swimming pool, which we called the Boys' House. The pump and filter for the pool were in the basement, but the Boys' House – just bedrooms and a bathroom, no kitchen – had been built for my brother and me. Pa had gotten the idea from his reading about the customs in various places. In parts of New Guinea and Africa, boys our age were housed separately from their parents and sisters in "bachelor houses."

"Make all the noise you want," Pa often said. "I don't want to witness your excesses or your indiscretions." He would then smile and say, "Nor do I wish you to witness mine."

Yet there'd been a vibration from their marriage that was unmistakable to us, the way friction sends out a burning smell: we had heard him hissing upstairs with Ma when we were in the main house before meals.

With plenty of space for ourselves in the Boys' House, and a guest room too, we played the Victrola, stayed up late, lit candles, sometimes smoked, and had our friends over. At mealtimes we gathered at the main house to eat, and after Ma left, to try Pa's latest dish. "This is a reduction sauce," and "Osso buco presented on a bed of polenta," and, holding a forkful of sun-dried tomatoes, "Loaded with micronutrients."

Later in that first year without Ma we got neighbors, one at the foot of the hill facing the sea, the other one on an adjoining piece of land. We hardly saw them the summer they were building; we only heard the hammering and the country music from the workmen's radios. But when the leaves were blown from the trees in October, the neighbors' houses were visible –

white, large, and the more conspicuous for the way the owners had cleared their land. They'd cut down all their trees, and they'd already begun to set rolls of sod for muddy lawns. We seemed now to be on our own wooded five-acre island, because none of our trees had been cut.

It was then that we saw more evidence of the animals, more scat, more scratchings, and Pa sniffed and squinted. Driven off the neighbors' property and robbed of their habitat, the creatures migrated to our land. How many we didn't yet know: we had not so far seen even one of them.

"You don't see them during the day," Pa said, and he seemed to be quoting someone when he added, "They are chiefly a nocturnal animal."

A few days after he said that, when we were sitting on the back porch, Pa paddled his hands, saying, "Shush." I thought, and hoped, that he'd seen Ma. He crouched and pointed to a slow hairy shadow moving beneath low juniper boughs, and this big shadow dragging a cluster of shadows behind it, two small ones, her young.

Raccoons. Pa whispered that we were lucky to see them in daylight, the plump mother raccoon with a black eye mask, tottering a little and poking her snout along the edge of the brick apron of the pool, keeping out of the sun. It was as though we were seeing strange visitors. Yet they didn't seem strange at all, more like self-possessed residents who knew their way around the property.

"There's a real mother," Pa said, and sounded tearful. He was still whispering into his hand.

Sam said, "Two kids?"

Pa hissed. "I said, two *kits*."

As we watched, they poured their supple bodies beneath the side slats in the deck that served as a seating platform on the far end of the pool. And now we knew that when we were in the deck chairs we were sitting on top of a family of raccoons.

Pa still wore an amused and even tender expression, but soon he became rueful, with a faded smile, as though thinking about how Ma had gone off with her friend – the worst day of my life. Long after the raccoons had gone, Pa kept squinting at the spot they'd slipped from, as you do a sunset.

That night after dinner, Pa said he wanted to tell us a bedtime story. The Boys' House was out of bounds to him, so we sat in the library and read from *Old Mother West Wind*. He put special emphasis on the character of Bobby Raccoon, giving Bobby the even, reasonable voice of a very good boy.

And for the next few days, he'd stop and peer at those slats in the deck from where he sat on the porch; or else, when we'd be eating outside, or playing cards at the picnic table, Pa would glance over, and I knew he was hoping to see them. Even in the shadow of the junipers, the mother had been a strong presence – large, healthy, busy, snouty, and deliberate in her crawl, with an air of belonging. The little ones were frisky, their coats were sleek, and they had a fat side-to-side noiseless way of gliding.

Not seeing them, Pa put out some leftovers for them, describing them in the way he served up food. "Chicken," he said. "Bones from the stockpot. Some bruised kiwi fruit."

The scraps were gone in the morning. "Must have been that mother. Or maybe Bobby. Like a pit bull on a pot roast." I was sure that Pa was sorry he wasn't able to stand over the raccoons and see them gnawing the bones, eating the chicken, doing a better job of finishing the food than Sam and I ever did, Pa saying to the raccoons, "Citrus chicken with a grapefruit salsa . . ."

They got into the garden and left symmetrical bite marks on the eggplants. They didn't touch the overripe tomatoes on the vines. But by now, frosty October, the garden was over. They ate the mushrooms that sprang up overnight in the dampness near the pitch pines.

"Looks tidier without that dog-vomit fungus," Pa said in the morning, seeing that they had cleared the yard of the growths that were like twisted pieces of dirty Styrofoam. "How do they know it's not poisonous? Just smart, I guess."

Halloween was costume time at the Harry Wayne Wing School. Pa bought us black eye masks and furry hats with tails. "Go as Bobby Raccoon." But we refused and went as pirates.

We eventually found out how many raccoons there were. I was feeling sick and sleepless one night, and wanted some sympathy from Pa. I got out of bed – it was about two in the morning – and, without turning on the light, I opened the front door to our house. In the moonlight on the slightly raised deck in front of our Boys' House I saw a number of lumpy plant-like shapes, big and small, each one in a different position, sitting, lying flat, creeping, in dark clusters, eight or ten of them – no, a dozen or more, very calm, a nighttime gathering that did not disperse as I watched. Most of them were still, like a whole collection of stuffed toys. Even when I stamped on the deck boards and clapped my hands they hesitated rather than fled, seeming bewildered to see a stranger on their territory. But when I made more noise, waking Sam, the raccoons tumbled away.

The sight of them startled me into health. I went back to bed. In the morning, breakfast in the main house, I told Pa. He just nodded in his preoccupied way, as though he was pretending to listen. It was around this time that Ma had called. I only heard Pa's side of the conversation, but I knew it was Ma on the line because, between the *miao miao* at the other end, Pa was saying, "What do you want? . . . Haven't you done enough? . . . We're cozy, we're a unit . . . Just fine," and hung up.

But he had heard what I'd reported about the raccoons. He put out some leftovers – tomatoes from yesterday's sauce – then set his alarm. At two in the morning he went out to see if what I'd said was true. He counted eighteen of them, big and small, and had watched for almost an hour.

"They act as if they own the place!" In a sour and disgusted voice he added, "Some of them standing on their hind legs. A few making babies."

But what seemed to bother him most was that they hadn't eaten the carefully cooked tomatoes he'd put out. "Those were heirlooms." He was insulted that, instead, they'd chewed the cedar shingles on the side wall of his office.

Seeing so many of them made him believe that he could smell them everywhere on the property. "It's a damp and dungy dead-dog stink that I can't get out of my nose."

He stopped the bedtime stories, and the talk about "little families" and "good mother," and now and then went rigid and sniffed and said, "Coons." And it got worse. Sam left the garage door open one evening after dumping some household trash. The next day we found the barrels we kept there overturned and the plastic bags torn open and picked through – clamshells, Parmesan cheese rind, kale stems, duck bones, and all the rest of the garbage that reminded me that the raccoons were pawing through Pa's gourmet food, eating some of it but not touching the tomatoes.

"Get a broom, Sam," Pa said to the garbage scattered on the floor without any emotion, which meant he was furious.

Out of the blue, at dinner that evening, he straightened his head and spoke to the window. "I hate the mindless punctuality of vermin. I hate it that they're welfare-fussy." Then loudly, "If those damn people down the hill hadn't put up those ugly houses and cut down all the trees, we wouldn't have this problem. I never minded our coons, but we have all their coons, too!"

Three wild turkeys often strutted in the underbrush during the day and roosted in the trees at night. The raccoons killed all three. They didn't eat them; they clawed at their feathers and gashed their necks with bites.

"Mugged them," Pa said. "Consider the spite of a fanatic."

He bought a trap, which was built like a metal cage, and after a few tries – it was sprung without capturing anything – he caught a fat raccoon. In sunlight it was sleepy and pet-like and shy. Pa loaded it into the back of the van and released it at the marsh four miles down the road.

On the way home, he remembered that he needed an inspection sticker for the van. At the filling station, the mechanic asked about the empty trap. Pa told his story. The mechanic smiled and said, “It’ll find its way back. They’re not stupid.”

This was in the office of the filling station, Pa paying for the sticker. Overhearing him, a woman, also waiting, said, “I just hope it’s not a nursing mother.”

“She rescues raccoons,” the mechanic said, laughing.

“There’s too many of them,” Pa said.

“Too many people, you mean,” the woman said.

“They have diseases.”

“People have diseases!”

“Whose side are you on?” Pa said.

The woman had been sitting quietly, but now, blinking in anger, she looked insulted and hurt. She said, “I have a shelter for them. I care for them. They are living creatures. Killing them is cruel.”

Pa said, “Maybe it would be cruel if I were killing them without a reason.”

The woman had been reaching into her bag and stirring the contents. She took out a leaflet and gave it to Pa and left in a hurry. She said, “I know who you are”–probably because of the well-known child custody case. Pa opened the leaflet, a brochure for her animal shelter, where she was shown nursing a baby raccoon with a nipple bottle.

The raccoon he’d let go at the marsh returned to our house, as the garage man had predicted. Pa knew that because he caught it again in his trap. He said it was not a boar; it was the mother raccoon. He released it even farther away, on the far side of the highway. Then he went to the Town Hall with Sam and me, and talked to the wildlife control officer to ask for advice.

The man in Fish and Game wore a khaki shirt with epaulets, a brass badge on his pocket. He looked like a scoutmaster, his hair a buzz cut we called a wiffle. He said, "There's a two-hundred-dollar fine for what you did."

"What did I do?"

"You moved it. Against the law."

"Oh, right. I'm illegal. They've got rights."

"Section twenty. Relocation of wildlife. That's an offense."

"You're protecting coons?"

"We're too busy for that. Coyotes are the real problem," the man said. "But raccoons out in the daytime might have rabies."

"What if I catch a rabid one?"

"You could call us. Or you could deal with it the way we do. Which is destroy the animal. You employing a suitable trap?"

"Yes. A kind of cage trap." Pa smiled unhappily. "Sometimes I bait it with squashed tomatoes. They don't eat them. Fussy!"

"Omnivores. Eat anything that fits in their mouth. But the acid in tomatoes doesn't agree with them. Use peanut butter on crackers." The man stood to give himself room to explain with gestures. He pushed up his khaki sleeves and said, "Get yourself a barrel. Yay big. Fill it to the brim with water. Making sure the trap is well sprung, immerse the trap containing the animal in the filled barrel. Problem solved."

The sight of a pop-eyed clawing raccoon fighting for its life, drowning at the top corner of a mostly sunken trap, was something Pa wanted us to see. What I saw was that it is a silent animal except in desperation, and the gagging sounds it made, of hissing and harsh gasping, baring its yellow dog-like teeth, terrified me. It clutched at the cage with hands like mine, black fingers hooked in the mesh.

"Bobby," I said.

Pa scowled at me, then turned and watched with satisfaction, seeming to relax, as the animal died and sank in its own bubbles, and that night, much happier, Pa made one of his special meals, short ribs, serving the dark meat with, "It's a delicacy." But I couldn't eat, and Sam hardly touched his. Pa said, "All the more for me."

He reported what he'd done to the wildlife control officer, who said, "Could have had pinworm. Roundworm. You don't want that. Your raccoon is a host to a lot of parasites."

And he explained that anyone breathing the dust from the scat of an infected raccoon might die a horrible death from organ failure. Pa bought rubber gloves and a mask and acid, and he went after the scat, scouring it from the decks. After that, whenever someone questioned him for killing the raccoons, he showed his teeth and said, "Pinworm!"

We should have been glad that Pa had something to care about, to take his mind off Ma, but his mood got darker as the raccoons became harder to trap. Judging from the scat piles and the scratch marks, they were just as numerous. Infuriated, muttering "They don't like tomatoes," Pa would bait a trap with the remains of one of his meals – herb-crusted salmon, the pounded lobster shells he'd used for the bisque – and the raccoons would eat them without tripping the door latch of the trap, or worse, would trip it without being caught.

"In effect, by sheltering them and feeding them my own food I've made them lazier," he said. "They think they belong. They are eating my house. They do no work. They are living off my labor."

He put out poison in a dish. They ate it all – rat poison heaped like the pellets and crumble we had fed the wild turkeys. Within a week, the dungy dead-dog smell hung over the deck. We had to pry up the boards to locate the corpses of the raccoons that had hidden themselves under the deck to die.

The animals seemed to fight back. The ones that Pa had poisoned we buried in the garden, but they were dug up and eaten, torn apart by other raccoons. In the stink, the flies, Pa, flailing with his shovel, hissed, "Cannibals."

We saw more of them in the daytime. "Rabid!" They climbed

onto the roof and crept down the chimney. One rainy November day we saw across the yard some wet raccoons, their heads poked above the chimney of Pa's office, staring down at us.

We didn't tell Pa. In the past we would have alerted him, but now we knew that he'd stiffen and howl, he'd hurry the meal, burn the croutons, forget the sauce, collapse the soufflé, or else he'd serve us leftovers. Yesterday's mac and cheese looks the same, but the leftovers of a gourmet meal are unrecognizable and garbage-like. If we objected, he'd insist that we were at war and demand that we help him. He wanted us to be like him. So: we saw evidence of raccoons all the time – scat, scratch marks, chewings – but we became secretive and didn't say anything.

Sam said in the dark, "I miss Ma."

I said, "She's with her friend."

One night, to cheer ourselves up, we played "Shanghai Lil" on the wind-up.

The door flew open and Pa came in and snatched the phonograph arm so hard he dragged the needle across the record.

"That's enough of that!"

This was like an invasion: he'd never come into the Boys' House before. He must have been crouched outside, listening in the dark. But at midnight?

Pa began fighting with the neighbors, and the talk became abusive. He got estimates for a perimeter fence. But when the salesman from the fence company heard what the fence was for, he said, "They'll climb it. They'd get over it even if it were twenty feet high. They'll tunnel under it. Hey, I want to sell you a fence, but no fence will keep them out. Fences are porous."

Pa sent him away, and the next raccoon he caught he kept in the cage, starving it until it could barely move. Then he released it, and when it stumbled he killed it, hacking it with the blade of a shovel.

He bought a powerful air gun. He unpacked it and unfolded the leaflet of directions. *"Cette arme n'est pas un jouet,"* he read. *"La supervision d'un adulte est requise.* That's me. All we need is a coon." He tried out the gun on the next one he trapped, but the animal cringed, clutched itself, and buried its head in its fur. And didn't die. Then Pa bought a .22 rifle and fired through the mesh of the trap until the animal was motionless and leaking.

But he knew he was losing. He had been so busy with the raccoons he neglected the usual chores. It was well into fall and he forgot to remove the screens from the sliders. The raccoons clawed and tore holes in them. When Pa got the bill for the repairs to the screens he lectured us loudly on loyalty and vigilance.

In the cold weather, climbing the tree next to the Boys' House, raccoons got onto the back roof and clawed and chewed the shingles, trying to get into the attic. Pa cut down the tree and called a contractor to send some men over to reshingle the roof.

"And what do we have here?" he said, staring up at the roofers.

His eyes were dark in the daytime and yellowish at night, something I had never noticed before. They were black now as he spoke to someone on the phone: "You sent me Brazilians. I don't want fruit pickers. I don't want illegals!"

The frightened men crept away, carrying their ladder. Other workers came in white overalls. The roof cost seven thousand dollars to fix.

"And you want to protect them! You and that crazy old lady with the animal shelter!"

We said we didn't, we were afraid, and his meals made us anxious. "Coq au vin," our father said angrily. "Potatoes dauphinoise." And in the same breath, "What if they get inside? They'll crawl into your room and eat your face while you're asleep. You're a delicacy to a coon."

Sam began to cry and said, "I hate them."

"That's more like it. That's what I want to hear. Henry?"

He knew I was resisting him. And so, when he discovered that some raccoons had torn out a board from under the threshold of the side door and were living in the Boys' House basement, he said, "Henry'll take care of it."

He set me to work emptying the basement of lawn chairs and chewed life vests and clawed-open cushions and piles of black scat, so much of it that I thought I'd come down with the pinworm disease. I stopped hating Pa for his cruelty and began hating the raccoons for making me do this filthy job.

Thanksgiving came and went. At Christmas, Pa said, "I was going to make herbed turkey again, with oysters. Savory yam purée soufflé. Stuffed mushrooms – breadcrumbs, cream cheese, and Parmesan. But I'm just roasting a bird and mashing some spuds. You can do the rest."

The phone rang. We knew who it was.

"Let it ring."

Emptying the trash that night in the garage, I felt the hot doggy stink of wet fur against my face. We had an old Jeep, Pa's favorite vehicle, for summer rides. I saw that two raccoons were asleep under the back seat. I knew what he'd say. I opened the garage door and pushed the Jeep into the dark driveway.

Pa saw me from an upstairs window and was soon beside me, carrying his rifle. When he poked the animals with the barrel they shrank deeper under the seat.

I said, "They'll go away if we leave them. After midnight."

"You think that's a solution. To let them sneak out of the Jeep. But they won't go away. They never go away. They'll stay and have babies. Where will that leave us?" He raised the rifle but didn't fire it. "How can I? This vehicle is a classic."

The next day, in sunlight, they were gone. Yet we knew there were too many of them to trap, that we'd never get rid of them. Knowing they were around made us fear Pa the more. Pa got pleasure out of killing them, even if he wasn't winning. He said that he'd find ways of making them die slowly – poisoning them, dunking them in a three-quarters-full barrel of water and watching them exhaust themselves, starving them in the trap. "Know what? I'd like to crucify one."

He had one subject only. He'd strike up conversations with strangers just to hear their views on raccoons. "Got any coons over your way?" Or, instead of "coons," he'd say "vermin" or "bandits." If they didn't agree with him, he raged.

"Everything is sorcery," he said one morning. His eyes were reddish. He hadn't slept. He'd stayed awake at night to spy on the animals. He'd begun keeping raccoon hours. "Business. Law. Religion. All sorcery." He took a deep breath. I thought he was going to cry. He said, "And all of this."

Until now he'd kept Ma away – refused her calls or put the phone down. But one night after dinner, we heard him say, "You again," in the whisper we recognized from before.

I signaled to Sam to duck down by the window. We couldn't see him, but we could hear him clearly.

"You think I don't know you're back," he said. "But I do. I could smell you before I saw you, and now you think you're going to take over the house while I stand idly by."

We became hopeful. Ma was home. He was talking with the bullying confidence of a lawyer, facing the darkness outside the screen door where a shadow was apparent.

"You think I'm just going to throw my hands up and surrender after all the work I've done," he said. "It's not going to happen. I warn you – I'm dangerous."

Fearing for Ma, we crept around the house to the door, and it was then we saw the masked face and the snout and the greasy fur.

He made sketches for a complicated mobile trap that was built into our van, that would lure them inside, and once they were inside he'd poison them and drive them to the dump. "Efficiency." He knew, as we did, that they were intelligent: they could smell a trap, and they were smarter in their way than Pa. And sometimes it seemed as though they knew that Pa was after them and they were deliberately targeting him as a result, out of pure spite – chewing his chairs, fouling his vehicle, clawing the weatherstripping at his office door.

They were a nuisance, but Pa called them evil, and in his frustration and fear he seemed worse. All that the raccoons knew was what raccoons knew, but Pa had the advantage of being a whole man, a once powerful attorney. He'd lost interest in investing, or maybe the investors had lost interest in him. Sam and I didn't pity him anymore. He slept in his chair during the day and stayed up at night, monitoring his traps, and he'd stopped his gourmet cooking, or any cooking.

"I eat anything that fits into my mouth."

He woke up after we got home from school. "You can fix yourselves something. Just don't make a mess." But the house was always messy, and the outside was booby-trapped. He did not repair the clawed shingles or bitten doorframes anymore. He wanted them as proof, he said, to justify his methods.

One of his cuff links went missing. "They like shiny things." He believed that a raccoon had taken it, and his keys too, when he couldn't find them.

I tried to recall our first sight of the raccoons, as furry masked cuddly creatures. But I couldn't. I could only see them as vicious and bewildered and pathetic, like Pa.

Sam stumbled into a trap and sprung it and cut his leg on the sharp metal edge.

"Serves you right," Pa said. "Now I have to set it again."

One winter day Pa's chair creaked as he sat up straight. He had been sleeping but heard something, a car in the driveway. He squinted as though a raccoon was approaching, and he eyed Ma slipping out of the car as if he had eyed an animal.

When she came inside the house, he said, "Where's your friend?"

"Away," she said. "For various reasons." We hadn't seen her for a year. She was wearing a warm fleece jacket that we recognized, and ski pants, and sturdy shoes. But her face was sad and pale, and she seemed uneasy. "What's that funny smell?"

"They have scent glands in their armpits," Pa said.

She hugged us, and when I felt her arms I could tell she was thinner. She pressed her head against us as if in prayer, then said, "Let's go outside."

The day was still and cold, ice crusts on the brown grass, frozen dewdrops on the dead leaves, an animal smell in the windless air.

"We've got raccoons."

"I wish I could help," she said, but she looked nervous.

Pa had followed us out to the gravel path. He said, "Everyone's got raccoons. You'd just make it worse."

Ma stared at him, surprised, as though seeing a stranger. That was not the sort of thing he'd ever said to her before. He was awarded custody because he was kind, reasonable, helpful, forgiving – nurturing, was how he put it to the judge. But he had a thin, mean face now, dimly lit and sunken eyes, unshaven cheeks, and discolored teeth. Normally he would not have been awake at this time. Ma had disturbed him.

She said, "I've missed you boys so much."

We told her we'd missed her too, but in a low voice so that Pa wouldn't hear.

"I've got a job now. I do counseling. I have a full caseload." She shoved her cuff back from her wrist and looked at her watch. "I'll have to leave pretty soon."

Sam said, "Can we come with you?"

She saw that I had the same question on my face. She didn't say anything. She looked up at Pa, who was standing like a sentry with his hands behind his back.

"Take them." His eyes were weirdly lit, and he was pale and spiky-haired from sleeping all day. "What good are they here?

They think it's all a joke. They don't realize how much is at stake." He turned away. "I've got my hands full."

Without another word, he crossed the lawn and headed back to the house, leaving the lights off, as he did these evenings, so that he was better able to see the animals. When I looked back, I saw him staring with yellow eyes at Ma leading us away from him.

Mrs. Everest

ALTHOUGH I WAS not prepared for it – but how could anyone be? – Mrs. Everest introduced me to the work of the artist Felix Gonzales-Torres, specifically a piece composed of about nine dollars' worth of light fixtures: two bulbs on extension cords twisted together, hung against a bare wall, and plugged into a socket at the baseboard. I expected her to say, "It's *supposed* to make you angry." But Mrs. Everest called it an eloquent depiction of grief.

"As an artist yourself, you can appreciate the depth of meaning here."

I said, "This means absolutely nothing to me" – the wrong answer, because she then told me that she was negotiating to exhibit this genius's work at her gallery, and I'd been hoping that she'd show my work too.

Instead of changing the subject, she reminded me of how little I knew by describing another of his works, this one consisting of 175 pounds of wrapped candy heaped against a wall. When I smiled, trying to imagine this, she said, as though to a child, "It represents his friend Ross, who died. That's how much he weighed. Gallerygoers eat the candy and make him thinner. See?"

And the extension cords, *Untitled (March 5th) #2,* one of a series, was said to depict the two men, Gonzales-Torres and his lover, entwined. Mrs. Everest showed me the catalogue entry from a museum where the installation was on view.

> The work is open to a wide range of interpretations – naked and vulnerable, or poignant and warm. The implicit ro-

manticism of the work's metaphor of two luminous bodies, tempered by the knowledge that at any second one of the bulbs could burn out, with the other left to shine on alone.

"When I think of luminous bodies, Andy Wyeth's Helga paintings come to mind."

I dared say this because many of my paintings have been compared to those of Andy, who was my friend.

Pretending to be deaf is a conventional form of passive aggression – Mrs. Everest claimed she could not hear any of my comments, squinted when I repeated them, and instead of answering merely shrugged, implying that they were too banal to address. In what I realized later was her belittling my work, she talked in her odd chewing way about an upcoming show at her gallery, praised – overpraised – the artist, a man who collected and exhibited used footwear, mainly the shoes of industrial workers.

This is perhaps the place to say that the art she promoted always needed an explanation: you had to be educated in the circumstances of the artist's life, the jobs, the peculiarities, the miseries. You felt no solitary aesthetic satisfaction in her gallery; instead you were possessed by a faint dizziness of bewilderment. J.M.W. Turner's long, eccentric life is unknown to the average museumgoer, yet none of Mrs. Everest's artists could be appreciated until an immense amount of biographical information was supplied as context, something Mrs. Everest was eager to offer, as in, "His lover weighed 175 pounds." People gathered around the works, discussing the minutiae of the artist's life.

My paintings were praised for their impartial realism, but not by Mrs. Everest, who regarded my portraits and landscapes as so self-explanatory as to be banal, the instant gratification of the human face or a cluttered room. My life was not public, my wife's weight was her secret. I often painted portraits, but my self-portraits I kept to myself. Every picture I've done has a history, but I intended each one as complete in itself. Why would you need to know more?

She smiled at the idea that I was still using a paintbrush, and I suspected she believed that my work lacked depth. She could be severe with people she disapproved of. "I have a mental list of people I want to kill," Mrs. Everest used to say, and her gargling old-actress voice made her sound more murderous. "Not die a natural death – I want to deal the fatal blow." She would then name the wished-for victims: a talk-show host, a celebrity humanitarian, a new neighbor, an art dealer – one of her competitors, usually a woman. "Quite a long list. I keep adding to it."

We always encouraged her with our laughter. Isabel and I were among her best friends. In the beginning we thought it was a joke, and later it became too awkward to say anything.

"I'm putting him on my list," she'd say at a party, and friends like us always knew what she meant.

We were summer people on the island. When our house was finished and we moved from the mainland, someone said, "Mrs. Everest wants to meet you." The implication was that I was lucky she was taking an interest. She was prominent on the island, where she spent the season in a house built by one of her ex-husbands – "the third or fourth," people said. I was told that she thought highly of my work. "Thought highly" was intended as a kind of catnip. Mrs. Everest was a well-known collector, and art dealer. I had never met her. Though I had been successful in my work, I was on the periphery. Her gallery was busy, the openings always packed with people. Until then I had not been exhibited in her gallery nor invited to any parties.

I knew she dealt in whatever was in vogue in New York City, installations, giant photographs, acrylic artifacts, rusted hubcaps, even color-coded condoms arranged in menacing mandalas. All of this was a far cry from my monoprint etchings and the portraits of, for example, the people who had worked on my house – the carpenters, electrician, plumber, roofers, plasterers – my *Workmen* series. No one mentioned these pieces; they talked about Mrs. Everest.

Whispers tend to enlarge the unmet person. She was one of those people who was preceded by an enthusiastic prologue of buildup, someone whom everyone spoke about and quoted – quotes always delivered with force, but so unmemorable you suspect the enthusiast to be somehow in thrall to the person. "You mean you haven't met her yet?" And then you meet the person and she never quite matches the talk, but you find so much else that no one mentioned, perhaps didn't notice, and you wonder why, because it doesn't seem like the same person at all.

In the case of Mrs. Everest, the quotes were slight but always repeated with gusto, usually how she had been sharp with someone, teased them or dispatched them with a word, the rudeness repeated with a shiver of approval. "She has a list of people she wants to kill." I smiled and said I couldn't wait to meet her, but I was also thinking, I don't get it.

Then the party came – the Callanders, her friends, a room full of people, a table of food, waiters offering filled wine glasses from trays. A lull in the conversation and glances at the entryway meant that she had arrived. She was greeted by Biff Callander and his wife, Lara. She took a glass of champagne, but didn't drink – it was an accessory – and she was shown my way.

No one had said how tiny she was, and misshapen, slightly bent over, almost hunchbacked – probably her age, some sort of fused vertebrae or twisted spine. She was ugly in a startling way, an ugliness that gave her authority, the ruined face, the staring, wide-open blue eyes, the elderly fingers, the walnut-sized rings, putty-like makeup and heavy jewelry, ropes of beads, dangly earrings. She looked like a crone from a folk-tale – untidy, her hair tousled, her battered suede jacket a poor fit, and she limped a little. No one had mentioned that she was doddery and uncertain, pawing the air as she shuffled along, or that she tried to make this oddness into a kind of majesty.

I felt a bit sorry for her. She knew she wasn't beautiful, was no longer young, was noticeably frail.

The first thing anyone said about her was the predictable reference to her mountainous name. "One of her husbands" was the explanation – at least four of them, all of them out of the picture. You didn't think of Mrs. Everest with a man. Her best friends called her "Dickie," though no one asked how she got that name.

By way of greeting, in that first meeting at the Callanders', she snatched up a platter and said, "Walter Rainbird! Have some cheese!"

This disarmed me and made me laugh.

"You're so much bigger than I expected. I wish I could have you in my gallery."

Some people are blunt because they're shy. Shyness can even turn them into shouters, if sufficiently riled. Then I thought about her forthright remark, and it became ambiguous: Did she mean that she wanted me, or that she couldn't possibly exhibit my work? Perhaps she was not so blunt after all.

No one could tell me where Mrs. Everest came from, or her true age, or what her real name was, or how she'd spent her first thirty or so years. She must have been attractive long ago, and being small, still had the pursed lips of a flirt. In the beginning, I asked about her – just wondering aloud. No one would say more than "I really don't know."

I was struck by her defiant opinions. Her confidence extended to her business activities: her gallery with its looks-like-art was a success, and was a vortex for the best parties. She knew her own mind, so I thought, and never hesitated to damn something. "I hate it," she would often say of anything she regarded as conventional. I guessed that she hated my work. Yet I represented money to her, and though she had perhaps a smaller net worth than her clients, she had the big investor's sense of insecurity, the wealthy person's fear that without warning she might lose it all.

She respected my financial success more than (if I may say so) my artistic achievement. This was the point: I seldom had shows because my pieces were spoken for in advance, not commissioned but sought-after. Always on the lookout for buyers, she habitually cultivated the rich. She tolerated my wife, Isabel; she never mentioned my work. This was a common occurrence in my life: the way my fame made me a magnet for philistines. People wanted to know me for my success rather than my paintings, because I was good at something and made money off it. As time passed I knew fewer and fewer people who were passionate about art, and more and more socialites, many of them Izzy's friends, as I smiled in the role of a preoccupied spouse, not a painter at all but rather like someone with a secret vice or a private income.

Though we had no friends on the island, I knew a handful of artists. I made the mistake of introducing Mrs. Everest to two of them. Morrie, who was a sculptor, showed her his studio and then said, "I've got some more pieces out back." She said, "I've seen enough." She was offhand with Marsha, an etcher. I asked her what she thought of Marsha's work. She said, "Lipstick lesbian." After this, Morrie and Marsha were cooler toward me. I didn't blame them.

When she went about wooing me, I was struck with self-conscious fascination, realizing that this little woman, being obvious – but offering attention, grand meals, glittering occasions – was actually succeeding. I saw myself succumbing and wanting more – and getting it; and then I was in her orbit. In ignoring my work, she seemed to imply that she was making an exception in liking me, and that I should be grateful for that. Meals were central to our relationship, food was important, cheese was a theme.

"What they do, no one has ever done before," Mrs. Everest said of a husband and wife whose photographs she exhibited. Each was a transvestite. They photographed themselves in costume. "That is the proof they are artists."

At this early stage of my knowing Mrs. Everest, I did not examine this remark. It seemed debatable. My paintings had never been done before. Yet I decided that I liked her conviction. I wanted her to say things like this about me. She didn't, yet my credentials – the ones that mattered to Mrs. Everest – were soon established.

It happened this way. One weekend in our second year on the island, my wife and I were visited by Andy Wyeth, with Helga Testorf in tow, stopping off on their annual early-summer migration from Pennsylvania to Maine. He flew into our small airport in a private plane. This quickly became news on the island. Where was he staying? What was he doing? Whom was he with? Mrs. Everest had the news early, but it was not until Andy left – he hated socializing – that I revealed to her that he had stayed with us, that I was putting the finishing touches to a portrait of him that I had begun the year before in Port Clyde, Maine. Mrs. Everest only wanted to know about the Helga detail. She said she hated *Christina's World.*

"What about Betsy, his wife?" Mrs. Everest asked.

"There's Betsy's world and Helga's world, and Andy proceeds from one to the other," I said. "Think of it as a kind of informal polygamy."

This complex shuttling romance bewitched Mrs. Everest, who had the old coquette's weakness for steamy gossip.

She wanted to see my painting of him, his lined, deeply tanned face like a landscape, his kindly smile, his luminous eyes. In the foreground, one of his hands was lifted, his delicate fingers crooked in the manner of a painter gripping a brush. He had the leathery look of a sportsman, and although he was in his eighties at the time, he seemed much younger – his smile gave him everything, youth and intelligence and confidence. I posed him standing at a window, his sloping meadow and the harbor just visible beyond.

"Why didn't you give a party for him?"

"He doesn't go to parties," I said.

"Helga was so beautiful in those pictures," Mrs. Everest said. "She must be really old now. Is she fat?"

When I said that Helga was lovely Mrs. Everest took it as a rebuke. I mentioned that Andy had a painting with him, of a cataract on a woodland stream, he called *The Carry*. He had showed it to me, saying, "I fell in," and he pointed to the place where, as he had stood painting, he'd stumbled into the water. The picture was real to him, the experience a vivid piece of his history; but he had made it, not installed it.

She wasn't interested in that, and she frowned at my portrait of Andy, as though concealing her reaction, like a wine snob swilling a sip. They were not the sort of pictures that she would ever exhibit. Yet I had been given face, in the Chinese manner, by this visit by the master of my school of painting. I tried to explain to Mrs. Everest that to me much of Wyeth's work, especially the later landscapes and coastal scenes, verged on abstract expressionism, or were studies in color. But she wasn't listening. She cocked her head at my portrait and looked closely, asked more questions about Helga and the Wyeth marriage, and seemed annoyed by my upbeat replies. But this was a turning point for me, my validation, the Wyeth visit.

Confident of her friendship, I saw more of Mrs. Everest, nearly always in the ritualistic restaurant-going way, and the paradox was always her ordering three courses and seldom eating anything. Junior's restaurant, where we often met, was a casual place, with excellent food, that was nicknamed "the kitchen" because the old-time islanders gathered there. In the summer, no one made lunch at home, and the islanders were sociable, so it was always lunch at Junior's.

A meal in most societies on earth represents a peacemaking gesture. But you have to eat something – anything, a nibble is enough. Mrs. Everest seldom swallowed. I took this to be hostile. A concentrated thought darkened her face, and she used her fork and knife as though she was killing and mutilating the food on her plate, lingering over it, always with her mouth open, seeming to utter a curse. And then at last the slow, disgusted way she ate, masticating it like a gum chewer, not swallowing. She had a habit of spitting food onto her plate, turning her whole meal into dog food. No one mentioned this, perhaps because, like me, they stopped looking. And here is the irony: she once said to me, "I hate watching people eat. And I can't stand to see them laughing."

My wife was off-island for the day. I was sitting with Mrs. Everest, and we were about to order, when I saw at a nearby table a man I had met in England on one of my trips, an American Foreign Service officer, Harry Platt. He'd kept in touch as he'd been moved from one post to another, and over six years or so he'd been to three countries in the Middle East, Turkey the most recent.

Seeing Harry Platt's face from far off in our local seafront restaurant made him seem gaudily familiar, like an apparition. He must have felt the same about seeing me, because he smiled broadly and got up. He was with an older woman, who stared but did not rise from her chair.

"Well met!" The pretentious expression was not pretentious the way he said it, but suited his old-fashioned Ivy League manner. "How great to see you. What brings you to the island?"

"My wife and I have had a place here for a few years. She's away at the moment."

He explained that he was catching the ferry in the morning,

and then he became self-conscious and nodded at the older woman at his table.

"Will you join us? This is my mother."

I glanced at Mrs. Everest, who had been eyeing the other woman, perhaps sizing her up. She said, "Absolutely not."

Harry Platt was an experienced diplomat, a charming man in his late fifties. He had been helpful to me, putting me in touch with various people, once helping with a visa, another time explaining a tricky piece of foreign policy. He knew presidents, he had sat with prime ministers. But hearing Mrs. Everest's rebuff (and his mother had heard too), he became flustered, his face reddening, his eyes frantic, as though he'd been slapped. His mother looked furious and chalky-faced.

"Maybe I'll see you tomorrow," I said.

"We're leaving at seven," he said with a desperate smile.

At that, his mother got up and went to the door, and Harry seemed to lose his balance, actually to topple, as if yielding to the gravitational pull of his mother in her heaving herself out. Harry's embarrassment made him fumble his farewell, and I saw, just a flicker – the glint in his eyes, the set of his mouth – that he was enraged.

Mrs. Everest said, "I think I'll have the peekytoe crab salad. You should have the lobster mac and cheese – it's one of Junior's specialities."

She did not allude to Harry or his mother, but the whole encounter upset me so badly I couldn't eat.

There were the men she called "the boys." Tony was an antiques dealer and a stickler for decorum. "Dickie's such a goddess. She served a raw ahi amuse-bouche without putting out fish knives." He was a name-dropper – Jackie this, Gloria that – but a reliable friend to Mrs. Everest, and like her, a gossip.

Tony fed her stories. She was in general not a listener, except to malicious tattle, and then she was all ears, smiling in anticipation, her mouth half open like a dog awaiting a treat. It might be something simple. The Callanders, for example. Biff had been in the State Department, and Mrs. Everest liked to say, "He was in the CIA." She said this with an admiring whisper when they'd been on speaking terms, and when she rejected him she said it as blame, revealing his disgrace – the spy as sneak – taking away his power by stating the fact: *I know his secret.*

But Tony had a better piece of gossip. Biff's wife was Peruvian. At one of the dinner parties Tony was seated next to Lara, being charming, asking all the right questions, mentioning how he had gone to Cuzco and loved Machu Picchu, letting Lara talk, refilling her glass, smiling, probably a bit of "Jackie once told me . . ." and the question he asked all couples, pure hostility masked as genial inquiry, "You must tell me how you met." That had to have come up, because afterward he had a present for Mrs. Everest: "Guess who was a flight attendant before she married James Bond?"

Another of Mrs. Everest's boys was Sanford – Sandy – whom no one liked. Even Tony was afraid, always steering clear of him, and he warned me to be careful of Sandy.

Sandy was small like Mrs. Everest, very thin, rather vain in his choice of shoes ("I have hundreds of pairs"), stylish in his clothes – expensive black suit with black T-shirt – and his skin was a strange color, possibly the result of a tanning salon that over the years had turned him a shade of purple, or maybe he had poor kidney function.

He had a hostile habit of starting sentences, "Don't take this the wrong way," and then following it with something insulting. In his talk he was much noisier than Tony, and he won the gossip competition. If Tony knew a mild scandal about someone, Sandy knew a disgrace. This disposed Mrs. Everest to Sandy, who was in his sixties but had the look – skinny, pouting, bug-eyed, small – of a bad boy. When I saw him with Mrs. Everest, he put me in mind of Iago, his purply face twisted in telling a story, his hands contorted and shielding his features like a mask of claws. I thought of the expression "motiveless malignancy." I did a sketch of Sandy, which I titled *I Am Not the Man I Am.*

Perhaps there was a motive, and it might have been Iago's motive too. Mrs. Everest was Sandy's only source of income. He was no better at his installations (hand-fired bricks) than anyone else she exhibited, but he was a far more malevolent gossip, and that was something that delighted Mrs. Everest. Like Tony and some of her other boys, he acted as her formal male companion, her walker. Even so, she was outrageously disloyal. After one party she said, "He was at it all night with that young waiter, dropping hairpins."

Knowing that Sandy would quote me, I was wary when I spoke to him. I made a point of praising Mrs. Everest's taste, her hospitality, her humor, her food. I spoke approvingly of Tony, because in those days Tony was in Mrs. Everest's good graces.

And why was I part of her circle? Perhaps it was my success: other people – important people, Andy Wyeth – cared about my work. And she had something to give, lunches, the dinners, the parties, with us in attendance. We were glad to belong, and then – knowing her better, becoming uncertain, seeing how she cut or dropped people – we were even better behaved.

I said to Izzy, "She's awful, but that's not the worst of it. My fear is that to keep her friendship we'll become just like her."

Even after all my travels I realized that I'd never known anyone like her. On an impulse, just doodling, I roughed out in pencil a sketch of her, with Tony and Sandy and some of the others, a capriccio of faces. But when I added some emphasis in ink, I got scared and tossed it.

Perhaps to purge it of memories, she had gutted her house near the harbor and at great expense redecorated it to display her art collection: Jasper Johns, Rauschenberg, Louis, Olitski, and some installations. Her friends, especially Tony and Sandy and Amadeo, raved about it, praised her for keeping the shell and rebuilding the interior, as a kind of museum, where my work was not welcome.

"That house has great bones," Tony said.

But with obvious secrecy she never invited anyone into the house. Whenever she was picked up by a car, she met the person in the driveway or stepped outside before the driver knocked. No one was allowed inside. Once, meeting her to give her a lift, I saw her kitchen through the window. A pile of laundry had been stacked, unsorted, on the stove, and her cat was asleep on the kitchen table in the sunshine, the cat's bowl near it. That said everything about Mrs. Everest's eating arrangements.

"I used to be a gourmet cook," she said. "I gave lavish dinner parties."

Was this true? No one I knew had ever eaten her food or been to a dinner party she'd given. She only ate in restaurants, presiding over the table. She ordered three courses and picked at them, hardly eating, never finishing. But in those rare moments when she chewed some food, a hidden part of her personality became apparent – a wolfish energy and appetite, her yellow teeth champing, her turned-down mouth working, an alertness the whole time, her gaze widened as though to ward off an intruder. Then she spat. After that, she'd pass a knuckle across the crumbs on her lips, push the plate aside, and say to the waitress, "Take this away."

She was always offhand with menials, and her brusque manner made them excessively polite.

"Yes, right away, madam. Shall I wrap it up for you?"

"Absolutely not."

At the end of the meal she would suggest another meal – dinner tomorrow night, lunch the following day, Sunday brunch. She only saw people for meals; she was unavailable at any other time. She went out occasionally, to movies, to see friends, to shop, but was covert about it, and generally huddled inside her grand house, except at mealtimes or gallery openings.

Her friends, especially those shrieking men, praised her sense of style, and yet she only wore the old suede jacket and junk jewelry. No one remarked on how rumpled she looked; on the contrary, her shabbiness was regarded as a sort of defiant fashion.

She had the big-city habit, which was like a vice to me, of going to the movies in the afternoon, even on the sunniest day. Although her house was by the harbor, she never went near the water, did not swim or go sailing.

Speaking of an adulterous woman on the island, she asked me what I thought. I said, "Emma Bovary," and she corrected me: "No, her name is Alice." Other instances like this convinced me that she had no education, but her coterie saw this as a virtue. "Dickie dropped out of high school!" This was more praise, but it was clear to me that she was unlettered: all she knew was from talk, from something she'd been told, from anecdote and chat. But she taught me that no one could be more condescending than a high school dropout. Books put her to sleep, print was a soporific to her. She loved big bold paintings of stripes, the oversize archery targets that were in vogue in the sixties, the grotesque photos in tabloids. Anything less bored her. Her gallery reflected this tendency. I remember one show with car crashes and crime scenes, forensic photos, bloody bandages.

Sooner than I realized it, because I did not dare to dislike Mrs. Everest, she made me doubt myself. I did not lose faith in my work, yet I felt browbeaten and stupid because of her. Just being with her, a whole lunchtime, say, would turn me into a dope. I'd learned not to contradict her or put in a friendly mitigating word for the woman she disparaged or the man she maligned.

Having listened in silence to Mrs. Everest's venomous remarks, I always felt ashamed after one of these meals, avoiding the front window as I left the restaurant, turning away from the reflection of my face. We were, as I say, summer people. Had I fallen foul of her and been ostracized, we would have had nothing – no parties, no society. Yes, I see that I was cowardly and deluded, but I was fascinated too. Ethical satisfaction is not the same as aesthetic satisfaction, or plain curiosity. I studied her and did sketches, compulsively planning her portrait.

It never occurred to me that, out of my hearing, she might be disparaging me. That was strange: she was disloyal to everyone I knew, yet I believed she would be loyal to my wife and me.

When this thought occurred to me, I saw my naïveté, but of course by then it was too late.

Someone Mrs. Everest had fallen out with – had in fact rejected – said to me one day, "She's an alcoholic, you know," as though this (if it were true) explained everything.

Perhaps it explained her famished stare, her fuss and obsessiveness, her bleak moods – little eclipses when she darkened and became impossible to please. Perhaps it explained her sweet tooth, which dry drunks are supposed to have, and her conspicuous regard for holding a glass – not drinking it but treating alcohol as if it were a magic potion, forbidden, tempting, poisonous, transformative. In her mood swings, which were frequent, she could turn on a person and, blinking, bare her teeth and deliver a sudden insult.

But a history of alcoholism could not account for the pleasure she took in someone's downfall, her love of bad news. The alcoholics I had known who'd taken the pledge were humbled, always haltingly explaining their weakness, or in a low-grade fever of atonement, constantly treading the tightrope of sobriety.

Not Mrs. Everest. She looked thirsty and pitiless, and on many occasions, clapping her hands like a child on hearing something disgraceful, relentless in her ill will, she was triumphant, reckless, and often wore the delirious expression of a predator, eyes aglow, as though she wanted to feast on her victim – had indeed already weakened the prey and would wait until the poor creature fell flat so that she could straddle the corpse and take a big bite from the haunch.

People do not fail without an element of struggle, but when it happens their failure is often undramatic. Failure comes in stages, like illness, a prolonged weakening, and finally a decline, with a whisper of extinction that is indistinguishable from death. This slowness and delay, the resilience in the human condition, the dying fall rather than the sudden plunge, is the reason I suspect tyrants, impatient for triumph, become murderers; why they carry out pogroms, persecutions, mass starvations; why they promote famine or reduce their enemies to slavery or captivity.

It is not enough to rejoice over the natural death of your enemies; their end must be hastened. Impatience is one of the besetting sins of the tyrant, an effect of blood lust; it is impatience that turns the conventionally cruel leader into a mass murderer.

And in order to be satisfied, Mrs. Everest wanted to have had a hand in it. "I want to kill them with my bare hands," she'd say, pretending to be joking. And the person must fail completely, be rendered naked, homeless, ruined, exposed, the house burned down, the dog lying dead in the driveway.

Hearing stories of people she'd destroyed, I studied the look on her face – her glittering, slightly drunken eyes, her nostrils flared, her lips apart, her teeth showing, her tongue thickening with hunger. I should have been warned, but Izzy and I remained on her guest list, fascinated, and also fearful. On this island we were isolated in the true sense of the word. One of the stipulations of Mrs. Everest's friendship was that her friends were mine, and her enemies too.

Some people, not many, received financial help from her. They were always wounded, a bit lost, abjectly grateful. Just as she could be cruel to some people who were vulnerable, she could take others under her wing and protect them. That was part of her paradox, that – so hardhearted – she knew how to offer help. She fed stray animals; she gave money to a ranch in Idaho that cared for horses rescued from circuses.

There was a woman who cleaned for her, to whom she'd given a car (not a new car, but serviceable) and paid someone to sort out her taxes; an old feeble gay handyman whose partner had died and who was indigent; an alcoholic chef who was just out of rehab and was trying to put his life back together ("I can start him off with a little restaurant"). They were all lost souls, they were no threat to her, and in truth she could not have been kinder to them; though each of these people served a purpose – the cleaner, the handyman, the chef.

She had no children, so I suppose all her maternal feelings were directed toward abused animals and these sad people who, in their tentative dependent lives, were like children, who also performed chores for her with some ability.

She was entirely self-invented. This is not a simple trick of the ego; it takes work, persuasion, money, boldness, willpower, and imagination. You have to admire it. And so, because of my portraits, my giving these images life, I began to find her of much greater interest, hideously compelling at times, for the way she had made herself, the life and the pretenses she had created, all her fictions.

Just as she could whip around and turn cruel or unfeeling, with "She is hideous" or "Lipstick lesbian," or might laugh like a witch at someone's bad luck, she could be unexpectedly concerned, sympathetic, even deeply moved at the plight of an unfortunate person, such as one small girl, Selma, the stepdaughter of a Brazilian roofer. The child disappeared from the island. It was not known whether she was with the man's estranged wife. The roofer was evasive and then he too disappeared.

"I'm worried sick," Mrs. Everest said. And she looked sick – gaunt, hollow-eyed, desperate.

"She might turn up," I said. I could only offer platitudes.

"You don't know," she said to me. "That man has done something with her. I know he's abused her, and I don't mean 'touched inappropriately' – I hate that expression. What does he care? She's not his natural daughter."

As I write this, about her kindness, I realize that I tend to revert to her cruelty, that I find it hard to believe that she had a soft spot. That cynicism is the influence of the woman herself on me, that I have difficulty bringing myself to believe in her kindness because she had taught me to be cynical. She made it impossible for me to believe in her.

She was a collector, an accumulator, a significant trait of the very wealthy, hoarding as investing – property, paintings, even people if they were powerful enough, stacking them up, displaying them as trophies – from the group photograph ("class picture," she called it) that was always taken of the guests at her annual summer party, to the objects on the shelves in her office. "That's scrimshaw, they're all whales' teeth," she'd say, reminding me that there is no pedant like an ignoramus.

Any person's collection of chosen objects is a glimpse into her mind. I liked Mrs. Everest better when I saw some folk art she'd collected, because folk art is innocent-looking and highly colored, purposeful, inventive, always seeming to evoke what is happiest in childhood. It was also the opposite of the hideola that she exhibited.

• • •

Another lunch at Junior's, a fondue this time. As always, she led the conversation. She was excited about the art scene, she said; she wanted to go in a completely new direction. It occurred to me that she was going to ask me to show my work at her gallery. But no, she began to speak about a man who worked in sand.

Thinking I had misheard, asking her to repeat this (*sand?*), she detected the incredulity in my tone and took it for hauteur. She said, "No one has ever done what he's doing."

She chewed, she spat, she made garbage of the fondue, and at the end she patted her food-splashed mouth and said, "I have a feeling. When I have a feeling about something, I'm invariably right."

"Tell me," I said.

"I have a feeling that you're going to do my portrait."

This teasing statement was typical of Mrs. Everest. She wasn't commissioning a portrait; she wasn't asking a favor of me. She was mentioning a rapture she'd had, that I was going to paint her picture.

She turned to look out the front window of the restaurant. But she was listening, tremulous with attention.

"Wouldn't it be marvelous if your portrait showed me holding a bouquet of flowers?" She was persistent. "Each flower with its traditional meaning – daisies for innocence, pansies for loving thoughts, tiger lilies, and so forth. A whole message in blossoms."

I did not say that one could not improve on a Henry William Pickersgill masterpiece. I did not say no. No one said no to her. But she did not hear yes, and my silence meant I wasn't interested. My pride would not allow me to do a portrait of someone who thought so little of my work that she refused to show it in her gallery. Or perhaps I was rebelling against her taste for installations and looks-like-art.

Long before she suggested that I do her portrait, I made a short and bitter ink sketch of her, rather dark, a mushroom on a dunghill, but close-up it was a little twisted woman on a money box, rendered perfectly. Her hatred of figurative painting was an inspiration to me, the sort of contempt that turned my every brushstroke into a calculated phrase. And it made me resist her.

A passerby glancing through the restaurant window at the three of us – Izzy was also there – would have assumed we were old friends having an intimate meal together, never guessing that this was a ritual of farewell. The passerby would not have noticed that Mrs. Everest had asked me nothing about my painting, nothing about our plans, our travel, our health. That she did not meet my gaze or even look my way.

After her monologue about the new show she didn't mention meeting again – nothing about the future, not even next week, never mind next month. She didn't eat a mouthful of the salad she had ordered. She poked the crab cakes apart, scattered the lettuce, punctured and pushed the cherry tomatoes, mashed the avocado. She ordered a glass of Prosecco, but without taking a sip, her eyes brimmed with gluey reproachful tears.

In the most low-key way, just chatting, making small talk, she conveyed indifference with the slightly perturbed and preoccupied air of someone who couldn't linger, with an unmistakable suggestion that, though she might see us again, we no longer mattered to her.

This invitation had been Mrs. Everest's idea. She wanted a portrait from me. She had even described it: Mrs. Everest posed in a sun-drenched window among symbolic flowers. All that remained was for it to be hung. And listening, just smiling, I had sent a message of disapproval, which was like a foul smell.

When the check for the meal came, the immensely wealthy Mrs. Everest frowned and turned away from it.

"I must run," she said. "Don't get up. Leonard is outside."

Leonard, her driver, greeted her with a groveling smile and a little bow, and then he helped this old lady into the car.

And when they drove away, Izzy said, "She seemed in a funny mood."

I saw Mrs. Everest one more time. This was at Sandy's house on the bay. He had invited us, but said nothing about Mrs. Everest's proposal that I should paint her portrait.

She was standing in her usual posture, as I would have painted her: old suede jacket, tousled hair, a glass in her hand, the elderly face of a wicked child.

She hadn't expected me to say hello, and seemed startled by my small talk. I was enthusing about the plants I had bought, annuals for the summer, enumerating them, describing their colors – dahlias, delphiniums, Shasta daisies.

"Verbena," I said. "Zinnias."

"I hate verbena, I hate zinnias," Mrs. Everest said, and frowned and coughed a little, like a cat choking on a mouthful of fur, and I translated that cough as *I'm through with you.*

After a short spell of being ashamed I had ever known her, I began to wonder why I'd endured her for so long. People say, "It's all good," and "I have no regrets," and "It was a learning experience." But I do have regrets. I want years back, I want days back, I want the hours back that I spent sitting over meals with Mrs. Everest. I regret knowing her. I didn't hate her; I felt sorry for her having to drag her damaged soul through life. I hated myself for knowing her, for pitying her. I hated myself for my appetite.

Have some cheese! she said the first time we met. That was the beginning of many meals that ended in my refusing to do her portrait. And I had wanted to do her portrait!

I mentioned this when I complained about her to her friend Sandy, because I knew he'd tell her everything. He listened with his fanatical stare, then said, "Don't take this the wrong way," and sounding like Mrs. Everest, added, "The only free cheese is in a mousetrap."

Another Necklace

"We are quite fortunate to have with us today one of the most illustrious English writers of our time, and now a fellow resident of Boston," Mrs. DeWicky was saying at the brightly lit podium. Backstage, in semidarkness, just at the edge of the heavy pleated curtain, waiting for her to finish, Raleigh Crindle smiled at the technician seated before the bank of lights and switches. He pointed to himself with a slender stabbing finger and, with a pop-eyed, self-mocking face, whispered the word "illustrious." The technician made his own hand into a pistol and cocked it at Raleigh and mouthed the words "You the man."

Then, noticing something, the technician came closer and squinted with concern and inclined his head – it was all mumming and dumb show here – as if to say, "Are you all right?"

Advancing in the heat, the man had loomed with a ripe animal smell and thick inquiring fingers, and Raleigh's chest tightened. His breathing became arrhythmic, he missed a beat of air, then gagged and whinnied a little as though with fear or ecstasy. He placed his hand against the welt on his neck and managed a smile and a whispered sibilance, "My necklace." The man opened his mouth and mimicked laughter, his big tongue working like a dog's.

Raleigh was fastening his collar button when Mrs. DeWicky at the podium said, "Mr. Crindle's perfectly marvelous fictions," and he was annoyed with himself, even in this heat, for noticing that Americans used the words "quite" and "perfectly" around English people in the belief that it made them sound more English, and sometimes said primly, "We took tea," in a way that English people seldom did. Raleigh wanted to be more grateful: coming here had saved him from obscurely vegetating in Slowland.

"For the past two decades, in novels and stories and travelogues, Raleigh Crindle has written powerfully of London, and of the English class distinctions he has called 'Asiatic subtleties' in his recent collection of essays, *How to Be English*."

But he was thinking, Travelogues?

"Mr. Crindle has won many awards and prizes, and for his portrayal of the quite delicate social misunderstandings, he has been called . . ."

This part of the introduction Raleigh knew so well from his published and much-quoted biographical note that he smiled again at the technician. Just as he heard, "I'd like to present tonight's guest," his cell phone buzzed against his thigh. He slid it from his pocket and flipped it open with his thumb and read the text message: *This is no damn joke. Im comin for u and u gon be damn sorry.*

He heard a disapproving hiss. Raleigh lifted his pale face from his cell phone to the technician. In rapid scolding hand movements, the man indicated to Raleigh that he must turn off his phone. And then the curtain parted.

"Ladies and gentlemen, Raleigh Crindle . . ."

He was dazzled by the lights and the density of brightened faces. He approached the podium, thanked the woman, and in a practiced gesture he slipped a folded piece of paper from his inside pocket and, his damp fingers twitching with anxiety, smoothed it in front of him on the sloping surface under the microphone.

"After that wonderful introduction I can hardly wait to hear what I'm going to say," Raleigh said, and after the ripple of laughter, he added, "If anyone wishes to accompany me to the Charles River at the end of this talk, they can watch me walk on water."

That sacrilegious second remark fell flat, but when he recovered and said, "I am proud to call myself a Bostonian," he was so surprised by the vigorous applause that he pursued it, saying, "As you know, many of my fellow countrymen – and countrywomen – have fled Britain for New York City. There are more bossy, high-profile English people in America now than there were before the Declaration of Independence!"

To yelps of laughter, he went on, "As the Londoner said of the GIs during the war, 'I don't mind the Americans. But it's those white people they brought with them.' I seriously wonder whether there are any English writers left in London! Perhaps it's understandable, since a knighthood means more in America than it does in Britain, but an English accent is still a questionable asset. Hearing my accent, some Americans ask me, 'Are you English or gay?'"

His accent was plummier in America, or sounded so to his ear, like an old voice on the wireless. And there were other words he had to avoid, like "schedule," or else had to learn how to say them differently. He had become acutely aware of his manner of speech, his gulping and stammering. Sometimes in shops he attempted an American accent, and even then was not understood. "'Cans,' not 'tins,'" he told himself.

"It is simply not true that when you ask an Englishman the time he tells what it is to the minute, and when you ask an American the time he explains how to make a clock." That one didn't work. He began again, affecting a confidential manner, lowering his voice. "But it *is* true that when you step on an Englishman's toe he's the one who says sorry." He continued, in the same tone, over the laughter. "On my second day in New York City I was walking down the street and saw a stack of newspapers and the big black headline 'Queens Mother Raped'" – he let this sink in, he repeated the headline in a shocked voice – "and I must admit it gave me a turn – you know how headlines have a way of seeming like boasts. But this was an outrage, until I realized of course that Queens is a borough. But to avoid any further misunderstanding I decided that I would not stay in New York a moment longer, and came to Boston, where I have been very happy ever since. Besides, my fellow Brits have claimed New York as their own and are shamelessly looking for celebrity there."

He paused for the crackle of appreciation to die away, then said, "They've forgotten what Dr. Johnson said about thirsting for wealth and burning to be famous." He smiled and used his confidential tone again, saying, "'They mount, they shine, evaporate, and fall.'"

Leaning against the podium he spoke into the silence. "Little do they know the pleasures of your city, which is not a city really, but a small town surrounded by smaller towns."

He knew from a muffled pause, a withholding, a silence and suspense, the very quality of the air in the hall like a drop in pressure, that he had just said the wrong thing. It was so easy here to blunder, and you were so quick to know it.

"Of course all cities are built up of townships, and Boston has bags and bags of character," he said, backing away; and explaining, praising, he recaptured the attention of the audience, who, as he always felt, were sitting in judgment upon him.

But he was glad for a chance to speak, grateful to have been asked. He needed this audience to take him on trust. He had come here to stay and found Boston to his taste. He could live in a house here, he could own a car; it was only twenty minutes to the woods in one direction, or to the ocean in the other. He could know the whole city, and no one knew him. The line about the fellow Brits – and the middle-aged ones he knew well – claiming New York as theirs might have sounded jokey, but they had rebuffed him in the stately city.

The English had come, they closely guarded what they had found, they didn't share, there were as cliquey in New York as they'd been in London – cliquier, really, and slyly competitive in being part of the scene, not so much class-conscious as wicked one-uppers. Some behaved like expats in a savage colony, praising the place in public but denigrating it in private, mocking the locals in exaggerated have-a-nice-day accents. Yet they had possessed it, crowding him out, and he found it hard not to resent them. The first English person seems unique, and then you see the second one and realize it's a whole identical tribe. There were just too many of them now. They were telly faces and wireless voices, they had strong opinions about everything, explaining America to Americans, who listened to them, and they were cock-a-hoop because the UK had stopped listening.

Raleigh had visited the States before – book tours, the lecture circuit – but that was a different routine: hotels, handshakes, expensive meals, free laundry service, key to the minibar. This, the monotony of a resident, seemed to occur in another country, of bills and frowns and strangers and inconveniences. And it was odd how a Pakistani or a Jamaican, or the Haitian taxi driver who lived in the house next door, also considered themselves resident in the same way, hanging on, never intending to return to their homeland. It disconcerted him to think, They're just like me.

This litany of grievances played in his head as he smiled and spoke, a silent counterpoint to everything he said aloud. His subject tonight had been billed as "Anglo-Boston": English writers who'd visited and written about Boston – notably Dickens, Trollope, and Kipling; and Bostonians who'd visited and written about England – Hawthorne, Henry Adams, and James.

The names were like chloroform: hearing them, the audience smiled and drowsed, but remained upright in listening postures. The writers he mentioned had felt at home, had made friends, had written their experiences, and were quotable. He meant to flatter the listeners, but also tactfully to educate them by reminding them of these traveler-writers, and he implied that these men had shown him the way, that he was one of them, for he wished to make a place for himself in Boston.

"They had secret lives," Raleigh said in a pleading tone,

hoping to rouse. "Dickens was in an adulterous love affair with an actress, Henry Adams was a ferocious anti-Semite, Hawthorne had an incestuous relationship with his sister, Kipling was at war with his American brother-in-law, Henry James was desperately lonely. But Trollope was a happy man."

Had they heard? He said, "And I am happy too." But it sounded insincere, like a protest. He added, "Almost without trying I have found a routine, and a routine is like a one-word definition of a life."

He glanced at his watch and saw that thirty-five minutes had passed, his allotted time was almost up, his cue for his prepared closing, about there being a Boston in Lincolnshire, but that it was little more than a market town with a cathedral tower so odd they called it the Stump. "Your Boston is the real thing, and I am grateful that you've welcomed me here."

He reached into his pocket for his handkerchief, and his fingers snagged on his phone, which was tangled in it, and he removed them both. His face and neck were damp in the hot bright June evening, and he knew his cheeks were pink, his face flushed. He wiped his face with one hand and with the other undid the top buttons of his shirt and opened the collar.

Mrs. DeWicky, who had introduced him, now appeared at his side and shook his hand in thanks, and when she looked more closely, with concern, he touched his throat and drew his collar together.

"Questions," she said into the microphone. "We have ten minutes before I turn you into the furnace of Arlington Street."

He glanced down at the phone and read, *U cant git away, I find u and buss u face. U be real sorry,* and shut it off with such force that the flesh under his thumbnail throbbed.

"Yes?" he said to a woman in the front row with her hand raised.

"My husband and I go to Britain almost every year," she began, and he was sure it would be a question related to travel.

But he smiled and listened, and when the woman was done, he repeated the gist of what she'd asked – destinations in Scotland – and he offered several suggestions.

After that, more hands, more comments. One thanking him for writing *Lifers,* his book about English prisons ("But I felt at home there because I'd been at an English boarding school," Raleigh said), another asking whether he knew any of the English writers who had relocated to New York ("Many of them are my Oxford chums," Raleigh said. "We're all *enfants terribles* in our sixties now. We can misbehave here to our heart's content"), and the inevitable English pedant ticking him off about his reference to Boston in Lincolnshire and elaborating on Saint Botolph. When he tried to signal an end, a man stood up at the back and spoke loudly.

"Do you think you'll be writing something about Boston?" he asked. "Or, um, what sort of work will you do here?"

"I have found a welcome here." His hand was in his pocket on *U cant git away.*

"Maybe some kind of book?" the same man said, persisting.

"I can only quote Henry James," Raleigh said, and sensed the same slackening of attention when he spoke the name. Why was that? Because they hadn't read him, or had read him and found him dull? To try again to rouse them from their torpor, he spoke with whispered urgency: "We work in the dark – we do what we can – we give what we have. Our doubt is our passion and our passion is our task. The rest is the madness of art."

When they applauded – and he suspected they were applauding his theatrical delivery rather than the message – he thanked them for being there and said he looked forward to seeing them again.

As he left with Mrs. DeWicky, several tried to detain him, just to chat, and he listened and smiled and edged toward the door, seeking to be free of them, and at the same time feeling that, apart from that one comment about *Lifers,* there had been nothing else about his books, no mention of his novels, no indication that anyone had read his journalism. But that was all right. He was holding his cell phone in his damp hand.

The taxi was waiting for them. At the foot of the stairs, glancing back, Raleigh said, "This is a first for me. Speaking in a church."

"Unitarian Universalist – it's a Boston landmark," Mrs. DeWicky said in a correcting tone. And in the taxi, "You must be thirsty! It won't take us long. It's just on Commonwealth Ave., but I've had a hip replacement, so I'm quite compromised. It's quite wonderful of you to have come."

Raleigh's phone vibrated again, but instead of looking at it, he tightened his hand over it, and now he could feel the buzz rudely interrogating his fingers.

"My pleasure," he said, and sat back, waiting for a compliment on his talk. He believed he had done a good job, had been witty, helpful, most of all patient with an audience he had regarded as mostly inert, ignorant of his work. As a cue he said, "Lovely audience."

"Perfectly marvelous," Mrs. DeWicky said. "They always ask great questions." Her smile faded as she turned to him. "What have you done to your neck?"

"Yard sale," Raleigh said.

"I have no idea what that means. English people are so verbal."

"I'll explain inside," he said, because the taxi was slowing down, the driver maneuvering it toward the curb.

"It's just a small group," Mrs. DeWicky said. "But it's a good group. Book lovers. They're the sponsors, and very eager to meet you."

He saw them as soon as he mounted the front stairs of the brownstone. They were gathered in a first-floor room, visible in the bow window.

The room soared, with a ceiling like a vast clamshell, lighted paintings on the walls – a somber landscape, a portrait of a child wearing red mittens – a Chinese long-necked vase, a celadon salver slanted on a stand at the center of a refectory table on which there were hors d'oeuvres and trays of drinks. Behind the guests – about a dozen – there was a wall of fine bindings, a ladder propped before them.

"You'll never remember all the names," Mrs. DeWicky said. "Eventually you'll get to know us well. You're a Bostonian now."

"I'm indeed a Bostonian," Raleigh said with a gummy tongue.

He was introduced to each person, some standing on their own, others in groups. One man shaking Raleigh's hand held on and said, "Are you all right?"

"Fine."

"You're feverish. I'm a doctor. I should take your pulse!"

"No need," Raleigh said.

But he did feel harassed and hot, and these people were calm, serene, coolly sizing him up.

Another man said, "Sorry I couldn't make your talk. Tee time."

"I know Bostonians are punctilious about their tea," Raleigh said.

"Golf," the man said irritably, as though he'd been mocked.

None of them, it seemed, had been to his lecture, and because this was so he felt slightly hostile toward their casual manner and felt no compunction to stay for long.

"Mr. Crindle has a story for us," Mrs. DeWicky said.

"But first I must use your –" He didn't know what to say next. He settled on "gents."

"We're all gents. Take your pick."

They'd been drinking.

"The restroom is down the hall on the right," one man said.

There were framed prints inside, and an old map labeled *Back Bay.* Raleigh locked the door and looked in the mirror. He touched his neck, tracing the welt, and then he turned his head left and right, all the time keeping the redness in view.

He opened his phone again. *U r in deep truble. I will find u. I will destroy u.*

He wondered if he was paler when he returned to the room. They were waiting for him, looking tipsier, perhaps having guzzled in his brief absence. Some of them were seated, and Mrs. DeWicky looked pleased, taking charge again, making another announcement.

"In the taxi on the way here, I remarked on a redness on Mr. Crindle's neck. He became very obscure! He said, 'Yard sale.' He has kindly agreed to explain this to us."

The man who'd said he was a doctor took a step toward Raleigh and inclined his head, appraising him, searching his neck.

"Heat rash," he said. He made a reflective gesture, chewing his lips. "Allergy."

"Yard sale," Raleigh said, and brightened as he began to explain. "I thought everyone knew this expression."

"A kind of rummage sale in front of your house," a woman said. "Stuff you don't want."

"That's the general meaning." Raleigh was still smiling. "You're skiing, shall we say, and you're on the slopes. You hit a bump or someone thumps you and – whoopsie!" – he flung out his arms – "your poles go left and right, your gloves get yanked off, your skis are stripped from your boots, there go your goggles! Your bobble hat is gone like a shot off a shovel. And you're on your back with all your kit scattered on the slope. Just picture it – yard sale!"

"Yes, yes," Mrs. DeWicky said. "Very good."

The doctor said, "And did that happen to you?"

"That was my point," Raleigh said, touching his neck. "It's left rather a mark. I call it my necklace."

"Abrasion," the doctor said. "This pressure bruise on your wrist is a little more serious. Could be a hematoma."

Raleigh slipped his hand into his trouser pocket and held his cell phone to steady himself and said, "I'm sure you know the story 'The Necklace' by de Maupassant." He sensed another slackening of attention, almost boredom, and the paradox was that it manifested itself by the guests leaning closer, as if Raleigh had begun to speak in a foreign language they were pretending to translate.

"Yes, yes," Mrs. DeWicky said. "We read it at school."

"Lovely old tale. And there's a delightful story by Maugham called 'A String of Beads.' Variation on a theme. What is it about necklaces? Henry James's story 'Paste' is written in that tradition, and our V. S. Pritchett also wrote a short story called 'The Necklace.' Theft was involved."

The names numbed them. Some of them winced as though finding the names hostile. Raleigh was sensitive to listeners tuning out. They had not read the stories, would probably never read them, but never mind: they had no need of literature – they were too happy, too social, too busy to need books or care about the madness of art, the madness of life. They were whole people with no desperate secrets, and he was broken and exiled. Even now they were smiling at him as if he was a lunatic, and for that reason they would care about him, and he knew he could always depend on them.

"I must take this call," Raleigh said, and snatched his phone from his pocket and jammed it against his ear.

But there was no voice. As soon as he stepped into the hall, he looked at the text message on the small screen. *U cant hide. I no were u r.*

"I'm awfully sorry," Raleigh said, reentering the room. "I am afraid I'm going to be terribly rude and uncouth and make my exit. Something incredibly boring has just raised its tedious head."

They were smiling as he spoke, liking his stagy apology, and perhaps relieved that he was going, so that they could resume speaking about other matters, things they cared about, and in their own language.

"I could drop you," Mrs. DeWicky said.

"I will not uproot you from this delightful bower," Raleigh said, and got the same smiles, like dogs hearing music, some opening their mouths in thanks.

"I wish we could do something," Mrs. DeWicky said. "You've been so sweet."

"Invite me back," Raleigh said. He kissed her on both cheeks and gave her shoulders a squeeze. "That would be such a treat."

"Soon."

"If I am spared," he said.

He lingered, feeling tearful, because he had meant it about wanting to come back. Then he hurried out of the house, and seeing a stoplight at the end of the avenue, near the Public Garden, he walked down the sidewalk. He glanced around and then cautiously opened his phone again. *U r dead meat*. He was glad to be away from them. He had a sense that the blood had drained from his face, that had he been among those people someone would have said – why did Americans always speak their thoughts? – "You're so pale. Are you sure you're all right?"

And he would have had to protest, "Yes, yes, I'm fine," and invent another story, and go paler.

He began to give the taxi driver the address through the side window, as he would have done in London. But cutting him off, the driver – foreign – said, "Hop in."

He spoke the address slowly, stammering a bit.

"Where's that?"

"Roxbury."

"Cost you extra."

"No problemo." And Raleigh laughed, saying the word.

Alone, sitting in the back seat of the taxi, he felt safe at last.

And when, after all the traffic, the taxi dropped him and he stepped into the hot street, then made his way to the shady side and turned into the alley, he was free again, his heart pounding.

He found the doorway and knocked. There was no answering voice, and he was anxious until he heard a sound, a chair being scraped backward across an uneven floor, the bump of heavy shoes. And then the door opened a crack, and he saw the cruel mouth and bloodshot eyes.

"Git on in here." The voice was fierce.

Thrilled, averting his eyes, whinnying a little once again, he obeyed.

Incident in the Oriente

WE WERE SITTING, heads bowed in prayer, waiting for the local Indians, Secoyas, to come barefoot into the mess container with the platters of food. When Max Moses said grace, as he was doing tonight, his terrifying vitality shone in his bulging eyes. Yet, rumbling on in his old smoker's vibrato, he did not raise his voice. His slight speech defect made him seem truthful: there was a babyish innocence in "daily bwed." His lazy tongue turned and snagged with a soft fruity catch on words like "church" or "chicken," and instead of "gravy" he said "meat juice," probably for the slushiness of the sound. It was "Wab" when referring to Silsbee's dog, a Labrador retriever. He said grace standing.

I was always surprised when Moses stood up, because the man I regarded as a giant was almost as small as the Mbuti pygmies we'd had on the payroll on the Uganda job. His tenacity and godlike resourcefulness in getting his people to obey him seemed to enlarge him. Though he could be chivalrous even in the worst conditions, we knew our lives depended on our obedience to him. Whenever strangers asked me how he was able to command unswerving loyalty, I used this meal as an example – every incident that had led to it.

In a world where many private companies were chasing the money from little countries to complete development projects, Moses was a rarity. His record of success was brilliant, his costs were low, his estimates fair, and he always had work. "I sometimes surprise myself." You think of charity or foreign aid as the deciding factor in the completion of these projects, but no, it is always the private contractor. "I want to surprise you, too. We are all in this together. If someone fails, everyone is accountable."

Moses' rule was to oversee every job himself and to be judicious in the matter of corruption. He had an odd neutrality when it came to bribes ("Cost of doing business – think of it as a tax"), always paying off the top man, whoever that happened to be, and depending on him for protection at lower levels. He used local labor at slightly above the going rate, and local materials whenever possible, even to the point of dismantling abandoned buildings if it meant a ready supply of steel or timber. Most of the others imported expensive building materials. Moses often used scrap, recycled wood, made bricks using local concrete and molds, bulking out the bricks with rubble that we crushed ourselves from the broken buildings. He rehabbed heavy machinery, so you would see an old bulldozer or cement mixer, good as new. "Found it. Fixed it up." That also meant profit. He had the frugality of a junkman, and the foresight too. We lived in steel shipping containers.

All this depended on cooperation. He often said that his business model was a traveling circus. The circus arrived in town with all the rides, the tents, the cages, the food stalls, and local labor was hired to raise the tents, bolt the seating, fetch water, sweep, scrub, wash dishes, feed the animals. The talent was in the circus; the muscle was local, and cheap. It meant the circus could travel light, picking up labor along the way, paying them off, leaving them behind.

Moses said, "If I were a general in a foreign war, I'd recruit soldiers locally."

No one dared to ask what he would do if they refused to obey, yet he answered the question anyway.

"In every man there is something – a sentiment – that you can tap into to make him take orders. It is often an anxiety. It's sometimes sacrificial."

Moses applied the traveling circus principle to his development contracts. A country secured a loan for a new road or a bridge or a clinic, and it hired his company to build it.

"Wars are fought with private companies, doing security detail, providing meals, putting up barracks," he said. "Someday all soldiers will be mercenaries, as they've been in history. Even now, money is a motivator – for scholarships, or the big payout at the end of the tour. This is the era of the private sector helping governments achieve their goals with somebody else's money."

In another age Moses would have been the captain of a clipper ship, or a general, as he said, or an explorer in the pay of a king who wanted gold from a far-off jungle.

We were in Amazonas, in a jungle now, oil depot work, on a river, the Oriente province of Ecuador, in the mess container. Moses sat at the head of the table like a chief, with a glow of satisfaction on his face. If he had said to any of us, "Stick your hand in that candle flame," we would have done it. But he was too practical for that. His rule, "Get up before dawn and be at my door at four-thirty, ready to work," was one we obeyed.

Five of us at the table, still saying grace, Moses, Chivers, Silsbee, Tafel, and me. The cook boy, Hong, was still outside with the Secoya servants. I was struck by how pious Silsbee and Tafel were in their prayers, murmuring along with Moses, sitting far apart tonight for a change.

Silsbee and Tafel had been the problem from the beginning. First time I saw them I knew it wouldn't work. Tafel had been with Moses for a year, Silsbee was a new hire. He'd been overseas on jobs before, an expert welder. Moses wanted him to teach locals this skill so that Silsbee would have a team. It worked at first, when we refitted a floating dock on the river, but when we got to rebuilding the bridge, two problems arose.

The friendship between Silsbee and Tafel was one – their instant liking for each other, talking, laughing, lollygagging. The average person thinks, Great, harmony. But harmony wasn't Moses' way. Friendliness and good humor relaxed the locals (was how Moses put it). Instead of working to a deadline, we were working as the locals did. "It's why nothing got done before. It's why we're here."

Work was social in places like this, Moses said; work was a party. "People love going to work, to meet their friends, to have a coffee break, to share meals. It's nothing to do with finishing a job. The job exists to support a social framework – they want to get out of the house and talk."

He did not say the easy relations between Silsbee and Tafel set a bad example. He could convey this with looks. He watched the two of them with a trace of astonishment.

Moses said, "I can take insolence from the work gangs, but not from my own men."

The other problem was Silsbee's dog, Gaucho. It was a Lab mix, big and sleepy. The idea that this dog did nothing infuriated Moses, who saw it as no better than a three-legged village mutt. It didn't earn its keep.

Silsbee had a way of blinking that showed a thought was passing through his mind. He said, "My dog makes me happy."

"That's exactly what I mean. Why isn't it doing something useful?" And in a kindly way Moses asked, "What is the insufficiency inside you that is satisfied by a dog?"

When, one day, some propane tanks were stolen by locals from the depot, Moses said, "Didn't even bark!" and held the dog and Silsbee partly responsible for the theft.

"Labs aren't like that," Silsbee said, and looked at Tafel for approval.

Tafel was a darkly handsome man who could have been Arab, with a sharp indicating nose, thin lips, close-cut hair, a narrow chin, and slender fingers, like a superior type of stern-faced Gypsy woman. He had been a foreign hire who'd stayed on with Moses. His specialty was supervising the work gangs, organizing the way they gathered material – posts, planks, struts, trusses, the usable fittings like window units, or if we were doing a steel frame, the plates and pipes.

"We are creating something," Moses said. "We are leaving something behind. Our names will be forgotten but these structures will be here long after we're gone."

We were leaving monuments, was his view.

Chivers drew the plans at Moses' direction, and did the paperwork and the accounts too, paying the men every two weeks. That Moses paid in dollars was another reason he was sought out by the local labor, since dollars were spendable anywhere.

But this job was going slowly, and the concern that showed as a knot in Moses' forehead was Tafel and Silsbee. Tafel had been one of the most loyal of Moses' men. I knew that because I prided myself on having Moses' trust, and I was competitive in this. Staging was my responsibility. In the Oriente province the scaffolding was fist-wide bamboo poles lashed together with split cane or hemp rope to make skeletal towers of frames and ladders.

Silsbee's welders set one of the scaffolds blazing. Moses told Tafel to reprimand him, which he did, but not long after that the two men were seen together laughing. The Lab killed some chickens. "We can't eat them now!" The local Indians sometimes seen laughing with Silsbee infuriated Moses. He asked, "Is this a social occasion?" in his jaw-twisting lisp and slipping tongue. The dog intimidated the locals but otherwise just slept in the shade. "That Wab."

A month into the job we were already behind schedule. Moses knew that he had no power over Silsbee, that he was losing Tafel, and that the laxity of these two men was undermining the project.

Moses gave a talk after dinner about the role of the private contractor, how essential it was, how it was accountable to the institution paying the bills.

"It is government work for money – not patriotism or justice. No abstractions. We aim for results. I have spent my whole working life as a contractor, in Kuwait, in Uganda, in Brazil."

Our core group was small and efficient, but the hundreds of local laborers became our teams. In western Uganda we had Mbuti pygmies sealing the insides of three-foot casings. A whole flotilla of Malay fishermen were signed on for the barging of cement for an offshore fuel dock. In Kuwait we extended the frontier fence – no Kuwaitis on the payroll but plenty of Filipinos and Bangladeshis, who had nothing in common but hunger. In Iraq we worked inside a great enclosure of twelve-foot blast walls to put up modular housing, and after that it was boreholes in Sudan.

"The type of government doesn't matter as long as we are paid in dollars. Most of the world is in the hands of megalomaniacs. We were hired to complete this job and by God we'll accomplish it. Think of us as commandos."

You would have thought in all that laborious lisping that we'd gotten the point. But the next day a tap was left running on a fuel drum, and two hundred gallons of stinking diesel oil drained into the sand. We had to use all our solvent to neutralize it – a mess. And there were more thefts.

Chivers, who was English, said to me, "He should sack them."

We never used Moses' name.

I said, "If he does, there's no way we can finish this. We'll have to find a master welder to replace Silsbee, and a wrangler like Tafel who also knows how to operate the backhoe."

Moses, working on tight margins because of the lost time, had invested all the money he'd been advanced. He needed Tafel back as a loyal worker. He needed Silsbee to take orders. He had to find a way of dividing these two men. Tafel might listen, but Moses had no control over Silsbee, who was too new to his command to care. And we were miles up the Aguarico River, on a deadline with the oil drillers.

Chivers said, "I wouldn't be surprised if he just beat them unmercifully about the head and shoulders."

I had known Max Moses for many years. I had no idea what he would do, only that he would have a better answer than that. In his mental leadership manual there was a different answer for every problem. Each situation was unique; each person was. Had Moses said, "Everybody's the same," that would have meant he was afraid or contemptuous. Everyone is different, was his philosophy.

"He's going to flog Silsbee," Chivers said.

"He never touches his people," I said.

"Then he'll read the riot act to Tafel."

"He doesn't raise his voice, but even if he did, Silsbee would still be a friend to Tafel, and the problem won't go away."

Seeing us talking together, Moses frowned, and from that moment on I ignored Chivers. At breakfast, Moses said to Tafel, "A needy person is someone you're always meeting for the first time," which enraged Tafel and made Silsbee sulk.

That same day he laid out the schedule, the deadlines, the inspections. He said, "At this rate we won't make it. We're going to work faster."

"It's the locals," Tafel said.

"It's us," Moses said. "It's you." There was conviction and even eloquence in the slushy suck-sound of his lisp.

Nothing else happened until later in the morning. Tafel was summoned to Moses' container. He wasn't long. He was soon striding out, nose forward, carrying a rifle.

The work site was over a little hill, past the shade trees where Silsbee usually sat chatting with the Indians, among the welding torches and the masks and tanks.

Chivers said, "Crunch time."

Within minutes we heard a gunshot, and after that, "No!" Back came Tafel, not angry but frightened and looking friendless and paler. Moses, at the entrance to his container, took the rifle from him and must have given an order, because Tafel said, "Yes, sir."

When Silsbee appeared with hatred and sorrow on his face, carrying his dead dog in his arms, Tafel walked past him without a look. Moses called out to the cook boy, and Hong took the dog by the hind legs, the way you hold a dead chicken.

Without any orders, we completed our day's objective long before the bell sounded at five. In the evening we assembled in the mess container as usual, Moses leading the grace, and at the end of it saying how confident he was that we would finish ahead of schedule and there might be bonuses. But we'd have to be quicker in taking orders. He let this sink in, then he signaled to Hong.

"Let's eat."

In the silence that followed, the stew was served. We ate without speaking, though a village dog began to bark. I wished it would stop, because it sounded triumphant, like mockery. I chewed the meat gratefully, and I smiled at Max Moses to show I wasn't paying attention to the barking. I was not surprised when he didn't smile back at me.

Rip It Up

WATCHING THE BLACK locomotive come chattering out of the tunnel, one-eyed, trailing smoke, its sharp chin forward, worrying back and forth on its seesawing side cranks, and looking lethal as it bore down on the solitary figure standing on the tracks at the level crossing, I turned the music up and said, "So long, dead ass."

John Burkell was biting his necktie in fear. He murmured, "No," into the wet stripes, as though I had asked a question.

Walter Herkis lifted his uncertain eyes to me, and now the music was so loud I just shrugged and made a face, meaning, "So what?"

"Okay, die," Walter said, turning back to the train.

As Burkell chewed his tie, the train shoved the little figure along, toppling it sideways and off the table. And I felt a kind of joy, watching Walter's big confident hand on the transformer, now slowing the train.

"So long, dead ass!" Walter screeched. The other screech in the room was the phonograph, a 45 of Little Richard singing "Rip It Up."

Walter's mother called out, "What's all that racket down there?"

"Nothing!" Walter looked at me for approval as he put another figure on the track, one of the toy pedestrians from the scale-model station. I was energized by the brainless clacking train and Little Richard, by Walter's high spirits, thrilled too by John Burkell's fear.

"Vito Quaglia would shit a brick if he knew you just killed him," John said. "Even in fooling. He's psycho."

"He's a banana man," I said. "Who's next?"

"I hosey Ed Hankey," Walter said.

"Hankey's a pissah. He can rotate on this."

John stuffed his tie back into his mouth and looked around as though expecting to see big lisping Ed Hankey bulking at the back of Walter's basement behind the model train layout, the toy hill, the toy town, the level crossing, where the train was bearing down on the image of Ed Hankey. Walter pushed the transformer handle to Full Speed and the front wheels jumped, almost derailing the shivering train, until the plastic figure spun on its back into the plastic trees.

"'And ball tonight,'" Walter said, with the song. "That bastard. Let's do the jocks."

"I have to go home," John said. His eyes, crusted with what he said was conjunctivitis, made him look sleepless and even more fearful. He slung his green book bag over his shoulder. "See you tomorrow."

When he was gone, Walter smiled at me. "He's having conniptions."

"Candy ass," I said. "He's wicked scared."

But even so, I knew that we were much the same, anxious pimply fourteen-year-olds gathered after school, taking refuge from the ball field and the bullies, safe in Walter Herkis's basement. Burkell chewed his tie, Walter bit his fingernails, I wore glasses and tried to rub the nearsightedness out of my eyes – my first year of glasses. We were miserable in much the same way, and misery made us friends. We hated school, every bit of it, the tough boys, the coy girls, the sarcastic teachers, the terror of the older students. The smell of the oiled wooden floors, the varnished desks, the urinal candy in the toilets. And the schoolwork itself – hated it most of all, because we were so good at it and made ourselves so conspicuous we pretended to have lapses of memory when we knew the right answers, Burkell in history, Walter in science, me in English, though I loved cooking chemicals in science, too. This infuriated the teachers, who seemed to know we were playing stupid. But it was dangerous to look bright.

"And here's the rest of the jocks," Walter said, dropping six small figures onto the tracks as he pushed the handle of the transformer once again, and the speeding train plowed into them, scattering them.

The music had stopped. I swung the arm of the phonograph and set the needle onto the edge of the record.

"Burkell's chickenshit," Walter said, picking up another figure. "Here's Evelyn. Your girlfriend."

"She's not my girlfriend."

But the music and the sound of the train drowned out my words as the locomotive sent Evelyn Frisch off the tracks.

"Don't make me come down there," Walter's mother yelled. "What are you doing?"

"Nothing!" Walter called out. "Did you finish the book?"

"Yeah," I said. It was the homework, *The Human Comedy* by William Saroyan.

"I don't get it," Walter said.

"It's junk," I said, and Walter looked shocked. "Homer's a banana man."

We were eighth-graders at Miller Baldwin Junior High. Walter was new to the school, someone the others had never seen before, a Seventh-day Adventist. He was depantsed the first day at recess, and cried. Then they knuckle-punched his arm with noogies. He was mocked for being tall and, his first day, for knowing the answers in science. He liked me because I didn't mock him. He wore his pants so high you could see the tops of his white ankle socks. I was his only friend. We hiked in the Fells most Saturdays, we built fires at the Sheepfold. I liked him because he had more comic books than Burkell, and Elvis records, and a ham radio. And a whole big table of model trains that he ran with a transformer lever he worked with his thumb.

After he knocked some more figures down, he played "Rip It Up" again. I sat on his stool and touched the transformer.

"It's hot."

"Because it's a transformer, shit-for-brains," he said. "It's the coil. The coil heats up from the molecules that are backed up by the wire density."

I squinted at his precise explanation.

"It's the resistance of the eddy current in the coil, because it's stepping down from AC to DC at a lower current. Ask Hoolie."

Mr. Hoolie was our science teacher, someone we exasperated by pretending not to know the right answers. I was impressed that Walter used the terms so easily: "voltage," "molecules," and "wire density." The idea that electricity was reduced by flowing through tight coils of hot wires was something new to me.

We were unhappy, restless, lonely boys, and this wet afternoon in October was typical, taking refuge in the stinks and sparks of science. Walter was hunched over the transformer. He then disconnected the wires from the side of the track and lifted them, making a bright arc.

"Spark gap," he said, smiling at the thread of smoke. "Now there's no one else left. Just us."

"You wish."

Almost the first person I saw the next day was Vito Quaglia, and remembering how we had run him over with Walter's train, I began to smile.

"The fuck you lookin' at, four eyes, you fucken pineapple."

"Nothing," I said, and tried not to show my fear.

Quaglia was a skinny yellow-faced boy given to casual violence – not strong but reckless and slow-witted, usually open-mouthed, with a chipped front tooth that gave him a fang. He wore his shirt unbuttoned, a dirty T-shirt under it. His wild hair made him look fierce. He was always in trouble and had nothing to lose by more trouble. Though he was failing in most classes, Quaglia excelled as a soccer player – fast, a ruthless kicker – and as a result was popular with some of the teachers. His friends were either almost as tough as he was or else his fearful flatterers.

"Pineapple was making a face at you," Angie Frezza said.

"You make one more face at me and I'll put my foot so far up your *culo* you'll have to open your mouth for me to take my shoe off."

Frezza laughed at this and then said, "*Mannaggia,* look at the knockers on her, Vito," offering him a picture torn from a magazine.

Quaglia opened his mouth wider, as though to see the picture better, showing his chipped tooth.

"Where's your fairy banana man friend?"

Though I was hot and anxious, I pretended not to hear, made myself small, and slipped away as he looked closer at Frezza's picture of a woman in a tight sweater.

He meant Walter, who was bullied because he was new, because he was weak, and especially because the word got out that he went to church on Saturdays. "Your wacky religion" – he couldn't go to soccer games on Saturdays. Everything about him was noticed: he couldn't eat meat, didn't drink Coca-Cola because of the caffeine, couldn't go to dances; he was a little too tall, and his clothes didn't fit. His ears turned red and he went breathless and silent when he was bullied, suffering it, his ears reddening even more, and hadn't fought back when he was depantsed.

"Quaglia hocked a louie at me in the corridor," Walter whispered in English class. "At the bubbler."

"He's a pissah," I said. "Tell him to rotate."

Vito and Frezza always sat at the back of the class.

Mr. Purcell said, "Jay, do you wish to share your thoughts with the class?"

"No, sir."

"Then sit up straight and pay attention." He was holding a book. "Has anyone finished the book?"

He meant *The Human Comedy.* I did not raise my hand. I simply sat, breathing through my nose. It wasn't that I hadn't liked the book; I knew the book was bad. I could not have said that of the previous book, *Silas Marner,* but this one was unbelievable, sketchy, sentimental, and written like a lesson. I knew the fault was with the book and not with me.

My certainty that it wasn't good made my head hot, as though I had been told a lie. I could have written an essay on why I didn't like it. Instead, all of us had to write about why it was good. That was another reason I hated school, finding it unfair. But my disliking the book was a secret that also made me feel powerful, superior to school, but also out of place, like an outlaw. I believed in Little Richard more than I believed in Homer Macauley.

"Do you have something to say, Jay?"

"The teacher calls Joe Terranova a wop in chapter twelve," I said.

Quaglia slammed his loose desktop and said, "*Mannaggia!*"

"Quiet," Mr. Purcell said. "But the teacher was reprimanded for it. And what did the principal say?"

I had said enough. I had only wanted to shock the class by using the word "wop." I shrugged, as though I didn't know.

Mr. Purcell was holding the book open. "He said, 'This is America, and the only foreigners here are those who forget this is America.'"

"And go to church on Saturday," Vito said in a harsh whisper.

In science, the next class, Mr. Hoolie showed us a large glass ball filled with water.

"I'm taking for granted that you read the assigned pages," he said, attaching a rubber tube to the glass ball. "This will show us two things. What two things? Anyone?"

"Air displacement," Corny Kelleher said.

Mr. Hoolie took up a piece of chalk and wrote *Air displacement* on the blackboard.

"And?"

The answer was lung capacity. But I merely sat, squinting.

"It was in your homework," Mr. Hoolie said.

"Air temperature?" Kelleher said.

"Lung capacity," Mr. Hoolie said, and wrote the words on the blackboard. "Who's first? Evelyn?"

We watched as Mr. Hoolie inserted a mouthpiece into the rubber tube, and then as Evelyn Frisch took the tube in her dainty fingers and placed it between her lips, there were murmurs from the back of the room.

"Settle down, people," Mr. Hoolie said. "Go ahead, Evelyn. Blow as hard as you can."

Vito muttered something, making his friends laugh.

"Mr. Quaglia, one more word from you and you'll be seeing me after school."

Evelyn had finished. The water in the glass ball had slipped down. Then it was Walter's turn. He did it, reddening from the effort, and gasped when he was done. The class laughed, and even Mr. Hoolie smiled.

Next Ed Hankey took the tube and blew, and the water level dropped sharply. He bowed to the class, making them laugh, then sat behind me and flicked my ear with his finger.

"Beat that, banana man," he said into his hand, and the class bell rang.

"Homework," Mr. Hoolie said. "The principles of the light bulb, chapter five."

Walter was hit by a spitball in history class. The teacher, Mr. Gagliano, was asking about the Louisiana Purchase, the previous night's homework, and called on Walter, who was wiping the back of his head where the spitball had hit.

"Can you tell us about the Louisiana Purchase?"

As Walter shook his head, Mr. Gagliano turned to me. "Jay?"

Thomas Jefferson. 1803. The French sold it after they failed in Haiti. Slavery. Napoleon. Fifteen million dollars. I said, "Nope."

Something at Miller Baldwin, a caged and hung-up feeling, and a jostling, and a gummy taste of failure I could not explain, made me wish to be mediocre and anonymous, and to hide my head from the ferocity of the school. It made me want to live in a foreign country. While depending on a hidden strength for no one to know me, I succeeded in keeping myself at Walter's level, though the assaults were worse for him than for me. The rest of the day was the same, the routine of avoiding eye contact, or any contact, threading my way through the students without calling attention to myself. We sat with Burkell over our sandwiches at lunch at a far table, and at recess we stayed by the fence. We knew we had to keep ourselves apart.

The end of the day was the worst class of all, phys ed – Mr. Gagliano also taught phys ed. The embarrassment of changing in the locker room among the shouting boys; the pushing, the actual nakedness, the towel snapping; then the run to Hickey Park for soccer. Two times around the track, and then kicking. The other boys, especially Quaglia and his gang – Frezza, Hankey, Zangara – were fast, deft, accurate in their kicks. Nervousness made me stumble, took away my coordination, and when two teams were chosen and the game started, I sat on the bench.

Gagliano liked the boys who were good at soccer, the Italians especially. Instead of teaching us the moves – passing, kicking, heading, stopping the ball, he yelled at us to do them, and blamed us when we failed. For the games he chose the good players.

I watched the boys on the field, and Gagliano shouting, and just wanted it to rain – thunder and lightning – anything to end this; for someone to be seriously hurt, someone to die.

After the game, two more times around the field.

"Pick up the pace, Jay!" Gagliano screamed at me.

Another awful day at school. Homework tonight, then the same thing tomorrow, a whole day of hiding the fact that I was afraid, afraid of being exposed, mocked, bullied. I was weak – I was reminded of it every minute. Walter was weaker, but that didn't make me feel any better. I was picked on because I was his friend. I slightly disliked him for being geeky and helpless, for depending on me, for not having a girlfriend, for not realizing his religion was weird.

"What's wrong with you?" my mother asked me on Friday afternoon.

"Nothing."

"What happened at school?"

"Nothing."

Saturday – a game day – Walter had to go to church. But neither of us was on the soccer team, so when he got home from church at noon, we went for a hike, usually a long hike, eight miles to the Sheepfold, to make a big fire at the campsite there. We sat and watched the ragged flames licking at the smoke, the fire like an expression of our anger.

"Weenie roast." I sharpened a stick with my jackknife and jammed a hot dog on it.

"You wouldn't believe the crap they put in those things," Walter said. "They've found human shit in some hot dogs. And thumbtacks."

This was his Seventh-day Adventist denunciation of meat. Another one was that pork gave you worms, and that coffee was like poison. He ate peanut butter and baked beans and nut cutlets and cheese. He was holding an aerosol can of Cheez Whiz, spraying the stuff on a cracker, as I cooked the hot dog over the fire.

I took the can from him and read the label. "'Contains cheese product. Salt. Artificial coloring. Emulsifiers.' This is crap, Walter." He started to laugh. "'Do not incinerate. Do not use near fire or flame. Dispose of carefully.'" Walter was smiling. "I'm incinerating it. Because you're too chicken to do it."

"No, I'm not. Give it to me. I hosey."

"It'll explode, you crazy bastard."

"Think I give a rat's ass?" He snatched the can and in the same motion flung it into the fire. We ran behind a tree, crouching, awaiting the explosion.

Nothing happened for a long while, long enough for us to suspect that it wouldn't blow. We got to our feet and tried to get a glimpse of the Cheez Whiz can discoloring in the flames, and as we peered, the can split with a disappointing pop, sending blue and gold sparks out of the fire pit, and an uprush of smoke and ashes.

"You're a pyromaniac," I said.

That pleased him. With pained eyes, his mouth twisted, his teeth clenched, Walter looked fiercely happy.

We were standing over the fire now, poking at the crater the exploding can had made in the fire pit. He jabbed his stick into the side of the split-open can and lifted it to admire it.

"I want to blow them all up," he said.

Finished with the futile voodoo of running over bullies with Walter's model train while listening to Little Richard sing "Rip It Up," we made that our plan. But an aerosol can was not enough. We wanted to make a real bomb. But how?

"What about match heads?"

We tore the matches from ten matchbooks and snipped off the heads.

"'Draw me,'" Walter said, reading the advertisements on the loose matchbooks. "'Learn to write this winter. Make money in your spare time.' It's not working."

The match heads fizzed and fumed, brightened and then shriveled black.

"Do I smell smoke?" Walter's mother called out. "What are you two doing down there?"

"Chemistry," Walter said, and frowning at the ashes, "This shits."

There was no bang, no sound at all, just the brightness of the match heads, little pills alight.

"We need a detonator," he said. "Not a fuse but something inside. A hot wire."

Yet we were happy. It was the pleasure of being in the windowless basement, listening to Little Richard screaming, not being at school. School was disturbing in ways I could not put into words but could see clearly: the throng of reckless boys, the short-haired jocks, bigger boys, scrutinizing and sneering girls, the more beautiful ones the scariest, the loud boys, all of them like monkeys, even the teachers. Every day was a struggle, and the all-day occasions of ridicule made me hate myself for having to cope with them. What sustained me was that it was so much worse for Walter, almost two months into his transfer to Miller Baldwin and still being picked on.

The teachers picked on Walter too, especially Hoolie.

"Herkis, still biting your fingernails? Get over here. Let me see."

He snatched Walter's hand and made a face.

"Bitten to the quick. Sit down!"

Walter couldn't help it. The more he was mocked, the more he chewed. He was mocked for not eating meat. Mocked for Saturday church. Mocked for not dancing. He was a freak. "You're going to hell, Herkis! You're probably not even an American." And I was his friend.

We had quit the Boy Scouts. We now liked dissecting frogs and mixing potions, heating test tubes over the blue flames of Bunsen burners. The lab was the refuge of the geeks at Miller Baldwin, and we were the geeks. Science class was one of the classes Walter liked, and I did too. It was simple science, but it was smelly and involved bubbly liquids in heated test tubes, a bowl of mercury, dry ice. I liked the stink of the room, the tadpoles in the aquarium, the model skeleton hanging by its skull, the jars of chemicals with yellow labels, the brass microscope, the lenses and prisms. The slop of a purple mixture in a beaker, the hiss of the Bunsen burner, the drip of osmosis, and "It's a bladder."

Even the wildest boys in the class sat still and watched as Hoolie melted lead in a crucible. We were all in awe of the unexpectedness, the sizzle and smoke of an experiment, the surprise, the dazzle of science.

I wanted to be a scientist, not for the discoveries, not for money, but to make fires and boil flasks and liquefy metals in a clay dish, to stir green smoking chemicals in a big black kettle and mix explosives. That was my secret: science, with its riddles and surprises, was the nearest thing on earth to magic.

Hoolie was turning a crank today, making a big clear light bulb flicker.

"Why does a bulb glow?" Hoolie asked. "Anybody?"

It was the hot wire coil of the filament, tungsten, a hard-to-melt element on the periodic table, sealed and mounted in a circuit in the vacuum of inert argon gas in a bulb with no oxygen. Chapter five.

"Because the wire is heating up?" Kelleher said.

"Good. What do we call the wire? Anybody. Frezza? Zangara? Miss Frisch?"

"The circuit?" I loved her lost tongue lisping in her pretty mouth.

"It's *part* of a circuit. But what do we call the wire, and what is its chemical composition? Walter?"

Walter shook his head.

"Jay, can you help us?"

"No, sir."

"This was your homework! I'm wasting my breath. Take out your notebooks." Hoolie sighed and wrote *filament* and *tungsten* and *conductor* on the blackboard, and he sketched a light bulb, the wires, with arrows indicating the electric current.

Frezza put up his hand. "So why don't the bulb explode?"

It was the question I would have asked, if I had asked any

questions. I listened carefully to Hoolie's answer, about the gas, the vacuum, the absence of oxygen, the circuit.

"This filament is a kind of bridge," Hoolie said.

At recess, in the schoolyard, Quaglia flicked a Zippo lighter in Walter's face and said, "Herkis, you pineapple, what's the chemical composition of this?"

"He bites his fingernails," Frezza said. "Herkis, bite my gatz."

Walter flinched and backed away, and then Quaglia lit a cigarette and palmed it and puffed it, eyeing Walter. "What are you looking at, shitface?"

Zangara said, "Plus, he's going to hell for his fucked-up Saturday religion."

On the way home, Walter nudged me and took a fat envelope out of his pocket. He lifted the flap and showed me the bright yellow powder.

"Sulfur. I hooked it from the lab."

It was important to Walter that we steal everything from Hoolie's science lab.

"For the bomb."

Later in the week, another awful day at school, Walter stole another envelope, this one containing gray powder. And a small jar.

"Powdered aluminum. Potassium permanganate."

That Saturday at the Sheepfold we mixed the chemicals in a little mound and lit it with a slow fuse of match heads and got a sudden bright blaze that surprised us with its force, crackling in the air. We looked around to make sure no one had seen us. We packed some more of the mixture into a metal cigar tube and used another fuse of match heads to light it. It flared, melting the metal, but did not explode.

"The detonator's crappy. It's just a fuse."

Later that day we went back to Walter's basement and worked the trains, the usual game of running over kids from the school and killing them, the bullies, the snobs, the jocks, the teachers, almost everyone we knew. It had begun as an excitement, but now it seemed a sad pastime, reminding us we were geeks.

"We need a hot wire, a real detonator, something to burn inside the tube. If it's sealed under pressure, it'll blow up."

It was the feeling inside me, a wire that heated and burned and glowed and made me angry, reddened my face, made my hands damp. Walter had one inside him too, a hot wire, like a filament in a bulb that made him breathless and hot and tearful.

The train was going round and round, knocking down the little figures on the track, Walter twiddling the transformer.

"A fuse won't work. We need to put a wire inside and somehow get it to burn."

"Like a filament in a light bulb," Walter said. "Connect a small wire to two thicker wires to make a circuit. The thin wire will burn."

"How do we set it off?"

"Control the flow of electricity."

Walter's thumb was pressed against the handle of the transformer. He began to giggle, as he did when he was watching a bonfire, the times I called him a pyromaniac, the excitement that made me happy and scared John Burkell.

"Use the transformer. Or are you too chicken?"

"Up your bucket," he said.

Walter detached the wires from the track. He snipped off a small piece of wire from a spool – the sort of multistrand wire we had on our lamp cords. He untwisted it and separated a single strand, then attached this narrow wire to the two thicker wires trailing from the transformer, connecting them, like the filament in a light bulb.

"Stick it on the floor," he said.

He pushed the handle of the transformer and all the lights went out.

"Walter!" his mother screamed from upstairs.

We put a new fuse in the fuse box, and the next time we used a narrower wire, which glowed and burned like a bright strand of hair when he gave it juice.

"The bridge wire," Walter said, poking at the ashes. "That's our detonator. Thanks, Hoolie!"

We made another one, twisting the wires into a circuit, then slipped it into a cigar tube. Holding the tube upright, we packed it with the mixture of sulfur and powdered aluminum. When it was taped and thick, with the loose wire attached like a fuse, it had the look of a real bomb.

"That's half a pound of crazy shit," Walter said. "That can do damage."

"Guy says, 'Hear about the guy who stuck a bomb up his ass?' His friend says, 'Rectum.' Guy says, 'Wrecked 'im—damned near killed 'im!' "

Walter pressed his lips together and laughed, holding the bomb, his shoulders shaking.

It was a week before we could test it, a week of school and wrong answers and "Nothing." A week of "You looking at me?" and "Homo!" and "Banana man!" and "You're going to hell, Herkis." And that was the week of the Hop, when I saw Evelyn Frisch holding hands with Ed Hankey and guessed they were going steady.

My head was still hot. I was silent with a pain inside me, the physical ache, the bright wire of misery. And even Walter seemed like a big silly boy who was inviting abuse. At home my mother smelled the burned sulfur on me and said, "Have you been smoking?"

The next Saturday, after Walter got home from church, we waited for his parents to go out.

He said, "You think we should?"

"Would you rather go down to Hickey Park and warm the bench with Burkell and those other geeks and watch Quaglia and Frezza playing?"

He was holding the bomb.

"You want to be a water boy?"

Just listening to me made him chew in anger, and his eyes got glassy with resentment.

We dug a hole in his yard near his mother's clothesline and buried the bomb, covering it with dirt, letting the wire stick out. We fastened a long wire to it in two twists and connected that wire to the terminals of the transformer, which rested on a small table in Walter's garage.

From the garage door we could see the pile of dirt.

"One, two," Walter said. "Here goes."

The ground erupted with a sharp bulge and bang, dirt flying up, and an elegant mushroom cloud rising, lengthening on a stalk of smoke but not losing its shapely cap that widened to a dome ten feet in the air.

"Bastards!" Walter was shrieking, his fingers in his mouth.

Out of smelly powder and old wire and junk metal we had made something deadly. It was a dark afternoon in late fall, the black bushes bare, the grass wet, and the large black hole we had torn in the ground was still smoking near the clothesline.

That was our first bomb. After another week at school, being jostled and mocked, we made another one. Walter came alive that Saturday after his church service. He giggled with excitement as he packed the wire and the powder into a bigger tube and buried it deeper. He dared me to throw the switch, and when I said, "Are you scared?" he dived onto the transformer and squeezed it and the ground erupted thirty feet away with a half-muffled bang, the spray of dirt, the symmetrical smoke cloud.

"Wicked pissah."

We spent so much time building the bombs that we became more neglectful at school and careless in our homework, so preoccupied that our science marks suffered. We weren't studying enough. We were failing the tests and pop quizzes that Hoolie gave us.

"What's wrong with you?" Hoolie said to me. He took

for granted that Walter, being new, wouldn't do so well, and also because Walter was teased so much he seemed to think there had to be a good reason for it, that Walter somehow deserved it.

We were both bullied more than ever. The reason could have been that we were happy. The contentment that showed in our faces seemed to invite hostility. We didn't care. Having a bomb made life bearable – more than bearable: it was the answer to all the teasing. I was mocked, Walter was threatened. Walter couldn't climb the rope in gym class, I couldn't kick the ball straight at soccer practice. He was flunking history, I was flunking math. We didn't have girlfriends, we didn't share in the jokes. He was gawky, I was small.

We were teased because we were friends. "Faggot." "Homo." "Percy." The teachers merely stood by: I deserved to be teased, I wasn't answering in class. They seemed to agree with the bullies. But I had no one else. We were singled out to be ridiculed, and the other boys joined in. We kept to our corner of the schoolyard with the other misfits, Burkell among them, and Chicky DePalma, who was flunking every subject.

Yet we weren't afraid. We had a secret: our bomb. Set off inside a desk, the bomb could shatter a wooden desktop and blow a student's face off. It could smash glass or tear a locker open with a bang that could be heard all over the school. It could blast the aquarium apart in Hoolie's lab, blind and maim any of those bullies, or blow a hole in Gagliano's Oldsmobile.

Having the secret made us feel powerful. And the bomb components were easily hidden – the jar of sulfur, the bottle of powdered aluminum, the potassium permanganate, the length of wire, the tubes, the transformer from the train set. The real secret was the detonator – the cord, the twist across the tips, the sizzle of the bridge wire. Anyone could make a pile of explosive powder, but we had invented a detonator.

The secret also made me silent.

"What's so funny?" my mother said.

"Nothing."

I had been thinking about our bomb, seeing mayhem – a bloody wrenched-off leg sailing skyward, teachers howling, the cloud of smoke, the deafening bang. All that made me smile.

We kept the loose pieces in a shoebox and were happy in the certainty of what we could do with it – shatter Hoolie's lab, blast the papers off Gagliano's desk, scorch the smile off the bullies' faces. In my imagining, Quaglia asked, "The hell's that supposed to be?" as with a big bang and a flash of fire his bloody fingers were blown in five directions. On the soccer field, under a car, in the schoolyard, the dirt flying up, the slow cloud rising.

We had our own bomb. But we didn't talk about it in a gloating way; we hardly talked about it at all, where it was or what we were going to do with it. It was enough to have it, an exploding thing, not a warm bright reassuring flare or fire, but a dark bomb that broke forth from underground with a bang like the crack of doom.

"You are such an asshole, Herkis," Quaglia said to us in the schoolyard. "And you're his faggot friend."

We kept smiling, were almost gleeful when we were bullied, because the bullies were too stupid to know that we could dismember them with our bomb. We had a weapon fiercer than their abuse.

We were proud of having devised a cheap and lethal way of getting everyone's attention, of making them afraid, of destroying them. That no one had the slightest idea of this made us even prouder.

Not much at school had changed. We were doing poorly in our studies. My mother blamed Walter. "He's a bad influence." Walter's mother blamed me, probably because I ate hot dogs.

But it was simple. We hated school, we saw no point in it. Even as, in Walter's basement, we were measuring chemicals, soldering wires, tinkering with the transformer, packing tubes with the powder, stockpiling bombs that resembled thick taped firecrackers, and – when Walter's mother was out – exploding them, we were flunking science and in danger of having to repeat it at summer school.

"You better smarten up, fella," Hoolie said to me.

The bullies repeated it. "Smarten up, fella!"

"I'm very disappointed in you," Hoolie said to Walter.

We reveled in his disappointment. We were not miserable anymore – we were confident, perhaps overconfident. Having the bomb made us insolent at times. "Bold," the teachers said, with a bad attitude.

"And that became known as the Westward Movement," Mr. Gagliano said in history class.

Walter smiled, hearing it.

"Mr. Herkis, what do you find so funny about that?"

"Nothing."

"Stand up!"

Walter stumbled getting to his feet, and stood there leaning, gnawing a bitten finger, his hair spiky, his chafed and knobby wrists showing beyond his shirt cuffs.

"We are studying American history. Lewis and Clark. Jefferson. The Westward Movement. And instead of taking notes, you smile."

"I was taking notes."

"Don't you talk back to me!" Gagliano was angry. "Get up here!"

As Walter stumbled forward, Frezza goosed him.

"Stand on one leg and repeat after me: 'I'm dumb.' Say it."

"I'm dumb," Walter said, tottering, wagging one hand for balance.

"Dumbo," Quaglia whispered, his yellow face forward, his chin on his hand.

"Dumb ass," Ed Hankey said, his scummy tongue between his teeth.

Gagliano was staring in fury while Walter leaned blotchy-faced in shame, his shirttail out, his ears red and veiny, his eyes wide open in fear, like someone about to be whipped.

I raised my hand.

"What do you want?"

"'Dumb' means you can't talk," I said. "So how can he say 'I'm dumb' if he's really dumb?"

"Stand up!"

I did so, trembling, feeling fragile, my throat burning, my face hot, my eyes glazed.

"Smart guy!" Gagliano said. His head was skull-like, bald with wisps of hair, his teeth discolored, his mole vivid on his pale cheek. "Know what you need? A swift kick. And I'm the one to do it. Know what we did with pipsqueaks like you in the army? Whaled the tar out of them, that's what. Sit down, the two of you. You make me sick."

Like that, we had new names, Dumbo and Pipsqueak. We were goosed and kicked in the ankles as we went from class to class. Burkell was so afraid he avoided us.

But we were defiant. We had a weapon.

Bombing was not a decision we discussed. It was an unspoken plan that we'd use our bomb against the school. The question was where? The science lab was too obvious, and though we were failing in science, we liked Hoolie. Maybe at morning assembly, but where to plant it? In the schoolyard at recess was easy, but the area was too spread out. How could we get the whole school watching? We somehow shared these thoughts without uttering them.

Sitting on the bench during soccer practice one afternoon at Hickey Park, we listened to Gagliano screaming, the muscles tightening in his throat and narrowing like cords.

"You gotta do better than that against the Hobbes," he yelled, as Frezza stumbled trying to head the ball.

The Miller Baldwin–against–Hobbes game marked the end of the soccer season, a day when the stands were filled with students, and even teachers and parents cheering, the whole school watching the junior varsity, Quaglia and Frezza and Hankey trying to impress them.

Staring ahead at the dank field, the dripping trees, the muddy boys, and tight-faced Gagliano, I said, "We can do better than that."

Walter looked at me. And, like that, the decision was made to explode a bomb at the soccer field during the big game, plant it somewhere everyone could see it. Not kill anyone but make a big bang, maybe hurt them a little, certainly scare them.

"Gonna rip it up," Walter said in a lilting way, "and ball tonight."

On the field, near the goal mouth, when both teams were massed at a scoring attempt, the whole school watching. The bomb would be buried about six or eight inches, and when the players were bunched in that area, as they often were during a close kick, we'd throw the switch.

I saw it all: the screaming fans, the game in progress, Gagliano clawing at his baldness, Quaglia booting the ball or Frezza heading it, all the cruel boys, and Evelyn and her friends in the stands, the sun shining, the band playing . . .

Then *boom!* Hell on the field.

We would be hiding behind the changing room, and when the bomb went off and everyone rushed onto the field, we'd simply unplug the transformer and leave the burned wires behind. The whole event would be so sudden and so loud, so smoky and concentrated at the goal, that we'd have time to slip away – just duck through the gap in the fence into Water Street, cut through back yards to the Fellsway, and take the bus home.

The wire would be found, but with nothing attached to it except, Walter said, maybe a message: *Up yours.*

I said, "They'd recognize our writing. They'd get fingerprints. They'd trace us."

"I don't care if they find me," Walter said.

"It's better if they don't."

"Why?"

"Because then we can do it again."

"Yeah, yeah," Walter said, biting his fingers.

We stole a spool of extension cord from the projection room of the school auditorium. We needed almost two hundred feet of cord, so that we could stay as far from the bomb as possible. And then we made more bombs, just for practice. The best were aluminum cylinders we found in Walter's basement – the same shape as the cigar tubes but fatter and longer. They were thin, so they blew apart easily. We had considered using iron pipes and glass jars, but we knew they were more destructive than we wanted. We could have made a killer bomb, filled a glass jar with explosive powder and rusty nails, one that would fling broken glass and metal and cause serious injury. We gloated about this and sometimes talked about the places we could set it off, the damage we could cause.

What we wanted most was the terror of a loud noise, a lot of smoke, and some minor injuries. We did not want to hurt anyone seriously or kill anyone. We wanted everyone to be afraid. *Who did this? What crazy bastard?*

We did not mind if we were suspected of doing it. We wanted to be feared for being crazy, being angry, for having the skill to make a bomb.

One day after school we went to Hickey Park and measured the various distances, to see if we had enough wire.

Mr. Gagliano came out of the changing room carrying a gym bag. "What are you boys doing?"

"Nothing."

"You know, if you weren't so lazy you'd be playing in the big game on Thursday."

This was a lie. There was no way we could have played. He wanted our school to beat the Hobbes. He was on the side of the jocks against us.

"You could make yourselves useful. You could be water boys."

We said nothing.

"Even so, I want you in the stands. Cheering for the team. You're going to be there?"

Saying yes was a thrill.

He started away and turned his head to say, "If you can't be athletes, you can be athletic supporters."

And he laughed. It was the sort of joke the others made. But we laughed too – we were gladdened these days when anyone teased or mocked us; it made us stronger and single-minded, because we could say afterward, *It's your own fault.*

We had no friends left, no one we could trust. Burkell hung around and said, "Want to come over to my house and read comic books?" Corny Kelleher said, "I'm looking for guys to collect money for the Jimmy Fund at the game." And Evelyn Frisch looked at me in a resentful way, because I had stopped talking to her.

Comic books! The Jimmy Fund! Girls! What were they to us, in Walter's basement, making extra bombs, filling cylinders, twisting wires, testing detonators. We felt like adults – we had power, we were to be feared, and we took pleasure in the fact that no one knew it.

Working on a bomb a few days before the game, we heard the sound of Mrs. Herkis's high heels on the floor – a sound I had grown to like for the way it suggested her swinging legs – and then her voice at the stairway: "Walter, I'm going shopping. Remember to lock the door if you go out."

When she had gone, Walter said, "Let's test this one."

"I hosey the transformer."

Walter smiled. We wired a bomb and carefully buried it in the usual hole, covering it with loose dirt. Then we crept into the garage. Walter handed me the transformer. I took it and started counting. I pushed the lever and the ground erupted. Dirt was flung up and a cloud of smoke began to rise as I dropped the transformer.

"Wicked pissah! Let's do another one."

"We only have two left."

"The last one's for the game."

"You do this one."

He rushed over, red-faced, laughing, to look at the damage to the hole, the burned wires, the flecks of metal, the hot steaming earth. He was laughing as he placed the new bomb into the hole. "I want you at that game!" He snipped off the charred strands of wire and peeled the plastic from the gleaming strands. "Okay, I'm going to the game." He began to twist the wires, connecting the bomb to the trailing wire to the transformer.

He was still talking as the bomb went off, a flash of fire, white and red in the middle of where his hands were, the bang and the brightness. We had never seen a bomb explode above the ground before, and this was very loud and very fiery, followed by a ball of smoke that swept across Walter as he fell back screaming.

He was not dead, but maybe he was dying. He was crouched, clutching his stomach. I ran to him, not knowing what to do. His screaming and crying somewhat reassured me – it meant that he was alive. But his face and his shirt were blackened, soot on his chin, the front of his jacket scorched. But what scared me most were his hands. Shreds of skin hung from his fingers, the skin blackened, his fingers and hands pink and raw, looking badly cooked, like hot dogs tossed on a fire. There was no blood, but the sharp smell of burned skin and hair was just as bad.

Kneeling there, Walter sobbing in pain, I heard a shriek – Walter's mother at the window. And in seconds she was out of the door, rushing up to us, pushing me aside and still howling, dragging Walter into the house.

I coiled the remaining wire, to hide it, and when I came to the transformer I saw that I had left the lever pushed forward. Walter had been connecting live wires. I could hear him screaming upstairs.

"You've been smoking cigarettes," my mother said when I got home.

"No."

"What have you been doing?"

"Nothing."

But the next day everyone knew. "It wasn't me," I said, but the way I said it hinted that it might have been. The news was so strange and unexpected that now I was teased in a different way, as equals tease each other, admiringly, almost affectionately. I said nothing more about the bomb, just sat, made no explanation. I wanted them to think that it was all my idea. That I had a bomb. That I had blown Walter up. That, if I wished, I could blow them up.

Hoolie said, "You think you're so smart," but I could tell that he was worried.

A few days later Walter came to school, his hands bandaged so thickly he looked like he was wearing mittens. Part of his face was burned, his chin peeled and red, his hair scorched. But there was defiance in his eyes. He lifted one of his mittens to Quaglia and said, "Rotate." I envied him a little, because, being badly injured, he looked like a hero. But I was his friend, someone else to be feared, who might do it again.

Siamese Nights

1

He knew before he'd been posted to Bangkok that you invented a city, any city, from the little you learned every day by accident. This one you had to make for yourself out of noodles and flowers, a glimpse of the river, an odor of scorched spices, office talk, moisture-thickened air that made you gasp, and neon lights shimmying in puddles – beauty in half an inch of dirty water. Or something you'd seen nowhere else, like the gilded shrines on street corners, flowers and fruit left as offerings, piles of yellow petals, people at prayer, their faces the more soulful for being candlelit in the night.

Then you flew back home and told people, and that was the whole city for them, what you remembered. In Bangkok, the availability of food, of pleasure, of people, made Boyd Osier a little anxious and giggly. Strangers smiled and seemed to know what was in your mind. *Take me! Taxi! Massage! What you want, sir?* You could possess such a place, the people were so polite.

Believing that it was his last assignment, his working life coming to an end, Osier was more attentive in Bangkok than he'd ever been, with the sorrowful clinging gaze of taking a last look. His company had sent him there. It made components for cell phones, the plant in an industrial area outside the city near the old airport, Don Mueang. The work was American; his life alone was something else. Or was he too old for another overseas assignment without his wife?

Osier's fear was that retirement meant his life would become a vacancy long before he was dead. If he wished to see where the years had gone, he only had to look at his unusual, carefully kept diaries. Instead of pages of scribbles, they were pictorial, a page of sketches a day. He had a small but reliable gift for caricature. His sketches were a relief from accountancy, though perhaps (he told himself) they were another kind of accounting, evaluating the day by illustrating it, the things he saw, the people he met, putting what they said into balloons. He told Joyce he did it for her, because when he was away she always asked, "What's it like there?" But he knew he kept the pictorial diary for himself, to test his talent without any risk, and to record the passage of time, in sketching that had the calming effect of autohypnosis.

Before he left for Bangkok, Joyce had said, "The place I want to live is somewhere I wouldn't mind dying." That rang true, because in other overseas posts, those short assignments when he'd been auditing the company's books, he'd thought, I would hate to die here – Ireland, Holland, Vancouver, the outsource centers they had developed. Something about the damp, the dark weather-pitted gravestones he'd seen under dripping trees, the insistent cheerfulness of people in the wintry gloom, indoors most of the time, so many of them careworn young people, resigned to their captivity. But Bangkok was his first hot country.

When he arrived, the two other Americans in the company, Larry Wise from Operations and Fred Kegler from Human Services, had befriended him, initiating him with what they'd found out. Their wives, too, were back in the States, so they were sympathetic to him, especially Fred, who cautioned him, telling him how to find a taxi, and a tailor, and what districts to avoid, and good places to eat.

"Sometimes you get a bowl of boogers or a dish of greasy worms that look like garbage, and you think you're going to collapse," Fred said. "But never mind, they're delicious."

Fred had an unembarrassed gape-mouthed way of talking, his visibly thrashing tongue turning "collapse" into *clapse*.

"They say they're not political"–*plitical*–"but they are. And sometimes someone's smiling and it's not a smile. Or they say no and they mean yes."

His distracting way with these and certain other words–*meer* and *hoor* for "mirror" and "horror"–made Osier mistrust anything Fred said.

Larry's line was always how simple it was to go home. "Hey, look how near we are to the States. I talk to my wife three times a day. We have conversations. Back home I talk but we never have conversations. Is this an adventure? I don't think so."

"It seems far to me," Osier said. "It seems foreign."

"Foreign I'll give you. But not far. You got here by going through a narrow tunnel at the end of the ramp at the airport in New York. And came out the other end."

Larry was right: the world was tiny. It was easy to go home.

They lived in the wholly accessible world, Larry said, the small, wired planet. "That's why this company's in profit. Look around. Everybody's always on the phone." So Osier never asked how he was going home, he only asked when.

But if separately Larry and Fred were sympathetic and helpful, together they lost their subtlety and were simplified, encouraging each other–rowdy, noisier, teasing, two guys at large in this city where, because they could so easily have what they wanted, they became greedier.

"Osier, want to go out for a drink? Get hammered?" Larry said, with Fred by his side.

"How about it? Do yourself a favor. You don't have to make a career of it," Fred said. *Creer.* This way of speaking also made him seem a mocker.

He went with them once. Larry and Fred brought him to a bar and supervised him.

The Thais did not carouse. They served drinks. They offered food. They offered themselves. Osier squirmed, feeling that he had nothing to offer in return. Every evening after that he said he was busy, because the men still asked. He had not dared to tell them that they'd embarrassed themselves.

Finally they took the hint, believing that Osier was virtuous and a bit dull. They resented him for not joining them, taking it for disapproval, and began to ignore him at work.

And now, as on those other nights when he'd claimed to be busy, Osier was sitting in the cathedral-like waiting room in Bangkok's central railway station under the portrait of King Rama V, going nowhere, as he told himself. Weeks of this – a month, maybe.

He liked the thought that because he was a *farang* no one took any notice of him, that Larry and Fred had no idea he came to the railway station waiting room to catch up on his diary. The diary was his refuge. It was less intrusive than aiming a camera at people, and it made him more observant. The Thais were so slight, so strong, so lovely, even the men and boys. He had learned to draw them in a few strokes, the slim-hipped boys, the slender girls with short hair, the crones who might have been old men. They glided in the muggy air like tropical fish, that same grace and fragility, drifting past him in pairs. The same profile too, some of them, fish-faced with pretty lips.

Their spirit compensated for the hot paved city, which was not lovely at all, the stinking honking traffic, the ugly office buildings. The river was an exception, a rippling thoroughfare of flotsam and needle-nosed motorboats. The temples, the wats, the shrines, housed fat benevolent Buddhas and joyous carved dragons, bathed in a golden glow. People knelt and bowed to pray for favors. This he understood, and envied them their belief. Why else go to church except to give thanks or ask for help? The rituals were full of emotion, addressing the Buddha obliquely with petitions and prayers: offerings, the gongs, the fruit and flowers, the physicality of it, the flames of small oil lamps, the odors of incense, seeming to celebrate their mortality. This veneration made Osier's own churchgoing seem like sorcery.

"How is it there?" Joyce asked from Maine, where she said it was raw. She spoke as though from a mountainside of bare rock and black ice.

How could he reply to this? They'd spent most of their summers in coastal Maine. Joyce looked forward to his retirement, and to the house they'd recently bought in Owls Head. But the mild summers of sea fog, relieved by the dazzle of marine sunshine, had misled them. Now he knew that the other nine months were winter: days of unforgiving wind that slashed your face, days of frost or freezing rain, a weight of cold that slowed you and lay on the night-like days like a stone slab.

"Fine," he said, shivering at her word "raw."

He kept to his pictorial diary, the doodles of hats and baskets, the carved finials on temple rooftops, because he had no words to describe the stew of the city – the heat-thickened air, the muddy river, the clean people, the efficiency, the unprovoked smiles, the signs he couldn't read, the language he couldn't speak. And so he asked her how she was, and she always said, "About the same," which meant her knee was giving her pain. She'd been healthy until her knee began bothering her, and then everything changed. She stopped going for walks, sat more, ate more, got heavy, resigned herself to a life of decline and ill health, and began to resemble her mother, who sat slumped in a nursing home.

Sketching was his hobby, but his work was numbers. Osier headed the accounting office, a job he loved for the order of its elements and the fact that no locals were involved on the money side – they couldn't be, company rule, payroll was secret, locals couldn't know how little they were paid, what profits the company was making, the low overheads. Larry and Fred were not involved either; only he saw the numbers, units shipped, cost per unit; and when the numbers added up he was done. It was forbidden to email any financial information or take any of the data out of the office on CDs. The office, too, was another world.

After phoning his wife, he improved his sketch of the noble portrait of Rama V, King Chulalongkorn, high up on the station wall.

He liked the idea that the orderly station was always in motion, a place of arrivals and departures. No one lingered here, no one to observe him. He was touched by the emotion of the travelers – families seeing loved ones onto trains, parents with toddlers, tense separations; and all the luggage they carried, some of them like campers, carrying bags of food and water. He was one of the few loiterers.

He loved looking at the girls and women – angel-faced, dolled up for their journey, slender, a little nervous, so sweet, waiting for their trains to blink on the departure board. He came to the waiting room twice a week or more, where he was licensed to stare because of his diary. He had a drink, he found food, he called Joyce. It was not a life here, but a refuge and, like most travel he'd known, a suspension of life.

The Thais were absorbed in their own affairs of travel. That was the beauty of the waiting room. No one was idle; the travelers' thoughts raced ahead, to the journey. Handling luggage, herding children, checking the clock, they were leaving this place. He knew these people somewhat. He saw them in the plant, at tables, in smocks and gloves, some wearing dust masks. Diligent little people, and when he was among them he felt – was it the business of outsourcing? – that his fate was intertwined with theirs.

2

He was sketching, smiling at this irrational thought, the night he noticed the beaky woman coming toward him. He'd seen her there before many times; her nose made her unmissable. She was, like him, another loiterer.

She was not tall but her features were so enlarged as to seem like distortions – menace in her nose, menace in her tangled hair, defiance in her chin. Among these tidy people she seemed like a freak for being so disheveled. But her shabby clothes seemed to inspire respect, even awe, in the passersby. She was someone from the lower world; she had nothing to lose. She had singled him out. Or was he imagining her menace? From a distance, shuffling, she had seemed so sad.

Ignoring half a dozen people near him, she scuffed toward him with a clapping of her plastic sandals. She didn't look like any Thai he had seen. He hoped that she would walk past him. But she stood before him, near enough to assault his nostrils. Her body odor seemed another kind of aggression: a hum of hostility in her smell.

She began to squawk. The people around him, all Thais, giggled in embarrassment hearing her, yet they were fascinated, too, at the sight of the foreigner being challenged. For those waiting for trains, this was a diversion.

One man said to him, "She talking you."

She was much too close: her dusty toes in the sandals touched his shoes. She wore a tattered wraparound, her lips smeared with lipstick. One cheek was cut cleanly, and though not a serious wound was crusted with dried blackish blood. She whined a little and nodded to get his attention, seeming to peck at him with her fleshy nose.

The bystander said, "She say, 'I not myself what you see.'"

This obscure statement made him look away. Without meeting the woman's gaze, but feeling disgusted as he brushed past her, Osier walked to a bench where a woman and a man were sitting with luggage.

Haunting him with her ripe-smelling shadow, the woman followed, legs wide apart, carrying a shoulder bag. Some of the

Thai travelers also followed. Osier turned away and pretended to be busy with his notebook, but still he heard the aggrieved voice.

Someone touched him lightly with a finger. It was the Thai man who had said, "She talking you."

The woman was gabbling in her sinuses. The foreign language had a twang of incomprehensible menace in it, too.

"She want money."

At first he resisted, but he got another whiff of her and dug into his pocket. He found a ten-baht note and handed it over.

The woman handed it back, gabbling.

"She want three hundred fifty baht."

Osier smiled at this precise amount, which wasn't much, but stopped smiling when he looked up at the woman. She was still talking in her scratchy voice. Her reddened eyes scared him.

"What is that language?"

"It Thai, but she *kaek,* from India. She want talk you."

"What about?"

His question was translated. Everything the woman said sounded like a threat or a protest.

"She say she special."

Osier reacted sharply, as though remembering, and shook his head. He said, "What's she doing here? I think we should get a policeman."

"No, sir." The man looked frightened. "That make her angry."

"Why does she want to speak to me?"

"You *farang.* You listen." The man laughed a little. "Thai people no listen."

Osier looked at the woman and said, "Hello."

But the woman's gaze did not soften.

"She come from far away," the man said.

The woman clutched her ragged wrap with heavy sunburned hands and turned her beaky face on Osier. She was chewing something, and then, as she began to shout, showing red teeth and dark gums, she grew devilish.

"You come from far away too."

"I don't understand."

"She wanting money. You have money."

Osier put his hands in his pockets, to protect his wallet.

"She say, 'I not normal.' She say, 'God make me different. People treating me in a bad way because I not normal.'"

The other panhandlers Osier had seen always repeated the same whiny phrases, pleading for food, saying, "No mother, no father." They made themselves pitiable. But this rough-looking beggar woman was making a speech, becoming angrier, denouncing Thais, proclaiming her abnormality, and, her voice going harsher, all of it seemed threatening.

"I someone else," the Thai man said, still translating, but slowly – he could hardly keep up with her. And because Osier did not understand anything she said, he looked closer, scrutinized her, and saw that she was not a woman.

She was a man in a woman's clothes, middle-aged, lined, muscled and graceless, clownishly painted with sticky makeup, in a torn wraparound and a dirty blouse, with big filthy feet and swollen hands, a wooden comb jammed in his matted hair, and demanding money, beginning to shriek, showing her green gummy tongue.

"If you don't give, sir, she will remove clothes. She will make nuisance and shame." The Thai man in his panic was clawing in his own pocket for money. "She will show private parts."

Seeing Osier counting twenty-baht notes onto his lap, the man (Osier no longer saw him as a woman) became calmer and licked the spittle from his lips. He reached out, his thick hand like a weapon, and snatched the pile of money.

"That's more than you asked for."

After the man in the wraparound whined his thanks and touched the notes to his forehead, after the Thai translator hurried away, after the crowd of onlookers dispersed, Osier got up and flapped his hand at the lingering cloud of stink and walked quickly out of the railway station, feeling banished.

He thought, Why did he choose me? But the sudden pantomime had been a shattering experience, much worse than being accosted by an aggressive beggar. He'd felt assaulted, and the smell, which was poisonous, wouldn't easily wash off. Then the unwelcome memory of the man who had provoked thoughts of mutilation and danger gave way to sorrow. It was not the menace he remembered, but the sadness.

He called Joyce and talked inconsequentially to calm himself. She said, "That's funny. You called me just a few hours ago and said the same thing."

3

He wanted to go home. He would have gone home, except that his work was not done. The hours to fill, from five to eight or nine at night, hours that were made bearable by his sketching at the station waiting room, he could not endure at the hotel. His room was small and poorly lit by a dim stylish lamp; sitting in the lobby, he felt conspicuous. He couldn't take the accounts back to his room, and he had to leave the office at five when all the others left. He'd been using a taxi, to avoid the questions in the company shuttle bus. But now he took the shuttle bus.

He'd turned Fred and Larry down so many times he didn't think they'd ask him to go with them anymore. He hoped that one of them would say "Drink?" Not because he wanted to carouse but because he wished their protection. He needed to stay as far away as possible from the railway station and the sight of the man-woman who was probably waiting for him.

The Thai workers were competent and hardworking, the

factory so well run by the local managers that he had time on his hands. So did Larry and Fred. Like Osier, they had wives back in the States, but it didn't stop them going to strip shows and massage parlors.

"Soi Cowboy! Great bars! The girls are hot – they wear boots and Stetsons!"

"Great little place called Angels. They're barely legal!"

They talked like excited boys. Maybe it was a feature of going overseas, a danger in outsourcing – you were infantilized by the efficiency of the locals. Larry and Fred were like teenagers. Had Bangkok done that to them? Even he felt it, the vitality of being among healthy hardworking people.

"Guess Bar – Soi Four. It's not far."

"Nana Plaza – amazing women, but they're all dudes!"

Joyce always asked what life was like in Bangkok.

"I don't know what to compare it to," he told her, but thinking of Larry and Fred he wanted to say, "It's like being young. I guess it's a kick."

Because when you were young you had a sense of choices, of not knowing how your life would turn out. Only the old foresaw the undeviating road ahead, and beyond it a darkness. That was how Osier had felt, but now his nights were empty.

In the shuttle bus Fred Kegler said, "Funny seeing you here."

"Just thought I'd hitch a ride."

"Maybe we can tempt you to have a drink," Larry said. But he laughed, because Osier had rejected them before.

"Maybe one," he said.

The shuttle bus dropped them at Patpong Road. They walked to a bar, Fred leading. "Here we are," Larry said. It was dark inside, smelling of beer and incense, with side booths. Osier squinted ahead, wondering if he'd be recognized. He liked the bar for being dark.

"Pretty soon you'll be out of all of this," Fred said.

He meant Osier's retirement. Were they gloating?

Osier said, "We've got a house. Near Rockland, Maine. My wife's already there." Out of fastidious sentiment he avoided mentioning Joyce's name in this smelly bar.

"A lot of guys opt for the severance package and stay right here in Thailand. You have a bundle coming to you. You're on one of the old contracts. You could have a second career."

Creer again; it jarred on Osier and seemed like satire. They didn't know the half of it, even Joyce didn't. Yet Osier said in an offhand way, "But what would that be like?"

"That would be a wet dream," Larry said, giving each word a meaningful lilt.

The bar was everything that Osier had objected to the first time, not just the rankness of beer and the slime of cigarette smoke on the clammy plastic cushions of the booth, the American rock music, and the Christmas lights, but the girls, too – six or seven of them, overfriendly, converging on the booth. They seemed to know Fred and Larry well.

Fred said to one of them, "This is our friend. Be nice to him."

"We be nice to him."

Each of the men had a familiar and favorite girl, who brightened at their arrival, almost like a steady girlfriend. Instead of talking to him, as he'd feared, they talked to these bar girls and took them aside, leaving him to nurse his drink with the remaining girls. The girls watched, whispering, as he took his diary from his briefcase. He sketched their pictures on a blank page. They laughed, but for a while they stood still, because he was drawing so carefully.

In the booth of four girls, only one was attractive – tall, thin-faced, slender, a bit aloof, possibly haughty or else shy, while the others fluttered around him.

Osier sketched her pretty fallen-angel face, her long lank hair, then said, "What's your name?"

But she turned away and wouldn't tell him. Sketching, he stared, and as he did, he heard Fred call from his booth to Larry in the next booth, "I'll mud-wrestle you for that one."

Fred laughed and said, "Reminds me. I told my ex-wife, 'When you're fifty you'll be standing on a street corner waving at cars.'"

Hearing their voices, Osier put his sketchbook away and finished his drink. Larry looked at Osier, sitting with the four girls, and said, "A bevy of beauties! Hey, Boyd, we're going back to the hotel. Are you staying?"

Surprised in his solitude, Osier said no and left with them in a taxi. This was all? A drink, a giggle, then back to the hotel? He felt kinder toward the two men.

Larry said, "They all have families. Like us. They send money home. Ask them what they want and they won't say a husband. They'll say, 'I want a coffee shop,' 'A grocery store,' 'A noodle shop.' Having a drink there, I figure we're helping the economy."

"Piss them off and you're in hell. Horror show," Fred said, and the *hoor* grated.

At the hotel, Osier said, "I'll pay." After Larry and Fred had gone into the lobby, he said to the taxi driver, "Take me back to the bar."

"Casanova? Patpong Road?"

"I guess."

The girls laughed when they saw him, the man who had just left, and that made him sheepish. Did they understand more of what was in his heart than he did? As though anticipating what he wanted, they made a place for him at the far corner of the bar in a small booth.

He said nothing, he hardly glanced at the tall girl, and yet one of the girls said, "You come back see her!"

They knew exactly why he'd come. They were so shrewd about men. But then, what was so complicated about men?

The tall girl emerging from the shadows looked even more like a fallen angel. She walked over, stately in her high heels, holding her head up, dignified, giving nothing away in her expression.

"Have a drink with me."

She seemed to hesitate. Osier was not dismayed, because after considering the offer, she chose him. She sat beside him and ordered drinks – beer for him, lemonade for herself. They drank without speaking, and for once Osier was glad for the loud music filling the silence and the space.

Finally she said, "You make picture?"

He showed her his diary, flipping pages. She put her finger on the sketch of the king and touched her heart.

"You like Bangkok?"

"I like the railway station." Though it no longer seemed safe to him.

"Nice station."

"And I like you."

She sipped at her lemonade and then looked away. "You not know me."

"But I want to know you." And as he sat closer, she made room on the bench, accommodating him.

I am out of my mind, he thought. What did I just say? Am I telling the truth? But at least the room was dark, the music loud, and he was alone. Osier was drunk, he could tell from his slowness, the numb warmth in his arms, his drowsy talk, a creeping weight in his body, his feet like cloth, all of it brainlessly pleasant, making him feel like a big fool. When he put his hand on the girl's thigh she reacted sharply.

"What's that?"

She said, "My knife."

She had to repeat the word before he understood. Smiling, he lifted his heavy arm and placed it on the girl's skinny shoulder. She shrugged but she didn't resist. Then he kissed her – on the cheek, like an adolescent's first smooch. She laughed and became shy.

"You're pretty."

She stroked her face with her fingertips. "What country?"

"America."

He wanted to kiss her again. He felt reckless enough, no one was looking – who cared in this place? He was as anonymous here as he'd once been in the waiting room of the railway station. He winced at his memory of it.

But, drunk, with his drunken sense of sliding slowly out of control, he felt that he was at the edge of a dark pit, a wide bowl of night, about to tumble in face-first. When he leaned to pat the girl's knee she recoiled again. That reaction made him hesitate and sobered him a little.

He drew back and said, "I have to go home."

She smiled. She said, "Everybody always go home," and as he left, staggering into the noise and fumes of the street, Osier reflected on the minimalism of her barroom wisdom.

Back at the hotel, alone with his guilt, he felt he ought to call Joyce. His cell phone was not in his pocket. The girl had stolen it. He deserved the anguish he felt. He used his room phone to call the emergency number to cancel his cell phone account. He was put on hold. Music played. He thought, I am off my head. He called his own number. After a few rings, a smoky voice.

"Hello."

"Who's that?"

He heard smoky laughter but no reply.

"You have my cell phone. I need it."

"I give you tomorrow."

"When? Where?"

She spoke the name of a bar, she repeated the street, but even so, writing it down, Osier was not sure he'd heard the name correctly. *Free* had to be three. What was *nigh*?

The next day was Saturday. Osier hailed a taxi after lunch and read the scribble he had written. The driver said, "I know, I know," but he didn't know. They discovered the *soi* in Sukhumvit, but he guessed at the bar – Siamese Nights.

From the outside, it was indistinguishable from six other bars nearby: neon sign, opaque window, strings of beads hanging at the entrance. But inside it was large, vault-like, and quiet, gong music playing softly, like the melody in a children's toy. Out of the back window he could see a canal, and plump lotuses in it, floating on their outflung petals, light falling across the water. He was looking into a Bangkok that was enclosed and placid and pretty.

She wasn't there; hardly anyone was in the bar. He sat in the mildewed air of midafternoon and drank lemonade – it was too early for alcohol. Besides, a beer would tire him, and this being a Saturday, he planned to spend the rest of the afternoon walking – not to the railway station or the big flea market, but simply to exhaust himself in the heat – then an early dinner and bed.

At a quarter past three he saw her. She entered the bar and without hesitating walked straight to him. He was reminded of the directness of the man-woman at the railway station who'd confronted him.

He was relieved to find her manner the same as the previous evening: assured, casual, undemanding, as though they knew each other fairly well. He was glad the place was dark. He'd thought of taking the cell phone and leaving, but now he felt like lingering. He loved her piercing eyes, her thick hair, her height – even sitting down she was almost his height, their eyes level. She was not a sprite, not kittenish like the other girls, but a cat-like presence.

"Lemonade," she said to the waitress.

A shaft of sunlight slanted through some boards near where they sat, and he could see through that crack the brightness of water, the glittering canal, the floating flowers, the bubbly stagnation shimmering in the hot afternoon.

"This is nice."

"Everything nice for you!"

She remembered that he'd said she was nice, but what he wanted to say was that he was less lonely. Her accurate memory made her seem intelligent, impatient with small talk.

"I meant it's quiet."

"Other bar too noisy. Too many people. Crazy people. *Farang ba-ba boh-boh.* This better."

"What's your name?"

"I Song. What you name?"

"Boyd."

"Boy," she said.

He smiled. "That's right."

The gong music seemed to slip through him and beat like a pulse, relaxing him. A small boy in a red shirt approached, selling single flowers. Osier bought one for Song, and he felt as he had on his best night at the railway station – serene, calmed, triumphant. The sunlight glancing from the *klong* glimmered in a bright puddle on the ceiling. He thought, This is all wrong, but this is bliss.

"I'm happy."

"Why not? Life too short."

She'd heard that from someone, another *farang,* and yet it pained him to hear it. It was true. He felt absurdly tearful, thankful to her for saying that.

And now he remembered himself at the railway station, mourning, seeing the travelers leaving on life-altering journeys while he sat sketching their faces, as though grieving for them. He had believed his waiting was a death watch for them, but no, he was grieving for himself, as he waited for retirement. I don't want to go, he thought, and glancing across at Song, he was creased by a pang, something deeper than hunger, like the foretaste of starvation.

"You're so young," he said, and heard fear in his voice.

"*Khap khun ka.* Thank you. Look young, but not!"

"How old?"

"I hate this question."

Impressed by her rebuff, he said, "Me too. Any children?"

She laughed and tapped his arm as if gratefully, and said, "No children."

"None for me either."

"We same!"

Bar talk, flirty, facetious, but a little more than that, with the revelations of foolery, Song emerging as clever and gentle and self-mocking.

Then Osier remembered. "My cell phone," he said. "Where is it?"

Song took the phone out of her bag but she didn't hand it over. She said, "You give me?"

"Why?"

And because he'd hesitated, she gave it to him.

But because she gave it to him so quickly, he said, "Why do you want it?"

"So I can talk you."

He loved that. He tapped her arm as she had tapped his. He said, "Yes. I'll get you one. Let's go."

He still sat. He didn't want to leave this shadowy place, Siamese Nights, the coolness of it, the girls huddled on the banquette, laughing, their knees together, the one other *farang* at the bar shaking dice onto the counter out of a cup and talking to the bartender. The watery light from the *klong* outside dappling the ceiling gave its fishbowl completeness an illusion of life's essence.

This is who I am, this is where I belong, this is a place where I can tell the truth. Guessing that Larry and Fred were consoled by places like these, he understood them better. He told himself that he had no wish to possess Song, but only to ease his famished soul by being with her, to relieve his gloom.

But this was peaceful. He thought, I have someone I can tell this to. He told her. She listened with bright eyes, saying nothing, not judging him, her skin so lovely he wanted to stroke her like a cat.

And when at last they were on their way to the cell phone shop, in the traffic and the heat, he wished he were back in Siamese Nights, sitting with Song, looking over her pale shoulder at the canal beyond the back window. Song had sat placidly with her hands on her lap. Osier liked her size, not one of those tiny bird-boned Thai sprites, but rather tall, angular, with a deep laugh, and a presence he hadn't associated with the Thais he knew. Song was a woman confident in repose, sweet without being submissive, with the melancholy he'd first seen that made him think of a fallen angel.

He said, "Why don't you have a phone?"

"They cancel. I no pay."

The clerks in the shop were so helpful, Osier let them explain the calling plans, though he knew most of the details by heart. He chose the simplest one, a six-month plan, renewable, inexpensive. Song picked out a red phone, and Osier signed the agreement.

Side by side in the taxi, he called her number.

"Hello, Boy."

"Hello, Song."

"You happy?"

"I'm happy." But he caught a glimpse of himself in the taxi's rearview mirror and turned away from that idiot face.

"Who are you calling?" he asked, seeing her tapping numbers into the phone.

"Mudda," and, hearing a voice, she smiled and broke into Thai. Osier heard gleeful croaking from the other end and was content.

For the next few days they called each other. He did so just to hear her voice. He didn't want to think why she called him, but she seemed happy to hear him. He remembered how, when he'd seen her in a group of five or six girls in a bar, Song had seemed the most feminine, the most mature, the softer, the more self-possessed, the only one not reaching out, not trying to catch his eye. She had not been looking at him at all; she'd been looking at the other girls posing for him, smiling slightly, and her narrow smile made her seem strong. She was not a coquette.

Her looking away had allowed him to study her body, which was fleshier than the others', heavy-breasted. Song sat straight, her legs crossed, and he saw that her makeup had been more carefully applied. He felt a connection: she was the first real woman he'd seen since arriving in Bangkok, and he felt as he had when he'd met Joyce long ago, a pang of desire that was like a seam of light warming his body.

In a reflex of self-consciousness he called Joyce.

"I miss you," she said.

Burdened by her saying that, with a catch in his throat, he could not reply at once.

He said, "I miss you too," and wondered if she heard the strain in his voice. They talked a little more, about some trees that needed to be trimmed in the yard, and then he said he had to go to a meeting.

Joyce said, "Please don't be angry. I know how busy you are."

Too confused to reply, he said, "Take care," and called Song a minute later. He said, "I miss you."

"You make me feel like a million dollar," Song said.

"I want to see you," he said.

"See you when I see you," she said.

Another of her catch phrases; she'd learned these quips from men. The thought made him vaguely jealous, but he was not possessive. He wanted her to be happy.

The next time he saw her – in the friendly bar, Siamese Nights, which was like a refuge by the *klong* – he said, "I'm going to the States."

"Always they say that to me." Though her eyes looked pained, she shook her head as if she didn't care.

"But I'm coming back."

"They say that always too. 'I coming back, honey. Love you!'"

"I mean it."

"Maybe you not come back. Maybe you be glad. 'No more Song. No more trouble.'"

What trouble? he wanted to ask. He didn't know whether he'd be back. He hoped so. The decision was not in his hands. There was a meeting in Boston – headquarters. Then he'd drive to Maine, swing by on the way to check on Joyce's mother. His return to Bangkok depended on the presentation of the accounts, whether his continued presence in Bangkok was justified.

Perhaps this bewilderment showed on his face. Song said, "You come me."

He knew what she meant.

"I get taxi."

Song gave the driver directions. They went through a district he recognized from its noodle shops and street life, not far from his hotel. Off the main road, down an alley, into a smaller lane to a courtyard and a doorway. Song paid for the taxi. A young man in a white short-sleeved shirt at the doorway gave Song a key on a wooden tag.

"You give him baht."

Osier opened his wallet, and Song plucked out the equivalent of ten dollars.

The young man led them to a ground-floor door, showed them in, switched on the air conditioner. Osier sat on a wooden chair and saw that the room had no windows.

"You want drink?"

"Beer."

Song left the room, and when she came back with a tall bottle of Singha beer and two glasses, she sat on the bed across from his chair and poured his beer slowly. They clinked glasses. Osier thought: This is how criminals conspire, this is how they behave, hardly speaking, over beer, in windowless rooms, rationalizing their heads off. Yet – giddy, defiant – he thought, I am happy.

Song said, “You take bath”– and she had to repeat it before he understood what she meant.

In the shower, he thought to himself, This is reckless, this is absolutely stupid. And then, Life too short.

When it was Song’s turn for a shower, she turned off the light in the room, left the light on in the bathroom, the door slightly ajar. A stripe of light from the cracked-open door lay across the bed, where Osier was propped against the pillows with his glass of beer.

Wrapped in a towel, Song crawled next to him. Her skin smelled sweetly of vanilla. Her full breasts were cool and damp against his arm. While he drank, saying nothing, she caressed him, stroked his chest. He put his drink on the side table and closed his eyes, loving her touch. And he touched her, not longingly or with any passion, but merely holding her breasts, weighing them in his hand. He made to steady her arm but she shrugged, she wouldn’t let go, her hand went lower.

When he did the same, she reacted with a sudden movement, pushing his hand away with the hand she’d used to caress him.

“What’s that?”

But she had buried her face on his shoulder, and he felt the heat as of a secret against his neck.

“It my knife.”

He became very still. He knew now, he’d heard it all, he even knew the word. He said, “You ladyboy?”

“Why not?”

He was amazed at his own calmness, and recognized a kind of strength in himself. He needed most of all to be kind. He said, “That’s all right.”

“You want me stop?”

Taking shallow breaths that he knew she could hear, he thought for a long time. He didn’t say anything. And then, when she stirred, he allowed it to happen, thankful it was night.

And it ended, a jostling in the dark – a clumsy farewell in a lane of noodle shops outside the room, Song urging him to take a taxi on his own, a sleepless night in his hotel, and he was on his way home through the silver tunnel to America, being shot from one end to the other. Lying on his narrow folded-down airline seat, half asleep in his twisted clothes, in the same posture in which he had been touched, he was flesh. Not weak or strong, but a helpless hot organism in a rapture of possession.

4

In a rental car, heading north from Boston, observing a ritual, Osier drove to the nursing home where Joyce's mother was a resident. She sat, her head tipped to the side, looking hanged, in a chair by the window, not so much white-haired as balding. A tang of urine in the air made him catch his breath.

She said, "Have you come to take me away, Roger?"

Roger was Joyce's father, her late husband.

Osier said, "No. I've brought you a lovely shawl, though. It's silk."

"I want to go home. Take me home. I don't want to die here."

He went cold, hearing this. He hated that she was so logical. Her house had been sold three years ago, to pay for this assisted care. He dangled the shawl to distract her, but she remained agitated and querulous.

"I want the key, Roger."

"What key?"

"The key for my toe," she said.

He continued north, ate a lobster roll in Wiscasset, and by midafternoon was in Rockland, driving toward Owls Head. Saddened by the leaves turning russet and yellow, by the chilly air, the dark water of the bays and inlets, he drove slowly.

Joyce's greeting was "Aren't the colors incredible?"

But the colors reminded him of something much worse than retirement. The next big storm or the November rains would tear all of them from the branches and beat them to the ground and blow them flat against the fence.

"Lovely," he said.

Death was the dry veins and the brittle curl in the withering leaves. These weren't colors. Color was life and heat; a naked body could have color; fish twitching in a tank had color, and when they were dead they lost this brilliance and went gray. He took a drive, parked at the shore, and called Song. With his eyes on three lumpy islands, he heard the purr of her warm voice, heat and sunshine in his head.

"You no forget me."

"I want to see you."

"See you when I see you."

When he got back to the house, Joyce was seated by the window, holding his pictorial diary in her lap.

"It all looks so amazing. Those temples, those flowers, those lovely people."

The images of his days at the plant were accurate, but after that first meeting with Song, he had disguised his nights, falsified his pictures, turned Siamese Nights into a temple, sketched Song as a slender boy, on one page a balloon enclosing "Life too short," and another, "Everybody always go home," and later, "See you when I see you."

Joyce's smile tore at his heart, because she didn't know anything, because she was happy, solicitous, believing he was overworked. He knew how murderers felt when they were in the presence of their unsuspecting victims: powerful, even perhaps pitying.

"I've made chowder. Your favorite."

He thought, That man is not here anymore.

Joyce made excuses for him because he was too ashamed to concoct any for himself. "Of course you're tired. You're not yourself. Think of the distance. Flying is no fun. All those security checks. Remember to get some exercise. Don't drink alcohol. And I really hope you make some friends there."

He was relieved to be summoned to Boston by Haines, the CEO, to hear the decision. It was up to them. His fate was not in his own hands.

Haines said, "We're extending you."

Which meant to him: Song. He called her from Logan Airport. He heard music.

"Where are you?"

"Waiting you. Siamee Nigh."

He contrived to see her the day he arrived – and, landing, he felt younger, hopeful; life was more complicated but richer. Meeting her involved a lie to Fred Kegler, which appalled him. But it was worth it to see Song's feline face, her straight hair stylishly chopped apart, her pretty mouth, her full breasts. Her secret ambiguity excited him. A ladyboy was more emphatically feminine to him in an old-fashioned way that reminded him of his youthful romances, and the pallor of her complexion made it seem as if he was always seeing her by moonlight.

They couldn't spend the night together – it would require him to tell another lie to Kegler. But he saw her on the weekend, not in a bar but by a lake in Lumphini Park.

She wore sunglasses, she carried an umbrella. "Thai people hate sun."

"What do Thai people like?"

"Like shadow. Like night." He laughed. She went on, "*Farang* like sun."

"I like shadow. I like night."

So he was no more than a *farang*? He struggled to make an impression, he talked about taking her on a trip. But he found wooing her like this a humiliation, because she didn't need him. She was always in a bar, always being pursued.

He wondered if, in spite of the longing he felt, he was kidding himself. How could he care this much for a ladyboy he'd met in a bar? Was it that he'd had a glimpse into his sexuality that he'd kept in a dark corner, a sort of corner like Siamese

Nights, where he'd groped Song and not been shocked? Or in the room. *It my knife.*

That night, alone, he went to Soi Four and chose a ladyboy bar at random. It was loud, filled with drunken *farangs,* some ladyboys in shorts dancing on a mirrored stage under a glitter ball.

"You buy me drink?"

"Sure, what's your name?"

"Me Nutpisit."

She was elfin, with eager eyes. But he knew she was a ladyboy, cute, rather small, pigtails, a miniskirt, knee socks. They drank together – she had a Coke – and later he paid forty dollars to the bar to release her. They walked to a hotel off a side street nearby.

"I give you shower." Nutpisit took him by the hand and switched on the bright lights in the bathroom. Through the open door, he saw himself in the mirror, his surprised face, the leering lipsticked boy.

"No," he said, and pulled his hand away. In a panic of self-disgust he began to apologize. The ladyboy Nutpisit, who had seemed so girlish, began to rage at him. Osier was frightened by the violent temper of someone so small. Nutpisit began to push him, then slapping him so hard, reaching for his face, she scratched his upraised arms. She raked his ears with her furious fingers. He pleaded with her, but she would only be quieted with fifty dollars.

Osier fled down the street like a felon, plucked at by the teasing girls sitting outside massage parlors. He had hoped he might respond to another ladyboy; then he would feel liberated from Song. But the experience had only served to show how much he needed Song.

He called her and heard loud music. He knew she was not at Siamese Nights. "I have to see you. Where are you?"

"Tomorrow better."

He agreed; how quickly she had power over him. It was physical, it was her flesh. *It my knife.* To show her he was serious and protective, that he respected her and was even proud of her, he took her to dinner at a restaurant by the river. Some people stared. They seemed to know.

"They say, Why you with *katoey*?"

He didn't care. This wasn't Maine. He said, "I want you."

At this she touched his hand, and he caught hers, and they held hands across the table like lovers.

"I never did anything like that before," he said.

Song said, "I understand."

The softness, the sympathy in the way she said it, the word itself, made him confessional. He explained what an ordinary life he had lived, the places he had been sent to audit accounts, that he had no brothers or sisters, that he had felt lonely when he'd gotten back to the States. She listened, she held his hand. He could not stop himself from talking – and it was more than he had said to anyone the whole time he'd been in Bangkok, more than he had said to his wife for years.

When he was finished, Song said again, "I understand."

They sat on the terrace, watching the narrow sampans that were powered by big square engines and long drive shafts that, plowing the river, gave them impressive waterspout tails. They ordered bowls of noodles, he drank beer, she drank lemonade. Strings of tiny bulbs, like Christmas lights, had been draped on the low hedges and spindly trees at the margin of the terrace. They cheered him as the same sort of lights had cheered him when he'd been a boy. Was this an effect of travel? That if you went far enough you found a version of your childhood?

"We go upstairs?" Song asked, pincering noodles with her chopsticks.

Osier knew what she meant – his hotel was nearby. He wanted it, but superstitiously he told himself that there was plenty of time.

The sidelong looks of people did not embarrass him, but only reminded him of how happy he was to be with Song. And a defiant thought that had entered his mind and that had been developing over the past days was that the very oddness of the affair, an older man and a ladyboy, such an unlikely pairing, had to be proof that this desire was real – not mere curiosity but passion. And if love was the feeling of generosity, of gratitude, of unending mutual possession, it was perhaps love, too, driven by a sexual desire that had a reviving power.

"We go upstairs tomorrow night," he said, to give himself the thrill of anticipation. "I have a meeting in the morning. Early. You know boss?"

"I know boss."

"Boss have meeting."

He had begun to talk in this halting oversimple way and was glad that no one but Song could hear him.

Song said, "I know meeting." She took out her handbag and applied makeup. "You business."

"Me business," Osier said.

She raised her head in a superior way, flashing her eyes, and said, "*Natang meehoo – pratoo mee da.*"

Osier smiled and leaned toward her.

"Window have eye – door have ear."

He said, "Where you going now?"

"Go to bar."

Something in his heart convulsed. Jealousy, and more than jealousy, a wrenching, like a sickness.

"Why not go home?"

Song shrugged. He knew that shrug – it meant, What about money? A certain cluck meant money. A way of rolling her eyes meant money. Men in the bar would buy her a drink. She might allow herself to be touched, or persuaded for money to go with them. What did he know?

"You want money?" he asked.

Song didn't speak. She was thinking hard, her face smoothed by the thought she was keeping to herself.

"If I give you money, do you promise not to go to the bar?"

She leaned toward him. "You think I like bar? You think I like men touch me?"

Her mouth twisted in disgust at *tuss me*. Osier, pleased by the energy in her response, was encouraged by her indignation, which was like proof of her morality.

"What about me?"

She touched his arm, then made affectionate finger taps on his hand. "My friend."

"I give you money. No bar."

"If I have money, I don't need bar."

He soothed her, saying, "I have money," and never in the whole time he'd known her had he enjoyed such rapt attention, Song's eyes fixed on him, her pretty lips moving as though murmuring a prayer, or soundlessly counting. Feeling powerful, taking his time, Osier agreed on a sum, the amount Song suggested, more than he had imagined. But he paid; he wanted to be certain of her. He couldn't bear to think of her being pawed in the bar.

Song said, "This for my mudda."

When he kissed her at the taxi stand that night she held him tightly.

"Tomorrow," she said.

All the next day he was so distracted by his work that he had lunch later than usual, in the empty cafeteria, eating as the staff was finishing the dishwashing and stacking the chairs for the mopping. Osier sat at the only free table, and as he began to eat he saw Fred Kegler enter the room.

"Mind if I sit here?" Fred was holding a Styrofoam cup of coffee and already seating himself. "You're having the chili prawns. I love the chili prawns."

This sort of chat made Osier anxious, because he felt sure it was intended to put him at ease. There was more of it: weather, an upcoming holiday, Fred's son in Little League, all insistently casual.

Then he began laughing softly, and said, "Spent the weekend in Pattaya. I know a guy there, American, married a local girl."

"It seems to happen a lot," Osier said.

"Big mistake. He's miserable. I've got this theory."

Someone announcing a theory was always unstoppable and usually wrong. Yet Osier listened, because his reputation was for being mild, a listener.

Still holding his Styrofoam cup of coffee, Fred said, "The more polite and submissive people are outside in cultures like this, the more rude and domineering they are at home." Fred was nodding, meaning to go on. "I'm talking about the women. These smiles, this sweetness. That's all for public consumption. In private it's the opposite, like they're taking revenge. Like they're corrupted. And not just here. I did a tour in Japan, different company. Those sweet little geishas turned into dragons at home."

Osier, hearing *crupted,* disbelieved him, and said, "That's a theory, but what's the proof?"

"My friend is the proof," Fred said, and sensing defiance in Osier, he seemed pained. "Hundreds of guys here are the proof." He lowered his head and spoke in a whisper, "Some of these girls here, let me tell you, they're not really girls. They're dudes."

This obvious warning by Fred had only made him more defiant. Larry had not said anything, but Osier had noticed that while seeming to avoid him, Larry was ever more watchful.

He could only call Song in the late afternoon. Song said she was in her room. He had no reason to doubt her.

He said, "I miss you."

"I miss you."

This echo worried him. Did she mean it as much as he did? He felt with such a person that they were only pretending to speak the same language.

"I want to see you."

"I want to see you."

I'm insane, he thought. But he didn't have the power to stop, because the worst of it was that she was stronger than he; she was dominant. She didn't need him, she could find the money from someone else. And she was a freak of nature, a kind of unicorn: he'd never find anyone like her.

He had never seen her room. He wanted to see her in it, to know her better. He waited for night to fall, then took a taxi to the address she had dictated to him. The room was in an old building smelling of fish sauce and hot cooking oil. But it was swept, it was tidy. What struck him about the room itself was the enormous calendar, the portrait of the king bordered in yellow for the royal jubilee, and the shrine in the corner, an image of Buddha, a flickering candle, some blossoms in a dish, a pair of amulets laid out side by side, and between them a slender tube of ivory chased in silver.

He was glad for the darkness, for the rattly air conditioner, because its noise killed conversation.

Song pulled the blinds and led him by the hand, like a child, into the bathroom. Dressed in a bathrobe and standing just outside the stall, she gave him a shower. Afterward she dried him and put him to bed. While he waited, buffeted by the air conditioner, it seemed to him that he was not in a room at all but another dark tunnel, being propelled toward its end and unable to do anything but allow himself to be tumbled.

Song had taken her shower, and in semidarkness she lay beside him and held him. She was the protector, she was active, while he lay safe, thinking, I am flesh, I am insane, I am happy, hold me.

"Magic knife," he said, touching her.

But she hadn't heard.

That became the pattern of their meetings: her room, the separate showers, the drawn blinds, the roaring air conditioner; and the pattern turned into a ritual without words. As a ritual, everything was allowable, and later he never thought about what had happened, having left everything in the dark: life with the lights out.

5

His floating dream-like indecisive life away from the precision of work matched the city with its smothering heat. The clasp of humidity and the gutter smell gagged him, and yet his mood swelled him with buoyancy. This, with the whole hot city pressed on his eyes, blurring everything around him, made him feel like someone bumping forward under water.

He stopped his diary, stopped sketching anything except market stalls and boats on the river, or the pepper pots of Buddhist stupas and the daggers of temple finials. He did not dare to draw any people for fear of being reminded how different he was from everyone else. Abandoning the diary and doing fewer drawings, he shook off the spell he'd cast on himself in his sketching.

That perplexed, oversimplified cartoon figure he drew to represent himself, wearing glasses, a startled question mark over his head, trying to make sense of Bangkok, no longer appeared on the pages of what was now a cluttered sketchpad. He could not bear to depict his confusion. He wanted to be a blank page. Ceasing to account for his days, he clouded his memory – memory, the useless ballast that gave the slow passage of his aging a heaviness that dragged him down. He was renewed each day by not remembering, stewing in a pleasurable anticipation of seeing Song, savoring the foretaste of desire, a creaminess of vanilla on her skin.

Now he knew why he had spent so many nights at the railway station. That waiting had been an evasion of this settled mood of acceptance. In a discarding frame of mind, flipping through the pages of his pictorial diary, he found a sketch he had made early on of the man-woman who'd demanded money from him. It had been done weeks before she'd accosted him, when he'd seen her as just another of the station's loiterers. He'd drawn her as a fussed and fretting creature, bird-like with her beaky nose, in a Gypsy skirt with a bright shawl. He had not seen her distress or the spittle on her lips. The sketch was colorful, even merciful. He let it stand.

Putting all his earlier life aside, not thinking of Maine, concentrating on the present – himself and Song – he was happy. He still called Joyce every day, or she called him. Song said, "Who?" because the calls were so frequent. He never said, "My wife." He denied he had a wife – he told himself he was sparing Joyce the indignity of mentioning her.

"Boss," he said. Song knew the word well.

Joyce was satisfied with the plainest details of his life in Bangkok. The more mundane details pleased her most; she understood them best, stories of power cuts at the plant, heavy traffic, a tummyache. Joyce was like an old forgiving friend, a link with another life, a different narrative. He could not tell her how happy he was. Where would he begin? She and her mother were consumed by ill health; they didn't complain; for every ailment there was a remedy, yet this speculation occupied the whole of their lives. Any mention of his happiness, his luck, his good health, would be a violation of their self-absorption.

He'd never believed he could be this happy. He had assumed he'd finish here, hang it up, go home, persist, try not to die. But this was life itself, and he had always felt he'd lived on the periphery. Now he knew he was isolated in his happiness. The others at the plant seemed to know. Strangers did not wish him well, and he sensed that Fred begrudged him.

One evening, saying, "I want to show you something," Fred had tried to reopen the cautioning conversation. He took Osier to a bar. He did not talk to the girls. The bar was on the same *soi* as Siamese Nights. It was as though he was demonstrating his superior self-control.

"Some people come here and take things so seriously," Fred said. "They see poor people and want to give them money. They see little orphan kids and want to try to rescue them. They even fall in love. Bottom line, collateral damage."

And with *clatteral,* like a slickness on his lapping tongue, Fred leaned across the table, seeming to peer into him, trying to determine if Osier had been touched by what he'd conjectured.

Osier said, "And some people come here and make generalizations. Most people do."

"Life can be so simple," Fred said, talking over him. "Just be a tourist. You can have a hell of a time here if you don't take it seriously."

Osier said, "You can have an even better time if you do take it seriously."

"You Catholic?"

"Fallen away, pretty much. But if I'm anything, I suppose . . ." He didn't finish the sentence.

"Me too. What about church?"

The mention of church in this bar, the girls leering from a banquette, offended Osier as much as mentioning Joyce's name here. He knew they were talking about Song without saying so, and that Fred was pained by the subject.

Fred left him there. He hadn't been specific, but Osier knew that someone must have seen him with Song. And everyone talked.

Osier walked to Siamese Nights and met Song, and while they were sitting, holding hands, Joyce called to tell him that spring had come to Owls Head, the snow had started to melt.

After he hung up, Song stared, the obvious question on her face.

"Boss," Osier said in a burdened voice.

"Boss," Song replied, more lightly, but eyeing him.

One afternoon Song called to say that she'd meet him after work at the plant. She had a surprise. She'd never come to the plant before. She was calling from a taxi on her red phone.

She remained in the taxi, parked next to the security fence, away from the guard in the security box at the gate, but even so, Osier knew that she'd been seen. She wasn't being indiscreet – showing up like this proved that she cared for him. She didn't go to bars anymore. She saw him most evenings, and on weekends he stayed at her apartment, marveling at the completeness of his new life. Still, she seemed suspicious, as though wishing to know him better, perhaps wondering whether he was withholding a secret.

"My mudda come," she said when Osier got into the taxi.

Her mother was at the apartment, cooking. Song wanted to prepare him for it – the old woman was staying for a week.

But she was not an old woman. She was probably younger than Osier, only mannish and careworn from a hard life.

"She have a farm."

She was no more than fifty or so, which meant that Song was younger than he'd guessed. The woman was faded, with a deeply lined face, sad eyes, and a laborer's coarse hands. He saw that Song was a refinement of her mother.

The woman, who was named Wanpen, did not speak English. She was active, eager to please, expressive in her movements, and through Song gave Osier to understand that she was glad to see him. Then, as if to show her gratitude, she labored in the kitchen cubicle, strands of damp hair against her face. She whisked vegetables in a wok and made soup and noodles and spring rolls.

Osier did not spend the night when Song's mother was

there, but he visited most evenings after work and was content in this secret nighttime life. He sat and was waited on in a rather formal way, the old woman calling to Song, and Song serving him; and it seemed to him that his life had never been this full. He was surprised when, at one of these meals, he got a call from Joyce.

He kept the call short, while Song whispered to her mother. And when he'd finished, Song said, "Boss."

"Boss," he said.

He was not apologetic anymore. He was grateful. Perhaps that was love, the sense that you were reborn, remade anyway, given hope.

"I've just been back to the States," Larry said, one lunchtime that week, taking a seat in front of him, setting his meal tray down. "Saw my wife. My kids. Just what I needed." This was the same man who had hooted, *Soi Cowboy! Great bars! The girls are hot – they wear boots and Stetsons!* Then he said, "You can go home too, you know."

Did he regret having taken Osier to the clubs? Maybe he felt he was responsible for whatever Osier was rumored to be doing.

Osier said, "One of these days."

Relieved, Larry began eating.

Osier could not tell him what was in his heart. He wished he were alone, that he were not part of this enterprise – the hotel, the plant, the company. It was too much like an encumbering family.

Passion had brought him to this point, and in the week of not being able to spend nights with Song, because her mother was there, he could see his life more clearly – not in the hot headlong way he had first felt, blinded by desire, but calmly, studying Song in his mind, and himself with her. It seemed incredible that the consoling softness of someone's skin and the contours of a body could change the course of his life – and so late in his life too, when everything had seemed so circumscribed by the inevitable.

Now – it was odd but not upsetting – nothing was certain. He was happy, he was hopeful, he felt lucky. He was amazed by the completeness of his life.

"She like you," Song said on her mother's last night. And Wanpen smiled, seeming to understand what was being said. "She ask who you talk to on phone."

The mother was that shrewd. Osier said, "What did you tell her?"

"I say boss." She laughed. "She not believe me."

With feeling and a flutter of helplessness, Osier said, "The boss tells me what to do."

Song spoke again to her mother, who answered solemnly. Song said, "She trust you."

Osier felt a burden of responsibility, the woman putting her faith in him.

"She always worry about me," Song said, and seeing that Osier was thoughtful, she added, "Because I different. I not like other people."

Osier wanted to say, Maybe I'm not either. Maybe I'm different too. But he said, "Tell her not to worry."

Repeating this in Thai, Song made her mother smile. The woman pressed her hands together and bowed in gratitude. She was small, sturdy, and seemed unbreakable.

Osier knew he'd made the woman a promise. He had spoken without thinking, yet he meant it. As on those other nights, he thanked the mother and said goodbye without kissing Song, backing up, clumsily chivalrous.

The following night they met at Siamese Nights, Song with a glass of lemonade, Osier with a Singha beer. Song said, "My mudda, she really like you," and it seemed to mean everything.

"She's a lovely woman. So energetic. You know?" He motioned with his hands. "I imagine your mother in her village, and I see sunshine and green fields and chickens and fruit trees . . ." He described the idyllic landscape he had seen from the train on his one-day trip out of Bangkok, which he'd sketched in his diary.

When he finished, smiling at the thought of what he had described, Song said, "I understand."

Later, at her apartment, she took charge of him, bathing him, scrubbing him, massaging him, exhausting him, being generous. It seemed that she was rewarding him for being so kind to her mother, but with a lavishness that approached debauchery.

Of course they suspected something at the plant, but they didn't know him, or were less sure of him. He was like a man receding as they watched him, backing away, growing smaller and simpler, blurring in the distance on a long road. Osier liked that. He was strengthened by his secrets. He knew now that a kind of happiness existed that no one could even guess at – unthinkable for these techies who assumed everything was thinkable.

Joyce, too. His happiness gave her heart. She could not imagine the source of his happiness, nor would he ever be able to explain it to her, yet she would accept it, as she accepted most things. She heard that note in his voice.

"I'm glad it's all going well."

Pleasure made him bold, passion made him guiltless. He did not wonder how she would manage without him. Already she was managing without him, and if she wanted to know what the future held for her, she only needed to visit her mother, as she did most weekends.

Osier's confident frame of mind made him more efficient, more observant of the routines at the plant, catching the shuttle in the morning, working on the accounts, making small talk in the cafeteria, heading back to the hotel in the shuttle with the others. Larry and Fred did not stop at the clubs anymore.

Some weeknights Osier slipped away to see Song, but that meant a late return to the hotel. Weekends, from Friday night to Sunday evening, he spent with Song at her little apartment near Siamese Nights.

One Friday at lunchtime, Fred sat heavily at Osier's table, commanding attention in the very act of seating himself – elbows on the table, arms upraised, trapping him.

"Great news. I just found out there's an awesome old church here on the river. Holy Rosary. Catholic. Services every Sunday."

Fred said this with the same gusto as he had in the past, shouting in a strip club, *I'll mud-wrestle you for that one.*

Osier said, "I had no idea."

"They've actually got a priest. I emailed him and told him about us. The company – American company, expat staff, Catholics. He was stoked. They got a pretty diverse collection of communicants."

Osier was not sure what Fred was saying, whether this was innocent enthusiasm or some sort of ploy. He'd winced at *clection.* He tried to think of an answer to the question he knew was about to be asked.

"So how about it? You want to come along?"

Had Fred suggested going to a market, or a concert, or an art exhibit, or even a Buddhist temple, Osier would have found it easy to say no. But a church service – Catholic – was another matter. He felt ambushed. He was the one who had been disapproving of the clubs, the one who had kept his nights a secret. He guessed that Larry and Fred had their suspicions. Why else had Larry harped on going back to the States? *You can go home too, you know.* A club would have been easy to reject, but how on earth could he turn down a Catholic Mass on a Sunday?

"Okay," Osier said.

And now he had to explain to Song. Sunday-morning Mass meant that he could not spend Saturday night at her apartment, because that would complicate meeting Fred in the lobby at seven a.m., as he'd agreed.

"Company business," he said, hating his lie. And sitting in Siamese Nights, he made up a story in which the boss figured.

Song listened, watching him with her smooth moonlit face. She heard what he said and nodded, but Osier knew that all her inarticulate alertness, her wordless wondering receptivity to every twitch and pulse, told her he was lying. But now it was too late for the truth. If he changed his story and honestly told her about the church service, she'd still be convinced he was lying.

She said, "When I see you then?"

"Saturday night's out. Sunday's a problem."

"I understand." And the way she said it, lightly, with no bitterness, he took to be a measure of her wounded pride.

Siamese Nights was quiet, the other girls gathered at one table, facing the front door for customers. Osier hugged Song to make a point. Normally he never touched her in public. She stiffened, resisting him as though violated, as though he'd touched her head.

"We can go to your place."

"No. You busy."

He wasn't busy. He knew this was a rebuff. And a moment later his phone rang. He had forgotten to shut it off. He looked and saw Joyce's number, and didn't answer.

Sensitized, Song noticed that too. "You don't want to talk to your friend?"

He said, "It's nothing. Nobody."

No one was more alert to a further slight than someone who felt rejected.

"Nothing. Nobody," she said.

And to prove it was nothing, he called Joyce back, damp and breathless with shame, Song watching, and before Joyce could speak more than a few words, he said, "I'll have to talk to you later. I'm in a meeting," and switched off the phone. Song was wide-eyed.

"See? Nothing. Just work."

"Nothing," she said.

"My boss," he said.

"I understand."

That simple exchange made him suffer. Saturday, he called Song. She didn't answer – no *Please leave a message,* either. He tried to calm himself by sitting in the garden of a temple, sketching a Buddha, but the picture was no good, the face lopsided, the eyes cruel.

No answer from Song later that night, even after five tries, the last at midnight. Imagining the most lurid scenes – scenes he himself had enacted – he couldn't sleep. Nor did she answer in the morning. And he reflected that in all the years of being married to Joyce he had never tasted such delight or endured such anguish as in his six weeks of loving Song.

"This is Missy," Fred said in the lobby on Sunday morning.

A woman of forty or so, freckled, in a blue dress, with kindly eyes, said, "Melissa DeFranza. I know Fred from Vancouver. I'm in sales and marketing. On my way to a workshop in Singapore."

"I mentioned I was going to a church service and Missy jumped," Fred said.

She said, "That's what I need. Spiritual renewal. So nice of you guys to include me."

In the taxi, Missy said that she hoped to do some shopping and wondered if the stores in River City were open on Sunday. Fred talked loudly about his family and said that he had managed to live as an expatriate in Bangkok because he had created – *crated* – a special relationship with Jesus. He talked; Osier tuned him out.

The church, Holy Rosary, near the river, had a pencil-point steeple and arches, the whole of it faced in cream-colored stucco. Osier, no longer keeping his pictorial diary, could not break his habit of drawing such buildings in his head, and it relaxed him to see that this one would have been easy to put on the page. The church was a study in straight lines. Flowers filled the altar, which was draped in white linen, its marble supports picked out in gold. The faces on the stained-glass windows had an Asian cast.

He felt it was blasphemous to resent having to attend, yet he wanted it to be over with, so that he could see Song and resume what he now saw as his real life.

Osier knelt and prayed for things to go right for him. He asked God to understand. Yet God knew he had come under protest. Osier would not have been surprised to see the lovely domed ceiling crack to pieces and fall on his head – or something worse – for his hypocrisy.

The priest, a Thai, or perhaps an Indian, murmured the prayers, soothing Osier with their familiarity. But at one point, turning to face the mostly *farang* congregation, he hesitated in his delivery. At the same time there came a moment of traffic roar. The front door of the church had been opened and shut.

Glancing back, Osier saw Song making her way up the center aisle. When their eyes met, Song pressed her hands together in veneration, as though in a temple, and took a seat in the pew just across the aisle from him.

Osier's heart raced. He struggled to breathe. Even in her best dress, a silk shawl over her hair, and wearing high heels, Song looked out of place – the dress a bit too red, the shawl revealing her lustrous hair, the high heels noticeably too high.

"Let us pray," the priest said.

The congregation knelt. Song followed their example, her eyes cast down. Osier was burning with shame and indecision. His hands had gone clammy. What if she stood up and screamed at him?

Utterly at peace, without a clue, Missy DeFranza, kneeling between Osier and Fred, said her prayers. Osier pretended to pray, and as he did, he lifted his head and saw that Song was staring at him. Her gaze was unreadable. Osier tried to convey his helplessness to her in a meaningful shrug, but she was unmoved. And when she sat, she seemed like a bright-feathered and flamboyant bird, conspicuous in scarlet, with silken plumage, too beautiful to be praying.

The priest mounted the pulpit and gave a sermon, full of pauses, its theme the parable of the Publican and the Pharisee. And when, after that, the priest led the prayers, Osier could hear Song in a clacking voice declaiming a prayer in Thai, and it sounded like blasphemy. Osier, terrified, tried to anticipate what Song's next move might be and how he might counter it. If she lunged at him, should he wrap her in his arms and drag her from the church? If she began shouting, denouncing him, ought he to hurry away?

But he saw, almost with disbelief, that Song was crying, tears streaming down her cheeks. And the priest at that moment was leading a benediction.

Had Fred seen any of this? Osier thought of making a run for it, just ducking out. But when the priest announced a hymn, and the people stood, holding hymnals, Osier looked across the aisle and saw that Song was no longer there.

This was worse. He endured the service to the end, then filed out with the others, squinting as the sun blinded him, and shielding himself, preparing to be accosted. But she had gone.

"Lunch," Fred said.

"Not for me," Osier said. He was choked with nausea.

"There's a great noodle place right near here on the river."

"I'll buy," Missy said. "I'm on expenses."

"I could use a drink," Osier said, and followed them, looking around for Song.

In the restaurant, digging at his noodles, Fred said, "Know where you find some awesome Christians? Korea." Because he said *Kree-ah,* Osier felt it was untrue. "That Mass did me a power of good." And, as though boasting, unashamed, he added, "I've done some terrible things in my life. Wicked things."

"It's all good," Missy said.

"No," Fred said. "It's mortal sin, pure and simple." He was

looking at a ladyboy who was sitting with an older *farang*. "She's not a woman, sentimental and afraid. She's a man."

Osier said, "What's your point?"

"She'll do what a man does," Fred said.

Osier, not eating, sipping at a glass of lemonade, suddenly stood up and said he'd just remembered that he had something urgent to do. He hurried out and took a taxi to Song's. His knocking roused the neighbor in the next apartment. She poked her head out and made Osier understand through hand gestures that Song had gone out.

He went to Siamese Nights, almost empty in the Sunday-afternoon somnolence, a trickle of music, a few girls at tables. He sat to calm himself, then left without drinking. He walked along the hectic sidewalk in the direction of his hotel, and at a wide intersection he saw he was lost. He stood among a row of parked motorcycles and called Joyce. She did not answer. This was not surprising. It was three o'clock in the morning in Owls Head. One of the motorcyclists agreed to take him to his hotel. And so the weekend ended in silence and humiliation.

Monday was no better – repeated calls, no answer. Tuesday – no answer. And this was the week of the quarterly audit. He had never been busier, and the numbers didn't tally. On one of those nights in his hotel room, walking quickly to the door, he caught sight of a figure in the full-length mirror. He saw that it was not him in his green short-sleeved shirt but a beaky woman in a sari, hands upraised to plead, lipstick on her mouth, a slash wound on her cheek, a comb jammed into her hair, imploring him. He was startled at first, then sad, seeing this sister abandoned to ridicule. He called Song again and got no answer.

In the cafeteria, Fred and Larry sat together. Osier was sure they had been talking about him. To discourage their gossiping, he sat with them.

Larry said, "You look like you've had some bad news."

Such bluntness always put Osier on the defensive. He began to protest.

"Just pulling your leg," Larry said. But Osier was sure that Fred had said something.

That night, the Wednesday, Osier went to Siamese Nights. He saw Song sitting in a booth with an older man, Indian possibly, or Arab. Osier did not hesitate. He snatched Song's arm and lifted her, and before the startled man could react, he dragged her out of the club and pushed her into a taxi.

"I love you," he said.

She sulked at the words. She said, "You a bad man. You lie to me. You take you wife to church."

"That wasn't my wife. I love you."

To prove it, he took her to his hotel. He had brought her there before for a drink – she even seemed to have an understanding with the doorman and the lobby staff, something in the oblique way they acknowledged her, familiarly, as an equal, not deferential. But this was a more conspicuous visit. He needed her to know that he was not ashamed.

In the bar, he ordered her a lemonade, and a beer for himself.

Song was looking over his shoulder. "That man."

Fred, leaving the bar, his back turned, but unmistakably Fred.

"You friend," she said.

"Not my friend."

"You boss?"

For simplicity – how could he explain? – he said yes, and as he said it, she looked again in the direction of the door. Osier didn't dare to look. He assumed that Fred was lingering, because Song was still watching, her head moving slightly.

"Maybe you boss see you."

"I don't care," he said, but a catch in his throat made him think that he did care.

"I go home."

"No. Come to my room."

This he knew was reckless, but he was determined to show her that he was not like any other man she'd met, not like anyone else who'd said, "I love you," and pawed her. He needed to be serious, even solemn, to reassure her. He had sworn as much to her mother.

He drew her to the bed and held her, both of them clothed, and said, "Tell me about your mother's farm."

"In the village," she said. "Grow rice, have chicken . . ."

And as she spoke, he could see it, greeny-gold in the sunshine, the graceful huts on stilts, in the thickness of banana trees, under the feathery umbrellas of palms. The rice fields, banked in big squares, filled with water, mirrored the blue sky. Her mother stood over the smoking cookstove under the house, stirring the noodles in the wok. The most durable sort of human happiness. Song mentioned the children playing, her brother on his bicycle, and Osier could tell that it meant everything to her.

"Go on," he said when she hesitated.

He easily fitted himself into that landscape. And when he fell asleep in Song's arms he dreamed of the village, and a detail she had not given him, a fierce dog barking at him.

He woke in the darkness. He was still dressed. Song had gotten into the bed. She'd had a shower. Her dress was folded on a chair.

"I'm going to the States," he said.

He could tell even in the darkness, by the way she breathed, that she disapproved. She held his arm as if restraining him, though he hadn't moved.

"If I don't go, they make trouble for me."

Song became thoughtful, then said, "What trouble?"

"Telling stories about me," he said, and because he was ashamed of speaking this way, he whispered, "They no like me."

He could tell he had her full attention, as when he had said, "I have money," and her lips had moved as though in prayer.

She said, "They make you go home?"

He didn't answer, but his silence was like a statement, and Song's eyes were on him.

"Who say?"

"My boss." He had to keep it simple – language was always a problem. But when he uttered the formula, she held on tighter, and he felt the desperation in her fingers.

"Boss," she said disgustedly.

He regretted the word, his lame excuse, but the truth – Joyce, his pension, his early retirement, all of it – was too complicated to explain. He longed for the time when no more explanations would be necessary.

"Don't worry."

"I coming back, honey." She sang it, as a kind of jeer, and that stung him. Her English had improved and was lethal in its accuracy when she was mocking.

Song said nothing more. The air conditioner restarted, filling the room with clatter. Instead of breaking the spell, the noise made any more talk impossible, and the mutter, with the blast of cool air, roused them. They made love joyously, but with defiance, too. Afterward he thought, How many more years of work? One or two. How many of life? Twenty or more. He was not old – Song had shown him that he was just beginning. He wanted more of life, more of Song. He craved that simple golden world of greenery that she took for granted, that he'd once imagined to be unattainable.

Even in Bangkok she was an oddity, and together they were a greater oddity, but they were alike.

In the morning he called Song a taxi, and he rode the shuttle with Fred and Larry. He was aware of their scrutiny. Had Fred said anything?

Fred said, "We're thinking of hitting a few clubs tonight. Want to join us?"

This from the churchgoer who had a special relationship with Jesus. All that Osier could think of was his plan to go back to the States, to announce his intentions. He had no words for what he felt, no name for the state he was in, no way of saying what it was that had happened in the night – none that made any sense to him. If this was love, it was something he had never known before. He sorrowed for Joyce, for himself – not for Song. He knew that when the period of grieving was over she would have everything she wanted.

"I can't go," he said. This was the same man who'd gotten him to go to church. But this was different.

"We figured," Larry said.

Osier looked at them both and said, "I know what you're thinking. But there's nothing wrong with me."

Where had that come from? He was sorry he'd blurted it out. That they had no reply was like a challenge to him.

He spent the day finishing the quarterly accounts and making arrangements for flights back to the States. He called Haines and asked for discretionary leave, a week. He called Joyce, saying that he would be coming. And that night he slept well, knowing that he'd made his decision.

His phone rang in the darkness. He guessed it was Joyce, perhaps fretting, a confusion in the time difference. But it was Song. She had never called at this hour, and whenever she called she was circumspect. But she sounded certain – odd for this predawn hour.

"Boy?"

He blinked at the name. "Yes?"

"No more trouble."

"It's four o'clock in the morning," he said. "Where are you?"

"No more trouble."

Her self-assurance gave him hope. Even if she was not love, she was life, and she had allowed him to discover something about himself. He was someone else, not the man he had been. Away from home, in the hot night of this city, he had become transformed. It was a glimpse of difference he would never have found in the States. It made him wonder, and that wonderment was his strength. Hearing Song's voice, he yearned for her.

"I want to see you."

"I want see you," she said.

"See you tomorrow."

"See you tomorrow."

Then he slept deeply, consoled by her confident voice.

Neither Fred nor Larry was in the lobby when the company shuttle drew up. The doorman said he hadn't seen them. Normally they were waiting for Osier, holding cups of coffee from the urn in the lobby.

He called Fred's cell phone number but got a recorded message. He tried Larry.

"It's me," Osier said when Larry answered. "Shuttle's here."

Larry sighed, a kind of whistling, and gasped a little, sounding like a weak child. "I'm at the hospital," he said. "I'll be all right. But I don't know about Fred. He's in tough shape."

"What happened?"

"Couple of guys jumped us last night. They went after Fred. If I hadn't intervened they would have killed him."

"What, a robbery?"

"No robbery. Just"–Larry's voice was weary, wounded–"mayhem. Screaming mayhem. The guys came at us with knives. They cut Fred real bad. You gotta call Haines. And Fred's wife. Maybe the embassy, too."

Osier stood in the courtyard of the hotel, the great hot city roaring around his head. The driver signaled from the van, querying with his hands, a gesture that asked, "Shall we go?"

Osier went up to his room but could not summon the nerve to break the news to Haines. To comfort himself, he called Song. "Big trouble," he said, and he was going to say more but he didn't trust his unsteady voice.

"No trouble," Song said.

He had hardly started speaking when she cut him off with uncharacteristic efficiency. She knew everything – the bar, the injuries, even the name of the hospital where the men had been taken. And after this explanation, "I want see you."

He had once thought, I can choose. People were happy who believed that. He was miserable, because he was no longer ignorant, because he knew he had no choice, and such misery seemed like a guarantee that life went on and on.

"Why did you do this?"

She hadn't understood. She said, "Wiv my knife. Wiv my friend."

He said, "I don't know," and the panic in his tremulous voice chastened him. Osier dropped his arm. He didn't want to know how things would turn out. That was an unfair abbreviation, like knowing in advance the day of your death. He tried to be calm. He lifted the phone to his face and said it again.

"But I know," Song said, with a steady voice of utter assurance, of insistence, taking possession of the whole matter. "Never mind. I love you."

The manly fury in her voice was dark, even the word "love" was bloody and hellish. He was terrified by her certainty.

"I want see you," she said.

"No." And when he said it, he heard Song snarl into the phone. The awful noise of objection was like the crackle of a harsh hot light, exposing everything he'd ever said and done, burning away his shadow. "I've got to make some calls." She made the noise again. "Okay – later. Siamese Nights. Where are you now?"

"I downstairs. Waiting you."

Nowadays the Dead Don't Die

LOOKING FOR BIG game, I had walked all day with the spearman Enoch through the low prickle bush and the bulging head-high termite mounds in the sand hills, kicking through clusters of black pebble-like scat. I could see frantic bird prints, and the scoring, like finger grooves, of the light gravel by thrashing snakes, but saw no animal larger than the hares that had left that scat and the marks of their pads in the sand among the blowing grass. No tracks of lions or hyenas, not even dogs.

"I will tell you," Enoch said, sounding ashamed, almost fearful. Then he explained.

We were asked, my brother and I, to take the elder, Noah, to the hospital at the boma, sixty-five miles away, in my brother's vehicle. It was a road of potholes and detours, and halfway there, shaken by the ruts, his swollen belly paining him, Noah died. This was the beginning of everything, though we didn't know it. At the time it was just a body to be disposed of.

Noah had no family. This was a problem. Among our people death is the occasion for a day of old specific rituals, first the washing of the body, smearing it with ocher, then wrapping it with herbs in a blanket, some chanting by the other elders, and finally carrying the body into the bush, where it is left to be eaten by animals, the lion, the leopard, the wild dogs, the hyenas. Dogs can be fierce in packs, but hyenas are the most thorough and will return to eat everything but the blanket.

We say, "The day the old woman disappears is the day the hyena shits gray hair."

The family pays for the funeral, and this includes the cost of the blanket, the strings of beads, the twists of herbs, a clay pot of beer, and the red ocher–smearing. The total can be a cow, or a month's wages for someone who works at the boma.

"He's dead," my brother said, stopping the car.

But Noah did not seem completely dead. We heard a rattle rise from his throat to his nose, the last of his life bubbling from his lips, and very soon he was silent and so skinny he seemed deflated.

The day was ending in a low portion of reddened sky, and we sat by the roadside, thinking the same thing: that he had no family, no one to bear the cost, and that the hospital at the boma would not compensate us for the journey, because he had died on the way. He was dead, and so he was ours.

Sitting on this verge of the bush road in previous years, we were usually passed by a speeding vehicle, a Land Rover on a night drive, hunters who'd use lights. Or creeping past us, the shadowy figures of poachers, rifles slung across their backs, heading into the last of the day, that red skirt of light and the gilded trees. We saw none of these men as we hesitated here. We were used to their movements, because we were hunters too. We sat as though in the heart of a dead land, only a few baboons creeping toward a tamarind tree, to climb it for the night. But hunting had been bad, so we used our hunting vehicle for transport, as a bush taxi.

We couldn't go farther. And what was the point in carrying the dead man to his empty hut in the village?

"That tree," my brother said. I knew what he meant.

A fever thorn at a little distance looked important, singular in its size, a fiery witch tree among the tufted scrub.

Without discussing the matter we dragged the body from the back seat. It flopped like a sack on the stony ground. We arranged it, stretching it out, and with each of us holding an end, we bumped it through the bush to the thorn tree, where we let it drop near the rounded tower of a termite mound. I was uneasy with the face upturned, and so I rolled the body onto its belly, its nose in the dust. It was warm under my hand, and a brownish liquid ran from the mouth.

"We should eat something," my brother said.

We had brought bread and chicken meat and fruit for the trip, but neither of us could swallow. Even a sip of water choked us, though we were thirsty.

Back in our village, no one asked what had happened. Noah had no family to inquire. People assumed that we had brought him to the boma, that we had been paid. We didn't volunteer the information that he had died, that we'd dragged him under a tree and left him.

After a week, feeling guilty, we drove back to the witch tree to make sure he'd been eaten. But he was swollen and stinking, still whole, his body bursting his shirt, his bracelets cutting his flesh, ants on his face and scouring his eyes. Fearing that he'd be found, we dug a hole and buried him, thinking, Where are the animals?

Burial in a hole was something new to us, but a necessity. The body broke apart like overcooked meat as we tumbled it into the pit.

From that day, things began to go wrong. The first was the vehicle, problems with the motor that made no sense – leaks, belts decaying and breaking. Milk thickened and went sour when I drank it. Clay pots cracked like biscuits, the thatch roof rotted, my cows stopped eating and two died, my youngest son developed a fever. My brother's experiences were no better, leaks, cracks, decay, and illness visiting his hut too.

My son died. It was a sadness, the fever worsening until he coughed out his life. And he was part of my wealth, a forager and a herd boy. My brother's wife was found with another man. She had to be beaten, and she was too injured to cook or work after that. The guilty man was ordered to pay a fine – a blanket, a cow, a purse of money, a thickness of copper bracelets, a gourd of beer. But he vanished into the bush, and my brother's wife had to be sent back on her bad leg to her family in disgrace.

My son's was the first death in our village in more than a year. He was buried in the traditional way: the usual ceremony and the body left in a field for the lions and hyenas. But a week went by and my son had not been eaten. I was so sorry to see him bulging in the blanket and disfigured, rotting there, like Noah under the witch tree.

We concluded that so many animals had been hunted and poached and driven off there were none left to eat our dead anymore. Or was it that we'd buried Noah, whose spirit was still among us, blaming and making trouble?

My wife was sorrowing; even the chief was at a loss. But I said, "We will bury him." We made a hole for my son and pushed him into it, as we had Noah in that first hole.

After that, there were many – buried bodies in the holes underneath the earth of our living places.

It was the only answer, but not a good one. We do not burn bodies as the Wahindi do. We prayed for the animals to come back, we used medicine, we left meat for the animals. The meat became infested by ants and flies. It seemed nothing would go right for us in this new ritual of burying, because in the ground they were with us, uneaten and angry.

The loss of the animals marked the beginning of the ghosts. And now nothing dies, the dead are always haunting us, and we spend so much time trying to settle their spirits, it has become our constant occupation, but without success, with no animals left to eat them, nowadays the dead don't die.

Autostop *Summer*

ALL THROUGH FIVE courses of the lunch, listening to Vittorio, I was thinking how long-winded people seldom become writers, how long-windedness itself is a form of indolence. The besetting sin of talkers is not the talk, which might be witty, but the evasion, the laziness in it. Talkers never remember what they say. Welcome to Italy, I thought.

I was facing Vittorio but, eager to get away and be alone, I wasn't listening. I studied the besieged look of the table, the sauce-splashed napkins, the oil stains on the linen, the spills of grated Parmesan cheese, the dish of ragged spat-out olive pits, the flakes of bread crusts lying where the loaf had been twisted apart, the lip-smeared wine glasses, the tang of vinegar-sodden salad greens flattening in a blue bowl. The cheese board came, and Vittorio picked up the peculiar notched knife and wagged it over a crumbly hunk of Asiago but didn't lower it.

The other guest, Tito Frasso, nodded at Vittorio and dabbed at the smallest breadcrumbs on the tablecloth, collecting them on the tip of his finger and poking them onto his tongue. Vittorio was dressed in stylish hunter's tweeds. Frasso, hardly more than twenty-five, had green hair and wore a stitched leather vest over a yellow T-shirt and bright orange sneakers. He had been introduced to me as a journalist. Earlier in the meal he said he had an idea for a book.

"I always found it hard to tell anyone I wanted to write a book," I said.

"Strange," he said, naïvely, I thought. Yet in contrast to his clownish clothes, Frasso was soft-spoken and serious and respectful of Vittorio, who had invited him along so that he could mention my newly translated book in his newspaper column. Frasso had added, "I would like to solicit your advice." He licked crumbs from his finger. "About writing."

"My advice," I said, "is give in to temptation."

He lost his smile, he squinted at me, and moving his lips he seemed to repeat the words I'd just said.

Being back in Italy always reminded me of my first visit long ago, my beginnings as a writer, my humiliations and little victories on the branching roads of the sunny, antique country that was then still its old self. It was a place of men in brown suits and old women in black, of rat-tatting Vespas and cigarette smoke as ropy as incense, the air thick with Italian life, the hum of freshly ground coffee as dense as potting soil, the rankness of damp paving stones in a piazza, the piercing fragrance of flower stalls, the chalky tang of old stucco house walls as yellow as aged cheese, the gleaming just-mopped marble floors of dark interiors, and the glimpse of fruit globes on terracotta platters, the confusion of odors making Italy seem an edible country.

"*Che successo?*" Vittorio said suddenly, lapsing into Italian as though from shock. He touched my shoulder to steady me, and Frasso leaned away to give him room.

"Nothing." But my memory must have shown as melancholy on my face. I forced a smile, I told him to continue, and this time I listened.

"*Bene.* As I was saying, if you have any friends in Florence," and he made an operatic gesture, raising his arms in welcome, and pleading with them to embrace a body, "please, I beg you, invite them to the dinner on Thursday when we launch your book."

I hesitated, because I knew that if I told him the name of the man I had in mind, I would have to lie about it, and the sorry business had such a strange history that I might regret it.

But I was at that later unapologetic stage of life when one can be bluntly curious to know how things had turned out for people met long ago on the road, people who'd been kind or cruel to me. How had they fared, and what had they forgotten, and who were they now? Mine was the vindictive nosiness and intrusion of a ghost, with the ghost's satisfactions.

"There's only one man, and he's a Fiorentino, but he might not be alive," I said. In a way I hoped he wasn't, because then I could explain the background to Vittorio. "His name is Pietro Ubaldini."

"I know him," Vittorio said, looking pleased. "Tito?"

Frasso shook his head and frowned. The name was apparently new to him.

"Tito is from Napoli. He remains a student of this place," Vittorio said. "I can tell you that Ubaldini is alive."

"That's good news."

Vittorio cocked his head at me, because I hadn't spoken with much enthusiasm. "A great patron of the arts from an old family. He is"–and he shrugged and twirled one finger–"*anziano* now. I will have an invitation sent to him." Vittorio folded his napkin, pressing it with the heel of his hand, and–more opera–from across the room asked the waiter in gestures for the bill, signaling with upraised scribbling fingers. "You're okay with this dinner?"

"I'm fine."

"You don't mind saying some few words afterward?"

"I'm looking forward to it," I said. "I want to talk about how Italy made me a writer."

"Excellent." Then he smiled, as though remembering something. "But how do you know the *grande nobile* Ubaldini?"

"Never met him. He's the friend of a friend from long ago. I was told I should look him up if I was ever in Florence."

That was a lie. I had met Ubaldini fifty years before, but not in Florence. I did not really care to talk to him again, but I wanted to look at him. If Vittorio had pointed to another table in the restaurant and said, "That's him," I would have been satisfied. I merely wanted to see his face, and I suppose I hoped he'd see mine. It was not an exercise in recognition, but in verification. So much time had passed that I sometimes thought I had imagined Ubaldini, but when Vittorio pounced on the name, I felt a bit winded, as if it had been an exertion to say it. It disturbed me to think that I would be seeing him again.

I had thought of him often over the years. It was in the fortified hill town of Urbino that I got to know what serious writing entailed. I had a free room, a job as a teacher, a small salary, and the love of a pretty woman who was studying at the university. But I had arrived there in such a roundabout way, I believed I was being plotted against.

In Amherst I had written stories, but many of my friends called themselves writers too. It was a comfort for us to be untested among bookish people in a college town, to talk about our writing and read our stories and poems to appreciative audiences at the local coffeehouse. We published them in our literary magazine, we complimented each other, and it was all a cheat for being self-serving.

Italy was the world, it was flesh and food and temptation, it was all those odors, the true test of my writing ambition. I hitchhiked to the coastal town of Fano and lived for a few weeks at the house of an American couple, the Shainheits. Fano was saturated with the aroma of grilled fish, the thick blue edge of the Adriatic Sea flopping against the hot sand. Benny Shainheit, a teacher of mine, was in Italy on a Fulbright and had invited me to stay. In the first week they were visited by another American academic, named Hal McCarthy. Over lunch at a café, McCarthy said he was headed inland. "Delicious Gubbio," he said, working his lips around the words, making the place name sound like soupy dessert you'd eat with a spoon. "And what brings you here?"

I said I was writing something.

"Sunshine and blue sky everywhere," he said, panting and slightly suppressing a furious giggle, "and you choose to sit in a dark room staring at a blank sheet of paper!"

"Not blank," I said defiantly, but still I felt undermined, my first taste of the hostile envy of an idle academic for a young writer. That neither of the Shainheits said anything in my defense only added to my annoyance.

During the day, I wrote in my upstairs room while the Shainheits were at the beach with their little boy, and in the evenings I sat in a café, bantering with the locals, practicing my Italian. Late one night, about ten days into living with the Shainheits, I came back and found them – Benny and Laurie – sitting together at the kitchen table, as forbidding as my parents.

"Please sit down," Benny said. He was stern, giving me an order. The "please" was hostile.

Seated across from them, I saw that Laurie had been crying, her face fixed and ugly with misery. For a moment I felt sorry for her, and then she gave me such a hateful look – dark glistening eyes, smeared cheeks, twisted mouth – that I knew they had something against me.

Benny's chin was lifted in indignation, and it all seemed stagy and portentous to me, intended to impress me with its seriousness. He reached below the table to his lap, found what he was looking for – a notebook, which he slapped on the table and poked across to me. I saw at once that it was my own notebook, dirty at the edges, ink-smeared, and with a familiar white label pasted to the cover.

"So this is what you think of us," Benny said. "After all we've done for you."

I put my hand over the notebook to prevent them from snatching it back.

"I'm bald and toothy, am I?" he said, and never looked

balder or toothier. "Neck flesh like a scrotum. Hairy ears. Chipmunk overbite. Goose-eyed."

"I don't know what you're talking about." My voice was high and unconvincing.

"I habitually stand with my prehensile feet pointing at ten minutes to two."

I made the mistake of smiling at that.

"And I'm beaky and old," Laurie said. "Beaky and old! Who do you think you are to write that about me? I'm thirty-seven. You think that's old?" But protesting she began to cry again with a scowling face, and she looked feeble as she clawed at her reddened eyes.

I said, "You have no right to read my diary. That's an invasion of privacy."

"You invaded our house," Benny said. He remembered something else. "The Punch and Judy show."

Laurie looked up from her hands. "Oh, and Jaunty's a homunculus, is he?"

Jaunty was their two-year-old son, a whiny stumbling child with an enormous head. "Homunculus" was a favorite word of mine at the time.

"You've abused our hospitality," Benny said.

"You read my private diary," I said. "I call that abusive."

"Laurie found it on the floor." He looked anguished, as protesting liars often do. "When she picked it up she saw a few pages."

"Bull."

"He's calling us liars," Laurie said. She cocked her head. "Ever think you might be crazy?"

"You're what we call a passenger," Benny said. "We want you out of here. You're just ridiculing us."

What surprised me was the coziness of the "we" and the "us." They were a couple who constantly quarreled – as I also described in detail in the "Punch and Judy" section of the notebook – who hated each other's company, who seemed to welcome me for the novelty of their having the diversion of someone else to talk to. And now here they were, side by side, facing me, united in their hatred of me, their common enemy. It seemed theatrical and false when Benny clumsily put his arm around Laurie, who was still tearfully hiccupping, and she looked burdened by the arm.

By then it was too late for me to go anywhere but to my room, where I packed the little I owned in my bag and lay fully clothed on my bed, sleepless and hot. At first light, before the Shainheits were awake, I crept out of the house and walked quickly up the Via Nolfi to the center of the town. I knew a cheap hotel there, the Albergo Due Mori, two black marble cherubs on its Moorish gatepost wearing turbans. I stayed for a week, writing about the confrontation with Benny and Laurie, and avoiding the public beach, where I might see them again.

This seemed yet another obstacle to my becoming a writer. It was bad enough to be mocked ("staring at a blank sheet of paper!"); it was worse for my privacy to be violated, indeed to have no privacy. But at the Albergo Due Mori I had something to write, and I was undisturbed. An Englishman staying at the hotel told me that Robert Browning had come here and was inspired to write a poem after seeing a certain painting in a church: *The Guardian Angel* by Guercino. I found the church and the painting, and I wrote a poem too, wishing for a guardian angel.

Early one morning, seeing Benny Shainheit's Volkswagen parked near the Albergo Due Mori, I checked out and walked to the coast road with my bag and put my thumb out – *autostop,* as hitchhiking was called, the random pickup. The first car that stopped held three Germans, two young men and a pretty woman, Johanna, going to Venice. I went with them; it was a day's drive. We walked around late-afternoon Venice, we flirted with American girls, and then we pooled our money and drank beer and bought fruit to eat, washing it in a public sink. When night fell we drove to a hayfield outside the city, where we slept, the men on a blanket in our clothes, Johanna curled up in the back seat of the car.

Come with us on the road north, they said in the morning, being friendly. "Find us some American girls and you can have Johanna." One of the men muttered to Johanna, who came over to me and shook her hair back with a movement of her head and kissed me on the mouth.

They all laughed, seeing how startled I was, and then I laughed too, but I said no. They dropped me on the main road south, where I stuck out my thumb – *autostop*. I got a ride from some men who said, "*Siamo comunisti,*" and when I asked them where they were from, one laughed and said, "Kansa Seety." They were from Bologna, and they left me a few miles south of it. Not long after, a red Alfa Romeo drew up and the man inside leaned over and said, "*Tedesco?*"

"No. American," I said, and patted my chest pocket, drew out my passport, and showed him.

He was in his late thirties, perhaps forty, a handsome man in sunglasses, who sat at an angle, driving with one hand and chatting to me. His English was good, but when I asked him what he did for a living, he laughed and said, "I am lazy." I took this complacency to mean he had money.

"You Americans are so free," he said. "Your passport in your pocket and *autostop*. That is all you need. You are lucky."

It was a beautiful day, a hot afternoon in July, as we sped toward the coast – and I did feel lucky, in this fast car with this smiling man who was taking me south. When he asked me where I was going, I said Fano, because it was there that I could get my bearings. We passed Rimini and Cattolica, which I'd seen from the northbound car with the Germans.

"You're a student?" he asked.

"A writer," I said. I disclosed my secret with hope, with anxiety, holding my breath. And I told myself that I could call myself a writer even if I was not published.

"*Bravo,*" he said.

That gave me hope, someone who didn't mock me, who believed me. We talked about Italian writers. I mentioned Moravia and Pavese and Primo Levi. He said that he knew Levi – he was from Florence. I asked him his name, and he told me, "Ubaldini," and I said, "As in Dante."

"Another Ubaldini. But maybe the same family. Who knows?"

We talked about Dante, we talked about the summer's films, *Otto e Mezzo* and *Che Fine ha Fatto Baby Jane?* He said that he dabbled in the film business. He did some writing – "but not serious, like you." He said he could introduce me to some publishers, and I thought: Yes, I could stay in Italy, keep writing, have an Italian publisher, raise an Italian family, perhaps near the coast here, in a villa, watch the sun rise over the Adriatic, live in the local way, in the slow, lazy, stop-go life of Italy.

We were then near Pesaro. Without a word, instead of continuing to Fano he jerked the car inland on a rising road. He must have seen a question on my face.

"This is better," he said with confidence.

The road narrowed, slanting into the hills, and for the next half-hour or so he seemed to use all his concentration to maneuver the car, taking the sharp bends by yanking the steering wheel, and speeding whenever the road straightened. We passed farmhouses, some small squat churches, and hillsides of cows, and I marveled that so much had happened since the Shainheits had tossed me out of their house.

All this time he was talking, with the casual enthusiasm of a benevolent Italian, about good food and great books and the lovely weather. And sometimes he was talking about nothing, but with such lazy pleasure he was exulting in his good mood and, in the Italian way, filled me – his passenger – with the confidence that happiness conveys. I was slightly tipsy from all the talk.

Then the car was slowing down and drawing into a widened viewpoint at the edge of the road, overlooking a village and the sunlit fields of rural Italy, the blue sea in the distance. We were parked on a parapet of land surrounded by poplars, outside time, as though he'd flown me from the sky to tempt me with the glorious view. I had no idea where we were.

He shut off the engine and turned to me, perspiring. He looked tormented, and his sudden seriousness alarmed me. When he wiped his face with his handkerchief he had to remove his sunglasses. His damp eyes were both lewd and benevolent.

"*Bella sole d'Italia,*" he said, seeming anxious, wearily wiping his face again in the heat.

"Where are we?" I asked.

He didn't answer. He said, "I am from Florence, as I told you. But I have a villa on an island. You know the Isole Tremiti?"

"No."

"Is very beautiful," he said. "You can swimming, you can boating" – in his apparent fluster his English broke down. "Is the sweet life. Good food. You can make writing there. Is perfect."

I said, "I need a job."

"What money you need, I give you."

It was a dream, it was everything I wanted: a house by the sea, the freedom to work on my book, comfort and happiness. But it was so voluptuous I knew there was a catch, and I suspected what it might be. "What do I do in return?"

"You make writing. You write fabulous!"

"Anything else?"

The sweat was dripping from his face, but he didn't wipe it. His tight shirt was plastered to his body. He seemed determined not to say anything more, and yet to elicit an answer from me. He turned to gaze across the russet tiled rooftops and through the slender pines to ocean below us, and for all I knew the island he promised me, where I would write, was floating like a lotus blossom somewhere in the glittering scales of that sea.

"Sorry."

"You say no because you never try."

"I can't do that." Then, as though to explain, I said, "I have a girlfriend."

"I sometimes have a woman," he said in a sour tone of rebuttal. "It is"–he curled his lip–"like stroking a cat."

"Let's go," I said. "You can drop me at the next town, wherever that is."

His face hardened, and he wiped it with his bare hand and flicked the sweat from that hand. He said, "You are a big stupid. You refuse me, eh? Okay, Signore Scrittore, write something on this little road!"

And in his anger he reached for me. I lifted my arm to block him–but I moved too quickly, and in the confinement of the small car I caught his chin with my elbow, banging his head against the doorpost and knocking his glasses sideways, so they swung across his face.

He howled, then said, "*Va via!*"

And as soon as I pulled my bag from the back seat he slammed the door and sped downhill, leaving me in the long shadows of the tall poplars in the late-afternoon sun on the empty road. He knew he was abandoning me, and he was furious because I had rebuffed him. My talk about being a writer annoyed him, as it had annoyed Hal McCarthy and the Shainheits. I thought, irrationally, that these people were actively trying to prevent me from becoming a writer, but instead of making me feel small, I was defiant and saw myself as wolfish and resourceful.

I stood on the road, the setting sun on my face, looking around, wishing to remember every detail of this abandonment. I didn't know which way to go, but because Ubaldini had gone downhill, I decided to head uphill. I walked for a while and saw a sign, *Gallo,* with an arrow, and kept walking in that direction, but I did not see a town, and no cars passed this way.

Then it grew dark, a car came out of that darkness, I made the *autostop* sign with my hand, and the car slowed down. It was a Fiat driven by an Italian man whose English was excellent. He was going to Urbino, some miles into the hills. He said he was a professor at the university there, and what did I do? Superstitiously, I said I was a teacher. "I am looking for a teacher," he said. I thought to myself, Another one. But when we got to the town, he dropped me at a *pensione* and said would I please visit his office in the morning? He had a job for me, teaching English.

I spent the next two months in Urbino. I fell in love with Francesca Porretta, one of my students–"Paolo and Francesca," I said, "*I celebri amanti.*" I tried to work on my novella, *Ticket to Hell.* Francesca tickled me as I wrote, she kissed my neck, some afternoons she lay on the edge of the bed and kicked her legs and laughed. "*Gli amanti condannati,*" I said. Francesca showed me the great painters of Urbino, Uccello and Raphael. I was blessed with luck: it was my luck that these people recognized and resented. I got very little work done, but I was learning.

Late in August I was notified by the Peace Corps that I'd been assigned to teach in Nyasaland, in central Africa. For my application, I was fingerprinted at the main police station in Urbino by an amused policeman, who smoked a cigarette between inking the right and the left set of fingerprints.

Kissing Francesca goodbye, I hitchhiked – more *autostop* – to Rome, then took a train to Naples, then a ship home, traveling third class in a cabin with seven Lebanese immigrants to Canada, who got off in rainy Halifax. From New York City I bummed a ride to Boston, starting from under the George Washington Bridge. A few months later I went to Africa. By then, Francesca had stopped writing.

At last my hitchhiking stopped. In a remote village of mud huts, among illiterates who lived on porridge and stewed greens, a place without pictures or books, all of it smelling of woodsmoke and the sour grass of its roofs and in the rains stinking of its red clay roads, I wrote every day. I went on writing, working, always in distant places. I traveled, I published my books, married twice, and raised my children. It was the life I'd wished for. And whenever I returned to Italy, I remembered the sunlit Italian roads and that *autostop* summer on the Adriatic and in Urbino, all of it like a banquet. And that was why, when Vittorio asked me in Florence if I had a guest for the dinner, I said, "Pietro Ubaldini."

Copies of the Italian edition of my novel were stacked on a side table at the restaurant, one copy upright, showing the cover. In a private room on the second floor, reserved by Vittorio for the dinner, a long refectory table was set for a dozen people.

I had climbed the stairs warily, watching for Ubaldini, but only one person was there, Vittorio's young assistant, Dialta, setting out place cards, smiling to see that I was the first to arrive. She poured me a glass of wine, and we waited. I did not know whether to stand or sit. Some more people came, two journalists, and then Vittorio with an attractive woman. Vittorio introduced me to the others. Tito Frasso, the young green-haired man from Vittorio's lunch, slipped through the door, padding in on his orange sneakers, in the same leather vest but a different T-shirt. He approached me and said hello. It occurred to me that he dressed that way, absurdly, defiantly, creating a street style all his own, because he didn't have much money.

I wanted to sit, I hated the delay, but I knew that an Italian dinner was a ritual, and the delay itself was part of the ritual, like the chitchat, the predinner drinks that we sipped standing, the laughter, the teasing. Everything that seemed inconsequential was part of the observance – nothing could be hurried. All this time I glanced around, wondering about Ubaldini.

At last, Vittorio sighed and said, "*Allora* . . ." The word was like an order, as people maneuvered to take their places at the table. I was seated at one end, Vittorio at the other. A chair stood empty near Vittorio, the linen napkin folded like a nun's cornette on the plate before it.

"I am so excited to read your book," the woman on my right said. She was a journalist, she would be reviewing it. "Is your first book?"

"No." I could not bring myself to tell her it was my thirty-fifth.

"*Parla Italiano?*" asked the woman on my left.

I said no, I didn't dare, and she smiled and sipped her wine, and the woman on my right told me of her trip to Eritrea: "Magnificent! Africa! But so sad, so poor."

I said, "I used to live there." But still she went on describing it to me.

And while she spoke, and the waiters served the antipasto, an old man came through the door, nodded at Vittorio, handed his coat to a waiter, and, sizing up the table, stepped to the empty chair. I would not have guessed it to be Ubaldini. He was slack-jowled, horse-faced, and his ill-fitting suit was too loose. He was smaller than I remembered, and with distorted features, his ears and hands much bigger. His only affectation was a stylish pair of glasses, tortoiseshell, with pinkish lenses. He tugged them down, surveyed the table, said something to the woman next to him – a pleasantry, I guessed, and a word to Tito Frasso, who sat across from him. When he smiled he showed his discolored teeth to their roots. Then he ate, daintily, in the Italian way, poking his food with a fork, not betraying any appetite.

After the antipasto came the soup course, the fish course, the pasta course, the meat course. I heard about Eritrea and the Red Sea, and poverty in Africa, and the animals – fantastic; and the dancers in Kenya – fantastic; and Somalia – a tragedy. More wine, more water, more bread.

Ubaldini kept his head down and picked at his food. I watched him closely as he ate with concentration, from time to time lifting his napkin to dab at his lips, and as he dabbed, meeting the gaze of the young man in outlandish clothes, and smiling at him with yellowish teeth, as though sharing a secret.

Waiters came and went, plates were gathered, glasses filled. The dessert was served, tiramisu, and the cheese set out.

As the coffee was poured, Vittorio rose and thanked the guests for being there, speaking in sonorous Italian; and then for my benefit he spoke in English, and the temperature of the room went down with the sound of the foreign language, the air becoming slightly stale.

"Tonight, my friend, our distinguished author, has joined us for the occasion of his new book – yes," and he paused for the light clapping. "And he has agreed to say some few words." He motioned to me. "Please."

I pushed my chair back and stood up.

From the moment Vittorio began speaking in English we seemed to slip into an amateur theatrical, a play in which we were unsure of our lines. I spoke haltingly, as Vittorio had done, but the slowness threw me and made me less certain of what I was going to say next.

"Fifty years ago I visited Italy for the first time," I said. "I was just a boy, really, but it was here, in the beauty of Italy, that I began to write . . ."

I did not say that it had been an *autostop* summer of obstacles and temptations. I described my arrival, my first impressions of Italy, the sunlight, the smells of food and hot oil, the glow of old stone, the texture of ancient marble, the way the whole of Italy had been sculpted and formed, every hill, every field, every town – none of it wild, all of it showing the evidence of the human hand, where eating was on everyone's mind; not books but food.

I glanced at the dinner guests as I spoke, and my gaze returned to Pietro Ubaldini, whose elbow was propped on the table, his hand idly cradling his head, his fingers stroking his cheek, listening attentively.

Then I risked it. "One day I was traveling from Venice by *autostop*. I was picked up by an Italian man in a car. We talked and talked, and finally we disagreed. He dropped me suddenly by the roadside at nightfall, abandoned me on one of the branching roads of Italy."

I looked squarely at Pietro Ubaldini. Still he stroked his cheek and stared through his tinted lenses.

"He didn't know me, and I'm sure he forgot me. Though I didn't realize it at the time, he did me a great favor. When you're young the world seems unknowable, and so it seems simplified by its obscurity. You have no idea how precarious the road is, or where it leads, and it's not until much later that you understand its complexity and how you found your way. Sometimes it is with the help of kind strangers, but more often perhaps, perversely, by the hostility of strangers. It was rejection that got me to Urbino and a job and a sense of myself. I arrived there through a series of accidents, one road leading to another. I didn't know where I was, only that I had to keep going. I knew one thing – that I couldn't go back. I was open to any suggestion – taking chances. I had to. I had no money."

As I spoke, Ubaldini stopped looking at me and began to look at the young man, as though I was offering encouragement and a promise in my own story to the young man, who was listening with rapt attention.

"I see it now as a series of expulsions. Each person I met believed he was frustrating me. It was not the great literary culture of Italy that made me a writer. It was the opposite, its philistinism. You say you want to be a writer, and Italy orders you another glass of wine and says, 'What's the point?' Italy's love of comfort, its taste for good food and leisure, its joy in talk, its idleness, its laughter, its complacent teasing cynicism"–and here I paused for the people at the table to savor this description and bask in it–"all these traits make it the enemy of art."

"Oh, no!" Vittorio called out, and Ubaldini nodded at the young man Frasso.

"But you give in to temptation, and you're tested, and that's how you learn. Italy's great complacency, the way it wraps its arms around you, produces the occasional rebel who does not want that embrace. That person writes a good book, or a poem, or makes a film. I said no to that embrace on a country road."

The scattered laughter, the uneasy murmurs, some of the whispers translations, made me want to finish.

"So I want to thank you for helping a bewildered stranger find his way. You didn't know what you were doing, and neither did I, but here we are – and all's well."

Knowing that I was done, feeling released from their bewilderment, they clapped hard in relief. Vittorio thanked me, some of the people left, and the rest milled around the table talking, another Italian ritual, the protracted goodbye, a way of showing gratitude or warmth, the period of hesitation in a culture where hurrying, or any urgency, even the urgency to be alone and write, is considered a vice.

I stepped over to Ubaldini and thanked him for coming.

"I was fascinated by your remarks," he said. "I appreciated the ambiguity."

"What do you do in Florence?" I asked.

"I do nothing! I am ancient!" And laughing, he again caught the eye of the young man. "Tell me, will you be here long?"

"I leave tomorrow." I looked for the lewdness and benevolence on his face, but saw the exhaustion of old age, and yet still a glint of greed in his eyes.

"A pity. I would like to invite you to my home. I have a library with many fine books. I have important pictures. I have a view of the river."

Now he was speaking as well to Frasso, who had drifted near. Ubaldini muttered to him rapidly in Italian. Each time he smiled he moved his tongue against his lips, as though he was tasting his own smile. The young man murmured his thanks, and I understood that the same invitation was directed to him, and that he was agreeing to a visit.

Before I left, Frasso came over to me. "Thank you for your advice," he said. "Where I come from, in Naples, no one reads a book or writes a poem. But here is different. And so –" He shrugged, the noncommittal Italian lift of the shoulders, then went to the door, where Ubaldini was waiting for him.

Voices of Love

CHEATING FOR LOVE

I was a graduate student, twenty-three, living in Princeton with my boyfriend. We were very friendly with a couple, Greg and June, and we spent a lot of time with them – maybe too much. Greg was always after me, calling me and slipping me notes. He said that June was frigid and so on. He was very hungry, and I had to admit I liked his attention. One day we ended up in bed, and that was the beginning of our affair. The odd thing was that the four of us were still friends, even though Greg and I had this secret.

We had plans for dinner at our place one night, the four of us. Greg called me and asked me to come over – "It's urgent." When I got there he was naked, and we were soon in bed. In the middle of it the door banged open. It was June, screaming at him, "You bastard!"

He had been on top of me in a tangle of sheets. He covered me with a sheet and began screaming back at June: "Get out of here! How dare you come in here!"

I was dying with shame under the sheet. June was my best friend.

I was still cowering under the sheet when Greg got up and pushed June out of the room. She went away sobbing. I got dressed and left. That night the four of us had dinner, as we'd planned. Greg and June were a little quiet, but were holding hands. My own boyfriend didn't know anything – he was cooking. We all remained friends. June never knew I was the other woman. But being discovered that way made me realize what a terrible thing I had done in cheating on her, and cheating on my own boyfriend too. I thought of it as the worst day of my life, taking that risk. But I had done it for love, and within a year Greg and I were married.

THE FIRST MOVE

I had been married about two months when I took a trip to Singapore for a series of high-level meetings. I was thirty-two, a field organizer for a development project in Asia, based in Kuala Lumpur. At one of the dinners I met a man who flirted with me and was quite frank about wanting to sleep with me. I fended him off, though he was very persistent. He knew I was married. He was married too. I let slip the fact that I had been married only two months.

He said, "Oh, God, I'm so sorry." He explained that if he had known I was a newlywed he would not have been so persistent. He wished me well, and he became very sweet and even protective over the next few days of our meetings. I began to regard him as a good friend. He also laughed at his earlier wooing of me and kept apologizing for his behavior.

But I kept thinking how, inevitably, my husband and I would be unfaithful. I imagined the day when he would come to me and say, "I've got something to tell you," or perhaps I would accidentally discover his infidelity. And then I would be unfaithful to him, but with whom? We loved each other, yet I knew that it would happen – because it so often does. I thought, I don't want him to be first. I was very sad thinking of these realities, especially in this lovely city.

I had dinner with the man in his hotel. I asked if we could go upstairs to his suite so I could use his bathroom. He was, as usual, very kind, now like an old friend.

When I came out of the bathroom I asked him to turn off the lights. Then I took off my dress and sat next to him on the sofa, wearing only my panties.

I said, "Don't be shocked." He said, "But I am!" I told him about the decision I had made. "I want to be first." I was afraid he might reject me, but we made love and I stayed the night. The Singapore trip ended and I never saw him after that. My marriage has been very happy and I was never unfaithful again. When my husband confessed to an indiscretion, I forgave him.

THE UNSUITABLE WOMAN

As soon as I met Rita, I knew she was unsuitable: not my type. And the odd thing was that she was completely willing – an agreeable companion, resourceful, submissive sexually, and game for anything. She was pleasant, but after one night with her I wanted her to leave. When sex was over I found nothing to say to her. A month later she called me and asked why I had rejected her. She said, "You hurt my feelings." I couldn't think of anything to say. She seemed a bit obtuse, unfunny, yet wanted desperately to please me. She was attractive, athletic, about thirty, a landscape architect. I felt that on some level she was incompetent and slow, but she was very good-natured. Afterward I hardly thought of her, and when I did I became anxious, because I could not imagine her with any man I knew.

I met her twenty years later. She had married a graphic designer, who was about her age, very intelligent and talented, and she was still a landscape architect. He loved her madly. It was obvious in everything he did – he adored her. They were a wonderful couple. He admired her talent and praised her. What had he seen that I hadn't? They had no children, they were devoted to each other, they seemed very happy and well suited to each other.

Their happiness made me think that I had judged her wrongly before, that the selfishness and incompetence I had seen in her had been in me – my faults.

I had been suspicious all those years ago when she had

been so willing. But she'd been sincere. She'd found someone who appreciated her, needed her, loved her, and his love had improved her too.

NO STRINGS

I met a woman in the local supermarket who said to me, "Are you the architect?" I had just done a big handsome building in town, and a piece about it in the newspaper had used a photograph of me.

"Yes," I said, and looked at her closely: attractive, about forty, with piercing blue eyes that were fixed on mine and a fearless, upright, almost defiant posture, which seemed boldly welcoming.

"I'm a huge admirer of your work," she said with a lovely smile. "I'm an interior designer myself. I feel I could learn so much from you, spending time with you. No strings."

I was on the point of giving her my address when my wife came up to us and said, "Let's go, Walter, or we'll be late." Not even a glance at the woman. She had sensed something.

Well, so had I. About a week later a letter appeared in my mailbox. In this rather long letter the woman said that as she was a decorator and I an architect, we might work together. "No strings." There was no stamp on the letter. This worried me: she knew my house. Somehow she had found out my address. She had written her telephone number under her signature.

I was sorely tempted. "No strings" sounded like the recipe for a guiltless adultery, and when a woman is offering herself in such a casual way she always seems to me more attractive for being so easily available. Yet, more out of procrastination than indifference, I didn't reply or call her.

One day at the local library, crouched down looking for a book, I was aware of a woman looming over me. It was she. "Why didn't you answer my letter? You didn't even call." She was hurt, she said. But she mentioned that she was "hooked up with a wealthy lawyer." Then: "He's so uptight. I love to give oral sex – my lips are so sensitive – but he says it embarrasses him. He thinks it's a big deal. It isn't. I love pleasuring men. But he's going to be history. I've told him, 'No strings.'"

Soon after that, I got another letter from her. She'd left the lawyer. She wanted to see me. *We can work something out. No strings. I'm free most afternoons.* And again she wrote her telephone number.

I began to dial her number, thinking, *My lips are so sensitive,* but before I finished I heard the front door open. My wife. "Walter, give me a hand with the groceries," and the spell was broken. I wrote a short note: *I don't think I can help you.*

That was not the end of it. Months later, I heard a loud knock at my door. It was the woman.

"I'm being evicted! I have no place to stay! You've done well – look at your nice house. I can't get any work. You owe me. People have helped you – you have to help me. I'm going to be on the street! Don't just stand there gaping at me. Do something, you bastard!"

Screaming, crazy, demanding. I was shocked, and as I closed the door on her ranting, I thought, What if I had acted on my temptation? And that night I wept in my wife's arms, though she had no idea.

EMBASSY WIFE

My husband, Byron, was a terrible diplomat. He quarreled with his colleagues, performed his work badly, drank too much at parties, and neglected me and the kids – and yet he got a promotion. This was in Germany, where he was a public affairs officer. The head of his department was a man named Jay, who was very dapper and good-looking and devoted to his wife, Marina. He and his wife went everywhere together, which made me feel bad, because I spent so much time at home looking after our three small children. My husband said that if I showed up at the embassy parties, his professional life would be easier.

One night we went to dinner at Jay and Marina's. I sat next to Jay. It was quite a large party, but after the other guests left, Jay kept filling my glass. He was very solicitous and complimentary. I must have had a lot to drink because after a while I realized that I was sitting alone with Jay. We were talking about Germany, and children, and the weather, and then he put his arm around me.

"Please don't," I said. "What if Byron sees us?"

Jay laughed. "Where do you think he is?"

I had no idea. I didn't know what to say.

"He's upstairs with Marina!"

In my drunken state it took me almost a full minute to work this out. Byron was with Marina, therefore it was permissible for me to go with Jay, and somehow Byron's job depended on my agreeing to this.

But I sat there coldly until Byron appeared. "Let's go."

"They're swingers," Byron said, as though that excused his behavior. Some months later, after Byron had been demoted for a petty infraction, I had a brief affair with the nineteen-year-old son of some embassy friends. Byron and I have been utterly faithful since.

SPLIT-UP REVELATION

After my wife and I split up, when we had nothing to lose by being truthful, she told me that she had suspected that I had a mistress, because I no longer made love to her with any passion or desire. And what convinced her was that I was so kind to her, as though because I was guilty of infidelity I was trying to cover it up with displays of kindness. I just smiled.

"Were you ever unfaithful to me?" I asked.

She shrugged and said that when she was sure I was being

unfaithful, she went one night to a bar alone. Naturally a man came over to her and asked her if she wanted a drink. They talked awhile. She did not go home with him, but she agreed to meet him again. That was the night they made love. "He was very rough with me," she said somewhat dreamily. He tied her to a bed, forced her to perform several extreme sexual acts, and then spanked her.

We had never done anything like this. Her describing it (in more detail than I expected) aroused me.

I said, "He sounds like an animal."

She said, "He knew how to please a woman."

I thought, What? And there was more, she said. He had a girlfriend. He made no secret of her. Sometimes they went out together, my wife, the man, his girlfriend. One night while drinking at his apartment, the man demanded that my wife and his girlfriend make love while he watched. My wife got into bed with the woman.

"What did you do?" I said.

"We cuddled. What women do."

"And then what did the man do?" The anguish in my voice terrified me.

She smiled but wouldn't tell me any more. "It was a couple of years ago. You had your own girlfriend. It was retaliatory."

But it wasn't. I had no girlfriend. My feeling had been that my wife had lost interest in sex. How I longed to be that man. And my wife – now my ex-wife: I had never believed this respectable schoolteacher capable of such debauchery.

MY LOVER'S FRIENDS

I had arranged to meet Susan on a particular evening. She was a successful advertising executive, highly intelligent and yet easygoing. "I've been too busy to get married," she said. But she seemed perfect to me. We had been going out for a few months and she gave me to understand that tonight would be special – in fact, that she was going to let me stay the night. Sex at last. And not only that, but the sex would be passionate. She wasn't subtle: she conveyed this to me by various expressions, by touching me, the look in her eyes, the tone of her voice – the wonderful anticipation of lovers.

"Let's meet at my conference and we can go on from there."

This was, she said, a weekly meeting at a colleague's house. I said, "Fine." I went to the house at the appointed time. The conference was all women, six of them. They were business types. At first they were polite to me, and then I could see that they disagreed with everything I said. It was just before a state election. They supported the most right-wing candidate. We talked about capital punishment. They were in favor of it – electrocution. "All murderers are men," one said. To change the subject I asked what they did for work. "I'm involved with start-ups." "I design websites." "I do marketing." Susan just smiled and mentioned an advertising campaign she was doing on behalf of a man. "People talk about his wealth, but he earns every bit of it." They talked about money, venture capitalism, interest rates.

On the way home, Susan and I got into an argument about her friends. I hated them. She defended them. But at her house, when she said, "Coming in?" I said no, made an excuse, and never saw her again.

MY GRADUATE STUDENT

I am sixty-two and know I look my age, but I am also the head of a well-respected department of political science at a famous university. I brought some of my foreign students to Washington, D.C., for a few days, to meet lobbyists, senators, and bureaucrats; to give these young people a notion of the political process firsthand; and to do some sightseeing. One of the students, Klara, was Polish, about twenty-four, rather small, with the classic Slavic look: clear skin, good cheekbones, a pouty mouth, and a slyness in her blue eyes. She stayed near me throughout the trip, was always friendly and respectful, but spoke to me only when no one else was around. She had read my work, she said; she was an admirer.

We were alone one of those days, walking along the Mall after visiting the Washington Monument. She said, "What if I told you I wanted to get you into my room and –"

And with a twinkle in her eye she described in detail one of the most extraordinary perversions I had ever heard. She was quite matter-of-fact, yet it was something altogether new to me and almost unimaginable.

This shocked me, but I managed not to show it. All I could say in reply (my mouth very dry) was "I suppose I'd ask you why you wanted to do this."

She said very seriously, "I want to do something to you that no woman has ever done to you before."

"Maybe we can talk about it," I said. Back at the hotel later that evening, I called her room. She said, "Are you ready?"

Of course we didn't do exactly what she had suggested, but we approximated it. From the moment I entered her room I was in her power. I long to relive that night, but what she did was so extreme I cannot imagine even mentioning it to any other woman, much less repeat the act. She was a virgin. She remained a virgin, but I think I lost my virginity that night.

TWENTY-YEAR-OLDS

In a way, I have been preparing myself for this event, this feeling, for years. As a painter, I know many older painters, sculptors, photographers – say, artists in my position. Something happened in the late 1950s and early '60s. They met younger women, always the same sort of woman. Maybe I'm wrong, but I know of very few exceptions.

This woman was in her twenties. A woman of twenty doesn't know if she has a place in the world, something about her age or our age. What will happen to her? Will she find a job? Will she find a husband? Will she ever have a child? Where does she belong?

She has no idea where she is going. She is anxious. She needs someone to intervene.

Here's where the artist comes in. A painter or a photographer at sixty has either made it or stopped trying. If he has made it, he looks powerful – more than powerful, as indestructible as his art. But one thing he does not have: his youth. And he certainly questions the diminishing of his virility, what the Dutch call "the shutting of the door."

He meets a twenty-year-old and is immediately smitten. She is so relieved to be rescued, like someone plucked from a deep sea, she believes she is in love with her rescuer. Not long after they meet, she is secure and happy, having been brought to safety, on shore at last.

Perhaps she has his baby, perhaps he leaves his wife, perhaps they live together and he paints her. Never mind, no matter – it is always a disaster. She leaves him. She has a life. He is destroyed by this love. And even if you know in advance what the consequences will be, you still pursue her, as I did. Her name was Lucy, and I was wrecked.

THE DANCER

Years ago, I had been a waiter in Provincetown. My life changed when I met Ken and we moved to the far north of Vermont. People in the village accepted us as a gay couple. Twenty happy years passed. Ken died suddenly of heart failure. I spent two years being lonely. Then I decided to go back to Provincetown, just to see.

Because of complications, I spent only a few days there.

The town had changed a lot. Rich gays had put up big houses. Many more people, but they looked nice, even outrageous in a nice way. They liked showing off. I heard one man say approvingly, "Look, billions of queens." The butch gays had muscles. The lesbians looked pretty to me. I was happy, but those years in Vermont made me an unsocial type. I am shy in large groups. And I don't drink alcohol.

"I'll have a soda water with lemon," I said at the Atlantic House. The upstairs bar was full of butch gays in cowboy outfits drinking beer out of the bottle. One was chanting, "Fudge till Tuesday!"– whatever that meant.

There was dancing in the downstairs bar. I just watched. One man on the floor was alone. He wore a fireman's helmet and yellow rubber fireman's trousers and rubber boots, but other than that he was naked. The rubber trousers were held up by suspenders. This man fascinated me. I had never seen anyone like him in my life. He danced so energetically he was covered in sweat. I loved watching him.

He must have noticed me. When the music stopped he came over to the bar. I was very worried, frightened that he'd talk to me, because I didn't know what to say. He looked me up and down and smiled. He said, "Very nice."

That's all. That was the moment. Ever since, I have thought about him constantly, especially when life is hard for me or I'm lonely. I think of him, how he was dressed, what he said to me, and I am happy.

MY OLD FLAME

I was trying to think of a way of breaking up with my girlfriend, Paula, who was uncommunicative, always saying, "I'm not verbal like you." In spite of this, she often corrected me. When I referred to a woman's sex, she said, "You mean gender." And she sometimes talked about her "goals." I am suggesting that she could be rather irritating. Or was it me? She was gentle and very kind to me and good company in a quiet, listening-type way. She was passive, and I think I was looking for someone to take the initiative. She liked torch songs – that's what she called certain love songs.

To break the news to her gently, I took her to an expensive club where a black woman sang these love songs. I thought I would offer Paula a good time, an expensive meal, the whole business, and later it would be easier for me to say, "We're not really suited to each other."

She loved the club. She loved the music. She sat transfixed, drank a little more than usual, and said that it was one of the most pleasant nights of her life. Back at her apartment, she interrupted me before I could tell her what was on my mind. She said, "Let's make love."

Not only was that unusual in this normally passive woman, but while we were making love, she said, "Can I tell you a secret?"

I must have said something. I was dazed. I hadn't planned to be making love, but the evening had swept us up.

"I wanted to go home with her," she said.

That was Paula's secret, spoken in the darkness of her bedroom. I was overwhelmed. It became our secret. We talked about it all the time. I could not leave her. In the end she left me, and I was heartbroken.

FIRST LOVE

Everyone was pretty much the same at my junior college, but after I dropped out to get a job, and started night school, everyone seemed different: it was the real world, much harder for me and much more complex. I was living with my meek old grandmother in Upper Darby, Pennsylvania. I felt like such a failure – working in an art supply store, living with my grandmother, going to night school. I was eighteen years old, the youngest student in the class. One man was over sixty. Many were quite old, one or two were middle-aged men, some older women, some housewives. “I deliver bakery goods,” the man sitting next to me said. “I guess I eat them,” the woman in front of him said. The class was Economics for Small Businesses. Everyone was aiming to start their own business, but somehow I knew we were all doomed to failure.

The woman who had said “I guess I eat them” saw me standing at the bus stop and offered me a ride home. This happened a few times, until one night she stopped at a house and said, “I live here. Want to come in?”

The way she screamed at her child, who was upstairs, scared me and made me obedient. She put the light out, unbuttoned my shirt, and said, “Let me, let me.” It was the first sex of my life. It was heaven. Night school was three times a week – I couldn’t wait to go. After every class she drove me to her house and we made love. And after a few weeks she met me outside the art supply store. I saw her sitting in her car and I was joyous.

Some days I had errands to run and couldn’t see her, but even so, she stalked me and asked me to come with her. “I can’t, I can’t,” I’d say, though I wanted to. Another day Grandma was sick and I had to stay home. The woman came to Grandma’s house and banged on the door and begged to see me. Although she was sick, Grandma yelled at her, while I hid. Grandma won, the woman went away, and Grandma said, “No more night school for you.” So I went to New York, where I became successful in real estate. That was my first love, and I suspect hers, too.

EPISODE IN BANGKOK

As a sculptor and welder of large metal pieces I was always invited to the unveilings, especially when a big company was involved as the sponsor or patron. My Bangkok gallery sold one of my pieces to a bank for its courtyard's inaugural, and I flew there for the opening. My translator was a lovely young woman, very slender and pale. Hardworking and sleep-deprived, she was attractive to me: her weary fortitude made her seem waif-like and aroused me. Yet she was strong—stronger than me. I tended to fade in the evening while she was still alert. She was always early at the hotel in the morning to pick me up. She said, "Call me Pom. My real name too hard."

She grew lovelier to me each day, and I found myself desiring her. In the taxis I would sit close to her. Sometimes I'd put my hand on her warm receptive hand. I asked where she lived. Far, she said. I suggested getting a room for her at my hotel. She said, "Not necessary." What did that mean? I tried to be as polite as possible, knowing how manners are so important in Thai culture. I thought my extreme politeness might work magic on her, but it didn't.

One day she was late. It was the only time she'd ever been late. She was apologetic but had an explanation. Her explanation took almost an hour of nonstop monologue. To summarize: after leaving me the night before, she had been accosted by two men who'd taken her in a car to a remote place and raped her, over and over. She spared me no detail, and her English was perfect, which made it all worse. It was a harrowing story of violent sexual assault.

"We must go to the police," I said when she'd finished.

She said no. "We will say no more about this." I could not read the expression on her face. It was not a smile. It was something so enigmatic it seemed akin to either ecstasy or anguish.

Soon after this, my sculpture was unveiled. I left Bangkok. It was only later that I realized she must have invented the story as a way of attracting me, but of course by then I was home with my wife, who is the love of my life.

SWEET TOOTH

Traveling around Japan, especially in the smaller provincial towns, I'd always stop in convenience stores for candy or a chocolate bar or cookies. I had a sweet tooth. Maybe it was the bland Japanese food I'd been eating that exacerbated my craving.

Invariably, the cashier at the convenience store was a girl in her late teens – slender, pale, with flawless skin, delicate hands, fine-boned, smiling, submissive, sweet, and obliging. I would linger over the transaction, often ask a question just to detain her, and if no one else was around I would ask her name, her age, and what sort of music she liked. She was always delightful. I am not talking about one or two girls like this, but twenty or more. It was like a whole social class of delightful teenage cashiers, smiling at me while they went about their dreary job. I always thought, If I were not married, I'd move to Japan and marry one of these beauties.

A year after my trip, back in my small town in Massachusetts, I wanted to have a desk built and went to a local cabinetmaker. The man, Arthur, showed me pictures of some of the work he'd done – in Japan. I got to know him better. He had lived in Japan for fifteen years.

I told him my fantasy of the cashier.

He laughed and said, "I married her."

He had fallen in love with the very sort of girl, nineteen, beautiful, a cashier in the convenience store in a small town near Nagoya. He too had a sweet tooth.

"It was horrible almost from the beginning," Arthur said. "Yes, she was submissive and sweet at the store, but most of these girls are the opposite privately from the way they are in public. As if to compensate for that public role of being obliging and deferential, at home they're nagging and dominant, hypercritical, unhelpful, frigid, and unpleasant. Mean with money – mine took charge of all my money. Her mother was the same. We ended it." He thought a moment, then said, "Maybe they're not all like that, but . . ."

GUESTHOUSE VOICES

Our son and his wife and their small baby visited one summer. I had to put off our old friends the Butlers, saying, "If it weren't for my son's visit, we'd be glad to have you on the Fourth of July. Come after that – the guesthouse will be free."

The Butlers said they'd visit the following weekend. I looked forward to their visit, because they were a happy couple and liked us and, frankly, Joe and I were going through a rough patch.

I should also add that my son and his wife were model parents, extremely attentive to their little six-month-old son, Freddy, who never gave a moment of trouble – usually slept through the night. And if he was fussed, they seemed to know it instantly, even when we were eating in the main house, kind of like parental extrasensory perception. I was amazed at how prescient they were to this infant's needs – changes of diaper, wakefulness, teething, whatever.

I said to my husband, "That's a lesson to us. They're on the kid's wavelength in a way we never were." We were sorry to see them go.

The Butlers came. Wonderful couple, no kids, devoted to each other. Ron Butler had been the best man at our wedding, one of our oldest friends. We had felt an emptiness when our son and his family left, but the Butlers perked us up. They'd driven a long way and said they were tired. I said, "Have a nap. Everything's informal. We have no plans. Let's do something tomorrow."

They went to the guesthouse and shut the door.

I poured myself a glass of wine and settled in front of the TV, but before I turned it on I heard, *I told you they're pissed off.* It was Ron Butler's voice. My husband came into the room and made a face. We heard from a corner bookshelf, *You're such an asshole. This is the last goddamned time. Did you see how they looked at us. They don't want us here.* And then the wife, *Oh, shut up, you queer.*

We sat, horrified, until at last we found the baby monitor my son had left behind, the apparatus under the bed, the receiver in our TV room, to hear whether the baby was crying.

That night my husband embraced me tenderly and said, "You are so precious to me."

The Butlers were their delightful selves, but we were not surprised when they said they'd have to leave earlier than they'd expected.

The Furies

I NOW BELONG TO an incredibly exclusive club," Ray Testa had said in his speech at his wedding reception. He savored the moment, then winked and added, "There are not many men who can say they're older than their father-in-law."

He was fifty-eight, his new wife, Shelby, thirty-one; his father-in-law was fifty-six and seemingly at ease with this older man marrying his daughter. He said, "She's an old soul."

Ray Testa was a dentist, and for seven years Shelby had been his hygienist. But "I'm thinking of leaving," Shelby said one day. Ray urged her to stay and finally pleaded, "You can't leave. I love you." She didn't smile. She swallowed air and said that she had feelings for him, too. Then, "What about Angie?"

He confessed everything to his wife, adding that he wanted to marry Shelby.

Angie took it badly, as he guessed she might, but unexpectedly she said, "Why didn't you leave me years ago, when I might have met someone who really cared for me?"

He hadn't imagined she'd object in this peevish way, for such a coldly practical reason, because his timing was inconvenient for her. He thought she'd tell him how she'd miss him and be miserable without him, not that she might have been better off with someone else.

Staring at him, her eyes went black and depthless and she seemed physically to swell, as though with malevolence. Ray expected a shout, but her voice was the confident whisper of a killer whose victim is helpless. "I know I should say I wish you well, but I wish you ill with all my heart. I've made it easy for you. I hope you suffer now with that woman who's taken you from me. These women that carry on with married men are demons."

She sounded like her mother, Gilda – Ermenegilda – sour, mustached, habitually in black, pedantically superstitious, Sicilian, always threatening the evil eye. He told himself that Angie was bitter, cruel for being grief-stricken, demented by the breakup, she didn't mean this. They had no children; they divided their assets in half, the proceeds of his more than thirty years of dentistry. Angie got the family house, the dog, a lump sum; Ray the vacation house on the South Shore – he'd commute to his office from there, Shelby by his side. Shelby wasn't greedy. She said she'd never been happier. Ray did not divulge to Shelby the vindictive curse Angie had uttered. He now had what he wanted, a new life with Shelby.

She was a treasure, unconventionally beautiful, not the fleshy new graduate she'd been when he first hired her but with the lean feline good health of the jogger she now was, tall and sharp-featured. Her mouth was almost severe – she hardly parted her lips when she spoke, and then always in a low certain voice that got his attention, as in, "What about Angie?"

With the unwavering judgment of someone untested, someone innocent and upright, Shelby was young, alert to the obvious. Her eyes were gray, blinkless, cat-like. Ray had desired her from the first, but thought that his feeling would diminish as he got to know her better. Time passed and his desire to possess her became a physical set of symptoms, like hunger, a swollen tongue, a droning in his head, a tingling in his hands.

Now she was his. He could not believe his luck, how she had come into his life, to lead him confidently into a future he'd hated to contemplate. He sometimes eavesdropped on her working on a patient in her concentrated way and he was almost tearful with gratitude that she was his wife. People said how a second wife was often a younger version of the first one, but she was in every way the opposite of Angie.

They had never argued, and so their first argument, a few

months after their marriage, came as a shock to Ray. It concerned his high school reunion, the fortieth. Ray wanted to take Shelby. She protested that she'd feel out of place. Everyone knew a high school reunion was hell for a spouse. She said, "I think you'll regret it."

But Ray became a big smiling boy with a boast, and Shelby agreed, even to their staying the night at the hotel in his hometown, where the reunion would be held in the ballroom.

Medford had changed: it was denser and now divided by the interstate, much busier, but still full of memories, as he told Shelby on their tour through the place, the two brick façades that had once been the entrances to single-screen movie theaters, the National Guard armory that bulked like a granite citadel, the basement stairs that had led to Joe's poolroom, the Italian cobbler, the Chinese laundry, the post office with the old murals of shipbuilding in its lobby. Now Medford had a new hotel, with a ballroom large enough to accommodate the high school reunion.

"One night, nonsmoking, king-size bed," the clerk said at the reception counter, tapping the check-in card with her pen, but she kept glancing at Shelby, uneasily, almost with pity, as though suspecting an abduction.

They drew stares later, too, as they searched the table for their name labels.

"I don't really need one. It's your night," Shelby said.

But as she said it, Ray peeled the paper backing from *Shelby Testa* and stuck the label to her beaded jacket.

A woman in a black shawl approached them as Ray was patting the label flat. The woman flourished a large yellow envelope and drew a black-and-white photograph from it, saying, "Miss Balsam's class. Third grade. Do you recognize yourself?"

"That's me, third row," Ray said. "And that's you in the front with your hands in your lap. Maura Dedrick, you were so cute!"

"Aren't I still cute?" the woman said.

Twisting her fingers together over the old photo, she was

small and thin and deeply lined, with weary eyes. No makeup, with a trace of hair on her cheeks, fretful lips, her open mouth like a grommet in canvas.

"Of course you are," Ray said.

Smiling sadly, as though he had satirized her with his sudden answer, appearing to dare him, wanting something more, she seemed to go dark with defiance. And she turned, because two other women had come to greet her.

"You remember Roberta and Annie," Maura said.

Ray said "You married Larry" to Roberta.

"He left me," Roberta said.

"I'm divorced too," Annie said.

All this time, Ray was aware that while they were talking to him they were eyeing Shelby. Annie was bigger than he remembered, not just plump and full-faced but taller – probably her shoes – and she was carrying a handbag as big as a valise. Roberta was heavily made up, wearing ropes of green beads, Gypsy-like. Ray had known them as girls. They were old women now – older than him, he felt, for their look of abandonment tinged with anger. When they became aware of his gaze they recoiled in a way that made him feel intrusive. They were fifty-eight, everyone in the room was that age, though when he surveyed the growing crowd he could see that some had fared better than others.

"May I introduce my wife?" Ray said. "This is Shelby."

The women smiled, they clucked; but Ray saw that Maura had narrowed her eyes, and Annie had leaned closer, and Roberta seemed to snicker. Putting his arm around Shelby, he felt her tremble.

Maura said to Shelby, "Angie was so mad when I went to the junior prom with Ray. Angie was my best friend – still is."

Roberta hovered over Shelby and spoke in a deaf person's shout, "He took me to Canobie Lake. He got fresh!"

"Remember what you wrote in my yearbook?" Annie said. "'You're the ultimate in feminine pulchritude.'"

"I guess I had a way with words," Ray said.

"You had a way with your hands," Roberta said, shouting again.

Maura said to Shelby, "I've known Ray Testa since I was seven years old."

Everything that he'd forgotten was real and immediate to them – the prom, the lake, the yearbook, Miss Balsam's third-grade class. He had lived his life without looking back, and he'd been happy. But had their disappointment made them dwell on the past, as a consolation?

He said, "Shel and I need a drink."

Maura said, "I'll get it."

"Don't bother."

But she insisted, and after she slipped away they spoke with Annie and Roberta. While they chatted about changes in Medford, he remembered the rowboat at Canobie Lake, the fumbled kiss, his clutching Roberta, the way she had snatched at his hands. And Annie – the summer night on her porch, her arms folded over her breasts, and "Don't, please." And when Maura returned with the drinks he recalled the back seat of his father's car at the drive-in, the half-pint of Four Roses, and "Cut it out." Horrible.

Maura handed over the two glasses of white wine. Ray sipped his, but Shelby held hers in both hands as though for balance, not raising it.

"Drink up," Maura said.

Shelby put her glass to her lips, and Ray did the same. The warm wine had the dusty taste of chalk and a tang he couldn't name, perhaps a metal – zinc, maybe, with the smack of cat piss – and he found it hard to swallow, but to please Maura he swigged again, and he knew he was right in thinking it was foul, because Shelby did no more than sip. And seeing Shelby struggle, Maura looked on with what he took to be satisfaction.

He remembered their flesh, and he sorrowed for what they had become, parodies of those young women. They had badly neglected their teeth. He felt grateful that Shelby did not resent his being so much older, but he was never more keenly aware of their age difference.

In the ballroom, where a small band played, some couples had begun to dance. His arm around Shelby's waist, as he steered her onto the floor, he could feel her body go heavy, resisting the music.

"How you doing?" he heard. It was Malcolm DeYoung, a high school friend. "Hey, who's this fine lady?"

"Shelby, I want you to meet my old friend Malcolm."

Malcolm said, "What about some food? There's a buffet over there."

They stood in the buffet line, and afterward they sat together at a table. Ray said, "I used to know everyone. But the only people I've met so far, apart from you, are those three"– Maura, Roberta, and Annie were at a nearby table. "The funny thing is, they were my girlfriends, at different times."

Malcolm said, "You got a target on your back, man," and he winked at Shelby.

"I really wanted to introduce Shel to my old friends."

Malcolm put his fork down. He stood up and said, "I don't drink these days. But let me tell you something. In a little while these people are going to get a little toasted. I don't want to be here then. I don't think you want to, neither."

Then he left them. Ray didn't speak again, nor did Shelby say anything more. She put her knife and fork on the uneaten food on her plate, and her napkin on top, like a kind of burial. Ray hugged her and said, "Ready?"

She said, "I was ready an hour ago."

They left quickly, not making eye contact, and in the hotel lobby Ray said, "Shall we go upstairs?"

"What did you do after the prom?"

"We watched the submarine races up at the Mystic Lakes."

"Show me."

He drove her through the town and to the familiar turn-off, then down to the edge of the lake, where he parked, the house lights on the far shore glistening, giving life to the black water. He held Shelby's hand, he kissed her, as he had in the first weeks of their love affair. He fumbled with her, loving the complications of her dress, delighting in the thought of her body under those silky layers slipping through his fingers, and now she seemed as eager as he was.

"Here?" he asked. "Now?"

"Why not?" She shrugged the straps from her shoulders and held her breasts, and as she presented them to him, their whiteness was illuminated by the headlights of a car, swinging past to park beside them.

"Cops," Ray said.

Shelby gasped and covered herself, clawing at her dress, and ducked her head, while Ray rolled down his window. A bright overhead light came on inside the other car, which seemed full of passengers.

"You pig." It was Maura Dedrick, her face silhouetted at her window, someone beside her – Annie, maybe – and someone else in the rear seat.

Ray was in such a hurry to get away, he started the car without raising the window, so he heard Maura still calling out abuse as he drove off, and the shouts were mingled with Shelby's choked sobs that made her sound like a sorrowing child.

Back at the hotel (the reunion was still in progress – fewer people, louder music) Shelby lay in bed shivering, repeating, "That was awful." Ray tried to soothe her, and in doing so felt useful, but when he hugged her, she said, "Not now."

Once, in a dark hour of the night, the phone rang like an alarm. Ray snatched at it, and the voice was a shriek, the accusation of a wronged woman, which Ray felt like a snatching at his head.

"Wrong number," he mumbled, and hung up, but was unable to get to sleep again.

In the morning Shelby said, "Show me whatever you're going to show me," and slid out of bed before he could touch her, "then let's go home."

He drove her to his old neighborhood and then slowly down the street where he had lived as a boy. The trees were gone, the wood-frame houses faded and small. Shelby sat, inattentive, as though distracted. But he urged her to get out of the car, and he walked her to the side of a garage where he'd scrawled a heart on the cinderblock with a spike, the petroglyph still visible after all these years. It was here, in the garage between two houses, that he'd kissed a girl – what was her name? – one Halloween night, crushing her against the wall, tasting the candy in her mouth, and running his hands over her body.

"Hello, stranger."

A great fat woman with wild hair stood, almost filling the space between the garage and the nearby house. She laughed and put her hands on her hips. She wore bruised sneakers and no socks, and when she opened her mouth Ray could see gaps in her teeth, most of her molars missing. She raised her hand, clapping a cigarette to her lips, then blew smoke at him.

"I've been waiting for you."

"Is it"– he squinted to remember the name –"Louise?"

"Who else?" she said, then, "Who's that, your daughter?" and laughed again.

Shelby said, "I'll meet you in the car."

"She's scared," Louise said triumphantly.

Ray was frightened too, but didn't want to show it. The woman was hideous, and her sudden appearance and her weird confidence made him want to run. But he sidled away slowly, saying, "Don't go away. I'll be back."

"That's what you told me that night. I've been waiting ever since!"

Had he said that? Probably – he'd told any lie for the chance to touch someone. She had scared him then, she scared him now. He had the sense that she wanted to hit him, and when she took another puff of her cigarette and tossed the butt aside, he feared that she was coming for him. She was big and unkempt and reckless-looking.

"Please," he said, and put his hands up to protect his face and ran clumsily to his car.

Louise did not follow him. She watched from the passageway beside the garage, potbellied, her feet apart, and as he started his car she shook another cigarette from the pack, fearsome in her confidence.

"I haven't seen her for years," Ray said. Shelby did not reply; she was mute, her arms folded, faced forward. "Imagine, she still lives there."

"Waiting for you."

"That's crazy."

But when they got home there was a further shock. Ray parked and noticed a white slip of paper thumbtacked to the front door. The idea that someone had come up the long driveway and through his gate and left this note disturbed him. And he was more disturbed when he read the note: *Ray, You must of gone out. Sorry I missed you – Ellie.*

"Who's Ellie?" Shelby said.

He was thinking *must of,* and he knew Ellie had to have been his college girlfriend. She'd become pregnant. "I missed my period." It had happened just about the time they were breaking up. She told her parents, who arranged for her to have an abortion in another state – it was illegal in Massachusetts then. When it was over they'd written to his parents, denouncing him, saying he'd ruined their daughter's life. He had not seen her since. And that was who Ellie was – Ellie Bryant.

But he said, "I don't know anyone by that name." It was the first lie he'd told Shelby in all the time he'd known her. Shelby seemed to guess this, and smiled in triumph. Ray said, "Maybe an old patient."

Another bad night, and in the following days, each evening he returned home with Shelby from the office, he expected Ellie to be waiting for him. Friday came. He knew something was wrong when he passed the front gate. The gate, always latched, was ajar – a small thing, but for a frightened house owner, alert to details, it had significance. And he heard on his nerves the creak of the porch swing at the side of the house.

Shelby said, "There's someone here."

"I'll check – don't worry," he said, and braced himself for Ellie.

She was on the porch swing, facing away. He saw the woman's back, her cold purply hands – it was November – on the suspended chains that held the seat, the kerchief tightened over her head. She turned and the swing squeaked again.

"You." The snarled word made her face ugly, as though with pain.

He had no idea who the woman was, and before he could speak, Shelby came up behind him and said, "What are you doing here?"

"Visiting my old friend Ray Testa," the woman said.

"Are you Ellie?"

The woman frowned at the name. She said, "No. Ask him who I am. Go on, Ray, tell her."

But he didn't know. Even so, he started to gabble in fear.

"Think," she said. "You used to visit me and my husband in New Hampshire. He was a photographer. You pretended you were interested in his pictures. You were very chatty. And then, when he was away, you visited me. You couldn't keep your hands off me. Always sneaking around, sniff-sniff." To Shelby she said, "This man drove two hundred miles to touch me."

And the effort seemed preposterous, because the woman was gray, with papery skin and sad eyes and reddened gums showing in her downturned mouth. He hated himself for seeing only her fragility and her age, but because of her defiance it was all that mattered.

He said, "Joyce."

"See? He knows who I am."

"What do you want?"

"Just to pay a friendly visit."

"Please go."

The woman said, "Isn't it funny? You drove all that way to see me – took half a day to get to my house, and all the probing, to make sure Richard was away. And now you can't wait to get rid of me."

With that, she stamped on the porch floorboards and hoisted herself from the swing. She stood leaning sideways, and she came at him, maintaining the same crooked posture, with a slight limp, a suggestion that she was about to fall down.

"This is how he'll treat you one day, sweetheart," she said to Shelby.

Ray let Joyce pass, then followed her to the driveway and kept watching her – where was her car? How had she gotten here? – but, still watching her, he saw her vanish before she got to the road.

Shelby was in tears, her face in her hands, miserable on the sofa. She recoiled when he reached for her.

"You know them," Shelby said. "All of them."

She refused to allow him to console her. She was disgusted, she said. She didn't eat that night. She slept in the spare room thereafter. He regretted their sleeping apart, until one night soon after Joyce's visit, he woke in his bed and became aware not of breathing but of a swelling shadow, someone holding her breath in the room.

He said, "Shelby?"

The soft laugh he heard was not Shelby's.

"You probably think you had a hard time," the woman said, becoming more substantial, emerging from the darkness as she spoke. "In those days, an abortion was a criminal offense. A doctor could lose his license for performing one. And it was painful and bloody and humiliating. It had another effect – I was never able to bear another child. I got married. My husband left me when he realized we'd never have children. I became a teacher, because I loved kids. I recently retired. I live on a pension. You destroyed my life."

Just as he thought she was going to hit him, she disappeared.

In the morning Shelby said she'd heard him. "Who was it?"

"Talking in my sleep. I was dreaming."

Certain that he was lying, Shelby said she could not bear to hear another word from him, and when he attempted to explain, she said in her unanswerable, dead-certain voice, "You keep saying how old and feeble they are, and how repugnant. But don't you realize who they look like?"

He gaped at her, feeling futile.

"They all look like you. I sometimes think they are you. Each person in our past is an aspect of us. You need to know that."

Ray called his ex-wife, but got her voice mail. "Angie," he pleaded, "I don't know how you're doing it, but please stop. I'll agree to anything if you stop them showing up."

For several weeks no women from his past intruded, and Ray believed that Angie had gotten the message. He even called again and left a thank-you on her voice mail.

Shelby demanded that they see a marriage counselor. Ray agreed, but on the condition that the counselor be in Boston, far from their home, so that their anonymity was assured. "I want it to be a woman," Shelby said, and found a Dr. Pat Devlin, whose office was near Massachusetts General Hospital.

On their first visit, after they filled out the insurance forms, they were shown into the doctor's office.

"Please take a seat," Dr. Devlin said. "Make yourselves comfortable."

She read the insurance forms, running her finger down the answers to the questions on the back of the page. She was heavy, jowly, almost regal, wearing a white smock, her hair cut short, tapping her thick finger as she read, and her chair emitted complaint-like squeaks as she shifted in it, her movements provoked by what seemed her restless thoughts.

"I'm afraid I can't take you on," she said, sighing, removing her glasses, and facing Ray, who smiled helplessly. "Did you do this deliberately, to make me feel even worse?"

Ray said, "The appointment was Shelby's idea."

Looking hard at Ray, the doctor said, "I thought I'd seen the last of you and heard the last of your excuses. Maybe it's unprofessional of me to say this – but it's outrageous that you should come here out of the blue after the way you treated me." She gripped the armrests of her chair as though restraining herself, and holding herself this way, her head back, she seemed like an emperor. "Now I must ask you to leave."

Shelby was silent in the elevator, because of the other passengers, but in the street she said, "Tell me who she is, and don't lie to me."

"We were at BU together," he said. "Premed."

"You're stalling," Shelby said.

He was. But he had been thrown by "Dr. Devlin." Her name was Pat Dorian – Armenian, a chemistry major. She was beautiful, with a sultry central-Asian cast to her face, full lips, and thick jet-black hair. He'd taken her to a fraternity party and they'd gotten drunk, and she'd said, "I feel sick. I have to lie down," and she'd fallen asleep in his room, in his own bed, only to wake in the morning half-naked but fully alert, saying, "Did you touch me? What did you do to me? Tell me!"

He'd said, truthfully, that he could not remember; but he was half-naked too. And that was the beginning of a back-and-forth of recrimination that ended with Pat changing her major to psychology, so that she would not have to face Ray again in the chem lab.

"I knew her long ago," Ray said.

"Don't tell me any more," Shelby said. She turned her gray eyes on him and said, "She looks like you too."

Shelby became humorless and doubting, and she was like a much older woman, slow in the way she moved, as though fearing she might trip, quieter and more reflective, seeming rueful when Ray passed the bedroom and saw her lying alone – her bedroom. He slept in the spare room now.

He wanted to tell her that most people have a flawed past, and act unthinkingly, and that we move on from them. New experiences take their place, new memories, better ones, and all the old selves remain interred in a forgetfulness that was itself merciful. This was the process of aging, each new decade burying the previous one, and the long-ago self was a stranger. But for these women, all they had was the past. They dragged him back to listen to them, to take part in this ritual of unfulfillment, the reunion of endless visitations, old women, old loves, old objects of desire with faces like bruised fruit.

Instead of telling Shelby, he called her father and told him some of this. He did not seemed surprised to hear it. He hardly reacted, and when Ray pressed him for an opinion, the man said, "I can't help you."

Ray said, "She's like a stranger."

"That's my Shelby," the man said, and hung up.

Shelby still worked with him. Her father's abruptness (he had also seemed grimly amused) had rattled him, and so he said to her, "You are everything to me now. Those women are all gone and forgotten."

This was in the office. There was a knock, the receptionist saying, "We have a new patient."

Ray went cold when he saw her tilted back in the chair, awaiting his examination. She did not even have to say, "Remember me?" He remembered her. He remembered his mistake. She was Sharon, from the cleaning company, and he was surprised that someone so young – no more than eighteen or so – was doing this menial job. Why wasn't she in school? He'd asked her that. "I hate school," she said. "I want to make some money." She seemed to linger in her work, and one evening when they were alone, Ray had surprised her in her mopping, and kissed her, hoping for more. But she'd pushed him away, and wiped her mouth with the back of her hand, and never came back. That same year Shelby had become his hygienist, so she knew nothing of Sharon. He'd never seen Sharon again, nor thought of her – it was only a foolish, impulsive, hopeful kiss! – until now.

She stared at him with implacable eyes; her very lack of expression seemed accusatory. She lay canted back in the chair as Shelby hooked on her earpieces and adjusted the protective goggles. Sharon's mouth was prominent and her cold eyes were blurred by the plastic. She seemed weirdly masked, with an upside-down face, from where Ray stood, slightly behind her with Shelby. Her mouth began to move, the bite of the teeth reversed.

"You got yourself a hot assistant now," Sharon said. "Bet you kiss her when no one's looking. Like you did to me."

"This is my wife," Ray said, hating the way Sharon spoke. "Now open wide and let me have a look."

"I can't do this," Shelby said. She gathered the loops of the suction device and tossed them into the sink.

"Shel," he said, then, seeing it was hopeless, that Shelby had closed the door behind her, he attended to Sharon, his fingers in her mouth, gagging her. He wanted to pull out her tongue.

When he finished the cleaning he said, "You've never been here before as a patient. I haven't seen you for years. You don't need any serious work. Why did you come?"

"Just a spur-of-the-moment thing," Sharon said. "Hey, you probably think that kissing me and touching me was something I'd forget."

He sighed, he was going to shout, but he forced himself to speak calmly. "I'm done. I've knocked some barnacles off your teeth. Don't come back. If you do, I will refuse to see you."

Now Sharon's goggles were off and she was upright, blinking like a squirrel. She licked a smear of toothpaste from her lips and said, "I won't be back. I don't have to. I've done what I needed to do."

"What was that?"

"Make you remember."

But it would be a new memory. He had not recalled her as so plain, so fierce-faced. She had been young, attractive, in a T-shirt and shorts, with a long-handled mop in her hands, and now she'd accused him of forgetting her. But he had not forgotten – he remembered her as a girl, alone in the corridor of his office, holding the sudden promise of pleasure. The shock to him on her return was that she had aged, that she was raw-boned and resentful and no longer attractive.

Before going home to Shelby that day he saw himself in the bathroom mirror and hated his face. He hated what time had done to it, he hated what time had done to these women. He had flirted and pawed these old women. *They all look like you.* He hated the sight of his hands. *I sometimes think they are you. Each person in our past is an aspect of us. You need to know that.*

Shelby treated him as though he was dangerous and tricky. She seemed afraid to be with him because of who might show up, to remind him of what he'd done and who he was, an old beast they haunted because they could not forgive him.

Shelby and he lived separately in the house, took turns in the kitchen, ate their meals apart, more like hostile roommates than a married couple – a reenactment of his last months with Angie.

He called Angie again, but this time her number had been disconnected. Then he found out why. A patient said casually, just as he'd finished putting on a crown, "Sorry about Angie."

Misunderstanding, Ray began to explain, and then realized that the patient was telling him that Angie had died.

It had happened two weeks before. He found the details online, on the *Medford Transcript* website. *Collapsed and died after a short illness.* Instead of going home, he drove the seventy-five miles to the cemetery and knelt at her grave. A metal marker with her name, courtesy of the funeral home, had been inserted in the rug-like cover of new sod. He told himself that he was sorrowful, but he did not feel it: he was relieved, he felt lighter, he blamed Angie for the swarm of old lovers. This feeling scared him in the dampness of the cemetery, where he suspected he was being watched. It was then, looking around, that he saw that Angie was buried next to her mother, a reunion of sorts.

He told Shelby that Angie had died –"It's a turning point!"– that they could start all over again.

"You actually seem glad that Angie's dead," Shelby said. "Poor Angie."

Shelby stopped coming to work. She didn't want to stay at home either, as though fearing a woman would appear unbidden, a hag from the past, to confront Ray, to humiliate her. She seemed to regard him as the monster he believed himself to be in his worst moments, the embodiment of everything he'd done, and now, from the return of these offended women, she knew every one of his reckless transgressions.

With the death of Angie, the visitations ceased. But, demoralized, humiliated, Shelby left him. She did not divorce him at once. She demanded a house, and he provided it. She asked for severance pay at the office, and got it. And by degrees they separated. They spoke through lawyers until it was final, and he was alone.

Ray is not surprised when, one night, he is awoken by a clatter, as of someone hurrying in darkness. It is a familiar sound. He awaits the visitation, hoping it might make him less lonely. Perhaps it is Angie, who has come to mock him. He hopes to beg her forgiveness. No, it is not Angie's voice. It is Shelby's, and it is triumphant. But the body, the hag's face, is his own.

Rangers

YOU'LL HAVE TO excuse us," the young woman said at the rounded pulpit-like curve of the gleaming bar. She wore a low-cut blouse and had been listening intently, as though taking an order from the man beside her, who turned away to speak on his cell phone. "We just got married. Plus, we're new here."

Her sudden blurted candor silenced the drinkers. There was only the low bubbling sound of the TV. The woman's face was pink-blotched and hot with exertion. She repeated what she'd said to a smiling man in a camouflage jacket and cap by the cash register, who had also been talking on a cell phone. He said "Doesn't that call for a drink?" to the barman next to him ringing up a sale.

"Just a Coke for me," the woman said. "I found out today I'm expecting."

A bottle of beer and a shot of whiskey were set before the man next to her. He smiled past his phone and nodded his thanks.

"It's Leon's girlfriend. I don't care – can I call you Sarge?" She tugged at her blouse, shaking her breasts loose at the barman. "I'm Beanie."

The barman leaned closer, open-mouthed, holding his fat hands back as you would restrain a pair of puppies.

"That's enough of that," Sarge said. "And you just married."

"Anyone ever tell you your husband's got your eyes and your coloration," a nearby woman said. "I'm a cosmetologist."

"He is also my best friend," Beanie said, but didn't smile.

"I'm making a donation to the jar in your name," Sarge said.

Then, solemnly, "Beanie." The jar was a large clear glass flask, with a colored Stars and Stripes label pasted on and a handwritten sign hung on its neck, *For the Troops.* The plugged and slotted lid was padlocked. You wrote your name on a ten-dollar bill. "More than two thousand in there. For the troops."

The cosmetologist said, "Funny how camo makes you conspicuous, rather than the other way around."

"Desert camo," Sarge said. "Ranger camo."

Seizing the barman's attention again with her breasts, Beanie said, "Like them?" and rattled a yellow plastic pharmacy container of pills. But the barman's face was unreadable.

They were back the next night, the serious man Leon and his cell phone, the woman Beanie drenched in light, showing her breasts and the pills, saying, "I don't even care!"

Sarge greeted them, then said to the barman, "But I'm not going alone," and at closing time, to Beanie, "My friend here and I are joining you for a party. You gave him a thrill up his leg."

Later, in the empty parking lot, under the light, the four of them were silent but for Sarge, who, taking a pistol from Leon, said, "Here's what I want you to do for us, buddy," and the barman looked up at the three severe faces.

Talking softly, the three approached a house with the sign on the lawn *For Sale by Owner,* and when the muscular young man answered the door and said, "I was expecting the married couple, like you explained," Leon said, "This is our friend."

"Can we talk to the owner?" Sarge said, frowning under his cap brim.

"You're looking at him, soldier," the young man in the doorway said, pleased with himself, and folded his arms as though to emphasize his tattoos.

"We don't want to waste your time."

"I was military too. I know about wasted time."

"Because you didn't embrace the suck," Sarge said.

"What'd you learn?"

"I learned there's more ways of dying than ways of living."

The man leaned back from the words. "You said something about scoping out the house."

They loped from room to room, the young man striding behind them, praising the features. In his confident voice he said, "You two look so much alike."

Beanie said, "He's like a brother to me."

Sarge said, "I don't think this is the one."

"Hardly gave it a chance." And the man pushed his sleeve up further to show the rest of the tattoo, a shapely blue mermaid. He said, "Rapture of the Deep."

They visited three more houses, *For Sale by Owner,* walking to the front door, full of compliments, seeming eager to move in. "Got a car?" Sarge asked at the first one.

"Out back. What's left of it."

The others were short visits too.

The fourth, a farmhouse off the road, lay in semidarkness.

"You mustn't mind us, we're both a little deaf," the old man said, letting them in. An old woman squinted from her chair and looked futile. She said, "Married sixty-two years."

Beanie murmured, "Awesome."

"But somehow it seems longer than that," the man said.

"Them are old. Them are nice," Sarge said of some objects on the mantelpiece – silver, some porcelain, a clock.

"Family stuff. Mother keeps saying we should insure them." The man smiled at Beanie. "What do you look so worried for?"

"Hope your car's insured, nice-looking ride like that," Leon said.

"I've always had a Caddy."

"Tell me about it," Sarge said. Then, "Let's see that cellar of yours. Maybe we can convert it."

Rolling down the window of the Caddy – Leon beside him, Beanie in the back seat – Sarge said to the skinny woman in white boots leaning against the door, "That's not sufficient. You need to turn a few more tricks, Suzie."

"Melba." The woman's smile set one of her eyes twitching. "But anyway, how about you? Feel like a party? What about your friend there?"

Beanie said, "You should do yourself a favor and get an intervention."

"You got his features," the woman said, as though trying to make a friend.

"I'm intervening," Sarge said. He crumbled a pill in his palm. "This here's for you. You can snort it or use it the other way, as an innuendo."

Leon said, "She's wasting our time."

"Give her a break," Beanie said.

But Sarge said, "Hop in, Suzie." And to Leon, "Regular cash flow. She's sitting on a gold mine." And when the skinny woman hesitated, and Sarge snatched her wrist hard, it was Beanie who let out a cry.

In the back seat, moved by the infant depicted on the box next to her, the woman said, "I used to have one of them baby monitors." Her eyes brimmed with tears.

That week they worked out of a motel, Beanie bringing men, one at a time, from the bars in town and turning them over to her. With the woman in a stupor they drove to the coast and set up in a condo near the harbor, Beanie managing the johns, saying to Leon and Sarge, "This is women's work. Keep off."

At the condo, Beanie said to the man she'd brought, "I want to introduce you to my sister," and unlocked the too-warm and dimly lit back bedroom. "And no rough stuff." Sarge, and sometimes Leon, listened for trouble, and stepped into the hallway to collect the money afterward from the startled man.

Sarge said, "Ever think – a guy will crawl across broken glass to get a woman for sex. But when it's over he won't spend five minutes with her for a burger. Do women know that?"

"It's why we say maybe," Beanie said.

Still listening, Sarge shook his head. He was looking out the window.

"They got boat rides here," he said. "Harbor cruises."

Leon said softly, "If Beanie's not coming, count me out."

"You look pretty buoyant to me." Sarge was smiling, not at what he said but at what he heard on the baby monitor. "But swimming was always your Achilles tendon. Hey, you could have been a Ranger too."

"As if it mattered over there," Leon said. "Because nothing mattered."

"Wrong," Sarge said. "It's when you get home that nothing matters." His head was still tilted toward the monitor. "No one's listening."

"Which one of them is your husband?" the skinny woman asked Beanie one morning over coffee.

Beanie frowned at her. "Neither one."

"Because both of them hit on me all the time."

The afternoon the john said to the woman, "If this is a financial transaction, then I have to inform you you're breaking the law and that you're under arrest," the three others hearing it on the monitor hurried downstairs.

"Suzie's nothing to cry about," Sarge said to Beanie.

"Melba," she said, and put her face in her hands.

"No more risks," Sarge said. "We've got enough money to get us anywhere – like California, maybe."

Beanie said, "I want to go back. I feel like something bad's going to happen to us away from home."

"That's old-fashioned," Sarge said. "It's what I always liked about you."

Leon stared, his eyes locked on him and going darker.

"Wish we still had that great car," Beanie said.

"You don't win by hunkering down. You win by moving. But that car was conspicuous trouble. And I'm never going back."

A safe car was the secret, he said. And clean plates. And not speeding, not getting stopped by the law, staying among transients in RV parks, one or two nights, then roll.

They picked up a young man hitchhiking, to tease him. Sarge reached for Beanie's blouse, saying, "Like these, kid?" and Leon, "Where's your job?" When the student said, "There's no jobs anymore," Leon stopped the car and screamed, "Get a job, loser!" Sarge got out, panting. He dragged the boy onto the road. "Drop and give me fifty!"

At a small town, they asked directions at the local police station, one of Sarge's dares. Leon whispered "Look" at the posted mug shots, *Level 2 Sex Offenders,* with details of their offenses and their home addresses.

Leon said, "A hajji."

They visited the man – Leon's idea, and he was the one who knocked. "Police," Leon said, the heel of his hand on his holstered gun. "We have a serious complaint," and stepped inside while the others waited in the car.

Afterward, trembling in the back seat, he said, "Beanie, while I was in there, did he touch you?" and held his raw swollen hands against his thighs.

Beanie pressed her lips together and faced him with widened eyes.

"I couldn't help myself." Leon's pale face showed pink-blotched cheeks. His wet hands had blackened the cloth of his jeans.

"Me, that's my problem too," Sarge said. "Thrill up my leg. I used to wonder why fat people are always hungry. I guess I know now."

At the RV park that night, Leon said, "Beanie and I need to talk. We'll be right back."

"Hurry up. Three whole days here," Sarge said. "This isn't the safest of places."

After their months of absence, Beanie and Leon resumed living in the family house. Whenever Sarge's name came up,

Beanie said, "It was all his fault. We should never have hooked up with him."

Leon said, "He was my buddy over there."

"Big buddy."

Leon shrugged. "One of those vets that keeps his gun."

But Beanie showed Leon that she had the gun. Soon afterward she got rid of it, threw it overboard from the boat at Hollins Pond.

"Why did you do that?"

"If you want it so bad you can swim for it."

Leon winced. Instead of replying, he gripped the sides of the boat and steadied himself.

"But I don't need a gun where you're concerned. I know what you did."

"Cut it out."

He said it again. He knocked and repeated it that night at her bedroom door.

When Leon drowned in the boating accident, Beanie alerted the police. The pond was dragged, but Leon's body was not found until a week later, swollen, buoyant, bumping the bars of the spillway where the river began.

The local newspaper reporting his death wrote that they could not describe Leon without describing Beanie. They were both twenty-two, graduates of the high school, and lived with their grandparents, who rarely visited the school, even when Leon and Beanie were performing.

In school, Leon and Beanie Turner were known as the dancers, and seeing them dance put the audience in mind of one person and a shadow, smooth and symmetrical their moves, the way they glided and swayed, old-fashioned, back and forth. They practiced all the time in the basement.

Leon had proudly served his country, and after his discharge had returned home.

They spoke of turning professional, calling themselves the Turner Twins.

The death of Leon utterly changed Beanie. She was still grieving, people said. She vanished, then reappeared months later with a newborn infant – not a surprise. But after the blood tests on the baby and the subsequent questions, there was a knock on her door.

When Beanie answered, she saw two policemen.

"I knew it."

Action

MY FATHER WAS a suspicious man – and, as a widower, wounded, too. My mother died when I was ten, and he was overly concerned about my welfare. He showed it in the following way: he would take my chin and use it to lift my head and smell it, as though examining a melon for ripeness. He was checking for cigarette smoke, a girl's perfume, the reek of the poolroom or a back alley, for the odor of disobedience. There was never anything. Even so, to test me, he'd say, "Where?" meaning, "Where have you been?"

He was thrifty in all ways, with money, with time; he always tore a stick of chewing gum in half and put the other half in his pocket for later. And he was thrifty in using the fewest possible words. If he wanted me to move out of the way he said, "Shift," or if I asked for a favor he said, "Never." He hated explanations.

Gruff with me but talkative with customers, he seemed to me to be two people. That did not surprise me. I was also two people, the obedient son stacking shoes at the foot of the stairs and, out of my father's sight, someone else, I was not sure who, but certainly not the person he was used to.

All through high school I worked for him at the shoe store, hating every minute of it, like confinement. He claimed he needed me, but business was slow ("Slack"). I knew he had me there, tidying the store, sorting shoe sizes, to keep me out of trouble. His letterhead was printed *Louis Lecomte and Son,* which looked important, but the reality was my father dozing in one of the customers' chairs upstairs and me in the basement stacking boxes.

My father's worry about me made me think I was dangerous. I could hear the tremor in his voice when he called out, "Albert," and if I didn't reply, he'd call again, "Al!" then "Bertie!" with growing alarm – where was I? – until at last I said, "Yuh?" and he was calmed. Cruel of me to delay like that, but I was trapped. I missed all the school football games. I never joined a team myself because I couldn't take time off to practice. My friends hung around Brigham's after school, looking for action.

My father had succeeded. Sometimes I felt very young, other times like an old man; no action for me.

As a menial (no pay, just pocket money), I dusted the shoes on display, helped take inventory, or polished the Brannock Device, which was a metal clamp-like contraption for measuring feet – the width and length. I also ran errands.

I was on one today; the errands were the only freedom I had. But it was always the same trip – picking up a pair of shoes, sometimes two, from a warehouse in Boston, near South Station, on Atlantic Avenue.

Before I left, my father raised his hand and said, "No Eddie," meaning, "Don't associate with Eddie Springer," whom he considered a bad influence. What I liked about Eddie was his saying, "I'm a wicked-bad influence."

I took the electric car to Sullivan Square, climbing the stairs, waited on the platform in front of *Spitting Is Forbidden,* then rode the subway to South Station, and repeated the shoe size to the man at the warehouse counter. He did not greet me or even comment. He made out an invoice by hand, measured a length of string, and tied the box while I leaned on the counter.

A woman at a desk behind him smiled at me. "You look just like your father."

I didn't know what to say. My father was more than fifty years old. I could smell her perfume, like strong soap, and I imagined that her blond hair, too, had a fragrance. Seated, she seemed small, doll-like, but sure of herself.

The man said, "Ask your father why he only buys one pair at a time."

The woman winked at me. She said, "His father only sells one pair at a time."

"And when is he going to pay me what he owes me?"

"I'll ask him." The suggestion that my father might be tricky did not dismay me; it reassured me in my own weakness and made me admire him.

As I left, holding the box with a clip-on handle, a wooden cylinder with wire hooked through it, the woman said, "Don't listen to Grumpy. Your father's a great guy. Tell him Vie was asking for him. Violet."

Maybe that was his other side, a ladies' man and a traveler, a man of the world now down on his luck as a widower and the father of a sulky teenager. But if so, that did not make him forgiving. It made him more suspicious. He knew what a boy was capable of, and was overprotective. He was puritanical and hated any kind of foolery – loud music and loud talk, mentions of girls, of sunny frivolous places like California or Florida, any sort of indiscipline.

But that woman Vie knew something about my father that I didn't, and this idea that he was concealing a part of his life made me dawdle in the errand, in my own concealment.

I cut through South Station and bought a jelly donut. The woman at the counter wearing a white apron and white cap lifted the donut with tongs from the tray and dropped it into a small bag.

"Ten cents," she said, and I gave her the dime. As I stepped away, a man with a mean face leaned over and said, "Give me that." He looked like a gargoyle, and his smell and his ugliness made him seem violent.

Handing over the bag, I held on to the shoebox and hurried out of the station as though I'd done something wrong. I went up State Street, walking fast, until I got to Milk Street. I had the sense that the man might be following me. I went into Goodspeed's bookstore. The old woman at the desk said, "You can't bring any parcels in here."

Near the corner of Milk and Washington I stopped at a shop that sold knives and cameras. I knew the shop. There was always someone, usually two or three men, looking at the window display of knives – all sorts of hunting knives, wide blades, jagged blades, shiny, bone handles, bowie knives, Buck knives, Swiss Army knives – and in the adjoining window the cameras were set out, all sizes.

A grinning man in a long coat and glasses said, "Hey, look at that camera, how small it is. That one down there."

Like a toy, a tiny camera, propped on a small box with a tiny red roll of film.

"You could get some swell pictures with that. Fit in the palm of your hand," the man said. "Take it anywhere."

I said, "I guess so. It's really small. Maybe German."

He put his face near mine as the man had done in South Station, demanding my donut. "I took some pictures of my roommate when he was bollocky." The man was smiling horribly and making a face, and he dislodged his glasses. He pushed them back into place with his dirty thumb.

But I was backing away. I said, "That's okay."

"I could take a picture of you bollocky," he said. "Wanna let me?"

"No thanks."

"You're probably too shy."

"No. It's not that. I just don't want to."

I walked quickly away into the sidewalk crowd and ducked past Raymond's department store. I crossed Washington Street and hurried up Brewer, lingered in front of the joke shop, then to Tremont, up Park to the black soldiers memorial and Hooker's statue, and down Beacon. Just as I approached Scollay Square, five black boys, big and small, came toward me, filling the sidewalk.

My heart was beating fast as I hurried through traffic to the other side of the street, and I kept walking until I got to the Old Howard theater. Ever since leaving the shoe warehouse

I'd been escaping, and it seemed strange that, trying to avoid trouble, I'd found myself here. I had come here with Eddie Springer one Saturday six months before. I'd bumped into him on another errand.

Eddie knew the corners of Boston and all the shortcuts. He had shown me the knife shop and Raymond's and the joke shop; my father had shown me the memorial to the black regiment and Hooker's statue and the Union Oyster House. Between my father and Eddie, Boston had no secrets for me.

It was all exteriors, though. I never went into any stores. What was the point? I had no money, I was afraid of being confronted. But Eddie knew all the stores, and had even been inside the Old Howard and seen a burlesque show and repeated the jokes. A stripper said to a heckler, "Meet me in my dressing room. If I'm late, start without me," which made Eddie laugh so hard he didn't notice that I had not understood.

We had come this way in the winter, this same route, from South Station toward the Common, then via Scollay Square – a detour – and along Cambridge Street to the back slope of Beacon Hill.

When I realized that in this afternoon escape I was retracing that winter walk with Eddie, through the same streets, making the same stops, I felt safer. I knew that I could make my way onward to North Station and Sullivan Square to the electric cars, to bring the box of shoes back to my father.

Eddie was a hero to me for his being so confident and for knowing Boston, which was like knowing the world. He had a girlfriend. We'd stopped to see her. He'd introduced me to her – Paige.

As on that day with Eddie, I had nothing to do and nowhere to go on this summer afternoon of hot sidewalks and sharp smells and strangers, the air of the city thick with humidity under a heavy gray sky. It all stank pleasantly of wickedness, and if I'd known anything of sensuality I would have recognized it as sensual. But I was fifteen, small for my age, soon to enter my sophomore year of high school. Away from my house I was not sure who I was; it was as though I was walking the streets searching for a self.

Eddie was three years older than me, a neighbor who was kind to me because he knew my mother was dead. He smoked, he drank beer, he had this girlfriend Paige, and it seemed that the farther I walked down the back slope of Beacon Hill the more I resembled him. I remembered Paige: blond, small – her smallness made me bolder. She had blue eyes and a lovely smile and didn't say much. Eddie claimed she was an Indian, from Veazie, Maine, on the river, and he said she was a dancer.

"You like her."

"She's action." Saying that, he believed he'd told me everything.

I wished he were with me now. These days, when I was alone, I had no self, nothing to put forward, no idea that I dared express, no voice, nothing but the bravado I'd learned from Eddie, even his sayings. "Eyes like pinwheels," he used to say. Or "She's easy," as he said of Paige. I had no self at all.

I remembered Paige clearly. She had a broad, blankish face, but kindly eyes. She listened and responded with her eyes. Her smallness made her seem girlish, but she was older than Eddie and much older than me, twenty-something. She seemed strong – experienced and sure of herself. She had no airs, she was friendly, though she didn't say much.

"She's action" was a sly way of describing her – something unspoken. But when I'd been with her I felt I was in the presence of an adult who liked me. She had treated me as an equal and had not mentioned that she was eight or ten years older. I think that Eddie took me to meet her to introduce me to a life remote from mine and to show me what a man of the world he was. Being with him, I felt that I was learning how to be a man of the world.

I liked the idea that she looked demure and patient – solid

and reassuring, small and close to the ground, the ideal of motherhood. But deep down she was wild, her other self hidden, to be awakened by Eddie, who described her howling when he made love to her.

"She knows a few tricks," he said. "And so do I."

Paige lived alone in a basement on the other side of Beacon Hill, not an apartment but one large room, the kitchen at the back wall, a double bed to the right, some heavily upholstered chairs near the front door.

On this late-summer afternoon, crossing town, carrying my box of shoes, I walked slowly downhill, looking for her door. But I didn't want to knock, nor was I sure which door was hers, because on that side of the hill the houses were so much alike. I walked down the opposite side of the street, glancing across, and saw that some of the basement doors were open. Encouraged by the open doors, I crossed the street, and when I passed her house I saw Paige inside, framed by the doorway, standing at an ironing board, shaking water onto a red cloth and then running her iron over it.

"Hi."

With the bright daylight behind me as I peered down, my face must have been darkened, because she looked uncertain, even a bit worried. She lifted her iron, holding it like a weapon.

Instead of saying my name, I said, "Eddie's friend. Al."

Still holding the iron, she angled her body a bit to see me sideways, away from the light, and then said, "You! Come on in!" and laughed in a gasping sort of way, as if in relief.

I walked down the short flight of stairs to the basement room and sat in one of the upholstered chairs, exactly where I had sat on that winter day six months before when I'd come with Eddie.

"I hope it's okay," I said, because she had seemed worried when she'd first looked at me.

"It's nice to see you," she said, and returned to her ironing – and I could tell from the smoothness of her movements that she meant what she said. She pushed the iron without effort across the red cloth, and with her free hand she folded the cloth in half and ironed its fold, giving it a crease, then deftly folded it again.

"I just happened to be in the neighborhood," I said. This explanation gave me pleasure, because it wasn't true, yet sounded plausible, even suave.

Paige smiled, clapping her iron down, and I suspected she didn't believe me. She said, "There's not much going on in this part of the world."

"I was headed to North Station."

She seemed to guess that it was a lame excuse – she was literal-minded and truthful in the way of a person with no small talk. She said, "How about a drink?"

"I'm all set."

"There's some lemonade in the fridge – help yourself," she said, tossing her head, loosening her hair.

I felt it was beyond me to find the lemonade and a glass and pour myself a drink. Eddie would have known. It occurred to me that I was out of my depth and that, had she not been ironing in the open doorway, I might not have approached her. Without a word, she went to the refrigerator and poured me a glass of lemonade.

To fill the silence, I said, "I haven't seen Eddie lately."

She bowed her head and went on ironing.

"He changed schools. I guess he wasn't too happy in Maine." She still said nothing. "I'd like to go there sometime." She nodded. "Like Eddie says, cold in the winter, and the summer's only a few days in July."

She worked the red cloth into a tighter square and pressed it with the heel of her hand before applying the iron.

"And I don't belong there. My mother said once, 'Just because a cat has kittens inside an oven doesn't make them biscuits.'" She didn't react. I now felt sure I'd raised the wrong subject. I said, "But my mother's dead."

This roused her. She looked pained. She said, "I'm really sorry. Please have some more lemonade?"

I showed her my glass was half full. I said, "How's the dancing?"

"It's okay," she said, and in the tone I'd used, "The dancing."

"Whereabouts do you do it?"

"You know the High Bar?"

"Not sure."

"Combat Zone," she said, frowning.

"Never been to the High Bar."

"You've got to be twenty-one," she said. She was about to say more, but folded the red cloth again instead. "It's kind of a rough place."

"I'd like to see you there."

"No, you don't," she said. "You're better off somewhere else. Like get a good education."

That was friendly. It reassured me, because I felt that I was getting to know her better, and something more might happen, and it excited me because I didn't know what.

She was a solid presence, standing with her legs apart in her loose shorts, one hand smoothing and folding the red piece of cloth that was growing smaller with each fold, the heavy iron in her other hand. Wisps of her hair framed her damp face. I was not used to seeing a woman dressed like this, almost undressed, in her own house, and that excited me too.

"So where did you learn to dance?" I asked.

She smiled again, shook her head. "It's pretty easy," she said. "The guys don't come there for the dancing."

As we talked, my eyes were drawn to her bed, which was neatly made, with plump pillows and a teddy bear propped up against them, and on the side table a book. I could easily read the gold lettering on the spine, because it was a title I knew,

The New Testament. That confused me. It didn't fit with the image that Eddie had given me, *She's action*. I saw us in the bed, doing – what? I'd never been in bed with a woman before.

"Darn," she said.

The spell broke briefly, but the way she put down her iron and fussed, hiking up her untucked blouse, looking uncertain, made her seem sexy again.

"I'm out of starch."

As she spoke, a shadow moved across her face, filling the doorway.

"Just thought I'd stop in." The slow way the man descended the stairs emphasized his bulk, as though he was climbing down a ladder, testing each step before taking another. But when he got to the bottom step – and I stood, my nervousness making me self-consciously polite – I saw that he was not much taller than I was, but twice as heavy.

"Vic."

He went over and chucked Paige under the chin. She jerked her face away as if she expected to be slapped. "You behaving yourself?"

"Have a coffee."

"I'll have what he's having."

"Lemonade," Paige said. "It's in the fridge. In a pitcher. I have to get some starch. I'll be right back."

"I should go," I said.

"I won't be a minute."

"Don't go," Vic said at the refrigerator, pouring himself a glass of lemonade.

Then Paige was out the door and up the stairs.

I sat down. Vic sat in the chair next to me, but only breathed, sighed, didn't say anything. A sound came from my throat – a nervous noise, a whicker of anxiety, *Heh-heh*.

"Heh-heh," Vic said, the exact sound, and he stared at me. His face was mean and misshapen, with full lips. He was hunched forward in the chair, looking fatter, and I could hear his breathing, like gas escaping. He said, "I know who you are. You're Eddie."

"No. I'm not Eddie." My voice was high and terrified, and the way I said it seemed to convince him that I was lying.

To calm myself, or maybe to show him I was calm, I raised my glass to my mouth, As I began to drink, he leaned over and punched me in the side of my face, cracking the edge of the glass against my teeth and jarring my head. I drunkenly set the glass on a side table and tasted blood and moved unsteadily to the stairs, just as Paige came down.

"I have to go."

"What did you do?" she said angrily to Vic, but she knew.

"You heard him. He has to go."

I hurried away, blind, stumbling downhill. I was so stunned by being hit in the face I could not think, and my head was ringing, my jaw hurt, and yet I felt glad to be away, and happy when I saw I was not being chased. My mouth was full of foul-tasting saliva but I did not spit until I got to the bottom of the hill, and then I bent over and spat blood. I had a tenderness on my tongue where my teeth, or the glass, had been forced against it by his punching me.

Passing a pizza parlor, I saw my reflection in the window and was surprised to see myself as normal: no one would have guessed I'd been hit in the face. But I looked so young, so pale, with spiky hair and a rumpled shirt.

That was how I looked. Inside I was sick, and the wound in my mouth, the taste of blood, made me afraid. I ran, feeling skinny and breathless, to North Station, pushed my token into the slot, and hurried onto the train.

It was at Sullivan Square, as the train drew in, that I remembered the shoes. I'd left them at Paige's apartment when I'd run, after Vic hit me. And I'd been so afraid I hadn't thought of them until now. On the electric car I tried to think of an excuse. The truth was awful, impossible, unrepeatable.

As soon as my father saw me entering the store, he said,

"Shoes?" in his economical way, not wasting words on me. But it struck me that he was his other self, the one the woman had described, the good guy. He seemed, as I thought this, that he was summing me up too.

"I lost them. I was on the train and looked down and they weren't there."

"What else?"–meaning, And what other things happened to you?

"Nothing."

He lifted my chin. The wound in my mouth hurt from his tugging my head. He leaned over and, sniffing my hair, he knew everything.

"Sure."

Long Story Short

FRITZ IS BACK

I was born in Berlin in 1937. My mother was eighteen. She hid me from everyone for a year and a half. My father must have been someone who was hated, a Jew or a Gypsy: I never knew who he was. My mother got permission to emigrate in 1943 under "refugee status" and married a man named Wolfie. We sailed to Australia. None of us spoke English. We were put in a rural refugee camp, living in dormitories. After a year, we were sent to a suburb of Melbourne, where we were happy, but six months later my mother and Wolfie crashed their car. Mother was killed, Wolfie was so badly injured he could not care for me.

When the authorities came to put me in the orphanage, the next-door neighbor, Mrs. Dugger, said, "We could easily take him. He's one of the family. Fritz is no bludger." My name was Fred, but, being German, I was Fritz to everyone in Australia.

Mrs. Dugger didn't insist. She watched me get into the car. Then she reached through the window and patted me on the head. She said in a strange tone, "Bye, Fritz. Mind how you go."

I was put into the Fraser Boys' Home. I was happy there, oddly enough. The bigger boys protected me. And I was terrified when, after three years, Wolfie showed up, limping from his injuries, to take me away. He arranged for us to go back to Germany. We went by ship. He was abusive for the whole voyage. I had no idea why he wanted me to go with him; I still don't know. He abandoned me soon after we got to Hamburg. I was taken in by an old woman, and for the first time in my life I was held in the arms of someone who loved me. We both sobbed – the tears were endless. I was still young, but Germany was rebuilding, and I got a job in a restaurant. When I had saved some money, I went to hotel school. I worked in hotels, I became a manager, and eventually I became head of the company, a large hotel chain.

Long story short, our company was negotiating to buy a hotel in Melbourne. Forty years after I left that city, I returned. On my day off I went to the old neighborhood. I found Mrs. Dugger. She was blind, sitting on her porch.

"I used to live here," I said. "Long ago."

The moment she heard my voice, she began to cry and said, "Fritz is back!"

She died soon after that. Her son told me that she talked about me constantly, and it was only when I came back and she knew I was all right that she was able to let go. All those years of remorse for letting me be taken away by the authorities.

AN OBSTINATE CHILD

I have had an unusual life so far, difficult in many ways, but not so difficult as that of my father, who is sixty-something. He was my tormentor for almost the whole of my childhood.

I had a bad case of measles at the age of four. I had developed normally before then, but after the measles I became disobedient and willful. I didn't listen. I didn't pay attention. I defied my father, who was a stern disciplinarian – Marine Corps, two tours in Vietnam. "Listen to me!" But I didn't. He spanked me, sometimes so hard I could still feel it days later. He smacked my hands, twisted my ears, pushed me into a corner, and forced me to stand. He made me call him "Sir." As I grew older, the punishments became more severe. The worst one was having to kneel on a broomstick. I did this for hours at a time. I was seven or eight years old, and it went on for years. I was rude, I was defiant, you name it – so my dad said. I was a wreck, but I couldn't cure myself of being an obstinate child. I was also terrible at school, where the punishments weren't as bad as my father's, but when he saw my report card he went ballistic.

When I was about thirteen, I was given an eye test at school. Everyone got one. I failed. The eye doctor gave me a prescription for glasses and also suggested that I get a hearing test. This hearing test was given to me many times over a lot of weeks. Some of the tests were administered by groups of doctors or with medical students watching. Sometimes they asked, "How'd you get all those bruises?" I said, "Fell down."

The results showed that I was extremely deaf, as a result of the measles. I was fitted with two hearing aids. My whole life changed, though I was still pretty rebellious. The other kids laughed at my "earphones." I improved at school, but my home life deteriorated.

My father became desolate and filled with guilt. Some days when I stop by, I think he is on the verge of suicide, and it takes all the energy I have to reassure him and coax him into better humor, which is a pretty big burden for both of us. He still apologizes. I say, "How were you to know?"

MY PRIESTS

I was a Catholic in the 1950s, a student at an all-boys Catholic school, priests for teachers. I never heard of any of us boys being messed around with by a priest. I knew that I was afraid of them and probably would have done anything a priest asked me to.

But there was something else about them that impressed me and changed my life. In the ninth grade, we made weekly visits to the YMCA pool, where all the swimming was done in the nude. I was embarrassed, but I was the only one. We were all naked. And I recall how the priests would come into the changing room and find a locker. They wore long black cassocks, birettas, and black socks. They would undress with us, carefully folding their clothes and tucking them into the lockers.

Stark naked, they led us into the swimming pool, which stank of chlorine. They dived, they gave us swimming lessons. They taught us to pick up objects from the bottom of the pool – "surface dive." They showed us lifesaving maneuvers. "Never let a drowning man grab you. He'll take you with him."

What I remember of the priests were their naked bodies, big and pale without robes or cassocks. They were men, just white skin and hairy legs. After a while I did not believe they had any power at all, and certainly not spiritual power. As time passed, I liked them less and less – for their bodies – and as an adult, reflecting on the YMCA visits, I began to hate them for pretending to be powerful. I easily lost my faith.

SCHOOL DAYS

Like many boys of my generation, I was sent away to school. My father was an officer in the Indian Army, based in Bareilly, and he had the choice of sending me to a hill-station school – say, one in Simla – or to an English boarding school. He opted for England. There I went at the age of seven, accompanied by my mother, who left me at the underschool, returning every two years to check up on me. I know this seems extraordinary, but it was quite usual then. The period I am speaking of is the 1930s, for I was born in 1928, and my prep school days ended with the outbreak of war in Europe.

My mother died. This I was told by the headmaster, who took me aside and was very kind to me. His wife, Winnie – we called her Poodle – made me tea.

"Your father is coming to fetch you."

I was ten, but a small ten, a white weedy boy with bony bitten fingers and spiky hair. I was too nervous to be dreamy or lazy. I was a whiz at maths, chess, and Religious Knowledge, humiliated in all sports.

The day came. "Your father is in the foyer of Ashburnham." I ran. I was in a panic. I saw two men. I clutched one and began to cry.

"Neville, I am your father," the other man said.

This man I hugged was laughing: my uncle.

Nothing was right after that with my father. I began to think, Who is he? And maybe my uncle is my real father.

AUNTIE ROSEBUD'S JEWELS

My aunt Rosalind, whom we called Rosebud, had a fantastic collection of jewelry. She had two habits related to the collection. One, she was passionate about collecting, continually adding pieces, delving in markets, attending auctions and estate sales, and dealing privately. The other habit was her always announcing her finds and acquisitions. This meant that we were all keenly aware of what she had bought and what she owned. In so doing, she educated us. This is a topaz, this is a sapphire, this is a yellow diamond, and that's a black pearl. We learned the difference between white gold and platinum as settings, the virtue of one stone over another, the variety of hallmarks, the price of gold and diamonds – specific numbers and scarcity value.

Auntie Rosebud's collection continued to grow while we watched, from a few boxes to many chests of drawers, glass cabinets, and trays. We became knowledgeable ourselves. That close attention was a way of pleasing Auntie Rosebud. We felt that she needed us to take an interest, that she enjoyed educating us, and I suppose our knowledge linked us to this valuable collection and gave us self-esteem.

We were young adults, in the working world, when Auntie Rosebud sold her collection of jewelry. It was like a sickness and a death. An auction house swept down and valued the pieces, photographed them, and in a few months the whole collection was gone. She said, "You can bid for the ones you really like." But we didn't: we couldn't afford it. It wasn't the money she wanted. She had plenty. After the big auction she was more powerful than ever, and more of a mystery, and we felt so weak.

THE CHILD WITH THE CROOKED SMILE

I was in Central America, visiting schools for an aid project. Leaving one small school in a village, my guide, Ramon, said to me, "Did you see that small boy at the front desk, who was so slow? Alone, writing after school in his notebook?"

The boy with the crooked smile – I had seen him, and he had seen me, too.

"His story is so sad. His mother was only fifteen when she got pregnant. She had no boyfriend, no fiancé. She was just a schoolgirl. She gave birth, and afterward she moved out of the house and went to San Pedro.

"A few years later, visiting her parents, she saw her father hugging and kissing her younger sister, who was fourteen. She screamed at him to stop.

"Her father said, 'It's nothing. We're just being friendly.'

"She said, 'I don't want what happened to me to happen to her. Leave her alone!'

"But the father didn't. So the older daughter went to the police station and said, 'My father is having sex with my sister. He had sex with me, and this boy is the result.'

"The little boy looked at the policemen and smiled. They could see in his smile that there was something wrong with his head.

"The father was arrested. He went to trial and was given fifteen years and is in prison now. It's so strange. How do these things happen?"

A few days later we passed a small house in the forest near that village. Ramon pointed.

"That's the house of Señor Martin. He had seventeen children. Imagine! And now that I think of it, his second son was the one who committed incest with his daughters. He lived there."

"Seventeen children in that house?" I said.

"Two bedrooms," Ramon said. "Fantastic, eh, how these people can manage?"

THE SHADOW

I plan to retire soon. I have high blood pressure, yet my life has been uneventful – two children, both married; my wife is a real estate agent. I have spent my life in accountancy and tax planning. I used to think, I should get outside more. And then when my health problems prevented me, I was somewhat relieved not to have to get any exercise.

All my life there has been a shadow over me, one I could not identify, weighing me down.

I was at the supermarket – this was just the other day – and saw a young mother with her three children, one in a baby carriage, one holding her hand, and the third, the eldest, trying to help her. This big boy was about ten. He wore a baseball hat that was slightly too large for his head and tipping sideways. His eyeglasses were the cheap kind that make a kid self-conscious. He was pale, bucktoothed, very skinny, with an ill-fitting shirt and blue pants – not stylish, none of it. It was a poor family but an earnest one, conscious of decency and order. The boy was carrying a heavy bag, because his mother was burdened with the other children and the shopping. She chose each item very carefully, weighing the thing, looking several times at the price.

The boy was ugly, foolish-looking, really pathetic, trying to look anonymous but obviously what his schoolmates would have called a geek. His glasses were all wrong, he was weak, he was worried, he was trying to be helpful, but anyone could see he was miserably self-conscious and perhaps terrified. He knew what it was like to be mocked: he anticipated it every moment, glancing aside. I knew that his father either was dead or had deserted the mother. The father would have shown this boy how to dress and would have given him a manly example. But his mother nagged him. "You're the oldest!" He was in despair – I could see the shadow over him.

Later I examined my sadness and my pity. I realized he was me. I understood my life after fifty years. I did not sorrow for myself but for that poor ugly boy.

THE MAN FROM 77TH STREET

I was living on the Upper East Side. Every morning I walked down Lexington to 77th Street and got the 6 train to Union Square, where I worked. I was at the station by eight, and without fail I would see a man reading the *Wall Street Journal* just inside the turnstile. He always smiled at me, and I kept thinking that he would talk to me one day. He didn't, but he kept smiling whenever he saw me. This went on for about a year.

I moved to East 13th Street, a short distance from my office, and never thought about the man again. But after my boyfriend and I split up, I kept the apartment, though I hated staying home at night alone. I was in the bar section of a café in Union Square and saw the man from 77th Street. He smiled at me. I smiled back. We began talking. We were instantly on the same wavelength, as I had guessed we would be all along. I felt that I had known him for a year. We talked for about two hours – four drinks each – and then he said, "I want to make love to you in the worst way."

That struck me as funny. I even made a joke about it, that

word "worst." We went to my apartment, and we devoured each other, making up for a whole year of eyeing each other and fantasizing. I was thinking how I would tell my ex-boyfriend that it was like a cannibal feast. The man from 77th Street pounded me and twisted my body sideways and made a meal of one of my feet, while I watched, not aroused but fascinated.

Afterward, exhausted, I fell asleep. When I woke up, I said, "I used to dream of you making love to me the whole time I saw you at the station on 77th Street."

He stared at me. He said, "I've only been there a few times. I live in Brooklyn. I've never seen you before."

ENGLISH FRIENDS

My English friend Jane – very proper – gave me the name of this woman in London who would be glad to put me up for a few days until I got my InterRail paperwork sorted out. I just knew her as Victoria. When I called her from the airport, she said the best thing would be for me to meet her at her office in Westminster. I was totally impressed. She was a British civil servant, some kind of undersecretary in the Ministry of Health. These are the people who keep the British government running: the politicians and cabinet ministers come and go; these people stay. They brief the ministers on parliamentary bills and MPs' questions in the House of Commons. All this Victoria told me as she tidied her office before we left. She was drearily dressed and had greasy hair and was wearing a white shirt and necktie, like a school uniform. She saw I was reading a framed certificate.

"That's my MBE," she said. It meant Member of the British Empire, a title. "I say it means My Bloody Efforts."

She then explained that she couldn't take any of the papers home, because they were secret.

"Lucky you," I said. "You can make an explicit division between work stuff and home stuff."

"Bang on!" she said, and she laughed harder than I would have expected.

We went to her house by tube. Her husband answered the door. He was Jamaican, named Wallace. He wore a wool hat in the house. He was a carpenter, he said. He said very little else. I tried not to look surprised. While Victoria made dinner, Wallace offered me a drink and showed me to my room. The room looked lived in, and I wondered where, in this small house, Wallace and Victoria slept.

After dinner, Wallace rolled a big fat joint and passed it to Victoria. She puffed and passed it to me. I didn't inhale much. I looked at her and saw the civil servant who had shown me her secret papers and her MBE certificate in Westminster.

"I'm tired," I said, but when I went into the bedroom they followed me. They looked pretty interested. I said, "I can't do this."

My English friend Jane said I really missed something.

THE UNIFORM BUSINESS

I am pretty conservative on the whole and have a sales-and-marketing degree, which my parents urged me to get so that I could help them with their business. They are also conservative, you might even say puritanical. That is one of the reasons they chose this business, which is school uniforms.

Mainly it is girls' uniforms, skirts and blouses, knee socks and blazers. What is thought of as an old-fashioned line of clothes is actually very up-to-date, since many schools these days are switching over to uniforms, not just Catholic schools but all sorts. My parents chose this business because they believed it was virtuous and fair, that they were promoting modesty. Uniforms are made to order, in batches: a certain plaid for the pleated skirt, a certain blouse and blazer. A lot of the sewing is outsourced to factories in the Dominican Republic and Guatemala.

When I graduated, I was put in charge of mail orders, generally orders from clients who found our website, or from schools or individuals we had not been in touch with before – random orders.

Many of these came from Japan, some from Great Britain and Germany, and quite a number from the United States. In most cases they were single orders, apparently unconnected to any school. I knew this from the patterns that were chosen. An individual would get in touch, specify colors and fabrics and sizes, enclosing the payment.

By tracking these orders, I found out some interesting things. The sizes were usually large, as though for a school for big and tall girls, adult-sized, and these made up at least twenty percent of our total orders. Some of the skirts were huge. The measurements did not make sense. Yet the customers were satisfied, and I found out that they were, most of them, repeat customers.

Where were these schools? Of course, there were no schools. A fifth of our school uniform sales were to prostitutes and fetishists – men around the world involved with sexual role-playing, dominatrixes, sadists, transvestites, and closet pedophiles. I did not tell my puritanical parents my conclusions, or they would probably have shut down the business, and where would we be then?

MY BROTHER'S MASK

My father became wealthy importing timber from Southeast Asia, mainly teak but other hardwoods too. He was one of the first to farm it, which meant that when he died the company still prospered. My brother, Hank, and I inherited everything, the big company and a considerable income.

My visits to the plantations got me interested in Asian antiques, and when I began to sell them, I was so busy that I needed Hank to help me out. Soon I saw that he was taking trips to Asia purely to buy drugs. Like Dad, he was an innovator – an early smuggler of heroin inside little Buddhas and carved temple finials in small, hard-to-detect amounts, for his own use. His wealth ensured he'd never have to resort to dealing or relying on dealers in the States. He injected: his arm, his foot, his neck. He said, "I have it under control," meaning that he could afford it.

But over time the heroin ate up most of his money, and he borrowed from me for a while. A very expensive habit, and destructive too, or so I thought. I made him a promise. I said, "If you give up the heroin, I will hand over half my own inheritance." I had doubled my money with my antiques business anyway. Hank said, "Leave me alone. I'm like a person with an illness. Just leave me to my illness. A lot of people are in worse shape than me."

But I begged him. Finally he agreed. Here is the weird part. As soon as he gave up heroin, after a long, painful process of rehab and treatment, he became very weak. As an addict, he had been full of life; as a clean straight guy, he was pale, feeble, prone to colds, and sometimes could not get out of bed. This went on for a few months. Very worried, I brought him to a specialist, who diagnosed cancer.

He said, "Your brother has had cancer for years, but his heroin use has masked it. If he had still been using it, he would have had a happy death – sudden anyway. Heroin has been keeping him out of pain."

The next weeks were awful. He died horribly a month later.

STERN MAN

A stern man is the helper fellow on a lobster boat, and he is at my dooryard at four-thirty every morning except Sunday, ready to go, and if he's not there, I'll go without him. He does lots of things – hauls traps, baits them, hoses rockweed off the deck, boxes the bugs, gets handy with the Clorox. When you haul in winter your stern man might say he's cold, and you say, "Goddamn, if you're cold, you're not working hard enough." The stern man gets fifteen percent of the profit on the catch.

I have had them all, the drug addicts, the numb ones, the stealers, and one was crazy as a shithouse rat. A Christless little son of a whore from Belfast went off with my punt. Another one phoned me with death threats when I fired him, and he also talked about cutting the lines on my pots. It is a hell of a business.

But Alvin was the best stern man I ever had. Never late, not a talker, a good worker. God knows where he came from. I'd ask him where he came from, and he'd go all friggin' numb or else change the subject. Also, he went quiet when I talked about women. Mention a piece of tail or a fellow's teapot or a pair of bloomers, and Alvin just began scrubbing the deck or hosing rockweed.

I was talking about Vietnam one day. He was the right age. My son was there, one tour. But Alvin said, "I didn't join up."

"Why not?"

"Couldn't."

"Nothing wrong with you," I nagged him a bit.

"Warner, I was in prison," Alvin said after a while. First time he ever used my name, but all this time he never looked me in the eye.

"How long for?"

"Bunch of years."

"'Bunch of years'! So what'd you go and do?"

"I killed my wife."

"She probably deserved it," I said.

I knew I was right, because he didn't say anything else, though he left me a month later. Damn, I never found a better stern man.

MY WIFE CHEYENNE

Everyone has always liked us. "Here come Mort and Irma." They'd see us holding hands. We are small of stature – Irma's barely five feet – like a couple of kids. We had no kids ourselves, so we never had to grow up. We considered ourselves good mixers and had lots of friends. But we went kaput, and here's how.

As I'm in restaurant supplies, I travel quite a bit, and it's no fun, those cheap hotels you have to stay in to keep the profit margin up and the overhead down. Many of my accounts are in Florida, so we relocated to West Palm. But Florida is a huge state, and I still had to deal with the hotels and lots of nights away.

Irma got a little blue on her own and talked of buying a dog, and she didn't even like dogs. One Friday I returned home from the road, assuming we were going out to dinner, as we usually did. But:

"Can't. I've got my group," Irma said.

Just like that, a women's group. She had joined it while I was away; some neighbor introduced her. It made her happy. Good. My turn to stay home alone.

The next week, same thing but a little worse. I say, "Hon, how about a juicy steak instead of the group."

"I'm a vegan." Just like that. "We decided."

They had all turned vegetarian, the group. It was wives of working guys and some divorcées, kind of a support group. I told her I'm all for it, and I am. Traveling and sales is no picnic, but if this made her happier while I was away, hey, great. Then the name issue came up.

"Irma," I says one Friday, and she stops me, makes a face.

"Don't call me that. I'm Cheyenne."

"And I'm Tonto."

I had to sleep on the couch. This was no damn joke. And that wasn't the end of it. How could I be so insensitive? She was Cheyenne. They were all something. She had new stationery printed. She says she can take or leave the holidays. Imagine that. I'm still traveling, but when I come home these days, I don't know this woman.

ROCK HAPPY

I had been married for twenty-two years, living on the windward side of Oahu in Hawaii. No children. Originally I had come to Hawaii, as a young salesman, to advise people on how to set up Jiffy Lube franchises, but when my consultancy work was done, I decided to stay. I got myself a franchise, realized this was where I wanted to live, and sent for Diana, my high school sweetheart. She had a lot of complaints about living in Hawaii – the rats, the cockroaches, the way people talked English like it was another language, the lousy food, the terrible traffic, and many more, which is maybe the point of this story.

I was happy. I would have done anything to make Diana happy. I hardly noticed her criticisms of me, although our whole being in Hawaii was my doing, as she said. I was in kind of a daze, but so what? I never got rock fever, like they say. I was rock happy.

We were driving one wet afternoon over the Pali, and just beyond the tunnel there was one of these speed traps. Cop flags me down. I drive onto the shoulder and get out my license and registration.

The cop was a big moke, six-something, way over two hundred pounds, hands like pieces of meat. But he was very polite, very professional. It was true, I had probably been speeding. I laughed and agreed with him while he wrote out the citation.

A horrible choking honk like an animal's sudden fury made him stop writing. But it was a familiar sound to me.

"Billy! You tell him we're going to court! You hear me, Billy!"

The cop took a step back and looked into the car, at Diana's pudgy purple face, the veins standing out on her neck, the spit on her lips.

"Is that your wife?" He said it in a disgusted and pitying voice.

I said yes, and I almost added, What's the problem?

He tore up the ticket. "I ain't giving you this. You got enough problems, bruddah."

After a few months we separated, and within a year were divorced. Diana's back on the mainland now.

THE BUS DRIVER

It was at the three-day wedding event for my eldest daughter, who was marrying a very nice man, Brian, a successful contractor in Oregon. Taylor said, "I want a huge bash. You only get married once." I kept my big mouth shut.

The bash was held at a resort in Hawaii and involved all the guests being shuttled to lunches, rehearsals, dinners, activities, and so forth, getting in and out of vans and minibuses, and doing lots of socializing. We were sent a three-page itinerary. Movable feast!

I went with Tim, my second husband. On the first afternoon there was an important cocktail party at a function room on the property. The van was parked where it should have been, near the porte-cochère, but there was no sign of the bus driver. I walked up and down looking for him.

A gruff-looking man approached the van and waited at the front passenger door.

I was annoyed that he was late and not even apologetic. I said, "Are you the bus driver?"

He said, "No," and a second later seemed to change his mind about getting aboard. This really annoyed me, because I was sure he was the bus driver, and I muttered something, which I wish I could remember now. He walked away. I waited awhile, and then it hit me.

That man, the gruff stranger I had spoken to, was my ex-husband, Taylor's father, to whom I had been happily married for sixteen years, until he went off with a much younger woman, who I heard had dumped him, couldn't stand his drinking. I looked back and did not see him. Later, we said hello but not much else. We never discussed my gaffe, which I think says a lot.

BLACK RUNS

I was unhappily married and living in Connecticut, your typical bored housewife. Then I took a course: radiology. X-rays, CAT scans, MRIs. Two years. I got my diploma and left my husband and came here to Maine. There's a lot of work in radiology, and the hours aren't too bad. I chose Maine because of the winters.

I spend the whole winter skiing, except last winter, when I had some medical procedures. I have five screws in my shoulder and a permanently damaged rotator cuff that screams in damp weather. I've broken both arms, my collarbone, and my left ankle. I need to have my knees replaced. That'll be fun. Basically, they make lateral incisions, sever your legs, put in metal, and give you some kind of ID so you can go through a metal detector in an airport.

The ankle was something else. I read my own CAT scan and opted for ankle replacement. Basically, they got me an ankle from a cadaver, and they removed my bad ankle and fitted me with this donor ankle. But it's too small. I'm getting pain. They might have to redo it.

I hate cross-country skiing. My ex was huge on it. I hated hearing him say, "Oh, look at that yellow spruce," or "Oh, look, a rose-breasted grosbeak," or "Oh, gosh, let's sit on that log and have a bagel." Cross-country is for, I want to say, fairies.

He didn't understand that pain is pleasure, if properly applied. What I want is black runs, all-day black runs. I want to ski straight down on black runs with my legs banging and the tears streaming out of my eyes and freezing on my face. And snot pouring out of my nose and streaking on my cheek, and my whole face burning from the cold. I am hardly able to breathe on a black run, which no man I have ever known can understand, which is also why I fired my husband, I've fired every boyfriend I've ever had, and basically it's just me and my dog.

A REAL BREAK

Mother and Grace – let's just say they weren't best buddies. So as the elder daughter, and single, I began to look after Mother when she began to fail. And she was a wreck. Got confused in stores, left the oven on, real muddled about time. I made her stop driving, so of course I had to take the wheel. God, the hills. I wrote Grace that I was moving in with Mother. The big Polk Street house had been in Mother's family for years; Mother was lost in it. Grace understood completely and said she was relieved. She had been in a Minnesota convent since taking her vows, though she sometimes spent extended periods in Nevada and Florida as a hospital worker, "and doing spiritual triage too," on Indian reservations. We seldom heard from her, but Mother sent her money now and then. Because of the strictness of her religious order, she was never able to visit us in San Francisco. "And just as well," Mother said.

It got so that Mother could only manage with my assistance. I resigned from my secretarial job, lost my retirement and my medical plan, and became Mother's full-time caregiver. I updated Grace on Mother's condition and mentioned the various challenges we faced. Grace wrote saying that she was praying for us, and she asked detailed questions because these infirmities were to be specified in the prayers, or intercessions, as she called them.

About three years into my caregiving, Grace called. She

said, "Why not take a few months off? My Superior has given me special dispensation to look after Mom for a while. It'll be a break for me. And you can have a real break. Maybe go to Europe."

Mother wasn't overjoyed, but she could see that I was exhausted. Grace flew in. It was an emotional reunion. I hardly recognized her – not because she had gotten older, though she had. But she was dressed so well and in such good health. She even mentioned how I looked stressed and obviously could do with some time off.

I went on one of those special British Airways fares, a See Scotland package. It was just the break I needed, or so I thought.

Long story short, when I got back to San Francisco, the Polk Street house was being repainted by people who said they were the new owners. Everything I possessed was gone. Mother was in a charity hospice. She had been left late one night at the emergency room of St. Francis Hospital. There was no money in Mother's bank account. Everything she had owned had been sold. I saw Mother's lawyer. He found a number for Grace – the 702 area code, a cell phone. Nevada.

"I'm glad you called," Grace said. I could hear music in the background and a man talking excitedly, a fishbowl babble, aqueous party voices. I started to cry but she interrupted me with a real hard voice. "Everything I did was legal. Mother gave me power of attorney. I never want to see you again. And you will never undo it." Unfortunately for me, that was true.

GIULIO AND PAULIE

Giulio was recommended to me as a hard worker, a good man, very skillful in all sorts of building. This proved to be the case. When I praised him, he said, "I come from Sicily. We build the whole house there – foundation, brickwork, framing, plastering, carpentry, roofing, shingles, tiling, plumbing." He could do anything. He worked one whole summer, first brickwork, then replacing shingles, then glazing the cracked windows, then painting – every job I'd put off at last getting done.

He was seventy-seven years old. He asked for $40 an hour – a lot of money, the weekly bills were high – but he earned it.

After the second week, he brought his son Paulie, a big, boyish fellow of forty-three, tattooed, potbellied, very funny, not a good worker but strong. He could heave the big sacks of cement, he dug holes, he lugged the bricks. He was also to get $40 an hour, but some days he didn't show up. "He's goofing around," "He's sick," "He's sleeping," Giulio would say, seeming both dignified and somewhat ashamed of having to make excuses.

Then, one day: "Paulie's in jail." It turned out he'd been in jail before, spent several years inside for theft, credit-card fraud, and receiving stolen goods. What astonished me was the contrast between father and son: the honest old man, so talented and hardworking; the lazy son, who was a petty thief and a druggie.

Time passed, Paulie stayed in jail, but as I got to know Giulio better, I realized that he was cheating me on his time sheet, charging me for tools he bought or broke, not quite truthful about the work, carelessly hiding the scrap wood and the mistakes, a subtle thief. And I began to see, first faintly, then powerfully, how prideful Giulio the sly worker was more like Paulie the jailbird than anyone could ever guess.

BIGOT ON VACATION

I left my small village in Norway as a young man – I was hardly seventeen – and became a student in the USA, first in Michigan, where I had an aunt and uncle, then in Massachusetts, where I attended MIT and where I eventually settled. My life's work has been in developing radar sensitivity – defense work, but I justify it to myself by saying that I was creating a shield, not weapons of destruction. This was not entirely true. Missiles are guided by radar. In this work, my colleagues were from India, Pakistan, China, Korea, Japan, and many other countries. I must emphasize the diverse nationalities and how well we got along – it is important to this story.

I lived through the 1960s in the USA, working on defense projects. Of course, I was seen as one of the bad guys. I married an American, raised two children. I am proud of the life I have made here. My interests are sailing, skiing, and gardening. I am now retired – a happy man.

Here is the strange part. About every four years I go back to my village, which is near Bergen. It is always a horrible visit. I become enraged when I see what has happened. It has gotten so bad that I dread going home. The visits disturb me, because I see that I am a bigot. My lovely village is now the residence of Pakistanis, Indians, Africans, Vietnamese – brown people, who have come there as refugees, so called, because Norwegians are so happy to provide houses and welfare.

When I was a boy, we had one religion, one language, one culture – one race. Now it's a filthy mess. Skullcaps, shawls, smells. There is crime. So many languages. A mosque! A temple! Not refugees but opportunists. I am so angry when I am there: my lovely village spoiled. I think I will never go back again. I know I am a bigot there, and I hate myself when I am home.

MRS. SPRINGER, OLD-TIMER

Mrs. Springer, a longtime resident of our facility, was born in 1900. She was vain about the date, being the same age as the century. She clearly remembered the First World War. "I was at school. The school bell rang when the war ended, and we were given the day off." She remembered talk of Al Capone and Prohibition, the Great Depression and Lindbergh's flight. She was married to a science-minded German, living in Munich when the Second World War started. Her husband's family was wealthy – Springer was their name. She volunteered for war work, knitting socks. She told us all her stories. She had met Hitler. "He had very fine hands, small and pale, like a woman's."

She became a refugee after the war. She went to Los Angeles; her husband followed her later, and he became a metallurgist for Hughes Tool Company. He died. She lived alone a few years and then entered our facility.

We went to her ninetieth birthday party. We predicted that she would live to be a hundred. She accomplished this, but it was a decade of failing health. She lost most of her hearing. Her sight dimmed. At her hundredth she needed to be steered to the cake. We shouted for her to blow out the candles, but she couldn't hear us or see the candles. Even so, she smiled and said it was a great day.

Her hundred-and-first she spent in her room. We were away a lot after that, and each time we got back, we were surprised to see her still alive. Her other friends were less attentive too, even a little irritated when they had to run an errand for Mrs. Springer. We missed her hundred-and-second birthday. That year I saw her once. It seemed inconvenient and somewhat unfair, her living into another century. Her nurse called and complained that no one bought her medicine anymore. Her son died, not of any specific cause. "He was getting on," someone said.

We forgot about Mrs. Springer, we guessed she had died, and we were astonished to hear that she had a hundred-and-fourth birthday. We were not invited. Only her nurse, her cleaning woman, and – somehow – the plumber were there. She kept to her room. People said she was alert, that she asked about elections and the weather. No one visited her. We were embarrassed and, I'm sorry to say, a bit bored by her, and none of us saw her again until her funeral.

THE CRUISE OF THE *ALLEGRA*

It was my first winter cruise. I was a waiter on the *Allegra,* most of the passengers well-to-do people who spent part of the winter cruising in the warm waters of the Pacific, from Puerto Escondido to Singapore and back, including stops in Australia and New Zealand. That winter we stopped along the South American coast too, from Guayaquil to Santiago, and then to Hawaii via Easter Island. Often the passengers did not bother to go ashore – just stayed on deck and looked at the pier and drank and made faces.

Ed and Wilma Hibbert avoided the others. They were in their mid- to late seventies, from Seattle. Always dined alone, did not socialize, Ed very attentive to Wilma, who seemed the frail type. I heard whispers. "Snobs," "Stuffed shirts," "Pompous," "Cold." They must have heard them too.

Wilma fell ill at Callao, stayed in her suite, and was taken to a hospital in Lima, where she died. Ed Hibbert left the *Allegra* but did not vacate his suite. His table was empty until Honolulu, where he rejoined the ship.

And then the invitations began, one widow after another inviting him to dinner, to drinks, to the fancy-dress ball. They were not amateurs but persistent and alluring seducers.

Amazingly, Ed obliged. He seemed to welcome the attention, not like a bereaved spouse at all but like the most discriminating bachelor. The same women who had made demeaning remarks now praised him and competed for his affection. And I had the feeling that in obliging them, dallying with them, without committing himself, he was having his revenge, perhaps revenge on his wife, too.

He went on two more cruises, same routine, didn't remarry.

EULOGIES FOR MR. CONCANNON

I did not know Dennis Concannon. I was invited to his funeral by a friend of his son's who needed a ride. As it was a rainy day and I had nothing else to do, I stayed for the service, sitting in the back. The whole business was nondenominational, according to Mr. C's wishes. The turnout was very large – the church was filled. A reading of his favorite poem, by Robert Frost, with the memorable line "That withered hag." Several sentimental songs. Then the eulogies. One man got up and said, "I never met anyone else like Dennis. I worked for him for almost twenty-five years, and in all that time he didn't even buy me a cup of coffee." He went on – people laughed.

A woman: "I used to tremble whenever I was called to his office. I never knew whether he was going to make a pass at me or fire me."

Another man: "The salesmen put in their expense reports that they'd had their cars washed. 'Salesmen have to have clean cars.' But Dennis said, 'This was the fourteenth of last month. I compared the car washes to the weather report. It was raining that day. I'm not paying.'"

Someone else: "His partner, George Kelly, would be sitting next to him at some of the meetings. One would talk. Then the other, but saying the same thing. It was terrible. We called it 'Dennis in Stereo.'"

There were more speakers, with equally unpleasant stories of this man. At the end of the funeral I knew Dennis Concannon as a mean, unreasonable, bullying bastard who had gotten rich by exploiting and intimidating these people, the attendees at his funeral – not mourners but people who were having the last word.

Neighbor Islands

1. ERSKINE: A HUMAN SANDWICH ALL HAMAJANG

This was all twenty-some-odd years ago. What I remember is the sound from my front door, which was shut, just off the lanai, the underwater murmur of voices from a TV set inside the house, and my thinking, We don't have a TV set.

I'd been making the run to Hanalei to see my deputy there, on a weekly basis, always on the same day, a Thursday. He was an officer named Barry Moniz, the chief's cousin, the one who had fished the key of coke out of Hanalei Bay. Usually we talked sports and went over his paperwork. But his voice sounded strange.

"Ho, get flu, brah. No can talk."

So I was home three hours early. From where I stood, hearing those gurgly voices, I could see across the sitting room that Kanoa's door was shut, the kid probably asleep. Even though I'm trained to be suspicious, I was at my own front door, which smacked when I closed it. The voices stopped. Normally I slipped off my shoes to enter the house, but instead I took out my service revolver.

The house was very quiet with a holding-your-breath stillness, and the ticking of Verna's auntie's old clock was like timing the silence. I kept to the carpet for stealth reasons and walked through the sitting room to our bedroom door, which was not completely shut but ajar, just a crack of light showing.

I waited about eight seconds, hearing nothing, considering my options, then took a defensive position by the doorjamb and kicked the door open. There on the bed was Verna with two individuals, both men, all of them naked, and they froze like statues.

The overhead light made their skin very pale, except the men's forearms, indicating to me they were employed out of doors. This was also a warning of their physical strength, in the event of resistance. They were half hiding their faces in fear, but I could see – studying them, because I had the gun – that they were a lot younger than Verna.

With those stacked-up bodies of this crazy pile, like kids, and my Glock on them, I could have let off one round and gotten all three, like a 9-millimeter toothpick, right through the human sandwich, all hamajang, except that was my wife in the middle.

Not a sound came from them. They were barely breathing. I didn't say anything – didn't have to. I was aiming at them and in my uniform, even wearing my hat, thinking, This is at least fifteen years in Halawa maximum security before all my appeals are heard and I finally explain my way out. And who are these guys? I'd have to take out all three, unless I separated them and killed them execution style, an idea that was going through my head, with my story, "I saw the hapa-haole guy move his hands in a manner consistent with going for one weapon," but their nakedness weakened the alibi.

And I loved this woman. She was weak, always saying "I so kolohe," such a fool, and younger than me, but up to that time my best friend.

In police work, in a tight spot, with no backup and not sure of your ground, or don't want to hurt bystanders, you shout, curse, threaten, "Let me see you hands, you fricken lolo!" and all that. But I was not in a tight spot. I was home, looking at my naked wife with two naked men, and smelled – what? – dope smoke and that sex smell of funky sashimi. Since I had the gun, and they were silent and I wasn't talking, I had time to think.

In the silence like a buzzing fly, not a single word, even as I leveled the gun. But the very act of aiming, and the silence, concentrated my mind and made the whole encounter so serious I saw clearly I could not do it.

I holstered my gun, walked out of the house, drove to my office, slept there that night, and the next day went to the chief's office.

"Eh, here my badge."

Chief Moniz said, "Skinny, I won't let you do that," and handed the badge back to me.

"I quit, brah. Pau already."

"'Sap to you," he said. But he made a disagreeing face. Then he praised me. "You one real shtrick buggah but you real shtrong."

And he begged me to ask him why. I told him everything.

"Ho, hamajang, brah! Dey no more shame or what. No even close da light!"

I remembered that one of the men was wearing a baseball cap backward, and I mentioned that too because it bothered me. The chief just shook his head. He said he'd transfer me to the Big Island. Why should I lose my whole pension over a messy domestic?

Next day the house was empty. I picked up some things and flew to Hilo.

2. MONIZ: ONE FUTLESS WAHINE

I had known about the whole shibai for a year or more. I was relieved when Erskine gave the reason he was turning in his gun and his badge, because I expected something a lot worse: I'd braced myself for him killing his wife and our losing him, probably the straightest cop we'd ever had. I hadn't told him about Verna, because it seemed to me that it would send him over the edge, and we'd lose him, or he might go at anyone for telling him.

"I geevum dirty lickings!" kind of thing.

I'd hired Erskine when he was a young man, not knowing if

a haole could do police work on an island like this. His father, from the mainland, was a hell-raiser. Erskine was closer to his mother. He might have turned out to be a hell-raiser himself – some of them do, from those households – but he was the opposite; and as the years passed he became more and more severe. He even gave the mayor a speeding ticket once. I said, "Skinny, why you so shtrick?"

"To serve and protect. No exceptions." And his eyes went dead. "Bodda you?"

I kind of laughed, but it was a moving violation and the mayor's insurance company was not too happy. Mottoes are scary expressions, and so is *No exceptions.*

I had complaints, not because he was lazy, like the others, but because he was so straight. No exceptions meant a citation to a float with a bad brake light in the Kamehameha Day parade; it meant a night in jail for the man who flipped him the bird, and that man had fought in Vietnam, two tours.

"Brah, da buggah just bool-liar," I said.

"Disorderly conduck," Erskine said.

No TV at his house. "If I get, I smash um already."

"Why you worry about one TV?"

"Tings," he said.

"What tings? Humbug tings?"

"Stuffs," he said.

He was still living at home, his father having had a seizure, face turned black, and died. His mother lived another ten years, and she died – lupus. At the age of fifty-two Erskine married Verna, who was barely twenty, and she was a local wahine.

The exception in his life, from Kekaha way, near the landfill, Verna had grown up in a trailer, her father calling himself a scrap dealer, which meant rusty cars in the front yard. She was wild and didn't make it through high school.

Erskine must have met her at her dad's trailer, one of the many domestics he'd been called there for, or might have seen her at Barking Sands, where the kids hung out. Verna was a handful, but Erskine was not fazed by any situation, and she might have had father issues, since she had affairs with older men. They got drugs and alcohol for her in return for favors. I know that to be a fact.

She was a little lolo, but "a little lolo" often describes a passionate woman. She was living in Erskine's family home, sleeping in the bed where Erskine's mother died, no TV, and eventually a keiki, Kanoa. But aimless, as she said – futless.

"You futless?"

"I stay so futless awready."

The story was, the kid wasn't Erskine's. Erskine didn't do his homework, or wasn't doing it very well, because it got around that anyone who knocked at the door when Erskine was at the station would get a friendly welcome, no matter who. And if they had something on board, like killer buds, Verna was like, "Eh, we burn."

Drugs are the sickness of this island. Everyone either has them or knows where to get them. It didn't help that when Erskine and my nephew Barry had seized some controlled substance after hours, Erskine stored it at home, because Erskine didn't trust his fellow officers. Verna knew that. The famous key of coke floating in Hanalei Bay ended up at his place.

The key of coke was the start of it all. But Verna would also be happy with a couple of OxyContins ground to powder and used as a suppository, don't ask me how I know. No TV! One futless wahine, who would say to me, "Skinny think my okole too big. What you tink?" There is only one answer.

Erskine didn't know the name of the two kids with Verna that night. One was Ledward Ho, the other Junior – most people knew, I certainly did – Ledward a meth addict with rotten teeth as a result, and Junior had more acid in his system than a car battery. Big-wave surfers gone bad.

They brought something – pills, meth, batu, crack, speed, pakalolo. Kids! And she would have obliged. Two at one time was something new, but I wasn't really surprised.

What surprised me at first was that he didn't blow them all away. Then I thought, He's law-abiding–what he did was by the book. You don't shoot unarmed suspects in the back on this island.

Only the gun not going off was also kind of appropriate for Erskine, like a symbol. He was on the plane too fast for me to tell him I'd take care of the kid.

3. VERNA: A LESSON IN "JUST A SKOSH"

Never mind Erskine called me "shelter dog" and kept his big plastic gun by the bedside. He bailed me out of that awful trailer up at the landfill, and I didn't even tell him that for a while up in Lihue we lived in a container in the industrial area near Nawiliwili Harbor.

My stepmother, Jen, grew up speaking Hawaiian on Niihau, called herself a functioning alcoholic, and was afraid of mirrors. "We never have one meer anyhow." I gave her one from the thrift shop and she screamed like it was a trick. "It's a present!" I screamed back. "Take it down!" And why? "Because there's probably some babooze behind it?" She had the idea that all mirrors were two-way: you were being spied on by a freak on the other side.

"That's not funny. You call that funny? It a meer!"

She made me afraid of mirrors, which annoyed Erskine. When he looked at me it was that face he made when he was checking his cell phone, noting the number, the "Howzit?" look. Then he'd always turn away with that shouldery big-dog walk, Officer Serious.

Everyone thought they knew about my father, that he was good at everything, saved scrap, had all the answers. "I cockroach that fuel pump from an old Honda." Several things they didn't know. That he was afraid of flying and had not visited a neighbor island since the passenger barges stopped in 1972. So my one wish was to take flying lessons, to see my father's face when I got in the cockpit and took off down the runway – maybe say, "Want to hop in?" beforehand. They thought he was a bully because he spanked me. But he liked to spank me – or anyone, and maybe I deserved it for being wild and quitting school.

"You panty," I would say, to pretend I wasn't afraid.

Or he told me I was adopted and that he'd give me back to the orphanage if I didn't behave. I believed him.

The container we lived in for a while had no windows and was like an oven in the summer when the trade winds dropped.

I smoked cigarettes. Jen said smoking is a filthy habit and to give it up. No smoking or drinking on Niihau. But smoking relaxes you, and anyone who doesn't know that has never smoked. I needed to be relaxed. I smoked pakalolo. It was easy to get; everyone grew it, and that too was relaxing. "Don't knock it," I'd said to Jen, who would have been mellower with Dad if she used just a skosh of weed, and I told her so.

"Just a skosh," she said, wily old auntie, and, "Here, why you no help me bake some cookies?"

She had me sift the flour and mix in the sugar and shortening and butter, and when it was smooth, the cup of chocolate chips. She could tell that I was enjoying the mixing.

"Your ma wen never show you how for make cookies?" she asked, pretending to be amazed.

Which was cruel, because my real mother was dead from riding in the back of a pickup truck that was rear-ended on Kokee Road.

"Not yet," Jen said, snatching the spoon I was going to lick.

And then she took me out to the yard and got a stick and poked it into a twist of dog doo, and back in the kitchen she dipped the stick into the golden cookie dough and stirred it.

"Now taste um."

She knew what I'd say, so I didn't say it.

"Just a skosh!" she screamed. "Same wid djrugs!"

But when he brought home the key of coke from that

Moniz cousin my life was changed, and I don't care what anyone says: it is the greatest feeling in the world, and not addictive like meth if you're smart, no more than candy, in fact just like candy. I wanted to be a functioning coke sniffer.

"It's spendy," the chief used to say. But he found some more, maybe the same key, and he made me pay for it in my own way.

He couldn't blame me for wanting more. Junior got some in Maui from his surfing buddy Ledward, and said, "Now what are you going to do for me?"

Erskine was always working, at the station or on calls. What was I supposed to do – and his boss the chief always hanging around?

"What you good at?" the chief asked.

"Nothing. I so junk."

That made him laugh.

"The junkest."

Having Kanoa didn't make him happy either. The chief held him more than Erskine did at the baby luau.

Junior was always around on the day Erskine was in Hanalei. When he said, "I want to try something insane," I knew I'd have to say yes, and met Ledward.

I knew Erskine wouldn't shoot.

4. NOELANI: NOTHING BUT STINK-EYE

When we met on the Big Island, all Erskine talked about was how unreasonable his ex was – demanding, petty, immature – and I was totally on his side. He did not miss his little boy Kanoa at first, but after we were settled and he moved from highway patrol to a desk job in Hilo, he said he wanted to get custody, that his ex was a bad influence.

Around that time I was thinking: Cop, killjoy, straight arrow, spanker, scold – what kind of kid would want to be in the same house with him?

I could just about stand him. He was a righteous bully, never wrong, knew all the answers, knew the law ("that's a Class-A felony"). I felt sorry for what he'd been through, but I didn't want to go through it myself. He was making plans to fly over to Kauai to visit the kid.

I called Verna. I said, "You don't know me."

"Who's this?" she asked.

"Noelani. But listen up. I just want you to know that Skinny is coming over to talk to you about joint custody."

"That's all I need."

And I heard a man in the background squawking and thought, Another one.

After that, Erskine said, "Every time I go over there she's not at home, the kid's not there, and no one knows where they went."

"Maybe at her parents' place."

Erskine said, "She doesn't have anyone in the world except me," and went silent.

That was more and more the case with me. My friends didn't like Erskine for his strictness. They enjoyed a little smoke now and then, they watched football, they drank beer at the beach. And Erskine frowned at them the whole time.

"Dis guy nothing but stink-eye."

He had no doubts. He was the law, and even on a neighbor island where things weren't so strict he enforced the pettiest law: no dogs on the beach, no ball games, no open containers of alcohol – even confiscated pakalolo and brought it home and maybe was testing me because he made a big show of locking it in a desk drawer.

In the pictures he showed me, his kid looked so different and so poi-dog I wanted to say, "You sure he stay yours?"

Not only the kid's different features but the kid's smile – Erskine never smiled. Plus the fact that after the first few times, Erskine seemed to lose interest in me. I was a lot older than

Verna – closer to Erskine's age – but even so, I seemed to have more in common with her, this ex-wife, than the man himself.

And she began confiding in me, saying how she'd let him down.

"Don't beat yourself up," I said.

Though I rarely went to a neighbor island, I went over there to see what she was really like. She was young enough to be my daughter, and that's how I felt toward her. She gave me a big hug, and we had coffee.

"Ma, I want do shee-shee!"

The kid Kanoa was just awful and looked local. But he was very well dressed, new shirt and slippers and surfer shorts. I felt sorry for Verna, but I didn't want him. So I kept tipping her off whenever Erskine was on his way over. I thought I was doing everyone a favor.

On that one and only visit I met her new guy, Junior, and recognized him from what Erskine had told me: hapa-haole, tribal tattoos, Raiders hat on backward, a big laid-back moke who worked an excavator. But I could also see the attraction. He was like, "Whatever," and that was not Erskine's way.

What ended it was this visit. I began to think: She's been through a lot, made a few bad choices and lost her looks living with this blalah, and was making the best of it. But time passed, and I lived with Erskine and got to know him better and became like her. He made me that way, and I knew exactly why she two-timed him.

If I stayed with Erskine that's how I'd end up, as a stoner and probably cheating on him and getting blamed, and so I fired him and went back to my own island, Lanai, and stayed in touch with Verna.

The last thing Erskine said to me was "I'll probably stay single. I'll be okay. I can't handle hooking up with a new wahine, telling her all my stories, listening to all her stories, and then there's dealing with her stuffs. I'm married to my job."

5. JUNIOR: DOG LUCK

I put it down to Erskine was a haole from the mainland, raised by his mother, and didn't always understand what he was looking at. Like the tourists who sit on the beach and don't see those upside-down bowls in the shore-break are turtles feeding on the rocks and far out the puff of mist is a whale blowing, and when the tourists turn their backs the turtles stick their heads up and the whale breaches, slapping itself down sideways. Or they see monster surf and say, "Hey, cool."

Such a know-it-all giving out speeding tickets is one thing. But when he busted me for possession, and I was still a kid: I couldn't work for the state or join the army or get back to Maui. So I negotiated a key of coke from some dealers in Oahu, but it ended up in the harbor. Barry Moniz knew, and told his uncle, the chief, and that was the end of my hopes.

When he came home early that night and caught us naked, all in the bed, the overhead light on, his gun pointed at us, I went dead all over, first chicken-skin, then just numb. And afterward I didn't believe he'd really gone. I thought he was waiting for us to come outside so he could ambush us.

"Buggah wen go or what?" Ledward asked in a whisper.

We sneaked out by the back door.

"Junior. I tink we makeh-die-dead," he said in the pickup.

I heard that Erskine was transferred to Hilo, and with him on a neighbor island, things quieted down. It was Chief Moniz who told me. He made a few visits to Verna, gave her some money, like he felt sorry for her.

"She no can get food stamp," he said to me. "Wass the happs?"

The happs was I never smoked another joint from that day and I got a job digging, working an excavator, but because of my police record, not at the landfill, a state job, where I could have made more money. Ledward said she could have gotten us killed, but I said, "It was our own fault. We were the ones that set her up."

"Because she wen ask for da kine chrabol."

I was annoyed that he was blaming her. I saw things I'd never seen before, that Verna was in a bind, and after a while I married her on the beach at Hanalei, her kid Kanoa there in a little aloha shirt, a luau, the sunset, a green flash. I never saw Ledward again, because he went to Molokai.

And Verna would get a call from time to time, I guessed from Erskine, she didn't say, and we'd go stay with my cousin in Kapaa until Erskine gave up and went back to the Big Island. He wanted custody. But I would have said, "Tough. You left her. I married her. This is my hanai kid now."

Ledward used to say, "Yes, I want to catch waves in a foreign country, maybe Brazil, if I can snort coke there and have sex on the beach."

He is in Kaunakakai, maybe shaping boards, maybe hanging out. And Verna talks about taking flying lessons, which will never happen. Kanoa is on Oahu, where Chief Moniz retired, and got him apprenticing as a roofer. Kanoa still doesn't see much of his father, and never knew how his mother almost got shot one night. Erskine's ex, Noelani, sends Christmas cards and sometimes a pineapple.

I'm glad Erskine just walked away. He did the right thing by not shooting us. Yet he wasn't innocent. I'd never be able to convince him, but he was responsible. Instead of revenge I ended up with Verna. She makes pickled mango, one of those older women on a back road, selling it in jars, and you'd never guess from her smile the things that have happened to her.

But what was it after all? It was island style, a period of drugs and freaky sex and getting out of hand that all people go through before they settle down, especially on the neighbor islands. Then it passes. But it was all dog luck, because I would have shot me.

The Traveler's Wife

IN THE CAR on the way home from the Willevers', Bree said, "It's funny–" and Harry Dick knew she was about to object to something. She became chatty and opinionated at the wheel, and he was sorry he'd had three drinks because he hated being a passenger, especially *her* passenger. And what was that odd smell in the back seat?

Harry Dick Furlong, the travel writer, dedicated his books to his wife, Bree; he praised her for her patience in awaiting his return, and the way she ran the house, and coped with the demands of his office when he was on one of his trips – and tonight, as always, at the Willevers' she had listened to his stories as though hearing them for the first time. He liked to say their marriage was a partnership that worked.

The evening had gone well. The Willevers were good hosts, and grateful to Furlong for agreeing to the dinner so soon after arriving back from his last long trip. In addition to being a reader and a friend, Ed Willever was the Furlongs' attorney. He was also a tease, and it was a mark of his trust in their friendship that he dared to tease Furlong.

At the meal, Furlong had done most of the talking. He was full of new stories, and though most of them were boasts they sounded authentic. "You couldn't make this stuff up!" About being starved, stranded, threatened by some rowdy boys, propositioned by a drunken woman at a bar. One about a snake, another about a scorpion. "As a traveler I often feel like a castaway." At times it seemed it was not Harry Dick at all, but a fictional wanderer named Furlong whom he was recalling with amazement and admiration.

His trips had given him an aura of wizardry, as sudden vanishings and reappearances often do, travel in his way like an accumulation of magic, overcoming dangers as he plunged deeper into the murky world. His books were reports on the extraordinary, news from distant places. His criticism of most travel books was "You could see that sort of thing without ever leaving home."

He immediately thought "It's funny –" meant Bree doubted one of the stories he'd told at the Willevers'.

"You don't believe I had a scorpion in my shoe?" It had leaped out, he'd said, just before he slipped the shoe on.

"Not that," Bree said. "It was when you talked about not wanting to be known."

Furlong refused all interviews; he never appeared on television; he avoided book tours – no autographs, never elaborated on his trips, did not answer questions. "It's all in the book."

Exasperated, he said, "Haven't we been through that?"

"But when Ed said, 'It's kind of a cheat, isn't it?'" Bree was driving efficiently, glancing in her rearview mirror, tapping her turn signal. "And then, 'Being well known for your desire to be unknown.'"

"He was trying to be funny."

"It got me thinking."

She had never doubted him before. Never questioned him. And it cut him, because her point – Ed's teasing remark – was too logical to refute. Was she doubting him now?

He said, "I like my privacy."

"And everyone knows it. And they talk about you because of it. Like Ed said, 'The well-known recluse.'"

"You're taking him seriously."

Ed had also said something about having it both ways, but she did not remind him. They were in the driveway now, yet Bree remained in the driver's seat, holding the wheel as though gripping it gave her authority.

"I'm just asking."

"I got stuck in that village. I told you. I wanted to come home sooner."

Still she hung on to the steering wheel. "And when Ed said that going on a trip was maybe not leaving at all but making yourself more conspicuous?"

"He was drunk," Furlong said, sounding drunk himself.

"Making a big deal about hiding from the limelight was a way of attracting the limelight."

"Please." The word meant everything, but especially it meant, "This conversation is at an end."

Bree said lightly, "I don't know."

But before he got out of the car, Furlong sniffed and said, "Do you smell something?" He made the clownish face of someone interrogating a smell. He said, "Cigarette."

"I had a smoke," Bree said.

"You – *what?*"

It was the explosive tone he would have used if she had said, *I have a lover.* He was shocked, almost disbelieving, but the odor lingered as proof, and *I had a smoke* sounded worse than *I had a cigarette* – more knowing.

"At Ed and Joan's, while you were talking. I went outside. Probably my coat still smells. It's on the back seat."

"I cannot believe this. No one smokes anymore."

"I took it up." She spoke promptly, as if she'd rehearsed the reply.

"I stopped twenty years ago."

"I had never tried it."

"It's dangerous."

"So is your travel."

"And it stinks."

"You won't smell it. You'll be away."

He was so shocked by her casual *I took it up,* he was too embarrassed to tell anyone. He felt he had to hide her smoking from people they knew, and Bree objected to that. Smoking relaxed her, she said. It aided her digestion. It passed the time. Your own smoke smelled different from other people's smoke. "Who knew?"

And it seemed to give her confidence. She began to whistle – tunelessly, which made her whistling louder, more intrusive. Her whistling said, I am on my own. It also said, I don't care. And: I am going to go on doing this until I improve. And it seemed to him, irrationally, as though she expected someone, a stranger, to answer her, whistling back. He had never heard her whistle before, and the whistle was like another voice, but someone else's voice.

"I never travel with Harry Dick – I'd just be in the way," she said the next time they were at the Willevers'.

Willever said, "He's an outsider. Two outsiders is one too many."

Bree said, "As an outsider, Harry Dick has a hatred of insiders. But if you spend that much time writing about yourself, how can you call yourself an outsider? You're too big."

"But what do you really think?" Willever said, as he often did, as another tease, not expecting a reply.

But Bree said, "Travel can warp your outlook."

Afterward, in the silence of the car – Furlong was driving – Bree said, "I honestly don't know why I said that."

Furlong examined her face. She did not look sorry. She was smiling softly, but with unshakable defiance, her lips everted, as though she held a cigarette between them, a smoker's confident pout.

Feeling whipped, Furlong said, "What is wrong?"

"I don't know what I was talking about." Bree spoke in an insincere, silly-me tone – or did she mean it?

He said, "I think Ed knows you smoke."

She laughed – the laugh was new too, a cartoon cackle that went with the whistle.

He said, "How will you explain it?"

"I'll say how much fun it is. I never knew that."

They did not have children, a conscious decision, because a child would have hampered his travel. To "Any kids?" Furlong said, "We've got a really energetic Lab. It's like having a five-year-old who never grows up." But it was Bree who looked after Lester when Furlong was away.

It seemed to him that Bree was content. She did not discuss her plans with Furlong. But this apparent reticence marked the onset of a new habit, like the smoking, like the whistling. Instead of talking about her plans, she made announcements when they were in the presence of other people, usually the Willevers, sometimes the Jimmersons, now and then the Woottens – his friends, not hers. When they asked about a book he was writing, Furlong said, "I'm in Addis Ababa." Or "Just leaving Rangoon."

This happened one night at the Willevers', soon after her whistling improved. "I'm still in Kunming," Furlong said, and when (to be fair) Willever asked Bree what she was doing, she said, "I'm going to Las Vegas."

"Good for you," Ed said.

Furlong laughed. "That's Bree. Great at improvisation." But in the car on the way home he said, "You're not serious."

She said, "I don't know. It just came out. After I heard myself say it, it seemed like a great idea. I might go this weekend."

Furlong felt carved up, as with the revelation of her smoking. He said, "You don't gamble. You hate shows."

"But you can smoke there. And I've heard there are a lot of restaurants."

"And you hate to go to restaurants alone. You've said so."

"I've gotten used to it. From you being away."

Furlong uttered a skeptical sound through his nose that was meant to convey disbelief. But on the day he drove her to the airport, she said, "You'll be able to work better with me away. You can do whatever you want. You'll be brilliant."

It was what he had said to her once on one of his departures. And he had also written how, in Italy, if a person praised a baby's health and didn't say "Bless him," the praise was like a curse. He felt that way now, that in praising him she was blighting his luck.

It was just a weekend, she said. He sat at his desk, imagining Bree in Las Vegas doing – what? She didn't call. He dialed her cell phone. No answer. But that had been their agreement. "I don't want to disturb your writing."

Her silence, her absence, did disturb him – terribly. He wrote nothing – or rather, he wrote pages that, after he reread them, seemed to him forced and unreliable and lifeless, and he tossed them. He walked Lester, and found the dog demanding and indecisive. He fretted. What did people do in Las Vegas if they didn't throw money away gambling? Did they gamble in other ways? He imagined himself in Las Vegas, and Bree at home, and he became anxious.

On her return, Furlong said, "What were you doing all that time?"

She said, "What do you usually do?"

She seemed rested and chatty, not about Las Vegas but about her next trip, a longer one, to Disneyland. "I've always wanted to go."

Disneyland! The word suggested a world of frivolity and wasted money and bad health, a relic from the age of smoking. But she went. And in the five days she was away Furlong could not work. Worse, in the middle of that week Joan Willever stopped in.

"I just wanted to see how you were making out with Bree away." A girlishness in her tone, something coquettish, disturbed him deeply.

"Where's Ed?"

"Home. I didn't tell him I was coming over. I thought he'd be funny about it."

Furlong could only think that when he was away Ed Willever dropped in on Bree, and that a pattern was being revealed to him. He wanted to say *Bree smokes,* but he was ashamed to, and she might blame him for her doing it.

"You don't need me?" Joan said.

What did this mean? He stared at her and said, "I've got work to do."

"The traveler at home," Joan said. "Strange concept."

After she left, he sat with his fists pressed against his cheeks as though trying to force a sentence from his head. Nothing came, or only falsehoods came, as he awaited Bree's return; and he hated the thoughts that were crowding his imagination.

The last sentence he'd written was "The Nepali in the shop sat under a long sticky screw of flypaper, its curls black with bodies." He could not continue, or extend it. He kept seeing it, more and more bodies accumulating on the hanging paper.

Bree said nothing to him on her return, but the next time at the Willevers' she spoke up, mentioning the rides, the restaurants, the features of the hotel. Furlong sat, dumb, confused, with growing anger.

Ed Willever said, "You've got competition, Harry Dick."

Bree said, "Of course not. I'd never write about it."

And that confused Furlong further. He could not help but think that in her absences she'd taken over his life, that her travels were his own trips, but with a difference – she didn't write about them, she hardly spoke of them, but in a fragmentary way he believed her to be editing, in a spirit of concealment.

When she said she wanted to drive to Seattle, Furlong said, "Take a plane."

"You can't smoke on a plane."

"I want to come with you."

"No," she said. "I want to smoke in the car and you won't like it." Then, "You have to write your book."

He did not have the heart to tell her that he couldn't write.

Bree drove to Seattle, whistling as she left the house. She

was out of touch for ten days. She vanished in the way he had always done; and when she was away a part of him vanished – the confident part of him, the risk taker, the wizard, the storyteller; and he was left idle, feeling undermined, staring at his unfinished sentence, following her progress in his head, knowing what he would be doing on that road.

He could only think she had another life, that she dallied with other men in motels and told them lies or half-truths. He made the accusation but she denied it, laughing, blowing smoke at him, tapping her cigarette into a saucer. That maddened him. He saw a wickedness in her smoking. When she told stories of her travels at dinner parties, he did not believe them. Surely she was embellishing, improving, falsifying. And that suspicion – that her real life was out there, wreathed in cigarette smoke – finished him, as a traveler, as a writer, as a husband.

The First World

NUMBER ONE, I am writing this because the people on this island hate me and they don't even know me. Number two, they are bound to write the most awful things about me after I am dead, which might be soon. Number three, I don't give a damn but the woman in question is innocent and not able to defend herself.

I returned to Nantucket and brought my money with me, because as a boy I had worked summers on the island and been treated badly by rich privileged people. Not revenge – I had never envied them enough to want revenge. I wanted something for myself. I had worked hard my whole life, built a company, ran it, and finally sold it. Isn't the whole point of starting a business in America to sell it at a profit? Retiring to Nantucket island was my reward. I needed in old age what I had craved as a child.

I saw hot-faced kids cutting grass or washing cars and I grieved for the boy I had been, not knowing where my life would lead. There are few situations more frustrating for a young man with no money and no prospects than working for an older man who has everything. It is the condition of a Third Worlder toiling for a billionaire, the cruel proximity, the daily reminders. It was suggested – "Don't stare, Jimmy!" – that I avert my eyes when the man's daughter appeared; I had to acknowledge that I was out of her league. Naturally her father was self-made, something in electronic goods, at a time when such things were still made in America. This dumb Mick from Southie regarded himself as an aristocrat.

The day I got accepted at Northeastern he said, "I suppose this means I'll have to find someone else to cut the grass."

The island was so flat and so far at sea that the mainland was beneath the horizon even on the clearest day. The sea around the island was dangerous and shoaly, hazards everywhere, littered with wrecks, some hulks bristling in the sand at low tide, corroded stacks, rusty ribs, and the wrecks themselves were hazards. The aboriginals – none survived – had called it, in their own language, "the faraway land" – Nantucket. It was easy for the islanders to believe that they were alone on earth. But "islanders" was a misnomer. The old-timers had been there for centuries, but there had always been locals and year-rounders and summer people, and every season new people, each batch richer than the last.

At night, most of the island lay in darkness – empty roads: who would go out, and where would they go? The wealthiest on the island were among the wealthiest on earth, the poorest just hung on, and there came a point when you became too poor to go on living there – many had been driven out. The island had a Main Street and many churches, a library, an athenaeum, a yacht club, and a golf club.

Fifty years on, the menials were now different: Americans didn't cut our grass anymore, they didn't vacuum the pools or look after the kids. Time was when a rising class of hard-up college students took those jobs. No more. It's all foreigners now, and even the Irish students are gone. It's Jamaicans, Brazilians, Filipinos, and a scattering of Asiatics.

Nhu was one of these – Vietnamese, a bit vague about when and how she had landed on the island, stuck for a place to stay, looking for a live-in housecleaning job. I suspected that she was desperate, that she had abruptly fled an employer, some tyrant taking advantage. I knew all about that. How enigmatic the wealthy are at a distance, how obvious close up, just brutes in many cases – outright bullies – or else they never would have elbowed their way into business and made their pile. Most of the newly wealthy men I met in my career were physical intimidators.

Later, Nhu said, "Him lie tuss."

"Really?"

"Weery."

"Where did he touch you?"

"Hakoochi."

"What were you doing in the Jacuzzi?"

"Crean it. Him say, 'Put the wa' in.'"

"Fill it up?"

"Ya. Then him tuss me."

"In the Jacuzzi?"

"Teet."

I gave her the job, for her scruples, for her puritanism, for her conscientious objection, and to demonstrate that we Americans were not all the same. Besides, her country had helped make me rich in the scrap metal business, not that she ever wanted to talk about Vietnam.

Then there were just two of us in the house. At the time I was planning a new house – my dream of inhabiting a house I had made myself, as I had lived the life of my choosing. I told Nhu. There was no one else to tell. She stared at me, probably thinking, What has this got to do with me?

I said, "There's a little apartment for you. Staff quarters."

She just stared again – didn't even nod. She never looked ahead – could not see past the weekend.

"I know you're thinking you don't need it. You can live on fish heads and rice."

"And teevy."

"You got it. Wide screen."

"Okay, boss."

Clever little doll. But that was at the beginning, before the world ended.

So, my life story, the short version. Born on the Cape, salesman father, budget-minded mother. "Money doesn't grow on trees!" Part-time jobs were more important than homework.

The usual public schools: punks and bookworms and bullying teachers. I bagged groceries in the winter and in the summer took the ferry out to the island and cut grass. After a while my friends were slumming Ivy Leaguers, whom I half hated and half pitied. "Joe College." Northeastern for me – though after-school jobs turned me from a student into a worker, and gave me a nose for business.

The army: Vietnam, the Delta. My first sight of mountains of scrap metal and, after my discharge, my first deal. The simple profitable truth was that scrap metal was available in the Third World and in demand in the First World. The Junk Man, they called me out of sheer envy, and I regarded it as a summing-up of the steel business. Scrap into steel, steel into engine blocks, which became scrap again. I loved the poetry of its transformation, I loved the way it rhymed and made me rich.

Four marriages, much like your one or two. A little bit of pleasure, some conflict, and a lot of monotony – I preferred the monotony. I was always too wealthy to attract a liberated woman, so I got the needy ones who said, "Feed me," and wanted a meal ticket for life. Strangely, no children of my own, though Number Three had baggage. I bought houses and lost them. My lust and greed were punished; why wasn't theirs? But I married these women. They did not bewitch me. Then I was sleeping alone and liking it.

I am old enough to remember when junk men were part of the foreground on the Cape, sitting on a wagon, tapping a whip on a horse's hindquarters and calling out "Rags and bottles," buying scrap metal and rags by the pound and handing over a few coins to people who would otherwise have thrown the stuff away. The garbage man sold your swill to pig farms.

The army had made me a traveler, travel had made me a merchant. I saw opportunities. Even after Barghorn Scrap Metal became Barghorn Enterprises I still could not look at a freight car full of twisted vehicles and junked girders without seeing money. Space and transport are crucial factors in this business. I shipped it, stored it, processed it, then sold it. The market in rags hardly exists anymore, but scrap metal is more profitable than ever. Is any of this interesting? It is to me.

By the time I got to the island and bought the old Chapin place I had sworn off marriage. Yet I was pursued. I was not the Junk Man then. I was a CEO on joshing terms with Tommy Hilfiger and Harry Johnson and John Sculley. At parties I would socialize and think: What terrific women! Always available! Funny! Accommodating! Positive! Eager to please! Always saying, "I'd love to!"

They wanted, of course, to marry me.

It was about this time, living alone, being pursued, that I submitted the proposal to build my dream house on the Neck. I was happy. I was being looked after by Nhu. "I crean poor . . . I fix Hakoochi . . . I make noodoos." She knew most of the people on the Building Committee – she had worked for them at one time or another.

She would say, "Da Miffs. He dwee and dwee, he get dwun. She pray gol."

But I knew them too. "Ernie Smith. He's always saying 'It sort of melds.' Trish Smith, I've seen her on the course. Wears rompers. What about the Rotbergs?"

"Lobbers – chee weery nye."

"What about him?"

"He nye. Dey nye peepoo. He lie fitching."

"So it's a slam dunk."

But it wasn't: I got slammed. The hearing was at seven, and by seven-fifteen they had denied me my permit – absolutely not, no way, never. I asked why.

They said, We're almost built out and you're proposing the biggest house on the island. Out of the question, won't harmonize, stick out like a sore thumb, trophy house.

I said, "I'll show you trophy houses. In their time, the merchants and whalers were building trophy houses up and down Main Street. Listen, I've hired the finest architects."

They said, It's a quality-of-life issue, and what about the setbacks? The elevation of my place would change the Neck's dune profile.

"The dune profile changes every winter with the nor'easters, and if the dune gives way, that's my problem."

They said, The Neck's fragile ecosystem was easily impacted by water and septic parameters – this from a plumber who was a high school dropout, but anyway – and what about the road?

"Berm it."

They queried the theoretical runoff from the proposed golf course.

"Executive putting green. I've put in swales and catchments."

They said my swimming pool design was nonconforming. Island code had to be followed to the letter.

"Lap pool. It uses treated seawater. Aerates it. No chemicals. It'll be the only one on the island that's nontoxic. Next question."

They said the copper sheathing on my mansard roof would not pass Historic District guidelines.

"Downstream, it will develop a rich patina and look distressed and gorgeous – blackish, greenish." I looked at Ernie Smith. "It'll meld with the dune grass."

But the answer was no – no to the cupola, no to Nhu's staff quarters, no to the bocce court, no to the helipad, never to this lovely home.

I said, "If I'd listened to people who said 'never' to me, I wouldn't have gotten to this island in the first place."

My rage made the committee members smile, they enjoyed the illusion that they were more powerful than me, thumbs-down to the Junk Man. And yet what pleased them most was the thought that, deep down, they knew they were all exactly like me – parvenus and opportunists.

"We wish we could help," Rotberg said smugly. The others agreed, they moved on to other business, and I drove home, still furious.

Nhu was at the kitchen counter, sorting beans.

"I need a drink. Vodka."

"Olinch?"

"On the rocks. Splash of tonic."

"Was a messis fom da pumma."

"About the Jacuzzi?"

"No. Hakoochi wuck okay. Da pumma fom da Bidding Mittee."

"I just left there. The Building Committee turned me down."

I felt a little self-conscious confiding my defeat to my Vietnamese housekeeper. But she didn't flinch, did not react at all, so I went on.

Just then the doorbell rang – Nickerson, the plumber from the committee. I looked at him and thought, "Ecosystem," "impacted," "parameters." I blocked the entrance of my house with my body and said, "Yes?"

He looked a bit chastened, facing me on his own.

"The thing is, Mr. Barghorn, you can resubmit your plan with appropriate changes. You left the meeting before we explained that."

"Why would I want to make changes?"

He blinked at me. "That way you might get your permit. Your plans have to conform."

"You mean I have to please you?"

"So to speak."

I laughed and banged the door in his face.

But the moment I was alone I felt isolated, as though I had shut myself out and was stuck here. I hated living in someone else's idea of a house. Yet to amend my blueprints, to build a house to someone else's specifications, was not how I had lived my life. I wanted my own or none at all, yet I could not summon the strength to fight them. And I began to think that I might have retired to the wrong place.

So I sat, uncomfortably, mentally rejecting them all, and I heard an almost inaudible cluck and saw, out of the corner of my eye, a creature in the doorway – Nhu.

"Soy," she said softly in a tone of regret. "Vey soy."

I was moved to think that she who had nothing was trying to share the disappointment of someone who had everything.

"Never mind," I said, embarrassed at being consoled by this skinny little doll crouching in the corner.

"Me may noodoo."

"Thanks."

"You wan nudda drin?"

"One more vodka."

"Olinch?"

"Orange would be very nice."

She brought the drink. I sat and felt calm. She brought noodles and some dishes on a tray, stir-fried shrimp and bamboo shoots.

"Where did this come from?"

"My foo."

She crouched by my chair while I ate and drank, and we watched a rerun of an old episode of *I Love Lucy,* and Nhu murmured with satisfaction. And while all this was happening I thought, I don't need them, I don't need anyone. And I slept better that night.

The next day Nhu was up early, baking muffins. She toasted one and served it to me, with green tea, on the deck overlooking the Sound.

I said, "They wouldn't let me build my house."

She shrugged.

"And they said no to the staff quarters, where you were going to live."

She shrugged again. She had a very convincing shrug that

conveyed utter indifference. This was the First World but she was from the Third. Her mode of survival was: Learn to do without. Don't get angry. Don't show emotion. Beware of needing anything.

"I have the feeling they want us to leave the island."

"No can sweem."

Funny! She made a face, wrinkled her nose – clever doll. But her lesson was salutary. I was the needy one. If I was to stay here, I had to learn to be more like her.

I said I had to go into town to buy groceries.

"I geev lees."

"Don't bother with a list. Why don't you just come along?"

And so she did, without a murmur, hopped into the Bronco, smiled as I drove, and at the supermarket hurried ahead of me, tossing items into the trolley that I was pushing. Back home she helped me carry the food into the house. I thought, She makes life easy for me. None of my wives had ever inspired such a grateful thought.

And what was Nhu's life? Living in the back room, sleeping in a narrow cot, sitting with her fists against her cheeks watching a tiny TV, smoking cigarettes, and slurping noodles. Or else it was fish heads and rice, and early to bed.

We drove one day to Siasconset, and parked facing seaward, and I sat looking for shore birds with my binoculars. Then she drove slowly along the coast, so that I could watch an osprey building a nest on top of a dead tree. I was eating a NutRageous bar. I gave her a piece.

"Rishus!"

I thought, Life could be this simple.

That night I continued to drink after dinner. Nhu had a waitress's instinct for appearing from nowhere when my glass was empty and asking if I wanted more.

"Sit here," I said.

She resisted, then she sat on the edge of the chair, like a bird teetering on a branch.

"Drink?"

She said yes with her eyes and a certain motion of her head, and then, "Bland."

"This brandy is twenty-five years old," I said.

"Lie me!"

The way she perched and drank made me anxious, for she seemed to be balancing rather than sitting. But after she had two more drinks, her manner of perching seemed a good indication that she could hold her liquor, a rare thing among the Asiatics I had done business with.

I put my arm around her. She stiffened and moved so that she was perched on an even smaller portion of the sofa, as though about to take flight. She faced forward and said, "Nup."

"What's wrong?"

"You want sess? No can do sess wee me. We flen. If we do sess, I no can wuck, no can crean, and wha. No be flen."

I remembered with shame the shocked and disgusted way she had said, *Him tuss me.* So I poured her another drink, which she held in her hand, and she looked serious.

"If we do sess, me pain here," and she touched her heart.

We had another drink and then she said good night and went to her room, and to my shame I heard her double-lock her door, the key, the dead bolt. Now I was another employer of whom she could say, *Him try tuss me.*

But she stayed. I was careful not to presume upon her, and after a while I began to feel a certain relief knowing the limits of my friskiness and the boundaries of my friendship. I reminded myself that I was her employer and how much she mattered to me, how essential her good humor and efficiency were to my well-being on this island.

That was how things stood between us for several summer months. In those months we worked out a routine: she cleaned, I read the paper, then did my desk work. On rainy days we had lunch at home – Nhu eating in the kitchen, me in the dining room. On good days we had lunch on my boat and then went for a run, and I drank beer and steered, and she fished, trolling from the stern. She was good at it – knew the lures, knew the bait, knew the best speed. After a while I would anchor on a shoal and she'd cast for stripers, and now and then caught one, or bluefish, or pollock. She drank beer, too, and after a few would tell stories about the islanders she knew – about cruel husbands, or drunken wives, or unruly kids. She seemed to know most of the people on the island, the millionaires as well as the locals. She did not envy a single one of them, nor was she dazzled by their wealth; her stories were always pitying or gently patronizing.

She was fishing one day on a shoal, the boat anchored, the ebbing tide bubbling with rockweed making the current visible over the shelf of rocks, the greeny-black water purling and frothing. With nothing to do, I propped myself on a cushion and drowsed.

I did not hear her fall over the side, the shoal was so splashy and loud. But something made me mutter to her, and getting no response I tipped up the bill of my cap and saw the empty afterdeck. Then I called out and heard nothing but the current coursing past my hull.

I ran to the side and saw, some distance off, her little head and sprawling hair and one reaching hand, being slapped by the chop and bobbing among the standing waves of the shoal.

I threw out a life preserver on a fixed line and leaped in after it, holding the line. I was yanked in her direction and easily reached her, because I was swimming and she wasn't. I snatched at her, lost her in the foam, then swam forward and found her kicking foot, so small I could get my whole hand around it. Then her ankle and arm, and soon I had her upright and she was choking and coughing – a good sign, I thought.

Keeping her faced away from me for safety, I held her under her arms.

"You okay?"

"Blaup!" She gagged, she spat, she struggled.

I gave her the life ring to hold, and still she choked and spewed water. We floated for a while in the stiff current of the shoal, and when she was calmer, breathing more easily, I tugged her back to the boat.

She tried not to show her fear, she said she was fine, yet the terror was on her face and in her eyes. She had never looked more like an animal, more helpless, colder, more frightened. She sat wrapped in a blanket – she would not take off her clothes in front of me – modesty even in a near-death experience. We went home without saying much.

I said, "You didn't catch anything."

"Catch coh. No fitch."

She insisted on making dinner for me, and it was a special dinner, stir-fried prawns and bamboo shoots and water chestnuts from her stock of delicacies and imported provisions. Soup made with fresh-picked lemongrass from the pot outside her door, mango pickle, and salted duck eggs from God knows where.

I had not noticed how she was dressed until after I finished eating and she came to me in the living room, wearing her Vietnamese ao dai, her blue and white gown, and looking angelic. I was on the sofa, working on my fourth whiskey, half stupefied from the meal and the boat trip and the effort of the rescue.

"Wan somefin?"

My glass was half full. I said, "This is fine."

"Wan some uvver? Uvverfin?"

I was bewildered. I was not hungry and could not understand her pampering manner, for I was fine. She was the one who had had a scare, not me. She lifted the sides of her gown and sat beside me.

"Want tuss?"

Only then I realized she was offering herself. I said, "You don't want that."

She nodded with such solemnity that I smiled.

"You say me."

"You were easy to save."

"You say my lie."

"I was glad to."

"Can tuss," she said, lowering her eyes in a way that was both coquettish and demure.

"You don't owe me anything," I said. But I also thought, If she feels that way, it's money in the bank.

That was a defining day. It was as though she was saying, You saved my life, and so I am here because of you, and therefore my life is yours. But I did not take advantage of her. I was careful to remind her that we were still friends, that she was an employee, that I was grateful to her for helping me. Of course she remembered my drunken and indecent proposal from earlier in the summer, the thing I had wanted. She was willing to grant that to me now, out of gratitude.

All I wanted was to sit beside her, drink with her, hold her hand sometimes, watch the terns diving over the marsh grass at sunset. And sitting there, I thought: This is perfect. I don't need that big house. I am happy here, doing this.

"You are Buddhist."

"Ya."

"But no temple on the island."

"Temper hee," she said, and touched her heart.

We had short conversations, and afterward long silences. The silences were the most telling, because they expressed our deepest contentment. I wanted nothing more and for nothing to change.

Not long after that, she woke me in the middle of the night, startling me until I saw her small figure shivering beside my bed.

"What's wrong?"

"Canna slee."

"Why not?"

"Bah dree."

"What kind of dream?"

"Folly offa bow."

A drowning dream.

"Say me. Plee, say me."

She got into my bed, and as with the business in the ocean, and the way we hung on to each other in the water, it wasn't just me, it was something both of us badly wanted.

Days of bliss followed. Weeks. We were more than a couple, we were a team! After we started sleeping together I didn't know whether to pay her more or to stop paying her entirely. I asked her. She said, "Same." More money was like prostitution, no money was presumption. I wanted to do the right thing, because I didn't want this to end.

The routine suited me – paperwork and phone calls after breakfast, a nap after lunch, a drive to the dunes after the nap, and birdwatching or else fishing, some effort in order to stimulate a thirst, a drink before dinner, and then early to bed, Nhu beside me.

One day early on in this blissful period, we went clamming at low tide out on the harbor flats. She dug a bushel. Her first time handling a clamming fork and she's hoisting twenty pounds of littlenecks and quahogs and I am hooting in admiration and hugging her.

"Why you lie me?"

"Because I've never known anyone like you," I said. "You're always, 'Okay, boss!' You don't bitch."

She was much too cheerful to care how I praised her and I could not explain how much she meant to me. She washed my car, she trimmed my hair, she mixed drinks for me, she cooked for me, she caught fish and fried it, she made me laugh, she aroused me.

How old was she? Mid-twenties, maybe, as she'd said – no memory of the Vietnam War but intimate knowledge of its aftermath.

"My fadda take me to jungoo. He see snae, bih snae! He catch snae and – yum! yum!"

Snake-eating in the thickets of the Delta.

"He plan rye. Me hep."

Father and daughter, knee-deep in the paddy fields, bending over their reflections.

"And then you came here."

"Bludda come. He hep me come affa."

Less than half my age but she had lived as much as I had. We were made for each other. When I was with her I forgot who I was, and I had the impression that when she was with me she was similarly euphoric. I hardly considered the strangeness of it all, that I was a multimillionaire cohabiting with my maid in a mansion on Nantucket, for I was happier than I had ever been in my life.

You tend to see yourself most objectively when you imagine how other people see you; other people's eyes are colder. But there were no other people around. We were isolated enough here so that I seldom thought about our living arrangement, and when I did think about it I was just grateful. More weeks went by, but time moved at a different pace now, because I was happy. I had stopped thinking about building the grand house on the Neck. I was reconciled to living on this island in this secondhand mansion, because this woman was making me happy, and this was possible because she was happy.

I wanted nothing more. She wanted nothing more. The Buddhists are right: eliminate all desire and you've found peace.

"I lie you. You happy. No worry."

When the person you love returns your compliments, you know all is well.

All would have been well – nothing would have changed – if we had stayed in the little clapboard paradise we had made, of meals and naps, noodles and clamming, early to bed and up at first light. All *was* well, but there came a change.

The Figawi Ball at the Club was an annual islanders-only gala, held around Memorial Day after the big Figawi Race from Hyannis, before the summer people arrived. I had avoided the event, because as a youth I had been a waiter and a hired hand at the Club, and I knew it would bother me to see the members and be reminded of the suffering menial I had been.

Going was Nhu's idea, but she raised the subject as an example of pure irony, which was how I knew that it meant a lot to her. We were at the market and she saw the Figawi Ball poster taped to the front window.

"Crab dan."

"A perfect way of describing it."

"We go togevva, yah!"

The very idea of going was out of the question, and so she joked about going, even joked about what T-shirt she would wear, and which sneakers, to the great island event, open to Club members only, the tickets hard to get and expensive. Even the Brazilian menials knew about it and tried to work at it, just to be part of the glamour.

"You want to go?"

"Crab dan?"

"Right."

"Yah. For dan and seen. Ha!"

Understanding the profound impossibility she was suggesting with this mockery, I said, "Okay, we're going."

We were in the car by then, driving back to the house. She went silent, she was pale, I saw she was terrified.

"No can," she said. Then she pleaded, "No crab dan."

"You're my guest."

"No got dreh for way."

"I'll buy you a dress."

"Cannot for dan."

"No dancing. We'll just sit. We'll eat. We'll drink wine."

"Adda peepoo!"

But she knew all the other people on the island – more than I knew, and she knew them intimately.

I had made my peace with the island. I had given up the idea of building my mansion on the Neck, but I had no intention of leaving. I thought: If I'm going to live here, these people will have to get used to me. They'll have to understand who I am and what I do. I am proud of my life. This was not a summer fling with my housekeeper. Winter had come and gone. Spring was here. Summer was coming. The rest of my life was coming.

She was just the right size to carry off a little black dress and make it seem elegant. This she insisted on buying herself with money she had saved. I gave her the money for new shoes, beautiful ones from a boutique on Main Street which added three inches to her height. Her Brazilian friend at the beauty salon did her hair and nails. The result was a vision of loveliness, a transformation, from a little Third World doll to a First World dragon lady of intimidating beauty, upswept coiffure, crimson talons.

I would never have guessed how much she liked dressing up, and not just putting on new clothes but being glamorous. Glamour is a little girl's game, played with costumes and mirrors. New clothes made her a different person, one she liked better, someone who fitted in. And this transformation took her mind off the main event and made her less apprehensive.

Driving to the Club the night of the Figawi Ball, with Nhu beside me smelling sweetly, I thought again, My life is complete.

She said nothing. Silence was also part of the transformation, a kind of dignity and drama – and I suppose she was terrified, too.

The valet parkers eyed her, seemed to recognize her in some dimly admiring way, but no one else noticed us. The foyer was filled with members – men in suits or club blazers, women in gowns – all of them shouting excitedly at each other. I hurried Nhu past them to the ballroom, lifted two glasses of wine from a passing tray, and toasted her. She was both excited and shy, dazzled by all the people, bewildered by what I now saw as the roaring men and their shouting overdressed wives.

She stuck close to me. Rotberg and Nickerson from the Building Committee came up to me and started talking, saying how nice it was to see me, all the while staring at Nhu. They had detached themselves from their wives, who were standing to one side, casting glances our way.

I was hardly listening. I found that I was seeing all this with Nhu's eyes, and I was keenly aware of being in a room of big loud oafs, who had nothing to say and not even the grace to apologize for opposing the building of my house on the Neck. Their attitude was: We're all buddies now!

"Barghorn!"

Seeing that I wasn't listening, they began bantering with Nhu.

Rotberg: "Hope you're treating him all right!"

Nickerson: "Don't wear him out!"

This seemed to me in bad taste, so I steered her away, but while I was getting more drinks for us, I saw a man approach Nhu and begin monologuing. He was Hal Walters from the Historic District Committee, his wife a little way off and glaring at Nhu.

They were all there, all the people who had turned me down, looking pleased that I had appeared at a Club dance for the first time ever. It was proof to them that I would not be a problem. I was one of them. I even had a woman in tow.

The music was loud, incomprehensible to me, but Nhu knew the lyrics and was murmuring them. Another revelation: she liked pop music. She seemed slightly drunk, but quite happy as long as she was by my side.

I monitored a few nearby conversations, all of them dishonest complaints – one bitching about the high price of real estate, another about winter storms, and one beefy-faced man was moaning that it was harder and harder for him to find parking space for his private jet at the airport. You had to be a resident here to know that all of this talk was a form of boasting.

Without warning, a woman blindsided us, and in a drunken and demanding voice said, "Aren't you going to introduce me to your friend?"

I had no idea who she was, but it took me only an instant to see that she was not talking to me.

Nhu blinked and said, "Miz Row."

That might have been "Lowell" – there was such a couple at the Club. Other women circled, seeing this Lowell woman close to us, and they hovered like hyenas.

Nhu smiled at her, and she seemed confused for, really, she had no name for me that could be uttered in a public place.

"I hope this doesn't mean what I think it means."

All the women smiled, hoping for a devastating remark from their friend.

"That you won't be available to do my windows."

After that, nothing mattered. I considered hitting her, or throwing my drink into her face and howling at her. But I smiled and steered Nhu to the exit, for I had a much better plan.

Only the feeblest, the weakest, the most naïve of them tried to stop me. The shrewdest, the strongest, the wealthiest, the truly connected ones did not lift a finger against me. They were smart enough to know that they would fail, that I would break them and bankrupt the Board of Selectmen – that it was much less costly for them to go along with me, to humor me, to praise my extravagant house.

And these fat ones also knew how lawless the rich can be. I was one of them. And the ways we break the law are trivial, mere nuisances, compared to the plunder and mayhem we get away with legally. The worst of us are seldom breaking the law. The law is on our side – it ought to be; after all, we are the ones who make it.

The ones who tried to stop me sent an emissary from the Building Committee, who appeared one afternoon on my doorstep, smiling and making small talk.

I said, "Now tell me what's really on your mind."

"Local ordinance, as old as the town. You can't build without permission."

"I'm building."

"Then you need to apply for a permit."

"I did that." I smiled at him. "It didn't fly."

"If you try to build, we'll have to stop you."

"How?" I was still smiling. "A lawsuit?"

He blinked at me, perhaps trying to summon the courage to speak. I knew what I was about to say would be repeated a thousand times in town and would become part of the island's mythology, so I kept it simple and memorable.

"Sue me," I said. "You'll lose. I've got more lawyers than you. I've got more money than you. I could tie you up for a hundred years. I could bankrupt your board. I could destroy you. Don't talk to me, talk to someone who knows me. People who know me would not dare to stop me. This meeting is over."

I did not shut the door in his face. I watched him stammer and sigh and turn away. He walked self-consciously down the path to the street.

Building a house on a small island is a public event. Every aspect is visible: the arrival of the container trucks, two a day, on the morning ferry; the deployment of workers, the coming and going of carpenters, plumbers, electricians – they filled the ferries, the commuter flights, the charter boats, the barges. The disruption of the island the rest of that year was constant; it continued through the spring and into the summer, season of shortages and stress and no space, and on into the fall.

Who could find a plumber or an electrician or a painter? I

had hired all the best ones. I had commandeered the stock in all the warehouses and hardware stores. Islanders were told, "We're out of cement," "We're down to our last roll of cable," "No more rebar." Other building projects on the island were put on hold because mine was proceeding. And there was nothing that anyone could do except reflect that they had brought this on themselves.

By Labor Day the house had risen and was clearly visible from town – although it was fifteen miles away. The talk reached me: the house was ugly, I was a monster, I was a junk dealer who had made money on drugs in the Third World, I was buying up the island, I was an interloper, I had a criminal record, I had physically threatened the Building Committee, I had committed similar outrages elsewhere.

The house was finished in time for us to spend Christmas inside. The wall around it was to code – four feet high – but behind the wall I planted Leyland cypress trees that would grow to twenty feet in no time, five hundred of them, a wall of greenery.

I was the subject of the most vicious gossip. The story was that I lived alone with my Third World servant. In one version, I was a tyrant who satisfied my lusts on her. In another, she was a shrew who tormented me.

All talk. At this stage of my life I am keenly aware of the malicious innuendo and falsehoods spread about reclusive men my age. The things that people say! Just listen to the crap they talk about other people. Are they so much more scrupulous when they talk about you?

Instead of accepting that, I am writing this. I realize that what motivates most other writers in the world is the desire to have control over their obituary.

The other facts, then. We married off-island, in Las Vegas – her choice, and the day she came off the payroll, Nhu revealed a new side of herself, her love for gambling and her winner's instinct for numbers. She won at blackjack, she knew when to double down or fold, she had a knack for remembering cards that had been played, she knew how to wait, when to collect her winnings, and when to quit. She claimed gambling was like fishing. I did not see that at all, which was probably why I was unlucky at both.

But I was lucky in having her.

She said, "I way you!"

"You might have had a long wait."

She said that she had decided upon me early on, and that if I had not acted, she would simply have worked for me, whatever happened; no one else would do. All this was in her mind. The plan was fully formed as an intention, but she could not presume; it was for me to make the first move.

No long after that, I was diagnosed with all sorts of ailments – macular degeneration in one eye, cataract in the other, a bad knee – requiring surgery. Ringing in the ears. I was forgetful. Fishing for a box of cookies on a top shelf, I slipped off the chair and broke my collarbone. I was falling apart. Nhu was in great shape, still smoking, working every day to keep the house spotless, fishing now and then.

This is the life I dreamed of. I am ill, but bearably so. I am mild. She runs the house, she runs me. She is wiser, more experienced, shrewder. When we go fishing I steer the boat, she fishes and determines the route, the speed, the duration. I am her servant. It is what I want.

We seldom go out. We see no one. We phone for groceries now. We might take the boat for a run over to Edgartown on a calm day with a fair tide, or even to the Cape. But the rest of the time we live behind our hedge in the huge house I built for her on the Neck.

She will outlive me. She will continue in this house as the Junk Man's widow. And I will rest easy knowing that long after I am gone, people just off the ferry will look east and, seeing our house, will make faces and say in shock, "What the hell's that?" It is a symbol of our love.

Heartache

MOST OF THE still-intact small towns of the Deep South have a local diner, brimming with the tang of hot fat, where everyone is welcome. Good manners prevail, the mood is cheerful. Unless they're saying grace, people look up from their food when someone enters. There might be a framed Bible verse on the wall or printed at the top of the sticky menu.

Louleen's, in Peavy, Alabama, was one. I took the writer Kate Collier Delombre there for lunch two days in a row. Her lovely old house was outside the town. On the first day she said to me, "I have a heartache," and on the second day, at my urging, she explained it, softly, with the fastidious pauses I'd found in her writing. She finished when we finished the meal. Perta Mae, her driver and housekeeper, listened with her head bowed over her plate.

"I wish I knew what to do."

"Write it," I said. "If you make it a story, you'll ease your pain."

"I'm too old for a long story." She was a month shy of eighty-nine. She was fully alert, not sick but aged, small, fragile, easily wearied. Yet she was immortal-looking, with the mummified features you see in the very old, giving her the dusty glow of an idol, and still with an appetite for catfish.

"It's been a furtive life," she said, with the bird claw of her hand resting on her throat. *Futtive* and *futtilize* were words she made her own. "How did I manage all those years alone? People don't ask. Twenty-eight stories published, and my memoir. So many stories started and put aside. The magic of getting it right – bliss for me, but who cares?"

"I do," I said, and Perta Mae nodded, still chewing.

"Peavy people see an old white woman in a town of young blacks. I'm the minority now. They look at me with hatred. And why? In the secret history of the South we're all related, by some ancient concubinage, persisting to the present. My work saved me. My work and Perta Mae. What makes me happy is my writing, like praying used to. I am speaking to readers as I speak to you. Readers listen, no one else does."

Six weeks later I got a call from Perta Mae. "Miss Kitty," and she swallowed, then a whisper, a sigh, "she pass." I remembered how she'd lain her fingers on the back of Kate's bird claw hand, black on white, to steady the menu. "Her heart give out."

I asked Perta Mae whether Miss Kitty had done any writing in those weeks. She said no, just suffering. She invited me to visit. There was no story. The heartache was mine now, an obligation unfulfilled, mine to complete, or else to suffer.

Kate had adored her son, Jack, the more so because he was all she had; she'd been widowed when she was thirty and her son was five. He was Jack Delombre Junior, adopted in the second year of her marriage when her husband confessed (tears, his face in shadow) he could not father a child. He begged her to understand. His confiding this was a burden, but the appearance of Jack Junior crowded out the secret. Her husband was delighted when they saw this beautiful boy, who'd been put up for adoption by an unwed mother in the nearby town of Cow Creek.

Jack Senior was an attorney in Peavy. He was balding in his twenties, he looked old at thirty. He was a frail man, even sickly, ill with anemia, needing transfusions. Kate, sensitive to words, recalled "blood disease" and "his blood's not strong," and when he died, the doctor's explanation: "a silent stroke."

The child took his place as her companion until, at the age of twenty-six, he met and fell in love with Brenda Palmer, from Chattanooga. An intruder, so she seemed to Kate in the beginning, a stranger in a culture where an outsider with different ideas is taken to be an agitator.

In her solitude – Jack Junior soon married – Kate began to write stories. Writing gave her a purpose, made the day matter, and helped her to see. People from Peavy spoke through her stories, and local incidents were reshaped in them, the new tensions too, the way the balance of power had shifted from white to black, the whites feeling powerless and unappreciated, unremembered or wrongly remembered. In one story an old woman like Kate cannot understand directions, because the familiar streets have been renamed. She knew Dr. King, but who was Matthew Henson and who was Denmark Vesey?

Alabamans bring presents when they visit, a bottle of blueberry wine or homemade cookies or pound cake. On her few visits Brenda brought nothing, and Kate wanted to ask, "Is that usual in Chattanooga?" But Brenda glanced at her as though Kate had done something wrong, and Kate recognized an attitude toward blacks in the squint she gave Perta Mae.

The Brenda visits diminished, and then on the few that occurred she was late, which seemed more insulting than her not showing up at all. Was it resentment or disapproval? She never smiled. Nervy people have no sense of humor. She blinked a lot. At last Brenda stopped coming, and Jack Junior's visits became less frequent.

Kate thought, To live with a humorless person is a martyrdom. But perhaps she didn't know her.

Kate's feeling of being snubbed, even shunned, gave purpose and vigor to her fictions. It was in this period of isolation that she sent stories to magazines, in the spirit of a loner posting a letter, yearning to be heard; and her first stories were published.

She wondered if anyone in her family, or in Peavy, would notice. No one did. Yet distant readers responded to her, and it seemed as though she was writing to them from a far-off land.

By now she had a granddaughter, Jackie. Kate had hoped to make her a friend, someone to whom she might leave her jewelry. But the girl was like her mother, sulky, disapproving, conveying a sense of blame in her squint. Kate was resigned to not seeing the girl and her mother; her sorrow was that she saw so little of her son.

Perhaps he was torn, but he sided with his wife, and when the child Jackie proved to be a problem at school, Kate said, Nothing to do with me. They'd detached themselves from her, and maybe the mother was the influence, but they were all complicit.

Kate had been shy at first in sending out her stories, but meeting with approval she was encouraged, and writing became a career and a consolation. She was a witness to an earlier time, a whispered insistent voice, who'd known white privilege and conflict in the small world of the country town, hardly altered in her house where Perta Mae cooked and cleaned, as her mother had done for Jack Senior when he was small. Perta Mae was more loyal to her than Jack Junior, and her warmth and willingness took the curse off the rift with Brenda, if you could call that silence a rift.

"You're like family to me," Kate said to Perta Mae. "Better than family, based on the families I know."

Perta Mae lifted her head as if to speak, but smiled and said nothing.

One of the stories Kate wrote was about an old white woman and her black housekeeper – the housekeeper the daughter of the white woman's childhood servant, as Perta Mae's mother, known as Mammy, had been to Jack Senior, in the same house.

To wish for her son back was hopeless. She mildly scolded herself for not being content and was reminded that her unease, her seeking resolution and order, impelled her to write. And she who desired her son's happiness could not object if he found it with his wife and not his mother. But if Brenda had some good qualities, they were indiscernible, and if that little family was tormented, Kate didn't see it. They were absent, younger people she'd once known, that was the whole of it, and being absent they defied interpretation. That was a lesson. Her stories as a consequence were impartial, without explanation or blame. But she ached over the words "my son," and she resisted thinking of his adoption.

Her readers visited her now and then. They marveled at the old remote farmhouse, full of books, at the edge of its empty fields. She gave these visitors lemonade on her porch. In the Southern way they brought her fruit or cookies. They asked serious questions and listened gratefully when she replied.

Sometimes she said, "I would trade everything I've written to have composed a ditty that people would go on humming," and then stared and hummed a tune that strangely vibrated behind her face.

No one in her family had read a word she'd written. Reading was such a pleasant pastime that their refusal had to be deliberate, or hostile. They could so easily know me by reading me.

They don't want to know me, she felt, and not reading her stories was their saying "See, we don't care." It wasn't her son's absence that pained her – it was his indifference. And what sharpened it was the attention of so many others, those strangers. She imagined herself an artist whose family refused to look at her paintings.

Returning home late one night, Kate stumbled on the front stairs and injured her lower back. "Trauma to your left kidney and some spinal bruising." In the hospital she was reminded of Ivan Illych in the great story, how a fall had injured him, how he lay dying, the mention of his "floating kidney."

Kate's fall seemed like that, provoking a fatal illness; in her physical pain she felt immensely old and feeble. She lay in bed in her hospital room wondering whether her son and his family would walk through the door. How did they know she wasn't dying?

On the second day – why the delay? – her son visited. "I just got the news" could not have been true. She stared, as you do at a lie. He held her hand and uttered the conventional formulas of concern. She wanted to tell him: I've written better commiserations than that.

"Not good," she said, to test him when he asked how she felt.

The next day Brenda came. She took the bedside seat, stone-faced, empty-handed, as if commencing a deathwatch.

"I don't know how much longer I have," Kate said, "but I don't want to die without saying this."

She could hear Brenda's breathing from the scrape of air in the hairs in her nostrils.

"I know you don't like me much," Kate said, without any bitterness, as though naming a color. "But I don't know why. I just want to say that whatever the reason, if there was ever anything I said or did to hurt you," and she paused, "I'm sorry."

At first Brenda said nothing, and the only sound was the protest of the nose hairs. She swallowed a little, and the way she swallowed changed her expression and shaped her mouth to a rueful smile.

She faced Kate, unsmiling then. She had become a heavy plump-jowled woman.

"I accept your apology," she said, barely opening her mouth, as if someone else inside her was speaking.

Kate Collier Delombre didn't die. She lived for ten more years – ten years of solitude, not writing, looked after by Perta Mae, a respected figure in Peavy and elsewhere. Her fame grew and she won awards when she stopped writing, a paradox that amused her.

I met her in that period, and she told me how she had lost the affection of her son. Could it have been as simple as his adoption? Hated by her daughter-in-law, doubted by her granddaughter.

"My heartache."

That was the lunch at Louleen's when I urged her to fictionalize it, to ease her pain.

But she didn't write it, she died of heartache, and I did not begin to write it myself until after I accepted Perta Mae's invitation to visit the old house outside Peavy, set in the desolate fields her husband's family had once farmed, the furrows grubbed and scabby in winter.

I took Perta Mae, who seemed much older, to Louleen's, so as to be away from Kate's aura in the house. But even so, her spirit lingered there in the diner. Why is it, on a return to such a homely place, you so often choose the same table? The familiar entrance, people looking up from their food, Perta Mae limping ahead of me.

Perta Mae ordered fried catfish and mentioned how Miss Kitty had liked it that way, with two sides, rice and gravy, coleslaw, and a biscuit, a sort of homage set out on a plastic tray.

"You were true to her," I said. "The only one."

"Had to be."

"She was so grateful."

"Never told her why." Perta Mae worked her biscuit apart with her thumbs. "Old Mr. Jack and me was kinfolk."

I thought, *What?* But I suppressed my shock. "Why didn't you tell her?"

"Heh. Tell that woman anything and you see in her eye she fixin' to make it a story." She became serious and added, "Later on, I tell young Mr. Jack."

"But he was adopted."

"That's why he need to know. For his wife sake too." And she laughed and lifted half a buttered biscuit. "That's why they gee and haw when they see me and Miss Kitty."

I'm the Meat, You're the Knife

I WAS WALKING DOWN High Street to the funeral home when I spotted Ed Hankey coming toward me. He said, "Jay," then, "Guess who's sick?" then blinked and, "Murray Cutler."

Sometimes bad news takes the form of a greeting. I hadn't seen Hankey for more than twenty years, and felt this abrupt announcement was a tactic to overcome his awkwardness. Another reason I didn't want to reply by saying that my father had just died, and that was why I was there. I wondered if he'd ask why I was in Medford Square after so long. Family tangles, bereavement, and failure send us home; seldom happiness. Perhaps he knew about my father's death and was avoiding it by mentioning Murray Cutler. I was headed to Gaffey the mortician to meet my mother and sister, to choose a coffin and arrange the viewing.

When I asked how sick, Hankey said, "He's at a hospice." His lisp made the word juicier and more emphatic. He cocked his head to look straight into my face, clamping his mouth shut and widening his eyes, and this meant everything.

Instead of replying, I took a deep breath and nodded, reflecting on the news. Murray Cutler had been our high school English teacher. He was one of those people whose death, I knew, would be a problem for me unless I was somehow part of it. I was resigned to my father's passing, though. We had no unfinished business, and he knew I loved him. What I dreaded were the futile formulas of consolation from people who didn't know him. I felt fragile in my grief, hypersensitive to sound. Voices on the car radio grated on me, so did music, so did pity.

I said, "Maybe I'll go see him."

"Visit the sick, one of the Corporal Works of Mercy," Hankey said, and he laughed. We'd been altar boys together, we'd been classmates, we'd sat side by side in English class, where Murray Cutler was a tease. "What can I do you for?" Or, showing me two copies of an exam, saying, "This is mine and that is urine." "Copper Knickers," he said, "he of the heliocentric theory." He talked about the Huguenots simply so that he could call them the Huge Nuts. He had the tease's gift for spotting a victim's weakness.

All this time Hankey was talking about his wife and children, reminding me that he had married one of our classmates, how happy they were. Then: "I never really knew Cutler. He was a funny guy."

"I know," I said. I debated again whether to tell him my father had died. No, a death is not something you mention briefly in passing to someone you bump into, even an old friend. And it was better to keep these two dramas separate. Individually they were tragedies, lumped together they were merely news.

"Everyone said he was a wicked-big influence on you."

"In what way?"

"As a story writer and all that."

"Do you read my stuff?"

A look of suffering or at least sheepishness in his eyes, the visible evidence of a temptation to lie, like pressure on his head, and at last he said, "My wife's the reader."

When I snorted instead of replying, Hankey said, "Cutler taught us the word 'procrustean.' All these years, I've never used it."

"And 'transpicuous.'"

"Whatever that means. You probably used that somewhere, eh?"

"Not yet."

He shrugged and said that the hospice was near the Winchester line, on South Border Road. "The Elms. Big old house. You can't miss it."

South Border Road, of all places, in the wooded Fells, where I'd spent so much of my innocent youth, where I'd left my innocence behind.

"Jay, we were worried about you," my mother said at Gaffey's as I entered the waiting room. She sat compactly, hands clasped, my sister Rose next to her, both of them pale and stunned, as though waiting to see a doctor.

Rose said, "They're getting the catalogue. For the caskets. It's real stressful. I never thought –" But she didn't finish the sentence.

In that awkward silence I said, "I just bumped into Ed Hankey."

"Oh?" my mother said in a high and querying tone, her way of asking for details.

"He sent his regards. He asked how you were. He was sorry to hear about Dad."

"Oh?" She wanted more.

Rose said, "I remember Eddie."

I could not turn away from my mother's imploring face. I said, "He claimed that when his father passed away his spirit still lingered. Eddie could feel it in the house, and sometimes it seemed to be inside him. Unconsciously Eddie became more like his father. Used the same expressions, began to be frugal, adopted some of his father's attitudes. It made him feel better."

"I can relate to that," Rose said.

"The memory of his father made him stronger. Helped him with decisions."

My mother was on the verge of tears, dabbing her eyes with a balled-up tissue.

"Eddie was a nice-looking guy," Rose said.

"Your father was so kind. He had no business sense." My mother was clutching her leather handbag. "Now you have to take his place. You're in charge now."

They stared at me, bereft. I sat closer to them and said,

"Don't tell anyone I told you, but Eddie had a couple of funny stories about online dating, things going wrong."

A sad smile floated across Rose's lips.

"One of the women posted a picture of her much prettier sister, wearing a tracksuit. 'I like working out,' she wrote under it. 'Get physical.' But when Eddie met her he didn't recognize her – he said she weighed about two hundred and fifty pounds. She ate a huge meal. He sat there dumbfounded."

My mother said, "Oh?"

"Another one met him for drinks. He said she seemed nice, but a bit goofy. Anyway, they ordered some salads at the bar. Then a strange thing happened. This woman got a nosebleed, but didn't seem to notice it. She says, 'Anything wrong?' 'Yeah,' Eddie says. 'You're bleeding into the caesar salad.' So she gets up, and he figures she's going to the ladies' room. He never saw her again!"

"Something druggy about nosebleeds," Rose said, smiling broadly as she hugged Mother.

"God forgive me," Mother said, holding her rag of tissues to her mouth, laughing.

"Everything seems like a good idea on coke," Rose said.

And then a solemn man in a dark suit appeared, and we were invited in to peruse the catalogue.

Driving along the road the next afternoon, I glanced to the right and moved through a map in my mind, from Bellevue Pond to Panther Cave to Wright's Tower and the Sheepfold, until the shadow of Murray Cutler fell over the memory, and I realized that I was coming face to face with the man after all these years. I had no idea what I would say to him, but I needed to see him before he died.

At a bend on South Border Road, a large old house loomed from between tall trees, fieldstone and brick, with a pair of heavy-lidded dormers on the roof and bosomy bow windows on the front, set back from the road. *The Elms: Hospice and*

Palliative Care appeared in green and gold on a swinging board at the opening of the circular driveway: a family mansion converted to a medical facility.

Inside, at the periphery of the lobby area, a white-haired woman in a blue sweater sat at a desk behind a glass partition and a slid-aside window opening onto a counter, like someone selling bus tickets. She stood and, plucking her glasses from where they had rested on her head and dropping them onto the bridge of her nose, leaned toward me. The odor of new paint and fresh flowers in the lobby and the way the woman greeted me made me think of their opposites, decay and deception and death, sinister and obvious distractions, especially the smile.

"Please sign in," and she indicated the visitors' book. I was reminded of the leather-bound visitors' book we had chosen the day before at the funeral home.

I flipped pages, searching the column under *Destination*. Murray Cutler's name did not appear on any of the pages I saw.

"Mr. Cutler's not getting many visitors," I said.

"Professor Cutler doesn't have family," the woman said. Professor! "He'll be glad to see you. He's in two-two-eight. Stairs on the left."

His door was closed. I tried the knob, pushing it open slowly, then stepping into the inert body odor that hung in the small room like a sour baggy presence. Murray Cutler lay in a bed facing the window, an elderly woman beside him bent over a book, but turning her face to me, frowning, looking punished, when the door clicked shut.

"Sorry to interrupt."

"You're supposed to knock. I don't appreciate it when people don't knock." She sighed and hoisted the book. "We're reading this. I'm one of the volunteers."

In this interval, Murray Cutler did not stir. His head remained canted to the side, his mouth open.

"I can take over from you."

"He taught English at Medford High." She glanced at him as though for approval. "Did he teach you?"

"Yes. He taught me how to tell stories."

"He loves stories."

"I have some for him."

In a softer voice she said, "He's got an awful lot of challenges."

That was when he looked at me, not moving his head, but lifting his eyes, and remaining expressionless.

Although I had not seen him since high school, I recognized him at once. Wasted, simplified, and revealed by illness, he was reduced to a skeletal caricature of himself, the way a sickness shows us who we really are by making us too weak to pretend. He'd always been thin, his close-fitting clothes made him a stick figure, but he was vain about his body. Teachers wore suits and ties then. His suits were well cut and stylish.

Exaggerated by his sickness, he was a skinnier version of a skinny man. His skin clung to his skull, a tissuey death's head, a corpse's face, yellowish, with dry split lips. When he drew a breath his eyes goggled from the effort. He looked weird and weightless on the bed, like a castaway adrift on a raft. His arms looked useless. Where there had been muscle, there was slackened sinew, less like flesh than old meat.

"I'll leave him to you," the woman said, rising from her chair and handing me the book.

Desperate Journeys, Abandoned Souls. I read the dark title aloud and made a face.

"Stories of survival and heroism," she said, buttoning her coat. "We've just done Alexander Selkirk."

"Robinson Crusoe and his man Freddy, the perfect partnership, he used to say." I looked to Cutler for a reaction, but there was none.

"He's had a stroke. Well, a series of small strokes. His

speech is impaired but his hearing is perfect," the woman said at the door. "His eyesight is challenged too, so please read to him – or tell him a story."

When she stepped out and shut the door I put my face close to his.

"Remember me?"

He heard me. He seemed to strain, to focus his yellow eyes on me, his mouth gaping. His hands were folded on his chest, claw-like fingers, and a needle was inserted into the back of one hand, taped flat and attached to a clear plastic tube.

"I was your student. Jay Justus."

In a measured set of whispered gasps that I had to translate, he said: "Had so many students."

"You told me I was special."

This took a moment to register, but when it did he seemed to smile, as though I'd teased him, and he opened his mouth wider, showing me what remained of his teeth, discolored stumps and raw gums. He was ill, but I could see that there remained in his shrunken body a distinct intelligence that was like an intimation of heat. I was convinced of it when he became impatient, and that spark kept me resolute.

"Story," he said, and, urgent, working his dry tongue, he looked reptilian, as corpses often do.

"You were always a reader. You used to loan me books."

Impatience surfaced on his bony face again, twisting his features at me, his bulging yet unastonished eyes.

"You went to Mexico one summer. You told us all about it. How the Mexican children called you *Papacito* and followed you everywhere."

He lifted his head as though to bat away my talk, and, slurring, he said, "Story."

His saying the word gave me so much pleasure I hesitated until he repeated it two more times, chewing it in his insistence.

"This is a story about my friend in San Francisco," I said, and Murray Cutler smiled and looked content. "He was lonely, he lived on his own, he worked in a cubicle, he found it very hard to meet people. One day there was an earthquake, which they get now and then in San Francisco. His office was evacuated. He ran into the street and found a doorway for protection. A young woman from his office dashed in and cowered next to him. Can you picture it, the doorway framing them? As the tremors continued he put his arm around her, not saying a word. She welcomed it – she was terrified by the earthquake, the screams of the people on the street. My friend began kissing her, and, in her fear, she accepted this. When the whole business was over she still clung to him, and instead of going back to work, he took her to his apartment and assaulted her."

Murray Cutler seemed to listen with his open mouth, widening it as if to understand better. When I finished he grunted with dissatisfaction.

"More," he said.

"Another man, another time, another story" – and Murray Cutler looked bewildered. "During a fire alarm at a hotel, a man in his pajamas and robe found himself standing next to a woman who was clearly very frightened. Firemen, hoses, sirens, men with axes, men in rubber boots. The woman recoiled from them. The man took the woman's hand and drew her close, and he spoke to her in a reassuring way. She too was in a single room in the hotel. An hour of this, and then the all clear – a false alarm. But the elevators weren't working. The man helped her find the stairs and led her to her room. 'I don't know how to thank you,' she said as she opened the door. He still held her free hand. He wouldn't let go. He kicked her door open and said, 'But I do.'"

I stopped talking, and in the silence I created so that this might sink in, Murray Cutler said, "Why are you telling me this?" in his gargly voice.

"I'm Jay," I said. "Remember me?"

I was not sure it registered, nor was I certain he knew who I was. I said, "I'll be back."

But two days went by, the days of the wake at Gaffey's. I tried to stay in the background as relatives filed in to greet my mother, to embrace her and remind her that she was a widow, to tell Rose and the rest of my siblings, Fred and Floyd and the others, what a great man their father had been.

My cousin Eva came up to me and said, "I dated a guy, Charlie Saurin, who was in Africa like you. Middle of nowhere. He was a medic in one of those jungle clearings. No roads. The only way in was by small plane. He said visitors made him feel lonely. Know how he survived it? He said, 'When you don't think about leaving, a place seems bigger.'"

"I used to fantasize about being in the bush like that, isolated and in charge. The solitary bwana."

"So where were you in Africa?"

Standing near enough to my father's casket, I could smell the heavy perfume of the flowers. He lay with his face lightly powdered, his cheeks rouged, his pale hands crossed over the handle of his Knights of Columbus sword. His presence, and that sword, cautioned me. He was a practical man who believed in the economy of the plain truth, that fiction was folly, and only jackasses and liars made up stories.

"I lived in a friendly city – Kampala. I was a teacher at a good university. I had a nice house and a lot of friends. I had a cook from the coast who was full of Swahili wisdom."

"Sounds wild to me."

"It was pretty tame."

After they closed the lid of the casket and the last mourner had left, my mother went silent, looking shrunken and depleted. Rose sat next to her and bent to whisper something, but this seemed to provoke tears and Mother's clotted voice saying, "I don't know if I can handle this."

I went over to them. I said, "I just remembered Eddie's

other story. He found another woman online who said she was single and looking for a date. They texted back and forth, sent pictures, and made a plan to go out to dinner."

"Eddie's a game guy," Rose said. "You could take some tips from him, Jay. What's his thing?"

"Maybe he's lonely," I said.

Mother said in a clear voice, "Did it work out?"

"He washed and waxed his car to make a good impression," I said. "Then he drove to her house. But as he entered her driveway a man jumped out of the bushes, yelling at him – a little guy, going ape."

"Who was he?" Mother asked.

"Ex-husband. He'd been stalking her. The woman came to the door and screamed at her ex. He threw his shoe at her. Eddie said to her, 'Hey, I didn't sign up for this. Call him off.' The guy rushed at him. Eddie told me, 'I punted him into the next yard and drove off.'"

Mother was smiling. She said, "Good for him," as Rose took her by the hand and led her away.

When I returned to the hospice the next morning Murray Cutler looked weaker, vaguer, but hearing me speak he became attentive, as though the sound of my voice woke a memory in him. If he did not remember me, at least he remembered my stories.

"Earthquake," he said. He raised a skinny finger and poked it at me. "False alarm."

In English class, if any of us pointed at him, or pointed at anything, he said, "Be careful. There's a nail on the end of that thing. That's not ambiguous – what is it?" And he'd answer, "That's transpicuous."

But I was also thinking, Wonderful, he remembers what I told him.

"Story," he said, slurring the word.

"Okay. I was in Africa, in a place so remote I could only get there by small plane in the wet season. I ran a clinic. This was in western Uganda, near the Congo border, the Ituri Forest. We were so far in the bush and so neglected that we had to be self-sufficient. The people grew cassava and maize. I ate the local food, *ugali* and beans, and occasionally we killed a chicken. No one thought of leaving. Apart from the clinic there was nothing, not even a school, and no church. The nearest mission was at Bundibugyo – and most people regarded that as the end of the earth. It was not a happy village, but it was settled and resigned to its solitude. We never got visitors. My contract at the clinic was for two years, but I agreed to another two. I liked being in the middle of nowhere, a clearing in the bush. When you don't think about leaving, a place seems bigger."

Murray Cutler shifted his hands, clasping them, looking satisfied, perhaps imagining the desolation of this African village.

"Over the patter of rain on my tin roof – a sound I loved so much for its mournful tap-tap that it sometimes put me to sleep – over that peaceful repetition, I heard a plane circling the grass landing strip. Usually a plane brought mail and medicine, but today it brought a big smiling man named Charlie Saurin. This was a surprise. His first words were '*Jambo, bwana – habari gani?*' He seemed to want to make a point, speaking Swahili to me. Swahili was the lingua franca in this nowhere place. I said I was fine, but that I wasn't expecting him. 'I was sent from Kampala. Mr. Bgoya's orders. I'm here to help.'

"Bgoya was a government minister. What to do with Charlie Saurin? He was older than me, about forty-five, but with a full head of prematurely gray hair, combed back and upswept in a way that made him seem conceited. I'm wary of men who are vain about their hair. They behave as though they're wearing a special hat. To keep him away from my bungalow and the clinic I gave him the small house the pilot used when heavy rain kept him from taking off. That pilot, Bevan, once told me, 'You don't really know anyone until you've seen him drunk.'"

I repeated this to Murray Cutler to see whether he'd been listening. He nodded and smiled, but this approval in such a sick man seemed like self-mockery.

"I invited Charlie Saurin to my bungalow for drinks – locally brewed beer served from a plastic basin. '*Nakupenda pombe,*' he said, 'I like beer,' sipping it from the tin dipper, and though he lapsed into Swahili from time to time – he was conceited about his fluency, too – he became gentler, more polite, more solicitous, speaking to me slowly and deferentially. 'Are you sure there isn't some way I can pay for this?' But he didn't repeat that in Swahili."

Becoming restless and impatient again, Murray Cutler shifted in his bed. He sighed and said, "And the point is?"

"Whenever he spoke from the heart he said it in Swahili. Just before he staggered home, he paused and hung on the doorknob and laughed, saying, 'The history of mankind in four words: *Mimi nyama, wewe kisu.*'"

"Whaaa?" Murray Cutler said, throwing his head back.

"He started to teach classes, using his house as the school – there had never been a school in the village. You'd think this was a good thing, but it disrupted the rhythm of the village. The children weren't available to hoe the gardens or bring water from the stream. But the children didn't mind – being in school freed them from the hard labor and menial chores.

"The parents began complaining about this to me. One of the aggrieved men brought his son, Junius. Junius said, 'The bwana Mr. Charlie is taking me to America.' Junius's father said it was a *tatizo kubwa* – a big problem, and that Charlie Saurin's being there was a *shauri* – an issue.

"So I invited him over to my bungalow again, but this time we didn't drink. I told him I had run out of *pombe.* We ate chicken and roasted cassava and a stew of greens. And I saw how he ate, English style, a fork in his left hand, a knife in his right, two deft hands at work, spearing the meat and cutting a small piece, then slicing a bit of cassava and adding that to the fork, and lastly plastering some limp greens to it and lifting the whole business to his mouth. He worked his implements with affected skill, raising his elbows, making a whole operation of it, squinting at the fork of food before he made it a mouthful, and then champing on it. That told me more than his drunkenness had, and I remembered what he'd said."

"What did he say?" Murray Cutler murmured, raising his head.

"I'm the meat, you're the knife."

His head fell back on the pillow, and he worked his lips as though tasting what I'd just told him.

"The boy Junius told the other children that he was going to America. I heard them repeating it at the clinic. I was too busy to pay much attention to the school – and Charlie Saurin had only been there a month. I sometimes saw him walking with the children past the gardens to the edge of the bush, sometimes singly, sometimes in groups."

I fixed my eye on Murray Cutler.

"I knew he was trifling with the students, either with promises or actual deeds. I was strict with them. I never mentioned the world beyond our clearing. But he apparently talked about it all the time, America especially, and by doing so he made himself bigger than me. There was nothing I could do. The students felt familiar toward him, they hung around his house, and they were so convinced of his affection for them that they began to take liberties with his house, his food, some of his possessions. It was the casual, entitled way of rural Africa – after all, he had a great deal, and they had nothing. And there were his rash promises."

Murray Cutler closed his eyes, and I stopped speaking. He opened them again and seemed disappointed that I was still sitting by his bed.

"When he discovered they were stealing his things, he was enraged. How dare they take advantage of him! He stopped teaching. He told them that no one was going to America with him, least of all Junius, who had stolen his alarm clock. The next time the mail plane came to our clearing in the bush, he got on board, and as we all watched him take off, he turned his face away from us. He said we had destroyed him. But of course it was we who were destroyed, or at least corrupted, which comes to the same thing. No one was the same after the visit of Charlie Saurin. The villagers began to resent me, and now spoke of wanting to leave the clearing, but there was no easy way out."

I fell silent, Murray Cutler squinting at me. He snatched at the cord that hung beside his bed, to call the nurse, and yanked on it.

"This one man ruined everything by his meddling intrusion," I said, staring at him in defiance. I got up from the chair and left the room before the nurse arrived. His last look was one of uncertainty, perhaps fear. I was relieved to breathe the sweet air outside the hospice.

But then, driving away, I remembered a better detail, how Junius's father had gotten to Charlie Saurin. Mistaking this man for someone important, he had encouraged Junius to go with him, and had entrusted the boy to the intruder, and that was why Charlie Saurin had so much access to the boy.

Mother said, "Is there something wrong?" when I saw her that evening, alone in her house. Rose had left her to meet with the rest of the family, to see to the arrangements for the funeral at St. Ray's. She had urged me to keep Mother company at this critical time, and so I slept these days in my old bedroom at the top of the stairs.

"I'm fine. I'm glad I'm here."

Mother seemed doubtful, and this uncertainty looked like anxiety. The way she sat, hands clasped, knees together, slightly hunched, was like that of a peasant on a hillside weathering a storm.

"This is where I was born," I said. "That's an amazing fact to me. I've been everywhere, and yet this is the only place on earth where I truly belong."

"Oh?" And she looked up hopefully.

"It's kind of humbling to realize that." Mother didn't seem to hear me. I said, "Did you ever hear the expression 'forgiveness is final'?"

"What does that mean?"

"This is what it means. A guy I know who's also a writer found out that a man who'd hurt him was suffering a terminal illness. The writer was down on his luck, not much happening in his life – vulnerable to any slight. He had always resented the man who'd hurt him, but when he visited the man, he said, 'I forgive you.'"

"What did the man say to that?"

"He couldn't speak. He looked like he'd been slapped in the face. He was disarmed. There was nothing he could do. Because forgiveness is final."

"That's beautiful," Mother said, and took my hand. "I'll cherish that lovely thought. You could write about that."

I looked away. I said, "And I keep meeting old friends here. Some of them are having health problems. I feel as if I can be useful."

"You've always been kind that way, Jay."

I returned to the hospice the following day. Murray Cutler looked at me with dread when he saw me enter the room, but he was too inarticulate to object, and, bedridden, unable to do anything but watch me seat myself and stare, he was the helpless one now.

"I knew a couple, very creative woman, very entrepreneurial man, partners in the trucking business" – just the sound of my voice made Murray Cutler hug himself in fear. "They split up. She said to me, 'You have no idea. He was always hearing voices. His mother visited him in his office. The voices said, "Stab her in the eye! Stab her in the eye!"' He explained this in detail to his wife. 'You need to know.' His father had died in a plane crash. He refused ever to get on a plane, but that was all right – his whole business plan concerned freight in long-haul trucks. His other quirk was that he had to take thirty steps whenever he entered a room, so if a room only used up twenty steps he marched in place for ten more, but very subtly. I asked her, 'What was the attraction?' She loved him, and she told me, 'He had the charm that all psychopaths have.'"

In the time it took me to tell this story, the tension left Murray Cutler's body, and when I finished he said in his usual mutter, with a half-smile, "What's the point?"

"No one knew that he was crazy." I shifted to be closer to him. I said in a harsh whisper, "Only she suffered, and when she told her story no one believed her. But I believed her. And as for the man, his punishment – he still heard the voices."

The door opened, one of the nurses pushing a trolley with food trays on it. I was near enough to Murray Cutler to whisper to him without being overheard, "I'll be back."

The day of my father's funeral was so scripted, and adhered so closely to the script, it seemed that his death was the fulfillment of a long-range plan, that this was the last act in the ritual. I was grateful for that, for the sequence of events that numbed me by their routine, following a set of cues: our designated seats, the vases of flowers, the chanting priest, the candle flames, the kind words, nothing jarring; and then the casket on wheels, the silent hearse sliding importantly to the cemetery, where the grave had been thoughtfully dug and the muddy hole disguised with a rectangle of purple satin fringed with gold ribbon; more prayers, more flowers, and then another procession, the withdrawal, all of it expected. We were sad, but no one cried. The nature and purpose of a ritual is to meet expectations; it is the unexpected that is upsetting.

Murray Cutler cringed when I appeared the following afternoon, later than I usually visited. He must have thought with relief that I was not coming, but then to see me at the end of the day, when he was tired and having to face another story, was demoralizing to him.

He tried to cover his face as I pulled the chair close to his bed and began speaking.

"I knew a woman who visited Greece on vacation," I said. "A man stopped her on a back street in Athens, where she'd been buying souvenirs. He said, 'I had a dream last night of Jesus Christ. Jesus said to me, "You must go to this particular street. There you will meet a beautiful woman." And here you are.' When she turned to get away, a man in a doorway said, 'Come here. I will help you,' and the woman fled into his house. The man locked the door and raped her. And when he was done, the other man was waiting to do the same."

Murray Cutler, seeming to undergo a seizure, raised his arms as though to defend himself, and he cowered behind a tangle of plastic tubes.

"Raped her," I said, leaning over and showing him my teeth.

Sitting beside my grieving mother, helping her answer the condolence notes, took almost a week. My father had many elderly friends, and none of them used a computer. Rather than send a printed card as thanks for these spidery scrawls, my mother felt – and I agreed – that it was best to write each person a reply that reflected their degree of intimacy toward my father. It was a sensitive business, but it brought my mother and me closer. When she grew weary she put her hand on mine as I was writing, improving her responses to these people, and said, "Everything's going to be all right."

Murray Cutler was much worse the next time I saw him, a few days later. I locked the door to the room, and he groaned when I sat down and started to speak.

"There was a man who, when he lusted after someone and didn't want to be caught, pawed his prey in public places – in the bleachers at baseball games, in the back rows at concerts, in popular campgrounds. He possessed them by pawing them openly, looking like a dear friend and benefactor, and that was the paradox, because the victim was too fearful to make a scene. And when the victim went home he couldn't report what had happened. He had to think of a story, but in his story he was not a victim. He was triumphant. He invented dramas and dialogue. He became such an expert at evasion that the oblique habit of storytelling became his profession."

Murray Cutler faced me and never looked more like meat, and he tried to turn away, but he was too weak. "Yet one story always stood for another. He invented the truth," I said. "Now you tell me a story."

I sat watching him, and it was as if a succession of episodes might be running through his mind, all their cruel details twitching on his face.

I returned to my own empty room in my mother's house. I relived all the hopes and fantasies one feels in a childhood bedroom. I suffered the overfamiliar ceiling, the walls, the window: like a cell I'd served a sentence in, that I was confined to again. I hardly stirred from the house until a month later, to accompany Mother to the gravesite. "I want to visit Dad," she had said at breakfast that day, cutting a sausage, then putting down her knife.

We were standing at the grave when Mother said, "Your teacher Murray Cutler died. It was in the paper."

I couldn't speak.

"Dad respected him so much. He was a Harvard graduate, you know. Dad was so proud that he took you under his wing. What's wrong?"

I had begun to cry, sniffling, then sobbing with an odd hopeless honk of despair.

"He thought the world of you," she said. "Dad knew that. He used to talk about it to me." And then she was comforting me. "Go on, let it out, Jay, I know how much he meant to you."